THE HOLLAND FAMILY SAGA
PART 4

THE FIVE DAUGHTERS
BY
CLEVER BLACK

ISBN:978-0-9853509-8-7

This is strictly a work of fiction. Any references to actual events, real people, living or dead, or actual localities, is to enhance the realism of the story. Events within the novel that coincide with actual events id purely coincidental.

All material copy-written and filed on site at The Library of Congress.

The Holland Family Saga Part Four

October 18, 2012

8:51 P.M.

I can't express the gratitude and humbleness coursing through my veins as I write at this very moment. It's hard to believe that what started as a hobby some years back, has come this far. I wanna thank everybody who's read, or will read this saga and I hope to continue to deliver quality stories time and time again. Although I enjoy minimal success, I have much to be grateful for. I've interacted with some beautiful people while bringing these stories forth, far too many to name, but each and every one of you readers are special to me. Special because you have chosen to enter my world, chosen to get involved with The Holland Family and learn of their trials and triumphs, and have given me the opportunity to express myself from a literary point of view.

When I first started out with Part One, I had very few readers. Oneday though, I put the ebook on sale for the low price of free. I saw a comment by Dama Cargle advertising. Soon, Gabrielle Dotson got a hold of it along with Carla Towns. The rest is history. No matter what happens, because I have high aspirations for my work, I will never forget the group that gave me a chance, that went in head first and put me out there on the scene—Black Faithful sister and Brothers. That group holds a special place in my heart and I thank them for being that springboard I needed to get things started.

Many readers have joined the journey and purchased a ticket on The Holland Express. I read the posts and I thank all those readers who deemed it worth the effort to reach out, you all inspire me. Readers and supporters like Knook Barrow, Ciara Collier, Rosalyn Reed and Rosalind Butler just to name a few, have gone hard and you ladies deserve a hearty thank you.

To the groups, Let's Talk Relationship and Books, United Sisters' Book Club, My Urban Books Club and Just Read Book Club bring joy nearly every day with their conversation and friendliness. I tune in sometimes while working and try to be involved as much as possible. A special thanks to those clubs, and every book club and member who supports me. I hope I've represented my beautiful Black women righteously and did all readers justice with this read. With that said, ladies, uncork your wine, punch your tickets and climb aboard The Holland Express because this one's for you. The Five Daughters is leaving the station...ALL ABOARD!

The Holland Family Saga Part Four

CHAPTER 1

A FAMILIAR FACE

The ringing of my alarm clock stirred me awake on a cool, bright and sunny Saturday morning in October of 2008. I was scheduled to meet two of my boys at The Holland House of I.D.E.A.S. for an inventory count, but I was seriously thinking about putting it off until Monday morning because I knew I was going to be busy for a good portion of the day. I.D.E.A.S. stands for International, Domestic, and Exotic Automobiles and SUVs. Whips get laced out here real proper like. Ferraris, Jags, Caddy's, Old School Chevys, Maybachs, Porches, whatever. We hook rides up—for a price. I'm the owner of The Holland House and Samantha's husband Tre` is my co-partner. This here business I run don't hit hard like the game—but it's legit. I have top-paying clients from across the country, too, including rap stars, athletes, Wall Street execs and spoiled rich kids born with silver spoons in their mouths. A Holland House ride is highly sought after. You bring your factory whip into the lab, and we turn it into something sick. On any given week, me and Tre` can easily clear ten grand apiece after expenses. During the spring we could clear twice as much; but on average, it's around ten grand a week.

I makes money in my sleep and that's no lie. I got a solid group of eight A.S.E. Certified Mechanics that were hand-picked from the streets by me and had their licenses paid for by me as well. I got a down crew, much like the crew I had when I was in the game. Me and these boys are all legit—but don't get

9

it twisted—we some soldiers if need be. I told myself if I was ever granted another chance at freedom I would live an upstanding life in honor of my parents and so far, I was staying true to my word. So long as nobody don't step on my toes, or clown around with my family, I'm cool. I ain't looking for trouble, but you better believe I'll turn shit inside out and bring to anybody that want it and I got a team of hitters behind me with a street resume identical to my dead homies from the days of way back to back me up without fail so it's best these other cats stay out the way and let me and my crew get this money in legit fashion.

I showered and dressed up in a pair of grey silk slacks, tan leather shoes and a tan silk shirt with a grey silk suit jacket, my hair draping down my neck hanging just above my shoulders and slid my fully-loaded nickel-plated Berretta .9mm into my tan leather pouch and zipped it up and stepped out into the hall. All was quiet when I stepped out from the master bedroom and walked down the long hall of the mansion leading to the spiral staircase. I was wondering where Katrina and my two sons, Ben Holland Junior, and Kenyan were right about now. They would usually be in the family room with Henrietta around this time, but the second floor was cleared out. I descended the stairs and made my way to the kitchen where I saw my wife and Celeste preparing breakfast.

"Hey, baby, how'd you sleep last night?" Katrina asked me with a wide smile.

"Slept good, boo. Samantha made it yet?"

"Not yet. But they on their way." Katrina replied as she puckered her lips and stood up on her tip-toes to give me a quick peck on the lips.

"Mmm. That's good stuff right there." she said after she'd licked her lips.

"Celeste, fix me something to eat please, baby." I said as I opened the refrigerator and grabbed a bottle of grape juice.

"My hands are tied. Katrina fix Mister Holland a burrito will you please?"

"His hands are perfectly fine! He can get his own plate!" Katrina said as she walked out the kitchen sniggling to herself.

This here is an on-going problem around the house. I'd adjusted well to the life I was now living. I was a married man with two kids and a beautiful twenty-seven year-old wife, had found my long lost sister, reunited with my aunt Henrietta and was a successful business owner and multi-millionaire. After all my trials, I had conquered every obstacle thrown my way, but for whatever reason, I couldn't get use to the fact that Celeste was there to tend to the family's needs. It took me the longest to ask the lady to do something for me. I had done a lot of wrong in my past—up to and including murder—and was the head of one the most violent drug organizations the south had ever seen—but I had the hardest time asking Celeste to do this or that because I felt as if I was ordering the older Mexican lady around. She was close to Henrietta's age and I would never command my aunt and I felt compelled to treat Celeste no different. Celeste was a part of the family though, and it didn't take long for her and Katrina to pick up my reluctance to ask the lady to do something; and for that reason, and that reason alone, I would get teased to high heaven.

I eyed Celeste, who only sniggled as she cleaned the counters just as Samantha entered the foyer with her husband and twin baby girls, Tabitha and Gabriella. We call them Tabby and Gabby for short. Henrietta came out from the gym and greeted her niece and nephew-in-law and helped with the babies. She placed them on the carpeted floor next to my sons, one year-old Ben Holland Junior, and two month old Kenyan Holland.

"Hey, everybody! Celeste, fix me and Tre` one of those burritos please," I heard Samantha say as she went and joined Henrietta in the living room with Katrina and the babies.

"Oh, sure! No problem, Samantha!" Celeste replied as she dropped everything she was doing to make a burrito for Samantha.

They clown me like this all the time. Samantha be in on it too; but I know exactly how to get to her.

"I just asked you for one of those." I told Celeste.

"Well, Ben, Samantha's a guest, you live here. Besides, you don't want to order an old lady around do you?" Celeste remarked as she and Samantha laughed.

"That's your problem right there Celeste. You been, 'round her," I said pointing to Samantha, "Katrina, and Henrietta too long."

"She's my friend, Ben! She only *works* for you!" Samantha stated as Celeste chuckled.

"Okay, see how friendly I am when that paycheck of yours bounce, Celeste!" I said aloud.

"Mister Holland!" Celeste stated as she covered her lower face and giggled.

"Umm, hmmm. Look at your face now! Fix my burrito. Please, ma'am."

"That's all you had to do is ask, Mister Holland." Celeste replied. "You're learning."

I sat and ate with Samantha at the island counter. Saturdays around the mansion were always laid back. We cooked out nearly every weekend, alternating between Tre' and Samantha's four bedroom Swedish Style split-level home, and me and Katrina's sprawling mansion. This weekend the family was cooking over to our place and Samantha was here early to help out. When Atom, Katrina's miniature Daschound ran into the kitchen, Samantha bent down and picked the dog up.

"Ohh, he's so cute. Man, I wish I had dog, Celeste. My brother, I think he said he was going to buy me one for my house-warming gift but he never bought it." Samantha said as she smiled and fed a piece of her burrito to the dog.

Samantha was a dog lover through and through. She had wanted a dog for her home ever since she and Tre' had moved in a while back and I had promised to get her one; but I'd been so busy, I never had time. Today, though, I was planning on buying her this pet she been clamoring me about for the longest.

"I was headed that way today to get that dog after I leave the detail shop. What you want a Rottweiler or a pit-bull?" I asked.

"I don't won't no beast like that, Ben. I want a nice dog, like a cocker spaniel or a Labrador, not a fighting dog."

"A pit-bull is a protective beast."

"I don't need a pit-bull, or a 'protective beast' as you say. I have Tre` and my M-16 for that."

"So if it came down to it, who'd you rather have looking out for you, Tre`, or the M-16?"

"I'd take Tre` blasting the M-16 with me right beside him handling my business, too," Samantha answered.

All I could do was laugh because I knew my sister was serious. Samantha had taken lives herself; but she was commissioned by Uncle Sam to do so during that time. When she settled down, she joined the N.R.A. and had become a licensed gun carrier. She and I went to the shooting range at least once a week to spend time alone as brother and sister. I had a nice collection of handguns and one assault rifle, a custom-made chrome Tommy Gun, known as a Chicago Piano because of the eight hundred rounds per minute it spit out, but Samantha and Tre` had an arsenal of vintage World War Two era weapons in their gun locker amongst others. They had three M-16's, a Garand M-1 rifle, and two PPD-40 submachine guns that fired 1,000 rounds a minute. Samantha was heavy into guns and avionics. She was due to receive her pilot's license shortly and was training to become an aero mechanic. I was proud of my sister. She was a very ambitious and self-sustaining young woman.

"Good answer, love. And you know daddy can handle his business." Tre` stated as he entered the kitchen and sat at the counter, joining in on the convo.

"Baby, Ben going get my dog today! Surprise me alright, Ben?"

I knew Samantha had a Doberman Pincher once; but the police had confiscated the dog when they raided Asa Spade's home. She didn't want a fighting dog, so I'm assuming she want something like a poodle or a stupid-looking Shitzu or something. I don't know. I dove back into the burrito and I could see Samantha smiling at me out the corner of my eye. I love my sister more than life itself; and she knew me, man. It was like she could see my thoughts.

"What Ben? You don't know what I want?" Samantha asked me as Tre` hugged her from behind. "That's alright. You'll do fine, brother. Tre, you know what I want, don't you?" Samantha then said sexily as she turned around and hugged Tre` and nuzzled her nose against his neck.

That was something else Samantha did that she knew I didn't care too much for—all the PDA with her and Tre`. Don't get me wrong, Tre` my dog, but these two love birds here? When they get going? They can go overboard. Katrina would sometimes try and do the same thing. I can get down with mines, but holding hands while walking through the house? Kissing at every red light? That's how Tre` and Samantha rolled. Not my style. And besides, me and Katrina black ass been in this shit. We old vets to love, but we still going strong. Samantha and I had a strong bond, but she was little sister. I could only imagine the things she would've done to me if we'd grown up together. Look at her and Tre`. Lip-locking at the counter. But it's all good. I got Samantha covered.

"Y'all gone make me chuck up this burrito right here on the kitchen floor," I said before I got up from my stool and walked towards the living room to see my nieces.

"Ben, on your way back from the pet store can you stop and get one of those play pens from Wal-Mart? Tabby and Gabby will need a comfortable place to sit once the cook out starts." Henrietta said to me. The perfect time for payback.

"I'm a be at the pet store, auntie. We can just get the little tykes a doggy kennel."

"Ohhh no he didn't! I know he ain't just say that about his own nieces!" Samantha yelled as she ran into the living room. "You ain't putting Tabby and Gabby in a kennel! You put baby Ben and Kenyan inside a kennel!" she said to me before I took off running through the library, disappearing into the mansion.

Okay. The deal behind this is, although I'm thirty-four years-old, and Samantha is twenty four, we still act as if we're kids from time to time. Henrietta picked up on it a year ago and she said it was because of the fact that me and Samantha had been separated for all but a year and a half of our lives. We had a lot of catching up to do, and from time to time, in true sibling fashion, we would heckle one another. This day was no different. It was no hard feelings—one-upping one another was only another way the two of us would tighten our bond.

Samantha stopped chasing me and walked back towards the living room where I heard her say, "Oooh! He always do that! And then take off running! Your nieces gone push you down a flight of stairs when they get old enough!" she yelled aloud.

I came back to the room and sat beside Samantha and saw that her skin was flush and she was sniffling, as if she was crying. I apologized. The last thing I wanted to do was upset her. She said nothing as she got up from the couch and I quickly followed.

"Samantha! Samantha, I was joking, come on nah!"

Samantha walked into the library and burst into tears. Now I feel like shit. I leaned in the threshold, my head hanging low and feeling lower than dirt. I walked over to her pleading with her not to be sad, repeatedly saying I was sorry for saying what I said about my nieces, under the belief that I'd gone too far this time. When I approached Samantha, her body began to heave. I felt terrible. Samantha turned slowly to face me and I was prepared to apologize again, but instead of crying, she was all laughs.

"Gotcha!" she yelled aloud as she took off running from the library laughing aloud. I caught up with her in the hall and tickled her until she begged me to stop. We ended with a hug and a "I love you," and walked back towards the living room and discussed her soon-to-be new pet once more.

After about an hour or so of just hanging around talking, I made my way over to the pet shop on the north side of Phoenix. When I walked in, I immediately noticed the woman behind the counter. She looked familiar. And from the way the woman was looking back at me, it was obvious she was thinking the same thing.

"Can I help you, sir?" she asked in a nice friendly tone.

"Yea, I'm looking for a friendly dog. Not no damn Shitzu or Pug. A cocker spaniel or something like that if ya' got one." I said, all the while eyeing the woman and trying to recall where exactly I knew her from.

"Ooohh, those are cute," she said to me. "You a pet lover I see. My friend Lubby love dogs too."

"That's where I know you from," I snapped as I slapped the counter. "Rolanda Jones! East Shore! 1983!"

"Ben Holland? I thought that was you! How you been, boy?" Rolanda asked as she gently hugged my neck.

"Great. Great. Rolanda, I been wondering…what happened to everybody when I left East Shore?"

"Man, we went through some shit after you left, Ben. I was umm, I was just about to take a lunch. You wanna sit out back and talk for a while? I mean if you have the time."

"That's cool. First help me pick out a dog for my sister."

"Your sister? How? Your baby sister passed away with your mother and father in 1984 right?"

"Nahh. We had it wrong about that. Everybody had it wrong. Look, we got a lot to talk about. I never forgot y'all ladies. Where my girl Lubby?"

"Lubby," Rolanda said as she smiled brightly. "She's around. We, umm, we do have a lot to talk about. I want to hear what happened to you, Ben. And I think I speak for the rest of the girls when I say I would be glad to tell you our story." Rolanda said to me. "What happened to Gabriella's sister, Henrietta? The smart, librarian looking lady?" she then asked.

I couldn't help but to laugh at her statement.

"What's funny, Ben?"

"Everybody says my aunt looks like a librarian. She's doing real good. Had a bout with cancer but she beat it. I'm married now and got two kids. I'm doing okay. Me and my family living good. It was five of y'all right?"

"Off top. The Five—that's what we called ourselves for a hot minute." Rolanda stated as her eyes shifted to the side and she produced a wide smile. I could tell she was reminiscing about days long passed and I couldn't help but to wonder what happened to her and her girls when I left the old neighborhood.

As I watched Rolanda in deep thought, I had an idea. "Next weekend, want y'all come down and we can have a East Shore reunion."

"A reunion sounds nice, Ben. I'll call my girls and see if they can get away. I'm sure they can."

"How y'all get way out this way anyway?" I asked, still amazed having had ran into an old childhood friend from back in the day.

"You'll find out soon enough. But we don't stay in Phoenix —we stay in Las Vegas right now. I just opened this pet shop down here. Business is good for me and Lubby."

"I'm feelin' that! I'm feelin that! I own my own business myself. Tell Lubby I said what's up and I can't wait to see her. Man it's a small word. What? Hurricane Katrina brought y'all out this way?"

"Nahh. We left several years before the storm. A change of scenery was definitely in order for us, Ben."

"Okay. Well, look, take my card. My number on there and I'm a write down my address. And don't forget to tell Lubby I said what's up." I said just before me and Rolanda began walking slowly through the pet shop.

Rolanda smiled and shook her head and said to me, "I'll tell her tonight old friend, I'll tell her tonight."

As we walked, I learned a little more about Rolanda Jones. She was now thirty-seven years-old. She was a slender 5'10" 150 pound dark-skinned woman with long, thick wavy black hair that she wore brushed over the left side of her face on this day. She had the most captivating slender dark eyes, full sensuous lips and a wide, bright smile. She was a beautiful dark-skinned woman. We walked around the pet shop for a while and entered the area where she kept the dogs and they all began barking at me.

"They making a lot of noise. They act like I pissed 'em off or something, Rolanda."

"They just talking, Ben. They are all begging for you to take them. Dogs can sense good and bad owners. They are vying for your attention because they believe you are a good owner. I believe that you know?"

"Believe what? That I'm a good owner?"

"That too—but I was referring to my belief that dogs can talk. My buddy Kilo used to talk all the time. Come out back and meet Sno-Ball." Rolanda said to me.

I followed her out back of the store to a small patio and found myself staring at a snow-white pit bull. Now, if I were into dogs, this is the beast I would get. Sno-Ball was a snow white, red-nosed muscular pit bull. The dog's chest was heaving as he stood on all fours, staring up at me with his tongue hanging out his mouth. He looked as if he would strike if he was given the word.

"He attacks on command, Ben. But he's gentle most times."

"Samantha would be upset if I were to show up with a beast like that. I think she want something a little less aggressive, you know what I mean?"

"Okay. I just received this cute and cuddly creature this morning. Wait here." Rolanda replied.

I watched as she reentered the pet shop and came back out a few minutes later with a black cocker-spaniel puppy that we both felt would be perfect for Samantha.

"Her name is Cleopatra, Ben. It's the only name she'll answer to. I got her from the humane society. Her owners lost their home in a house fire and put her up for adoption. You can rename her if you want to—but I think Cleopatra is a pretty name for her breed. She looks like royalty."

I couldn't help but to agree with Rolanda's statements. The dog was precious indeed. Samantha's going to love it I know. After purchasing the dog, me and Rolanda sat and talked for almost three hours. I told her what happened to me when I left East Shore, my days in the game and my six year incarceration.

Rolanda said she only knew of one story, one incident when one of her friends ran into me outside of East Shore and she'd never known what all I went through after my parents were killed. She was both shocked and touched by some of the stories I relayed to her.

"Man, I thought we had it bad. You was a straight up beast out there, Ben."

"That was back in the day you know? I did what I had ta' do to survive, Rolanda. Somewhere along the way, the shit got personal. People went down—on my side and the other side. The more I thought I could pull away, the deeper I sunk into that shit. I lost a lot of friends to the game. If I had ta' do it again and have it end this way, though, I wouldn't. I'm more blessed now than ever, Rolanda, but back in the day, I couldn't see from noon till night, which was as far as my thinking went at the time because nothing was promised. Now, I got more to live for than ever, and I'd die, before I put my people through that living hell again, ya' feel me?"

"No doubt about that, Ben. But for me, if I had to relive those days, I would do so."

"Why?" I asked inquisitively.

"Because. We were so innocent back then. We did some bad things to other people—but we mainly hurt ourselves. We really thought we had our act together. The Five," Rolanda said as she looked towards the ground sadly. "More like The Fools. We acted like pure asses sometimes. We had a lot of fun in the beginning—but we each paid a heavy price, in ways we never imagined, Ben." Rolanda said to me as she went into some of the stories about her and her friends' childhood.

As Rolanda related some of her childhood stories, Cleopatra, who'd been snarling at the pit-bull, began barking loudly when the dog finally acknowledged her with a husky growl. Cleopatra jumped down from Rolanda's lap and ran over and barked at Sno-Ball, who only turned and walked off with a look that said, 'Bitch please. You don't want none of me'.

Rolanda laughed aloud and said, "My girls never believed me when I told them dogs be talking to each other, Ben. But they do. I know they do." she said as she began scribbling in a note pad. She noticed the inquisitive look on my face and said, "I'm sorry. I'm working on a memoir."

"About your life?"

"No. It's about my buddy Kilo. Sno-Ball's father. He died a few years after we got to Vegas. This here is a doggy memoir in honor of Kilo. They are popular books with animal lovers, you know?"

"That's new to me."

"It's a new concept in a way. I tell the story through the eyes of the dog. It's a mature read with human qualities is the best way I can describe it. I be tellin' my girls about it and they offer input, but this is my own little project. You think Samantha would like to test read it for me when I'm done?"

"Knowing the way she loves animals, she'd be the perfect audience."

"Cool. I can't wait to meet her, Ben."

"Rolanda, we can sit all day and talk. I wanna finish, so, I'm inviting you and the rest of the girls back to my home in Mesa next weekend. I'll put y'all up in a hotel for the weekend or for how long y'all stay and we can all sit and talk about those days from way back. You up for it? Old friend."

Rolanda agreed to visit with her friends the following weekend and I couldn't wait. I was jubilant the whole ride home. I called Katrina and informed her of the fact that I had run into some old friends who wanted to meet the family. I knew inviting five females from my past was asking a bit much of Katrina. "I know you probably thinking I done lost my mind, but these girls here? They go way back you know? I was supposed to grow up with these girls. This was way before we even met. Way before Manny and Oscar. But, if you feel uncomfortable—"

"Ben, calm down, baby," Katrina said through laughter. "If you've run into some of your friends from back in the day that you want to reconnect with, then I see no wrong in what my husband is asking. In fact, I wanna see what kind of friends you had when you were a little boy. We'll talk more when you get in. I'm good with what you're asking, baby. Love you."

"I love you too, baby." I said before hanging up the phone.

Today was turning out better than expected. I called my homeboys Victor and Lee at the shop and told them to hold off on counting inventory until Monday and rode home a happy man. Katrina greeted me upon my arrival and we placed Samantha's dog outside by the pool. She'd gone to Wal-Mart with Tre` so she would be pleasantly surprised when she returned. The rest of the family sat in the pool house and began to plan a menu for the following weekend so we would be able to feed our guests properly.

****

Rolanda Jones, meanwhile, was still sitting outside the pet shop in north Phoenix, still trying to digest Ben's story as it was hard to swallow. Ben had done some horrible things, but he also had suffered great loses. Rolanda believed that a lot of what Ben did was because he had lost his parents. She remembered Gabriella and Sam, they were good parents. Rolanda believed in her heart that Ben would not have done what he had if they were still alive during that period of time. The Ben Holland that Rolanda Jones saw on this day had the characteristics of the Ben Holland she once knew; he was gentle, thoughtful and kind, with a cool and calm demeanor.

Rolanda then began to reflect on the lives she and her friends once led. She had not the heart to tell Ben the full story at the time; but she was glad Ben Holland had invited her to his home because the story she had to tell would take a few days. There would be many laughs, but it would take a while to digest some of the drama. Rolanda was not one to hold back what she had to say. And even more so, Ben had hinted around to her as to what he had done. He stole, he was one of the most violent drug dealers in New Orleans during his day in Rolanda's eyes, and had been accused of murder once, serving time in jail. The man had talked openly and candidly with Rolanda, and the way she saw it, if Ben could tell his story, then surely she could speak on all what she knew and had been through.

As Rolanda reflected on those thoughts, she began formulating in her mind exactly how she would convey the story to Ben, and by doing so, it caused the thirty-seven year-old woman to reflect on the life she and her friends once lived. She got up and washed her hands and fixed a hot latte and moved into the office of the pet shop, leaving her three workers in control of the floor. She took a sip of the latte leaned back into her soft, leather executive chair contemplating on how best to relay the story to Ben. As she did so, Rolanda Jones began to reflect on the life she and her friends once lived.

CHAPTER 2

ROLL CALL

"We wanna thank everybody for all our success down here in the city. I wanna especially thank the young folk, because they really make this all possible. If it wasn't for our younger fans this radio show wouldn't be on the air. So without further ado, because it's bedtime for all the young ears that's tuned in and Jammin with Jazzy on 105.9, we're gonna do our roll call so all my young listeners can call in and represent their respective schools and also shout out their friends and neighborhoods before bedtime," twenty-six year-old Jasmine Lewis stated across the airwaves on a cold and rainy October night in New Orleans, Louisiana in the year of 1982.

Jasmine Lewis, A.K.A. Jammin' Jazzy, was the host of New Orleans's most popular evening radio show called *Jammin' with Jazzy*. Nearly every child and teenager, and some grown folk as well listened to the woman's variety show. Jazzy was a diverse and hip woman whose radio show played the latest hits, talked the latest gossip, gave advice to kids and young adults, and she also had a piece called *Ear to the Street* where she would put various people and neighborhoods on air live in order to settle neighborhood disputes and conflicts. Jazzy did it all. From reading an article from *Right On!* Magazine, to discussing the lyrics to some rock and roll album with her fans, one never knew what he or she would hear on Jazzy's program, which ran from 7P.M. to 11P.M. Monday through Friday, but one thing was certain—everybody who listened would always be entertained. Jazzy had fans as far as the waves blasting from the antennae of WYLD's studio in downtown New Orleans could travel. She was a huge hit along the gulf coast region, including Biloxi and Hattiesburg, Mississippi and southern Alabama towns such as Dauphin Island and Mobile. She was an idol to all aspiring female Dee-jays, even though they were few and far between during her heyday.

Eleven year-old Dominique Franz and her friends Rolanda Jones and Tracey Sanchez, both eleven as well, were three of Jazzy's biggest fans. They had dreams of becoming a radio host and Dee-jay just like her someday.

"Rolanda! Hurry up and dial the number for roll call so we can represent for Bri and Lubby!" Dominique yelled aloud as she and Tracey ran into Dominique's bedroom and closed the door and turned the volume up on the radio in order to listen to Rolanda represent.

"Turn the stereo down so it won't feedback into the phone, Rolanda!" Tracey yelled just before closing Dominique's bedroom.

Rolanda turned the stereo down and ran into the kitchen and quickly dialed the number in order to get in on 'Roll Call'.

Jazzy had the instrumental to the hit rap song *The Message* by Grand Master Flash and the Furious Five playing in the background on this cold and rainy night in October of 1982. Rolanda grew excited as the phone began to ring. "It's ringing, y'all! It's ringing!" she yelled aloud from the kitchen to her two friends.

"Hey caller what's ya' name and where ya calling from?"

Rolanda said nothing when Jazzy answered the phone. "Hello? Caller where ya' calling from?"

Still nothing.

"Catch me next time." Jazzy remarked as she hung up the phone. "Next caller."

"Hello, Jazzy," the female caller asked shyly.

"Ya' got me, sweetie. What's ya' name and where ya' at?"

Dominique and Tracey looked at one another and the two eleven year-olds frowned and stomped out of the room. "Rolanda! Why you ain't say nothing?" they asked at the same time.

"I didn't know she was talking to me." Rolanda said surprised, her dark, slender eyes peeking from beneath her Jehri-curled black hair.

"Man, let me try!" Dominique stated angrily as she redialed the number on the rotary phone. "You worse than Lubby with that stuff! Sitting there playing dumb!" She ended.

Dominique tried and tried to get through, but she couldn't dial the phone fast enough, she kept getting busy signals. She and Tracey tried the whole fifteen minutes that Jazzy was representing but they couldn't get through a second time around.

"Rolanda, damn! Everybody at Little Woods was listening! We coulda been hittin' tomorrow at school! I'm a tell everybody you got scared on Jazzy's show! You run your mouth all day and when you had the chance to get on the radio you froze up! You a scary cat!" Tracey snapped as she pushed Rolanda back into the bread rack in Dominique's mother's kitchen.

Rolanda pushed Tracey back and she fell against the refrigerator. She balanced herself and charged at Rolanda, but Dominique stepped in between the two and said, "It ain't that serious, Tracey."

"It might not be for you, Dominique," Tracey retorted. "But I had bet Michael and Donald fifty cent a piece that we was gone be on the radio! Rolanda scary self messed it up for me! Now instead of making a dollar I gotta pay a dollar! And I ain't even much got a dollar!"

"A bet? With Michael and Donald? That's why you mad? That's your own fault Tracey." Rolanda stated.

"No it ain't, Rolanda! You owe half on the bet! Pay up!" Tracey said as she backed away from Dominique and Rolanda and placed her hands on her hips.

"Hey! Hey! Hey! What in Jehovah's name is all this racket coming from my kitchen?" Dominique's mother, Antoinette Franz, asked as she walked into the kitchen and placed a coffee pot onto her stove top.

"She gambling in your house, Miss Antoinette!" Rolanda said as she pointed at Tracey.

Dominique's mother was a devout Jehovah's Witness and had been baptized for over ten years. Rolanda, and all of Dominique's friends knew Mrs. Franz was a stern woman. She often reproached Dominique about her listening to Jazzy's show, calling it 'worldly music'. Mrs. Franz, who was a homemaker, was married to an over-the-road truck driver named Stanley Franz, Dominique's father. Stanley wasn't a Jehovah's Witness, but he attended the meetings with his wife and daughter when he was home, which was usually six days out of the month on average.

Dominique hated going to the Kingdom Hall. She viewed the place as boring. Mrs. Franz didn't give up on her daughter though; she would study the bible with Dominique every Saturday morning and take her to meetings on Sundays. Mrs. Franz hoped that the knowledge she was bestowing on her daughter would one day eventually sink in as time wore on.

"I know you are not gambling in my home Tracey Sanchez," Antoinette said as she stared at eleven year-old Tracey through stern eyes.

"There she go! Every time man!" Tracey said as she threw her arms up and walked around in a circle inside the kitchen and began patting her pockets. "Every time something happen over here she gots 'ta tell it! Rolanda 'Spill the Beans' Jones reporting for duty!"

Tracey, Rolanda, and Dominique knew what was coming next.

"Go get my bible, Dominique!" the three girls lip-synced in unison with Mrs. Franz as they knew they were about to get another lecture from Dominique's mother.

"And don't mock me! Now, unless you wanna be grounded

for the weekend, I suggest you go and get my bible, Dominique! And Tracey I'm gone tell Maria on you when I see her!"

"She worse than Rolanda with that rattin' and shit!" Tracey thought to herself as she sat down in a chair at the kitchen table just as Dominique returned to the kitchen with her mother's bible.

The lecture on gambling went on for nearly thirty minutes. Ms. Franz was preaching to the kids about not serving 'the god of luck' when she looked at the clock and said, "Oh God. It's almost ten 'o clock! You two girls need to get home! You have school tomorrow," as she grabbed her coat and umbrella to walk Rolanda and Tracey to their respective homes, which was only several houses away on the same block.

The following morning, Tracey, Rolanda, and Dominique were walking to the bus stop and Tracey again brought up the fact that she believed Rolanda owed her half of the bet.

"You buggin'! You betta kiss Michael and Donald and get it over with!" Rolanda told Tracey.

"Ugh!" Tracey snapped.

"Ugh my behind! Neither one of us got no money. And when I do get fifty cent I'm buying a popcorn ball from your momma." Rolanda remarked as the girls emerged from the cat walk and strolled towards the rest of the kids waiting at the bus stop on the corners of Star Street and Curran Boulevard.

"Well, when you get the fifty cent just give it to me. I mean, my momma gone give me the money anyway."

"Shoot! Maria ain't comin' off no snaps and you know it!" Rolanda stated.

"That's all right Rolanda. You gone buy a popcorn ball sooner or later and that change gone be mines. My momma the only one selling those things back here."

"Tracey, I ain't gone lie, your momma caramel popcorn balls be hittin'. I don't know how she make 'em, but they the best." Dominique stated as she and her friends made it to the school bus stop.

27

Dominique and her friends resided in Little Woods, a newly built subdivision in the eastern part of New Orleans. Little Woods was also known as East Shore to those on the streets. The neighborhood consisted of predominately Black families working nine to fives and trying to stay afloat and make the mortgages on their newly built brick homes. Everything was shiny and new in the Little Woods subdivision in 1982. The houses were clean, the yards were neatly kept, and the concrete that cut through the subdivision and separated it into neat square blocks was fresh. The neighborhood sat right beside Lake Ponchartrain. Haynes Boulevard, one of the main roads leading into the subdivision from the main section of New Orleans, ran alongside the lake and had a huge levee separating the salty waters from the subdivisions that lined the opposite side of the street. If you were coming from the east through Slidell, Louisiana via interstate ten just south of the neighborhood, Little Woods would be the first huge subdivision at a major interchange on the interstate in east New Orleans. One would exit and head north alongside the huge levee and the subdivision would be on one's left.

An old beach, Lincoln Beach was behind the levee on Hayne's Boulevard at the most northern part of the neighborhood. The beach had rides and swimming pools once during the sixties, but it had closed down years ago; still, the kids from the neighborhood would walk over the levee, cross two sets of rail road tracks and then walk through the wooded trail and pop out on the sandy beach and take to the pier and splash into the water during the hot summers.

Little Woods was a fun place to stay for kids. The neighborhood was so new during 1982, that there were still sand piles on empty lots waiting to be spread out to form the foundation of new houses waiting to be built, but despite its newness, East Shore was still heavily populated with kids.

Rolanda Jones and her four friends all resided on Emory Road, which ran parallel to Curran Boulevard. A catwalk connected Curran and Emory Road. If you were facing the catwalk, to the left of the alley three houses up was 11 year-old Brianna Stanford's house. She lived closest to the alley. Eleven year-old Tracey Sanchez's house was the furthest away from the catwalk; she stayed to the left of the catwalk on the same side as Brianna, but about six houses up from Brianna's home.

Tracey Sanchez had lost her father in Vietnam in 1975, six months after her brother was born. Tracey never knew her father; she only knew him through the many pictures her mother Maria had displayed throughout their three bedroom home. Tracey's mother was receiving a pension from the military via her husband's death, and she also sold caramel popcorn balls that were to die for. Tracey's father was an African American/Hispanic and her mother was from Latin America. Tracey was a Black/Latina. She was an exotic-looking, pretty, thick little girl.

To the right of the catwalk and across the street, four houses down, was Dominique Franz's house. Three more houses down on the same side as Dominique's home, was Lubby Williams' home. Rolanda lived directly across the street from Lubby. Because of the locations of the girls' homes, in the beginning, Lubby and Rolanda were real close and Brianna and Tracey were real close, Dominique was sort of in the middle. She hung with all four girls, eventually they all became friends and for over a year now, the five were an unbreakable unit.

Dominique, Tracey and Rolanda made it to the corner and spoke to other students and searched for their other two friends.

"Lubby!" Rolanda called out aloud over the crowd of about two dozen kids in grades three through six. "Lubby, you got the math homework from last night?"

"You got the English," eleven year-old Lubby Williams asked of her friend.

"Umm, no. We got into a lecture by Dominique house last night."

"Ooohh! I missed out on that?" Lubby asked sarcastically as she placed her Math homework back into her backpack.

Lubby Williams was the friendliest of the bunch. She was well liked by her peers, but the bright-skinned brown-eyed, short brown-haired, slender eleven year-old had a rocky relationship with her mother, the person whom she wanted to please the most in life. Mrs. Williams had a fair paying job at a candy factory back in the city, but she was barely scraping by. She was a vindictive woman with a nasty disposition. She was once a loving and caring mother, but all that changed when Lubby's father ran off and left her when Lubby was only two years-old. Mrs. Williams, blaming Lubby for her husband leaving her, soon came to resent her daughter. By age ten, Lubby Williams was practically raising herself.

Lubby was a survivor, though; she knew how to get by when she had to, and so long as she had her friends to lean on for strength and support, she knew she would be okay because they came through without fail each time, even in their young age. Lubby often had to wear her friend Brianna's old clothes because she had very little attire of her own. Brianna would give Lubby old Nike's and Reeboks to wear. She gave Lubby old jeans that looked new because she may have only worn them once or twice. Brianna also gave Lubby matching shirts as well. Brianna had more clothes than she knew what to do with and she gave Lubby some of her 'gear' and never made fun of her friend. Lubby was glad to have a friend like Brianna and Brianna was glad to be able to help keep Lubby dressing 'fresh' as she, Rolanda, Tracey, and Dominique all wore nice clothes. The five never spoke on Lubby's plight; it would be one of many secrets the five friends would keep to themselves. Lubby's mother was neglectful in the way she raised her child, but to Lubby's friends, Mrs. Williams just wasn't a nice person.

Cynthia Williams would condemn Lubby for the very things *she* was doing even though Lubby never acted like her mother in the least. Mrs. Williams would have a different man in her home just about every other week. Lubby would hear the moans and groans coming from her mother's bedroom and wonder who she was with on that night. Lubby also had to assert herself because on several occasions, she had been approached by several of Mrs. Williams' man friends who'd propositioned her for sex. Through it all, Lubby loved her mother dearly and desperately wanted her approval and acceptance; but Mrs. Williams hated the fact that she had a daughter. She felt her life would be much better if Lubby wasn't around. For that reason, Lubby could do as she pleased as she was paid very little attention to by her mother.

"Come on Lubby stop playing!" Rolanda stated.

"I ain't playing! Now I gotta do my English before we get to school, I suggest you do your math." Lubby concluded as she pulled out her English book to try and hurry and do her assignment.

"Ooohh! I be wantin' to hit her sometimes!" Rolanda said as she walked off from Lubby.

"Traceyyy!" a voice yelled aloud from the cat walk, leading out to Curran Boulevard. "That's my fuckin' girl right there!" the strong voice said before the person yelling ever came into view.

Tracey looked around to see Brianna Stanford pop out from the alley way. The last of the five friends emerged from the catwalk and made her way up the sidewalk. Brianna wore her jet black hair in a crop. Her short and petite ninety pound frame bounced happily up the sidewalk as she approached the bus stop. She did a little dance in front the crowd as she waved a brand new pair of grey leather Nike's she wore on her feet to the crowd. Brianna Stanford was a flamboyant little girl. Her mother worked at NASA helping to build the center fuel tanks used on the space shuttle missions, and her father, a Navy Submarine Officer, was lost at sea with twenty-six other men when their submarine malfunctioned and went down in over twelve thousand feet of water in the middle of the North Atlantic Ocean when Brianna was only four years old. Mrs. Stanford received a hefty settlement for the loss of her husband and she'd used the money to purchase a new home and car. Brianna, who was known as Bri, (Bree) was the only child, as was Rolanda, whose father was absent in her life, and Dominique and Lubby. Only Tracey had a sibling, a brother aged seven.

Brianna's mother spoiled her rotten. She dressed her daughter in nothing but the best, Guess, Polo, Gap and Jordache' jeans, Polo shirts, Reebok and Nike tennis, leather penny loafers and suede hush puppy dress shoes. Brianna always had money on her as well. She would treat her four friends from time to time and never threw it back in their faces. The five were all the same age, but their birthdays were sort of scattered. Rolanda and Brianna were the oldest by a few months, their birthdays were in early March, Dominique and Tracey's birthdays were in mid-June, and Lubby, the youngest of the five, celebrated her birthday in early August.

Tracey was planning on asking Brianna for a dollar, but everybody began jockeying for position when they noticed the school bus heading up the street.

"Move punk!" Tracey yelled aloud to a male student who was standing at the foot of the curb.

"Yea! Move back punk! You know the five get on first! Come on Lubby! Get up here girl!" Brianna remarked just as the bus pulled up.

The male student stepped back, but before he did he 'goosed' Brianna's rear end. Brianna turned around and ran to the back of the line and began wailing on the student. Tracey joined in and Rolanda began to comment on the fight.

"Ooohh! She caught that eye! Bri caught that eye!" Rolanda yelled, imitating Brianna and Tracey's blows as the bus driver stepped off the bus to break up the fight.

Tracey and Brianna were pulled off the student and he got up muddy. The kids laughed aloud as he took off running home. When students all told the driver that the boy had touched Brianna on the rear end, the driver shrugged his shoulders and let the kids board the school bus.

No soon as the girls stepped on the bus they heard someone yell aloud, "Traceyyy! Where my money, sucka?"

It was Donald sitting at the back of the bus next to his best friend Michael, also known as Mike. The twelve year-old was licking his lips as he waited for Tracey to pay up. Tracey was at a loss for words, she was about to explain what happened the night before until Brianna stepped up and gave Donald a dollar and shoved her into an empty seat towards the back of the bus.

They were joined by Rolanda, Dominique, and Lubby who sat in seats beside and in front of them.

"Rolanda called me last night. You didn't want to have ta' kiss them two ugly boys, right?" Brianna asked Tracey.

"Good looking out, Bri. I owe you big time!" Tracey said through a sigh of relief.

"Don't worry 'bout it. It's just a dollar. Besides, we friends Tracey." Brianna said as the two girls smiled at one another.

Donald knew if Tracey had loss, she wouldn't have any money. The deal was whenever someone loss a bet and didn't have money, the girls would have to kiss the boys on the lips for ten seconds; and if the boys loss they would have to carry the girls' books to each class up until lunch. Donald didn't want the dollar, though; he wanted the kiss from the pretty Tracey Sanchez. Michael, on the other hand, wanted the money, but he knew of Donald's hopes. He shook his head in disbelief over the fact that Donald would take a kiss from a girl over money.

"I don't want that dollar!" Donald said as he threw the bill back into Brianna's lap. "That ain't her money!"

"Man you buggin', Dee! Take the dollar! That's ten packs of now-laters!" Twelve year-old Michael said to his friend.

"I don't want no damn now-laters, Mike! Tracey owe me, not Bri! So that mean I get a little kiss from Tracey." Donald said as he puckered his lips and closed his eyes.

Just then, Brianna slammed the paper dollar against Donald's lips. The five girls burst into laughter as Donald blew the dollar from his lips and spat onto the floor of the bus. Michael grabbed the dollar off the floor and laughed as Donald sat back and pointed his middle finger at the five girls as the bus cruised down Haynes Boulevard headed towards Little Woods Elementary.

"Roll call!" Dominique yelled aloud from the back of the bus. "Everybody represent!"

Dominique, Tracey, and Rolanda often imitated Jazzy on the way to and from school and the kids on the bus thought it was fun. From the front to the back, they would yell their names and represent just like the callers on Jazzy's show. Tracey never said anything about Rolanda getting scared the night before, so no one knew she had a chance to represent for real.

"Hey, this Tiffany A.K.A. Big Tiff and I'm representin' East Shore!" a female student at the front of the school bus said as she stood up and pointed back at Dominique, Tracey, and Rolanda waiting for the next person to represent.

"East Shore in the house!" the three girls yelled in unison from the back of the bus.

The entire school bus went from front to back shouting their names and representing.

When it got to Rolanda, she knew she had to make up for last night. "This here is the sexy slim sister with the scoop from the hood—ya' girl! The one and only Rolanda 'I already heard that' Jones! And I'm representing for Emory Road with my girls Dominique 'I hate church' Franz, Brianna 'Superstar' Stanford—"

"Heyyyy!" Brianna said as she stood up and waved.

"I got my girl Lubby 'run that by me 'gain' Williams! And last but not least, Tracey 'bet a dollar' Sanchez! And we holdin' it down for…. East Shore…" Rolanda said softly as she closed her eyes and snapped her fingers and bounced her hips before sitting down.

"Rolandaaaaa!" students called out. "Hoot! Hoot! Hoot! Rolanda on point today y'all!" a student yelled aloud.

Tracey leaned over and dapped her friend. "Now that's a Roll Call! That's a real Roll Call, Rolanda!" she said as she and Dominique patted Rolanda on the back.

CHAPTER 3

HARD LESSONS

The school buses were unloaded in front of the elementary school on this cold Friday morning as the five friends began making their way to the school's yard before classes. All five girls were in the same class. The class's students remained together throughout as they switched classes five times a day. They had homeroom first with Ms. Bryant, who was also their math teacher, and then there was English, a two hour class, and then lunch. They would then have science, then P.E., and they would end the day with Social Studies/U.S. History.

As the five were walking onto the yard, Calvin Huntley, another eleven year-old in the five's class got out of his mother's car and spoke to the girls as they passed. He made it a point to acknowledge Dominique personally. Calvin, the skinny, caramel-skinned wavy-haired dark-eyed eleven year-old was secretly voted the cutest boy in the sixth grade by nearly all the girls. Although Calvin went to Little Woods Elementary, he didn't reside in East Shore, he stayed about a mile away from the neighborhood, but he was in the same school district. Calvin knew the five well, he liked them all; but he had a crush on Dominique something serious.

Calvin's parents kept him under close guard in order to keep him on the straight and narrow. His older brother, fourteen year-old Gerald, had taken to the streets already and Calvin's mother and father were doing their best to keep Calvin from following in his brother's footsteps.

"Hey Dominique. Hey the rest of y'all." the young kid spoke softly.

"What's up Cal! Hey, let me see your math right quick!" Rolanda replied.

Calvin looked over to his mother as she sat behind the wheel of their Lincoln Town Car. From what Calvin had learned, cheating was a bad thing. He was being reared to be an honest, god-fearing individual and he did his parents bidding without fail. He understood they didn't want him to end up like his brother, and he had no intentions of doing so. It was fair to say that Calvin was a momma's boy.

"That's cheating, Rolanda. I can't do that." Calvin said as his mother smiled proudly and crept away slowly in her car and headed to work.

"That was smooth Cal. She gone now. Let me see that math, brer." Rolanda requested.

"I wasn't frontin' for my momma, Rolanda. That really is cheating and I can't do that."

"Who say that's cheating?"

"God. At least that's what my momma told me."

"Say, Cal, how come whenever you say something is wrong you gotta bring God into the fold? Why it just can't be your momma or daddy said so?" Rolanda asked.

"Why should it be one of them?" Calvin asked as he walked with the girls on the school yard.

"'Cause she not gone question God, but she'll question your momma and daddy and try and challenge them." Dominique answered on behalf of her friend.

"Yea," Rolanda chimed in, "so next time we try and get you to cheat, say your momma said so so I can answer back because God is too big a person to challenge." she ended just as the class bell rung.

Once they entered into Ms. Bryant's class, the five sat in the back as Calvin sat in his seat at the front of the class.

"Alright kids after I call roll I want y'all to take out your homework assignments and swap with the person next to you so we can check the answers." Ms. Bryant said as she got up from behind her desk.

Rolanda looked around at her friends and frowned slightly. Dominique had her assignment, so did Tracey and Brianna. "How, how y'all two did y'all homework when we was up late last night?" Rolanda asked Tracey and Dominique.

"We copied Lubby's work on the bus." Dominique answered as she laughed.

"Lubby, just ta' let ya' know, and I mean this, from the bottom of my heart—I hope you get kept back this year." Rolanda said in a sincere, but joking tone.

"Well, at this present time you have a better chance of that then me. I got my work!" Lubby said as she rolled her eyes and popped her neck. "The deal was for you to do the English anyway, so, you get an F in math—and thanks to you—I get an F in English today so we even."

As the teacher called out the answers, the five friends, minus Rolanda graded their papers. They only had three of the twenty problems wrong. The teacher went around the class collecting the papers as Tracey, Brianna, and Dominique mocked Rolanda. "We got our hoooomework! You ain't got your hoooomework!" the three sang aloud in unison.

Rolanda sat with her hand resting on her cheek looking sad as she listened to her friends making fun of her; but they would get theirs in due time because Rolanda was not the one to readily accept defeat. When Ms. Bryant approached her and asked her where was her homework, Rolanda told the teacher she didn't have it.

"What happened this time?" Ms. Bryant asked as she placed her hand on her hip and awaited Rolanda's reply.

"The lights went out last night and I couldn't see. So I *couldn't* do it—because it was too dark in our house." Rolanda said.

"Sooo, you didn't do your homework because it was too dark

in your house?"

"Yes ma'am. The Jones's can't keep up with the Jones's if ya' can believe that one. We on hard times let me tell ya'. I guess my momma couldn't pay the light bill."

"Don't lie to me Miss Jones! Detention for you on Monday! And I *will* call your mother this evening to let her know that you are pretending that you are poor and depraved."

"De- what?" Lubby asked aloud.

"Depraved," Rolanda remarked. "That mean somebody ain't got nothing. Like how I was depraved from copying your homework this morning!" she said as she rolled her eyes at Tracey, Brianna, and Dominique and cracked a smile. Rolanda she knew she was about to get her friends into trouble at that very moment and she was going bonkers on the inside.

"Rolanda shut up!" Tracey said in a near whisper.

"We got our hoooomework! You ain't got your hoooomework! Remember that song?"

The teacher heard what Rolanda said, song included and knew right away something was astir. Knowing the girls were close, she collected Dominique, Tracey, Brianna and Lubby's papers as they all sneered at Rolanda. Ms. Bryant looked at the work and saw that everything was copied exactly the same, the girls had the same answers right and the same ones wrong, everything was identical.

"What the hell did *you four* do? Put a blank page over each other's work and just copy it like that?"

"What's wrong?" the four asked in unison.

"Besides the fact that you copied everything verbatim?"

"Ver-who? You umm, you wanna run that by me again Miss Bryant? Please?" Lubby asked inquisitively.

"Verbatim," Rolanda interrupted. "That means identical, the same, alike, you know like how I tried to verbatim your work this morning?"

"Oh, okay, depraved and verbatim." Lubby said as she wrote

down the definitions of the two words.

"You girls will learn hard lessons in life if you don't shape up." Ms. Bryant said matter-of-factly. She then eyed the five girls as Rolanda began to jump up and down in her seat whilst covering her mouth to conceal her laughter. "Three days detention next week for the four of you. Cheating will get you nowhere in life."

"I ain't cheat Miss Bryant! They all copied my work!" Lubby said in a disheartened tone.

Ms. Bryant only smiled down at Lubby. She was so sincere in her confession, the lady wondered if she'd even realized what she'd done was wrong. At the same time, Dominique, Tracey, and Brianna were shaking their heads in disbelief.

Rolanda burst into laughter and said, "She ratted on herself! Lubby, you *too* honest, girl!"

"If you wouldna said nothing! Now we all get F's!" Dominique remarked as she sneered at Rolanda.

"They gettin' F's too, Miss Bryant?" Rolanda asked nicely.

"What do you think?"

"I think they should all get F's since they went verbatim with Lubby's work and proceeded to deprave themselves of a formal education."

"That is a fine use of the English language, Miss Jones, unfortunately this is a math class, but I like your attempt."

"Thank you Miss Bryant." Rolanda said softly, trying her best to get on the teacher's good side.

"Every time, man!" Tracey said as she folded her arms and shook her legs rapidly. "Just one day—*one day* I wanna see you shut up about something! Catch yellow fever—get a, get a sore throat or sip on some crazy glue! Anything so you can stop blabbing!"

"What's yellow fever?" Lubby asked.

"Yellow fever," Rolanda snapped back. "Yellow fever is when you scared all the time!" she answered as the class laughed.

Lubby was beginning to write down the definition to yellow fever until Brianna blurted out, "Don't write that down, girl! That ain't the meaning of yellow fever."

"Yes it is!" Rolanda said as she eyed Brianna. "When somebody scared what they call them? Yellow! So yellow fever is when you scared *all the time*."

"Well get yellow fever and shut up!" Brianna snapped.

Brianna then thought about what Rolanda was saying. In her young eleven year-old mind, it did make sense. She really didn't know what to think about what Rolanda had said. Rolanda eventually had the whole class believing yellow fever was a scary person's disease. Some students grabbed Science books to look up the meaning.

"Yellow fever is a virus transmitted by a female mosquito bite and is found in South America and Africa." a student read aloud before the class all booed Rolanda.

"See! It's in America, but in the south where we at. So there!" Rolanda said.

"He said South America. That's another continent. We on North America continent." a student said.

"I know, boy! But I had all y'all believing that right there for a hot minute, though," Rolanda laughed. "Who you know scared all the time?"

"Scooby-Doo!" a female student at the front of the class answered aloud.

"Rooobyy Rooo!" Rolanda stated and then laughed along with the class.

"Alright, alright, enough of the silliness. Remember, detention for you four girls next week. Cheating, I say again, will get you nowhere in life. And you can laugh and joke all you want, but you five will still receive and F today!"

Rolanda sat up in her chair. "But Ms. Bryant you just said—"

"I just complemented you on your vocabulary, Miss Jones.

Stop sucking up. You got an F like the rest of your friends for cheating."

The four girls laughed at Rolanda.

"You thought she forgot!" Tracey stated aloud as she laughed at Rolanda.

"Cheating is a sin. Right, Cal? That's what y'all tried to do with the verbatim thing, so don't cheat! Now that's one ta' grow on!" Rolanda stated aloud to her friends.

"So is lying! That's why you in the shape you in blabber mouth!" Ms. Bryant concluded as she tore up the four girls' homework and walked towards the blackboard to begin the day's lesson as the class laughed aloud at the five girls.

The class ended and the group of twenty-four students filed into the hallway and lined up outside their English class. None of the girls had their English homework and they all received zeroes for the day. They were angry having received more detentions. The following week would have the girls spending the whole week after school. They all vowed to do their assignments from that point forth. Even if they failed, at least they could say they tried.

An hour later, the English teacher, Mrs. Prell, was preparing to leave the class for a few minutes while she and the rest of the sixth grade teachers gathered to put in and buy lunch for themselves, which was a Friday custom at the school for the sixth grade teachers. Mrs. Prell left Lubby in charge to write down the names of the students who acted up.

Brianna and Tracey looked at one another and smiled a slick grin. They knew Mrs. Prell would be gone for at least fifteen minutes, and they saw an opportunity to sneak out of class. The two had done it before and they would usually meet up with Mike and Donald and run to the corner store to buy candy and make it back before the teacher returned. The four of them loved to sneak away; to them it was a challenge to see if they could beat the teachers back. The store was only a block away, but the hard part was sneaking off the school grounds.

When Mrs. Prell left her class, Tracey and Brianna put on

their coats and jumped from their seats and cracked the door and watched and waited until she walked down the long narrow hall and entered Ms. Bryant's class and disappeared from sight. Lubby said nothing as she watched her two friends prepare to leave class. Tracey and Brianna crept out the class and ran to their right, opposite the way Mrs. Prell had gone. They then slowly pushed one of the steel doors open at the end of the hall and peeked out into the cold air, their breath producing a light mist as their heads swiveled left then right. To their left, they saw Mike and Donald peeking from the end of the building. The two young boys were hiding outside the sixth grade building behind the side wall. The corner store was to the right on the corner across the street from the school. The four would have to sneak pass the main building which held the school's office to make it there.

Donald and Mike joined the two girls and the four crept underneath the classroom windows in the sixth grade building. They dashed under the breezeway to the main building and hid behind some bushes that lined the building and crawled behind the row of thick bushes and made it to the front of the school. Only an open space separated them from the parking lot and all the cars they were planning on hiding behind.

"Go first, Dee!" Mike whispered.

"You go! I went last time!"

"Scary ass!" Mike said as he peeked from the side of the main building. A parent was walking across the drive separating the parking lot from the main building and Mike quickly ducked back behind the wall until the woman entered the premises.

"We gotta go, brer! We got like ten minutes left!" Donald whispered.

"Let's go on three!" Brianna then stated. "One, two, three!"

The gang of four quickly darted out into the open and scurried into the parking lot and knelt down beside the parked cars and crept and crawled until they reached the end of the lot. They were now a good distance from the main building and were hidden by trees lining the entrance. They yelled aloud as they ran up the sidewalk towards the store, crossed the street and entered the building. Brianna had four dollars left and she quickly grabbed ten packs of now-laters. The Chinese-owned candy store had a wide assortment of the tasty treat—pine apple, banana, chocolate, grape, vanilla, cherry and everybody's favorite, watermelon. Brianna, who was looking out for her friends, also grabbed a big bag of lay's potato chips, five rock 'n' roll stage planks, a pack of 'fun dip' and made her way to the counter where she scored the top prize of all—the beloved pig lip.

Donald and Mike had handfuls of Jolly Rancher Wine Candy in a variety of flavors and two boxes of Cracker Jack along with four moon pies. They also bought twenty-five cent worth of strawberry cookies. As the Chinese lady began ringing their items, her small wooden counter covered in junk food, Ms. Bryant and Mrs. Prell walked into the store. Unbeknownst to Brianna and company, the teachers were buying Po-boy sandwiches from the corner store this day. Upon entering the place, the teachers had to do a double take. They couldn't believe what they were seeing. Brianna and Tracey were supposed to be in Mrs. Prell's English class, and Donald and Mike were supposed to be in Ms. Bryant's math class. The four knew they were in serious trouble when they spotted the teachers walking their way.

Meanwhile, back in Mrs. Prell's class, Rolanda had the entire class singing the theme song to *The Jefferson's*, a popular TV show in 1982. Dominique was pounding on her desk top, providing a melodic drum line to the class' chorus.

"We moving on up...Moving on up...To thee top...Moving on up...We finally got a piece of the pie..."

"Break it down Miss Jones!" a male student yelled aloud as eleven year-old Rolanda jumped up out her seat whilst holding her dress up over her knees. Rolanda danced as if she was in church on Easter Sunday as she sung lead. *"Fish don't fry in the kitchen...Beans don't burn on the grill...Took a whole lotta trying...Just ta' get up that hill...Now we up in the big league...It's our turn at bat...as long as we live...It's you and me baby...And ain't nothing wrong with that..."*

Kids were out of their seats dancing and jumping around in Ms. Prell's class. They were standing up in their seats and running around like chickens with their heads cut off in a complete state of fun-filled delight. Lubby was trying to restore order without much success. She was warning the students that they were going to get into trouble if they didn't quiet down. She wrote down names, but the kids didn't care, they only continued to sing, dance and literally bounce off the walls in the class. By the time she was through, Lubby had written all twenty-two students' name on the blackboard, including her own.

"Forget this man, they having fun!" she thought to herself as she, too, joined the festivities.

Ms. Bryant's class was no better, students in her class had a tag-team wrestling match going on. The male students had moved the desks from the center of the class and one student pretended to be the Junkyard Dog; another pulled a ski mask over his face and called himself The Grappler. The Great Kabuki was on hand, and so was Precious Paul Ellery and the Fabulous Freebirds. Things had gotten totally out of control in two of the six classes inside the sixth grade building, which was separate from the lower grades. The four remaining teachers left their classes and rushed into the two classes and restored order and ushered the children onto the yard and had them stand silently before the lunch period began.

Back at the store, Brianna, Tracey, Donald, and Michael began to get watery eyed. The two teachers took off their purse straps and began to lash the four eleven year-olds as they stood before the counter. The Chinese lady covered her lower face and looked on as the four children thrashed about against the counter, spilling nearly all of their candy and snacks onto the floor. Brianna grabbed hold of the counter and screamed aloud as she stared at the Chinese lady, her young eyes pleading for help as Ms. Bryant lashed her petite body furiously.

Tracey lay on the floor screaming to the top of her lungs as she grabbed her arms and legs trying to relieve the stinging lashes she had received. Donald and Mike were on the floor rolling about. They were trying to crawl under each other to block the lashes coming from Mrs. Prell's purse strap.

"Watch out, Mike!" Donald yelled.

"Forget you man, that shit hurt!"

"And ya' cussin' too, Michael? You gettin' double!" Mrs. Prell yelled aloud as she continued to lash Mike and Donald. When Ms. Bryant knew she had beaten Tracey and Brianna into submission, she helped Mrs. Prell lash Donald and Mike.

"Y'all ain't even hit Tracey and Bri that long, man! Alright! Alright fuck! I give! I give! I give! I give!" Donald and Mike yelled aloud at the same time.

The teachers had the four students stand facing the wall outside the store when they were done whipping them. They were now planning to scare the living daylights out of the young kids. When the four saw two police cars pull up, they began to cry silently, now under the belief that they were going to jail this day.

Brianna was so scared she couldn't see straight. Her eyes were watery as she prayed not to be taken to jail. The police cars had their lights flailing as they got out, pretending to be angry as they were already filled in on what was going on.

"What the hell is the problem here ma'am?" one officer asked Ms. Bryant.

"We caught these four students cutting class today and we want to turn them in!" Ms. Bryant replied as she eyed the four kids angrily.

"Mister, wait! We just came to by some candy! You can't take us ta' jail for that!" Donald said.

"Cutting class is a serious offense. That's more than enough reason to take you downtown, young man."

"Downtown!" Mike said as he grew scared. Mike knew downtown was where 'big people' went when they got in trouble. He knew what could happen in jail and he wanted no part of prison. "I'm only twelve, brer! I'm supposed to go to the detention center!"

"That's downtown. Any way I don't have to explain, you'll

see when ya' get there," the officer said as he ushered Mike and Donald to the car.

The two twelve year-olds wrestled as best they could and began wailing aloud as the cops placed them into the backseat.

"Shut up! You wanna cut class this is the price you pay today!" the officer said as he slammed the door and watched Mike and Donald kick and flail about in the backseat.

"Officer, take me home! Just let my momma punish me. I don't wanna go to jail! My momma will punish me good, I promise." Brianna stated as she pleaded with the officer with puppy dog eyes.

"Next time you'll know better, little girl. Don't ever cut school again." another officer replied as he ushered Tracey and Brianna to the backseat of his car.

"Come on man, y'all buggin'!" Tracey said with watery eyes. "We just came for some candy! And we going ta' jail for that?" she asked as she and Brianna were guided to the patrol car.

Brianna was placed in the car without much fanfare, but Tracey put up a serious struggle. The husky eleven year-old had braced her legs against the inside of the open car door.

"Move your legs! Get your feet off my car or that'll be another charge!" the officer yelled.

"Hold up, officer! I'm tellin' y'all, y'all buggin'! How in the hell we get ta' go to jail for buying *candy*?" Tracey asked again as she continued to brace herself against the car door.

"Tracey just get in the car before they charge you again!" Brianna pleaded.

"We goin' ta' jail for buying candy, Bri! This is stupid!"

Mike and Donald were even yelling for Tracey to get in the car. It took three officers to place the ever-struggling Tracey into the backseat. "Hold up man! We had *money* ta' buy candy! How in the he—" the officer slammed the door on Tracey. Only then did she begin to cry loudly.

Once the reality had set in and they began to believe that they were actually being taken to jail, all four kids kicked and screamed in the back seat of either patrol car as they looked back at their teachers growing smaller and smaller as the cars drove away. The officers circled the block and pulled up to the school grounds where they scolded the four in front of the entire school, the school's principal and several teachers. Lunch had already begun and Rolanda, Dominique, and Lubby watched with scared eyes as Brianna, Tracey, Donald, and Mike cried out in sheer terror. The girls were worried that their friends were going to jail. Lubby began to cry as she watched Brianna and Tracey wail aloud whilst being held by the hand by the police officers. She was truly scared for her friends.

"The next time we have to come out here, the next time we catch you, or any of you other students, especially the sixth graders, ditching class, you *will* go to jail!" the towering police officer said to the four students and the entire sixth grade class as he turned them over to the school's principal.

Brianna, Tracey, Mike and Donald's act of defiance, along with the mischief in the two classrooms had ruined upcoming events for the entire sixth grade class. The good now had to suffer for the bad. The homeroom Halloween party and costume contest was canceled and the 'trick or treat in school' was canceled as well for the sixth graders. The five girls had learned a crucial lesson this day: don't play around in school.

All the friends, with the exception of Lubby, had good parents that cared for them, but they were ruining things with their bad behavior in school. The lesson sunk in when the five friends were separated from one another for an entire month. They only saw each other in school and even then they could barely hang together as the teachers had separated them from one another. They only hung out during lunch when they ate and that was for maybe fifteen minutes. At home they weren't allowed on the phone and Jazzy's show was off limits for the entire month for everybody except Lubby.

Lubby's mother could care less what her daughter did; but during the entire month when her friends were under lock and key, Lubby had punished herself. Even though she was allowed to go outside, it just wasn't the same without her friends. She stayed inside the whole month enduring her friends' punishment, having to listen to her mother, who would call her stupid every day.

"What the hell you gone do the whole month, Lubby? Send up a fuckin' smoke signal? Staring out the window like you a fuckin' hostage! You can leave this mutherfucka ya' stupid bitch! Go make some new friends! Shit, you hanging 'round here all day after school cock-blocking!"

Cynthia's words really hurt Lubby, but she endured the verbal abuse for the sake of friendship. She cried most days, but she knew her friends were missing her just as much as she was missing them. She couldn't wait to get back with her girls. The five friends were miserable during this period of time; and the sixth grade class had suffered as well. The students were all bored because the five friends, who were so much fun at school, were broken up for a short period of time. The girls had indeed learned a hard lesson.

CHAPTER 4

ON AIR

"Ain't no since in standing there with water in your in your eyes...Hoping that it stop her...From whipping your behind...I wish those days, would, come back once more...I wish those days would, come back once more... 'Cause I love them so..".

Stevie Wonder's song, *I Wish Those Days* blared across the airwaves a week before Thanksgiving break in 1982. The five were sitting over to Tracey's house sitting in her bedroom listening to Jazzy's show, having just been reunited a few days earlier. The cold air whipped about outside as the five friends drank tang, and ate caramel popcorn balls and laughed aloud while listening to Stevie Wonder sing about somebody catching a whipping.

"That's a funny song! Somebody gone get a butt whipping!" Lubby said just before the song came to an end and Jazzy's voice came across the airwaves.

"My man Stevie talking about a behind thrashing on that one friends. And umm, it's appropriate for the next discussion. Now, you all know I keeps an ear to the streets—and somebody representin' Little Woods Elementary school tonight friends." the jovial lady spoke across the airwaves. "For my fans in Alabama and Mississippi, Little Woods is an elementary school in New Orleans East."

The five began to scream when they heard Jazzy speak of their school.

"She talking bout our school! We on the radio! What she gotta say about us?" they said randomly.

"Yea, what Jazzy heard was that a Brianna and a Tracey ditched class and got caught by the po' po'! It was a bad move because they messed it up for all the sixth graders at Little Woods. They ain't have no Halloween party, no trick or treat and they were punished for a whole month!"

The five looked at one another and began to moan when they realized they were being talked about in bad way.

"We gone be the laughing stock tomorrow at school! How Jazzy know 'bout that, man? That was a month ago!" Tracey said with tears in her eyes, but she wouldn't have long to wait to find out the source of the five's embarrassment over the airwaves.

"I wanna give a congrats to a Donald and a Mike for holding it down. They tried ta' stop the girls from leaving that day, and as they say 'the good have ta' suffer for the bad'. Let that be a lesson friends, stay in school and always, *always* do your homework and respect the teachers. Now, a special request from a Calvin at Little Woods, because they suffering for what these two girls have done, he wants to hear Mister Telephone Man by New Edition. Calvin having problems connecting with his beau y'all! Anyway, we sending this one out ta' Dominique in East Shore, Calvin says he forgives you sweetie. Your phone calls talking about what happened at Little Woods Elementary coming up next children so stay tuned." Jazzy said as she faded the song into play.

"Mr. Telephone man...There's something wrong with my line...When I dial my baby's number...I get a click every time...Mister Telephone Man..."

As *New Edition's* song began to play on the radio, the five eleven year-old girls quickly rushed to the phone in Tracey's mother's kitchen. They just had to let Jazzy know she'd gotten it wrong about the events that took place the month before. Rolanda grabbed the phone and began to dial the number.

"Oh hell no! You froze up last time, scary cat! Gimmie that receiver!" Tracey snapped. She and Rolanda were tussling over the phone as it began to ring Jazzy's studio.

"Dominique, Calvin represented for you!" Brianna said excitedly as she walked with Dominique, who was in a dreamlike state, towards the living room. "That's your new boyfriend now! Y'all have to go together!"

Dominique smiled at the thought as Tracey and Rolanda wrestled over the receiver in the kitchen. She went into the living room and sat on the sofa and listened to the song, dreaming of Calvin with Brianna on her side.

"Hey, you on with Jazzy, who is this?" Jazzy asked over the phone.

Tracey froze up when she heard Jazzy's voice and Rolanda snatched the phone from her hands. "Hello? Hello?"

"Yea, you on with Jazzy! What's happenin' caller?"

"Jazzy this Rolanda Jones, and Tracey and Brianna is two of my best friends and I just wanna say Donald and Mike lying. They got they behind whip at the candy store that same day! And they was crying when the police brought 'em back to our school!"

"Rolanda Jones?" Jazzy inquired as she looked at the school's enlistment roll. "Okay, I got you right here, you wanna go on air and tell all our listeners what really went down?"

"Huh?" Rolanda asked in a surprised manner.

"If they fibbing you should tell the listeners what's really goin' on, young sister!"

"Right, right, go on air and tell it." Rolanda said lowly as the four other girls looked on. "Well, umm—"

Just then Tracey snatched the phone and told Jazzy they were willing to go on air. The woman put her on hold and Tracey and Lubby looked at Rolanda with wide smiles on their faces. "Why y'all staring at me like that?"

"You gotta spill the beans Rolanda." Tracey stated excitedly.

"Uh, uh! I ain't going on air!"

"You can do it Rolanda!" Lubby remarked. "You gossip girl! That's what you do! Tell everybody what really happened!" Lubby suggested as she patted Rolanda's back.

Rolanda was reluctant to go on air. She argued back and forth with her friends, trying to convince them that she wasn't going to be able to tell the story correctly.

Tracey wasn't hearing it. She grabbed Rolanda's hand with the phone receiver and put it to her ear and demanded she tell the story. "You blab everything else! Tell that stuff man! Or you gone let Dee and Mike lie on us like that? Run ya' mouth like you always do!" Tracey said seriously right before the song ended and Jazzy's voice came back on air.

"Alright we back with Rolanda, and Rolanda representin' for Tracey and Brianna. If Rolanda has to tell it, things didn't go quite the way Donald and Mike said it did. Rolanda tell us what really happened, honey bun."

Rolanda froze for a minute and Tracey was about to go into a fit. She reached for the phone to tell the story herself, but just before she was about to snatch the phone, Rolanda walked away and yelled out, "Donald and Mike is liars! They was, they was at the store with Bri and Tracey and they punked up! They was all on the floor screaming like girls when the teachers hit 'em! That's right I'm a tell it all," Rolanda said as she paused, took a breath, placed her hands on her hips and began to rock slightly as she began to speak more slowly. "They was crying big crocodile tears when they got out tha' police car. Wait let me back up, Miss Jazzy! Now, everybody know, when you scared, or when you getting beat like a dirty old dog, you hollar 'I give'. Donald and Mike said that four times and cried uncle. And when they got back to school they was begging. 'Don't take me ta' jail, don't take me jail! They cried like babies in front of everybody and that's the truth!" Rolanda ended calmly as her friends patted her back.

Jazzy and her staff laughed aloud over the airwaves, "We gotta good show tonight staff!" Jazzy said off air.

Jazzy then went back to the airwaves. "Well, well, looks like we gotta conflict going on in East Shore this evening friends!

They is blowing the lines up!"

"Them li'l girls is mad. I believe the li'l girls." Jazzy's producer said over the air, further instigating the children's' conflict on this night.

"Me too. I believe the girls," Jazzy chimed in. "Let's vote on it friends. And tonight, for this eight 'o' clock hour at least, we only taking calls from Little Woods Elementary students. Come on and let's get ta' the bottom of what happened out there last month because no matter what you do there are private eyes watching you kids, stay in school all my children!" Jazzy ended as she faded into the song *Private Eyes* by *Hall and Oates*.

The five ran through Tracey's mother house as the song played, dancing and singing along with the music as they waited the outcome of the vote.

The next morning, the five couldn't wait to get on the bus and mock Donald and Mike. They had won the vote and Mike and Donald were called 'fibbers' by Jazzy. The girls mocked the two boys, who could only sit quietly and take their taunts because they knew their plan had backfired.

"Nice move Dee!" Mike said in a sarcastic manner as he got up and sat in another seat.

All day at school Mike and Donald were made fun of by the sixth grade class. Donald's plan to embarrass the girls had backfired dramatically. Donald knew the girls listened to Jazzy's show, everybody did—and when the girls got off punishment, Donald just knew he was going to be put on blast by Brianna and Tracey. He'd simply out-thought himself the night before.

During lunch that same day, Calvin approached Dominique.

"Hey, you heard me represent for you last night?" Calvin asked as he and Dominique stood by themselves on side of the sixth grade building out of sight from the rest of the students.

Dominique, dressed in an evergreen knee-length skirt and white turtle neck sweater with a pair of white knee-high boots, stood beside the sixth grade building blushing at Calvin. Her straight-pressed black hair hung just over her ears. She pulled her hair back and smiled at Calvin. Calvin looked into her dark pretty eyes and smiled back.

"You ever kissed a boy?" Calvin asked shyly.

"Cal, your momma, and my momma will beat us both! But no. I ain't never kissed a boy. Especially one that's not my boyfriend."

Calvin reached into his tan Lee jeans and pulled out a letter and handed it to Dominique, who opened it and read in silence as Calvin stood by waiting anxiously. When Dominique saw that Calvin had asked if he could be her boyfriend in the letter, she laughed. Calvin grew sad and began to walk off.

"Calvin," Dominique called out.

"What? You laughed at me so I guess I was wrong about us."

"You weren't wrong, Calvin. I just thought it was the sweetest thing a boy ever did. The song last night, and now this letter? Yes. You can be my boyfriend."

After Dominique spoke, neither child knew what to say or do. They merely stared at each other.

"Let me give you my number and you can call me." Dominique said lowly.

"Umm, I was—I was, umm—"

"What, Calvin?"

"Can I have a kiss, Dominique?" Calvin blurted out in frustration.

Dominique stared up at Calvin as her heart began to pound. Calvin was sweating in the cold air; both kids were nervous as all outdoors.

"Okay." Dominique said as she closed her eyes and turned her right cheek to Calvin.

Calvin reached out and pulled Dominique's face to his and pressed his lips to Dominique's lips. For ten seconds his lips remained pressed tightly against Dominique's lips. It was their first kiss ever and felt wonderful. Their little hearts were thumping furiously when they pulled back and stared at one another. Dominique's eyes were glazed over and Calvin had a look of shear ecstasy in his eyes. He was hooked on Dominique all from a ten second kiss. Dominique wrote down her number and handed it to Calvin.

"I like you a lot, Dominique."

"I like you too, Cal." Dominique responded.

Rolanda had seen everything. She was peeking from the front of the sixth grade building, and when she saw the kiss, she jumped out into the open and shouted, "Calvin gotta girlfriend! Dominique and Calvin go together y'all!"

Brianna, Lubby, and Tracey, who were under the breezeway mocking Donald and Mike, heard Rolanda and they ran to the edge of the building.

"Bri, y'all missed it!" Rolanda said excitedly. "Y'all go 'head and kiss again so they can see!" she said as Brianna, Lubby, and Tracey ran around to the side of the building.

"I *knew* y'all was gone go together! Dominique y'all make a good couple!" Brianna said, happy for her friend.

As the bell rung for classes to begin, Calvin begged the five girls not to tell his mother and father. The five liked Calvin, he was a smart, cute, and cool kid to them; only he couldn't do many of the things other kids did from time to time. They all agreed to keep he and Dominique's business under wraps.

That same day, a week before Thanksgiving break, Brianna had gotten the teachers to allow her and Tracey to apologize to the sixth grade class over the school's P.A. System. Dominique and Rolanda were overjoyed when Brianna and Tracey came to them that Wednesday and asked them to write up an apology. Rolanda, and Dominique had then decided to turn the apology into a small broadcast—a spin-off of Jazzy's show, only they would do it over the P.A. system at their school. They had no idea if the teachers would cut them off once they knew what was going on, but they dared to try on pull it off anyway.

All day the five were telling the entire sixth grade class to be on their best behavior—no cutting class, have all homework done, and no fighting. When Friday came around and Mrs. Prell and Ms. Bryant left to get lunch, they were expecting an outbreak of mayhem again since the five were back in unison, to their surprise, however, everyone was on their best behavior. Upon seeing that, the teachers agreed to let the girls have their say the following Friday.

The P.A. system was turned on the following Friday in the sixth grade building fifteen minutes before school was to be released. All the sixth grade students sat quietly as the five stood in front of the microphone in the school's office, their voices could be heard as they tried to get Rolanda to lead off.

"I ain't even get in trouble! That was Tracey and Bri!" Rolanda stated. The kids back in the classes started laughing as Dominique sneered at Rolanda and took the lead.

"Good afternoon! This is Dominique Franz and I'm standing here with Tracey Sanchez, Brianna Stanford, Lubby Williams and Rolanda Jones and we have a message to all the sixth graders." Dominique spoke loudly, kicking the show off. "A month ago," she continued, "Bri and Tracey, along with Donald and Mike did something bad friends, and on behalf of the five, because we all feel responsible for what happened, we wanted to apologize for messing things up at school during Halloween. As Thanksgiving comes closer, we want to remember all that we have to be thankful for, God, our parents, and the teachers here at Little Woods who really care about us all. Ms. Bryant, Mrs. Prell, Tracey and Bri has something to say." Dominique ended as she stepped aside.

Brianna and Tracey apologized whole-heartedly and they left the sixth grade teachers and students with smiles across their faces.

"Also," Rolanda said as she bluntly stepped in, "Mrs. Prell, the homework that Donald told you he did at home was a flat out lie—he did it in Math class right before he went to your class, that's what happened, umm hmm. That's get back for lying to Miss Jazzy. Thought we forgot and I ain't through with y'all. Mahogany and Celestine had a fight on the park in East Shore and on the strength, Mahogany loss that one. That's why she ain't come ta' school Tuesday. She was embarrassed, umm hmm—but she and Celestine been friends since the Slinky came out so they good. Ain't nothing to that. And, and Donald and Mike stole some cookies from the corner store 'round our house and caught a beat down by Donald momma, umm hmm. Them two just all up in it—get it together Heckle and Jeckle! What else I got? Oh yea, Stacey and Ricky is a couple, Leslie and Jeffrey is a couple, but I thought Jeff was going with Rachel—not being messy, that's just what I heard! Anyway, Calvin was voted cutest boy in the sixth grade and Tracey Sanchez was voted the most popular. That's 'the talk on the yard' and I'm Miss Rolanda 'I already heard that' Jones signing off."

The school's librarian was on hand and she said nothing as she stared at the girls. She appreciated the girls' apologies, but she didn't know what to make of Rolanda's message. Was it a joke? Was Rolanda serious? What would Mrs. Prell, and Ms. Bryant, the two ladies who allowed the girls to talk on the school's PA system think about what she had done?

The five waited anxiously for the two teachers to approach. When they heard the teachers' laughter in the hallway, they stared at each other and smiled.

"Y'all gone be Dee-jays for real one day!" Brianna stated to Tracey, Dominique and Rolanda as Lubby smiled with excitement, happy for her friends.

Ms. Bryant and Ms. Prell thought what Rolanda did was cool, as did all the sixth graders. Rolanda's remarks had sparked conversation in their classrooms between student and teacher which was hard to do in those days. Teachers gave orders and students obeyed, period. That one announcement had the students talking about what went on not only on the school yard, but also at home. The girls asked could they do a weekly report and the two teachers agreed, so long as no one got angry. Rolanda knew what she was doing, at the tender age of eleven she already knew to check with the students before she told what she knew. The students, White, Black, and Asian alike, all thought it was cool to be mentioned by Rolanda over the P.A., to them it meant you were in the loop, you were popular and had something going on. Dominique was going to do a weekly news report on major stories in the news, and Tracey would announce and then play the school's song for the week on Brianna's portable radio. Usually it was a song she heard Jazzy play and had recorded onto Brianna's portable radio boom box.

Dominique, Rolanda, and Tracey began broadcasting at the young age of eleven with a weekly report at Little Woods Elementary School that lasted the entire school year. They had changed the face of how students behaved on the yard and at home with their weekly announcements.

CHAPTER 5

IT WAS A GOOD DAY

Summertime had come real quick for the five. It was now Mid-August of 1983 and the girls, all twelve, were heavy into the summer season. They all had gotten bikes this year. Rolanda had an old bicycle she wasn't using and she had given it to Lubby, whose mother had refused to by her a bike. The five girls spent most days riding through East Shore, but on this hot muggy evening they had decided to pay Calvin a visit. Calvin and Dominique were still boyfriend and girlfriend, but they only got to talk on the phone once summer had started because Calvin couldn't go too far from the house. He stayed about a mile away from East Shore just off Bullard Boulevard. The girls, all dressed in tank tops, shorts and sandals, rode to the front of East Shore, there, Curran Boulevard was cut off by a thick brush about a quarter mile long. On the other side of the brush was another neighborhood and Curran Boulevard would pick up from there and continue right into Calvin's neighborhood.

Brianna rode her new Diamond-backed chrome Mongoose bike with black mag rims ahead of the rest of the girls who were all riding red Huffy bikes as their mothers had gotten identical bikes on sale at K-Mart. When they got to the brush, they had to exit their bikes and walk beside them through the thick brush. It could be dangerous walking through the brush, bums often slept on the discarded furniture left by illegal dumpers. The five hurried through the brush and quickly hopped on their bikes and sped towards Calvin's street.

"Bet a dollar I beat all y'all suckas to Calvin house!" twelve year-old Tracey screamed as she sped past everyone.

No one except Dominique took Tracey up on her offer; she hadn't seen Calvin since the school year had ended and she missed him dearly. Tracey looked back and saw Dominique barreling down on her and she tried as best she could to keep the lead. As they approached Calvin's street, Stony Brook Drive, Dominique had taken the lead and won a dollar from Tracey.

Calvin's neighborhood consisted of lavish stucco, brick, or Swedish style homes that were much pricier than the homes in East Shore. The people in this particular neighborhood were well-to-do, upper middle-class families. The grass was greener and thicker, the cars more expensive and the homes twice as big as the homes in East Shore. The five rode up Calvin's street and in the distance up ahead, they could see a crowd of people outside of a neatly built light-brown large brick house.

"I never knew people even came outside around here!" Lubby said as the girls slowly rode up the street heading to where they saw Calvin, his brother Gerald and Gerald's two best friends Bobby and 'Tank' standing out front of a house with a crowd of other kids and some adults who were excitedly looking at the scene before them. The five could hear music up ahead and they pedaled a little faster to see what was going on that had everybody's attention. Calvin saw the girls coming and he quickly began flagging them to hurry up and come see what was going on.

When the girls rode up onto the scene, they saw three women standing in the driveway in front the house singing a song. A 'Happy Birthday' banner hung above the home's front door. The three women were singing *Juicy Fruit*, originally sung by Mtume.

"Candy rain...coming down...taste you in my mind...and spread you all around...Here I am...oh this loves for you...hey baby...sweet as honey dew..."

The three women sang harmoniously as the five, along with

the rest of the crowd, which consisted of both black and white adults and children, looked on in appreciation.

"Who is that?" Brianna asked Calvin as she stared awestruck at the lady with grey eyes, who was the lead singer.

"That's Gabriella Holland and her friends Charmaine and Yvonne. They practicing."

"For what?" Brianna asked.

"I don't know really. They been practicing all summer, though. They sing at a club. Go talk to her when they get through, Bri. Gabriella a nice lady, she'll talk to you." twelve year-old Calvin said.

The five enjoyed the melodic song and when Gabriella and her friends had finished, Gabriella invited everyone out in front of her home to come and have a piece of her birthday cake.

"Hey miss, I like your voice!" Brianna said in an excited voice as the woman handed her a piece of cake.

"Why thank you pretty lady. And what's your name?"

"Brianna Stanford. I wanna sing like you when I grow up. I want my voice to sound just like yours."

Gabriella's eyes grew wide and she smiled. The woman loved to sing; and to see a young child wanting to grow up and be a performer had indeed touched her heart. "Well Brianna, I tell you what—me and my friends will be rehearsing here for the next few months. If you want, you can come by. This is my husband, Sam," Gabriella said as she grabbed her husband's arm. "And this here shy boy is my son, Benjamin."

"I'm not shy, momma! I just don't know them girls yet! But I think that one pretty!" the nine year-old light-skinned, thin-framed little boy said as he pointed at Lubby, who was waiting for a piece of cake along with Tracey, Dominique, Calvin, and Rolanda.

Lubby looked around to see who Ben was talking about.

"He talking about you Lubby." Rolanda said.

"Run that by me again!"

"You! He likes—you!" Rolanda stated as she laughed. "Damn, Lubby you umm, y'all gone go together?"

Rolanda thought it was funny that Ben had a crush on Lubby. Although the five, who were all now twelve, were considered 'li'l girls', to the teenagers in East Shore and else-where, Ben, was a 'li'l boy' to the five. Rolanda thought it was funny that a 'li'l boy' had a crush on Lubby.

"I mean, y'all can like, color together and ride his big wheel! That'll be fun! And Oooh! Y'all can even watch Reading Rainbow!" Rolanda said as she made fun of Lubby.

"That's a 'li'l boy, Rolanda. But he's cute! I ain't riding no big wheel, though." Lubby said as she joked with Rolanda and waved at Ben.

Lubby's brown eyes were sparkling, her brown hair was neatly pressed as she stood in a white pair of shorts, grey shirt, and a pair of grey leather sandals, all given to her by Brianna at the start of summer. Ben thought Lubby was the prettiest girl alive. He went and stood next to her and grabbed her hand and tried to pull her away so he could ask her name.

"Hey Ben, leave that girl alone! She too old for you!" Sam said as he laughed aloud. "Excuse my son," the man stated as he tried to pull Ben away from Lubby. "I guess he likes 'em older than what he is—but he means no harm."

"It's okay Mister Holland, I think he cute! He can't be my boyfriend, but I'll be your friend Ben!" Lubby said as she reached out her hand towards Ben. The twelve year-old thought the boy was cute and sweet, but he was too young for her. Lubby talked and played with Ben the whole while they were at the Holland family home; they had become friends on this day. The whole while they were there, Brianna followed Gabriella around her yard asking her questions about music, and Gabriella kindly answered every question. The two of them had become friends.

As the sun began to set, Dominique yelled aloud that they were missing Jazzy's show and they had to hurry home to catch the rest. Ben, not wanting Lubby to leave, told the five girls they could listen to the show in his parents' garage. "They won't mind! Y'all come on! You too Calvin and Gerald!" he said aloud.

Gerald, and his two friends, Bobby and Tank laughed to themselves. The three of them were now fifteen years-old and they didn't want to hang around a bunch of youngsters.

"Naahh, li'l Ben. You go ahead with that right there." Gerald remarked.

"Man y'all scared of girls!" Ben said as he ran back to his garage and began to pull out folding chairs for the five girls and Calvin.

Gerald and his friends laughed aloud at young Ben. "Hey, he got a point there! We gotta go find some females! Shit, Ben and Calvin got five of 'em all to they self!" Tank stated as the boys hopped on their Mongoose bikes.

"Calvin?" Gerald snapped as the young teens sat on their bikes in front of young Ben's home staring back at Ben as he unfolded chairs inside his parents' garage. "Calvin a momma's boy! He ain't gone do nothing! Them girls a li'l too young right now anyway player. Later on though, I'm gone have ta' take Lubby from Ben!" Gerald then said loud enough for Lubby to hear as he rode off.

Lubby liked Gerald—a lot. She had a serious crush on the fifteen year-old. She ran into the driveway and shouted, "I'm more woman than you think, Gerald!"

"Say that a few years from now, Lubby!" Gerald responded as he and his friends sped off down the street.

"It's gone be too late!" Lubby yelled back as she watched Gerald and his friends ride down the street and out of sight.

Back in the garage, Ben, Calvin and the five girls sat and listened to Jazzy's show. Gabriella came out and had given the kids cans of Coca-Cola to sip while they listened.

"You like Jazzy, Misses Holland?" Dominique asked as she sipped her soda.

"Yes I do. Let me let you girls in on a secret," the woman said in a low tone as she knelt before the girls, "Jazzy is a friend of mines!"

The five girls' eyes lit up.

"You know Jazzy?" they all screamed in unison.

"Yes ma'ams. She comes to our club from time to time. I'm planning on recording an album next year and she's vying to be the first Dee-jay to play my first single on the radio."

The five all sat with their mouths open staring at Gabriella. She knew Jazzy, their idol. Gabriella was also going to record an album and Jazzy was going to play it on the radio. At that moment, Brianna had become inspired by Gabriella Holland. Without fully comprehending what she had done, the woman had given Brianna inspiration to follow her dreams—she wanted to sing, just like Gabriella.

The kids sat and talked with Gabriella for a while whilst listening to the show. Before long it was almost ten 'o' clock. Gabriella told the girls they had to go home as their parents were surely looking for them. They all sighed when they had to leave.

"Hey, I'm not going anywhere. You girls, and you too Calvin, are always welcome over here. Matter of fact, tomorrow, I'll be playing my piano. Come by around four tomorrow evening and we'll hang out okay? But you have to leave now because your mothers and fathers may be worried."

The five got on their bikes and Calvin followed them through the trail back into their neighborhood. When they got to the end of the trail, Dominique and Calvin stayed back.

"Y'all gone kiss again?" Rolanda asked.

"Rolanda leave those two alone!" Brianna stated as she, Tracey and Lubby pedaled down Curran Boulevard. "I'm a find out if y'all kissed on the lips! And when school start I'm a tell it!"

"Ain't nobody kissing! And if we do, don't say nothing!" Dominique snapped.

"Nothing?"

"Nothing! We don't want our business on air!"

"Can I watch?"

"Bye, Rolanda!" Dominique and Calvin said in unison as Rolanda rode off slowly, sniggling to herself.

Dominique made sure Rolanda was out of sight before she turned and smiled at Calvin, her dark eyes glowing with excitement.

Calvin smiled back and said, "I ain't kiss you all summer, Dominique."

"I know, I missed that."

"Me too. My momma and daddy told me ain't nothing wrong with kissing if you love somebody."

Dominique smiled up at Calvin as she stood with her bike between her legs. "You love me Calvin?" she asked as her young heart began to flutter. Never had words sounded so good to Dominique.

"Yea, I love you, Dominique." Calvin answered as his face grew nearer Dominique's.

Dominique knew this would be more than just a kiss on the lips. She closed her eyes and parted her lips, more than ready for her first 'tongue' kiss. Her heart throbbed, she began to shake and grow sweaty around her temples as Calvin's face grew nearer to hers. When felt Calvin's lips land on the top of her forehead instead of her puckered lips, Dominique opened her eyes in disbelief and asked, "What the hell kind of kiss was that, man?"

"What's wrong?" Calvin asked.

"That's not a kiss, Calvin! Kiss me, man!"

"Kiss me, man!" Rolanda mimicked from the woods.

Rolanda had been watching the whole time and Calvin knew it.

Dominique turned around and scowled as she stomped her feet. "Leave us alone, shoot! Go 'bout your business, Rolanda!"

"Dang! You ain't, you ain't have to say it let that!" Rolanda said, pretending her feelings were hurt as she ran over to her back and rode off to catch up with Brianna and Tracey.

When they were sure Rolanda had left the two sniggled and, with eyes open, they pressed lips together. Dominique eased her tongue forward and she felt it make contact with Calvin's tongue. She opened her eyes wide and pushed her head forward just as Calvin placed his arms around her back and drew her body close to his. The sensation was incredible. Dominique stepped off her bike and let it fall to the side. She closed her eyes and wrapped her arms around Calvin and the two held one another tightly, low moans emanated from the both of them during what had become a very stimulating, special and passionate successful first 'tongue' kiss.

Calvin smiled as he pulled back from Dominique, whose lips were still puckered. She wanted more. Calvin had had enough, however, because unbeknownst to Dominique, he'd grown an erection and had gotten embarrassed. He calmly said he would call Dominique the next day as he gathered his bike and walked beside it through the trial. Dominique stood and watched as Calvin made his way through the woods. She bit her bottom lip and smiled, watching her boyfriend hop onto his bike and ride back towards his neighborhood. From that day forth, Dominique believed in her young heart that she and Calvin would be together forever.

Dominique then pedaled her bike down Curran and rejoined her girls. She pointed her middle finger and brushed off Rolanda's taunts as Brianna pulled alongside her and asked her what happened.

"We tongue kissed, Bri." Dominique whispered. "He said he loved me, too! Calvin loves me!" she said happily as the girls rode down the street on their bicycles on this muggy summer night in August of 1983.

Brianna smiled, happy for her friend. "I told you y'all made a good couple, Dominique."

"We do. We do, Bri. Thanks."

It had been a good day for the five girls. They returned to their respective homes and turned in for the night in anticipation of returning to Gabriella's home to hang out with Ben, who was cool to them, and Gabriella Holland, who in the eyes of the young girls was the nicest grown person they had ever met.

CHAPTER 6

THE RADIO IDOL

It was another steamy hot summer day in New Orleans; the day after Gabriella had invited the five girls back to her home. It was just before noon and the girls decided to head to Lincoln Beach to have a swim before they went to Gabriella's home. The five ran up the levee laughing loudly; eager to dive into the cool waters of Lake Ponchartrain. They were toting beach towels, life preservers, and two paper grocery bags full of sandwiches and frozen juices. They headed down the levee and were about to cross the railroad tracks when they heard the blaring horn of a train. Amtrak and freight trains ran frequently along the two rail lines as it was a main entrance and exit out of the city. The freight train was barreling down the tracks and the five had stopped to wait for it to pass. As the five waited at the foot of the levee, Donald and Mike emerged at the top of the hill on their BMX bikes.

"Let's beat the train, Mike!" Donald yelled as he readied himself to pedal down the hillside.

Mike was reluctant. "That ain't a good idea, Dee. Let's just go down there and chill with Bri 'nem till it pass." he suggested.

"Man, you a scary cat! I'm a bunny-hop over the tracks and beat the train watch!" Donald stated as he pedaled down the levee.

The girls saw Donald headed for the tracks and they began

screaming. The Engineer spotted Donald headed for the tracks from a half-mile away and he laid down on the horn. Trains traveled at over fifty miles per hour along this stretch of track, but they looked like they were moving slower than what they really were. Their size actually created an optical illusion that gave them the appearance of moving at a snail's pace; but the massive machine was nearly wide open as it headed out of the city.

"Donald stop!" the five girls yelled aloud. "Stop, boy!"

"You bouta get killed!" Mike yelled to his friend.

Donald saw how close the train was and he panicked when he got nearer to the tracks. The five girls ran back up the levee as Donald passed them on his bike. They turned around and stared and began to scream, but their screams were overwhelmed by the train's horn and the screeching of its brakes. Donald's bike was laying on the tracks for a brief second until it was crushed by the iron wheels of the long freight train and dragged down the tracks, steadily being crushed under tons of steel.

"Ohh shit! Donald! Donald!" Mike screamed as he hopped off his bike and ran down the levee and waited for the braking train to slide by as sparks shot out from the steel wheels.

About a mile down the tracks, the train had come to a complete stop and the Engineers ran back towards the scene at a furious pace. When they got there, they saw Donald's twelve year-old body writhing about on the set of tracks next to the set of tracks they had been traveling. Lucky for Donald, when he panicked, he ran into the tracks and his momentum flipped him off his bike and threw him across the tracks the train was traveling and had prevented him from being hit. He was clutching his left arm and crying aloud.

When the five girls and Mike looked at Donald's arm, they could see the bone on his left arm sticking out from his skin. The Engineers called for an ambulance and Mike went and called Donald's mother, who arrived in her car just as the ambulance was carting her son towards the waiting ambulance. Donald's mother cussed at him all the way to the ambulance.

"The fuck you doing trying ta' beat a fuckin' train, stupid ass?"

"Momma I broke my arm! I'm hurt! Stop cursing me!" Donald cried as he was wheeled to the ambulance with Mike following close behind.

"That ain't all that's gone be broke! 'Cause I'm gone break your damn neck soon as Methodist Hospital send your ass home!" Donald's mother snapped as she walked behind the gurney yelling at her son. "Let that be a fuckin' lesson to the rest of y'all! Don't be an ass like this mutherfucka! Stay off the tracks when ya' see a damn train comin'! And as far as the railroad, I'm suing y'all bitches!"

Once everything had settled down, the five went on to the beach and enjoyed a cool dip for almost two hours before they realized they had to get ready to go over to Gabriella's house. As they were leaving, they heard another train coming. The five began walking slowly through the wooded trail and began talking about what happened to Donald. When they got to the clearing, they saw young Calvin and Ben atop the levee sitting on their bicycles. Ben's eyes lit up when he saw Lubby and he began to pedal down the levee just as the train was approaching. The five screamed aloud when they saw the nine year-old headed towards the tracks. Calvin hopped off his bike and quickly grabbed Ben's seat but the momentum was pulling the two down the hill.

"Hit the brakes, Ben! Hit the fuckin' brakes, boy!" Calvin yelled.

Young Ben slammed his brakes and the two stopped about ten feet from the tracks. The engine's horn was deafening and the wind from the speeding train had knocked Ben off his bike and had also knocked Calvin to the ground, but both boys were unharmed. Calvin Huntley had saved Ben's life this day.

When the train passed the girls rushed across the tracks to the two young boys asking were they okay.

"I'm sorry, Lubby! I was just trying to see you," young Ben said.

Lubby had tears in her eyes because she knew Ben had almost died, and he seemed unfazed by the event that had nearly taken his life. "You don't have to run to me when you see me around here or anywhere else, li'l Ben. When you see me and I see you, I promise to wait on you okay?"

"Thanks Lubby. I think you cool. Hey, you wanna ride my bike home?"

Lubby laughed half-heartedly. Ben had quickly put the event out his mind, but she replayed that image mentally several times over, glad Ben was saved by Calvin. Lubby knew young Ben Holland had a crush on her, but he was three years younger than she. She also knew what it felt like to have a crush on someone older than you as she had a serious crush on Gerald. Rather than be rude to Ben, she decided to remain nice to him, because Gerald, who was three years older than Lubby, was nice to her.

Ben and Calvin walked with the five to East Shore. Ben was riding his bike beside Lubby. From time to time, Lubby would ride the bike with young Ben and guide him by sitting on the handle bars, which elated nine year old Ben, who was happy to be close to Lubby. The group stopped and talked to a few of their peers along the way, telling some who weren't around what happened to Donald on the rail road tracks.

Lubby and Rolanda said goodbye to Tracy and Brianna as Dominique hopped onto Calvin's bike. She watched as Rolanda and Lubby chased Ben down Emory Road on his bike.

"Hey Cal, I heard you cussing back there by the levee." she said as she peddled slowly.

"I know! I was scared man! I saw Ben was about ta' die."

"That was awesome, Calvin. You a hero!"

"I don't think so. Look, don't y'all say nothing to Gabriella because she always tellin' Ben not to ride on the levee. I don't know what I woulda done had I let something happen to that li'l boy." Calvin said as Dominique paused in front of her home.

"Calvin you saved, Ben, man! You might not see it that way,

but he could have gotten seriously hurt. Look what happened to Donald."

"I see what you mean. But I don't wanna be called a hero. I'm just glad I was there."

"Me too—hero." Dominique said as she smiled at Calvin proudly. "Hey, we all going shower and change, you and Ben gone wait for us?" she then asked.

"Looks like I ain't got a choice." Calvin said as pointed to young Ben walking up the sidewalk holding Lubby's hand, preparing to enter her home.

"Who in the fuck is that? Don't tell me you fuckin' li'l boys now!" Cynthia snapped when she eyed Lubby walking into the living room holding Ben's hand.

"I ain't having sex momma! And Ben is just my friend."

"What the hell you bring his ass in here for? He ain't got a job or money! You need ta' find a man with benefits with ya' young hot ass!"

"Momma why you talk to me like that? You always hurt me! And I don't even be doing nothing!" Lubby remarked as she began to cry and usher Ben back to the front door. "Ben go back by Dominique and Calvin and I'm a ride my bike down there when I change." she stated as she stood in her doorway.

"What's the matter with your momma?"

"She just be buggin' sometimes."

"My momma don't never bug out like that. You gone come by my house today?"

Lubby looked back at her mother and saw Cynthia staring angrily at her and didn't bother to answer Ben's question. She just shut the door and locked it.

"I know you goin' over there! You oughta be shamed, fuckin a li'l boy! You need a man, like the one I got!"

"Ben more man than any of them suckas you bring in here." Lubby stated under her breath.

"What bitch?" Cynthia asked loudly as she pounced on her

daughter and began hitting her across the back.

"Momma! Momma! I ain't do nothin! Momma stop!" Lubby stated as her mother continued to beat her across the back and then shoved her into her room.

"You not even welcome to take a bath in this mutherfucka today! Get ya' clothes and get the fuck out! And bring some extra shit! Whatever rags that li'l flashy bitch Brianna giving your ass now-a-days! And don't come back to this mutherfucka tonight! Let one of them four hoes ya' fuck with take ya' ass in! Or maybe, or maybe your new boyfriend can put ya' ass up for the night after ya' through fuckin' his young-dick ass!"

Lubby sat on her bed and cried. She wanted to look presentable for Gabriella, but she was unable to take a bath. She smelled like salt water and her shoulder length brown hair was frayed and her light-tan skin was dry and ashy. She donned a pair of jean shorts, sandals and a tank top and placed some underwear and an extra tank top into her backpack and ran out of her mother's house. She couldn't understand why her mother treated her that way. Cynthia stood in the doorway with her arms folded and looked on at her daughter as she hopped onto her bike and rode up the street towards Dominique's house.

Truth was, Cynthia's so-called 'man' told her that twelve year-old Lubby was interfering with him and her relationship. If Lubby was home when he got off work this day, he would not pay her light bill. Cynthia was two months behind and she needed the money. To make matters worse, the man had propositioned Lubby for sex the week before. He wanted to break her virginity; offering Lubby money for school clothes. Lubby refused and threatened to tell her mother, but the threat was just a ploy because she knew her mother wouldn't believe her. That threat by Lubby, however, began to cause a rift. The man was now forcing Cynthia to choose either him or Lubby, and when it came down to it, Cynthia, who already viewed Lubby as a liability, chose an outside man over her own daughter. She slammed the door shut and dialed her 'man's' number to let him know Lubby would be gone for the night and he was welcome to come as soon as he was ready.

Lubby never told her friends whenever she and her mother had an argument; and although she hated her mother's verbal and sometimes physical abuse, Lubby, during this period of time, never bothered to reach out for help. She dealt with her troubled relationship with her mother, the best way she knew how, which was to tell herself that one day, she would make it better. No one, neither Dominique, Rolanda, Brianna, nor Tracey, nor either of the girls' parents knew of Lubby's plight. Lubby's friends knew Cynthia was a harsh and strict woman, but for that matter, in their young eyes, so were all their parents. The girls only thought Cynthia was just the same. Lubby hid her troubled state very well. She went into Dominique's room and asked her for some lotion before the seven friends rode off; at least she would appear to be clean when she entered Gabriella's home, but she would carry the weight of her mother's abuse this day with her for a long time. For a brief moment, however, Lubby would forget her problems once she made it to Gabriella's house.

When the seven friends arrived over to Gabriella's house, they saw a white limousine parked in front of the house.

"Ooohh! That's what I'm a have when I become a superstar!" Brianna stated as she rode up to the car and stared at it for a moment.

"I told y'all! My momma and daddy the bomb!" Ben said proudly as the seven laid their bikes on the lawn and walked up to the front door.

Ben was leading way, walking backwards staring at Lubby as he smiled and danced. "Momma! My friends here!" he yelled as he turned and pushed the door open and allowed his friends to step in.

The five girls and Calvin widened their eyes when they entered young Ben's home. The place was immaculate. White marble floors ran throughout. An oil-painting of Ben and his parents hung in the foyer. Ceramic tiles laced the kitchen and a lacquered southern white oak dining room set for eight laced the dining room. Inside the living room was a floor model TV that held various trophies; singing trophies that Gabriella had won during her high-school years. Pictures of Ben and his family were everywhere. The house had a built in fireplace that held more trophies on its mantle. The girls were in awe at the beauty of the home.

"This is how I wanna live when I grow up!" Brianna stated.

"Hey little girls and boys," a nice-looking lady with long brown hair said pleasantly as she came out of the kitchen with a plate of brownies.

"This my Auntie Henrietta. She pretty and nice! Grab a brownie, y'all!" Ben said as he ran through the house calling for his mother and father.

The girls, along with Calvin, grabbed a brownie and thanked Henrietta.

"Gabriella your sister, huh miss?" Rolanda asked.

"Why yes she is, Rolanda."

"Hey, lady? How you know my name?"

"Ben described all of you to me." Henrietta replied. "Rolanda he told me, was the tallest and the darkest and that she was very pretty. So that would be you pretty girl. The pretty brown-eyed girl is Lubby. My nephew has a serious crush on you, Lubby. You remind me of myself when I was a young child." Thirty-five year-old Henrietta stated as Lubby smiled a pretty smile. "The cute girl with the long ponytail is Dominique, who likes Calvin. Now, I'm having trouble between determining who's' Tracey and who's Brianna because both of these two beauties are brown-skinned with dark eyes and short black hair." Henrietta stated as she shifted her eyeglasses and smiled at the two girls.

"I'm Bri, and that's my girl Tracey." Brianna remarked as the group made small talk inside the kitchen.

"We have a problem here at Little Woods tonight friends!" a jovial voice then yelled out from the back of the house.

The five then looked at one another in surprise. They knew that voice. It sounded just like Jazzy. The girls grew excited when they heard heels clacking on the marble floors. "And these five girls is gone set this matter straight for all involved!" the voice continued to speak as the woman came into view.

The girls began screaming to the top of their lungs when they saw Jazzy walk into the living room. Rolanda had to take a seat and fan herself. Tracey went berserk—she was jumping up and down while clapping and laughing aloud. Dominique was frozen stiff—she'd become star struck. Lubby and Brianna's mouth was agape and their eyes were wide. Calvin merely stood and smiled. He already knew Jazzy was waiting on the girls to arrive. The five were beside themselves, and when Jazzy stretched out her arms and said, "Come give Jazzy a big hug!" the five girls made a dash for the woman's bosom.

"I bet y'all never expected to see me here today did you?" Jazzy asked as she hugged each of the girls.

"Today? We never expected to meet you in life!" Rolanda stated.

"Well here I am. Come on and let's go to Gabriella's music room."

When the girls entered the music room, they saw Gabriella sitting on her husband Sam's lap in front her piano lightly strumming her keys. She turned and smiled at the five girls as they ran up and hugged her neck and thanked her for allowing them to meet her friend Jazzy. The girls hung out with Gabriella, Sam, and Jazzy along with Henrietta and young Ben all day and had gotten Jazzy's personal number at the radio station. They could now call her directly when she was on the air. Jazzy warned them not to give her number out and not to call too frequently.

"I'm trusting you girls will be responsible with my number. You seem so nice and smart and I'd be real disappointed if you were to betray my trust. Remember I did a show on trusting your friends? I consider you girls friends now, so show me you can be trusted, okay?" the full-figured 'big fine' caramel-skinned, thin-eyed woman asked as she smiled down upon the five. Her 5'8" 150 pound frame towered over the little girls, except Rolanda, who was nearly Jazzy's height at the young age of twelve.

Jazzy wore a lot of accessories with the white silk short set she had on. Her black ankle-high boots were diamond studded and she had her name tattooed in big bold letters down the outside of her right leg. Huge diamond loop earrings were nestled in her ears along with a ring nose. Jazzy also sported four open-faced gold teeth, and what seemed like scores of bracelets were on either wrist. She made a lot of noise when she walked. Jazzy looked every bit the part she portrayed on her show. She had to leave at 9 that night as she had an appearance at a night club in the French Quarters. Jazzy often did appearances at night clubs and hosted parties in and around New Orleans. She was an early version of 'Downtown Julie Brown', who would become a popular MTV Dee-Jay Host in New York City.

The five walked Jazzy to her car and there, she gave them autographed t-shirts from WYLD and autographed pictures of herself. On top of that, Gabriella had taken pictures of the girls with Jazzy and she was going to turn them over to the five when she got them developed. There was also video footage recorded by Henrietta that day.

Gabriella had done a very nice thing for the girls, and had given them an experience they would cherish always. As they were leaving, the five thanked the woman repeatedly. Brianna, who was trailing behind the four other girls and Gabriella, tugged gently on Gabriella's shirt. When the woman turned around she saw Brianna had tears in her eyes.

"What's wrong sweetie?" Gabriella asked.

"I want you to teach me to sing."

"That's nothing to cry about, Brianna."

"Will you be my friend, Gabriella?" Brianna asked lowly.

Gabriella's heart was touched. She grabbed Brianna's hand and said, "Brianna, the first day you came around here and shared my birthday cake with me and told me you wanted to sing was the day you became my friend. I'd love to teach you to sing."

Gabriella took Brianna's number down and talked to her mother to set up a time when Brianna could begin her lessons. It was more of a getting-to-know-you phone call conversation for the two parents. Gabriella was a very good teacher to Brianna. She taught her how to sing from her stomach and not her throat. She pointed out various styles of singing cadences and variances to certain rhythms. Brianna was a fast learner, and over the next two months or so under Gabriella's tutelage, Brianna had made great advancements with her singing ability. She would often practice back in East Shore in front her friends, all of whom adored her voice, and would, from time to time go over and sit in on Brianna's music lesson. Most days, however, Brianna's friends would be outside playing with Calvin and Ben. The five rarely hung out in East Shore anymore since Brianna had begun her lessons, besides, it was much more fun inside Calvin's neighborhood. Dominique could hang out with Calvin, and Lubby could see Gerald and play with her friend Ben. They spent the rest of the summer and much of the beginning of their seventh grade school year inside Calvin's neighborhood.

As fall of '83 rolled in, the five were enjoying a playful and calm existence. Brianna was moving along with her lessons and Lubby's mother had even shown love by purchasing her daughter new winter clothes—something she hadn't done in almost two years. Lubby was glad she didn't have to wear many of Brianna's old clothes that school year. The fall season of '83 was turning out to be some of the best times the girls had ever had; but a sudden tragedy would impact the girls' lives years, and shatter established friendships that had become all-so cherished.

CHAPTER 7

GROWING PAINS

"So—she standing there staring at me—looking like Aunt Jemima without the head scarf—and I'm waiting for my change. I said, 'Lady, I gave you a fiver! You owe me three dollars and thirty seven cents'!"

"So what set everything off, Rolanda?" Tracey asked through laughter.

Tracey, Dominique, and Rolanda, now seventh graders at Fannie C. Williams Junior High School, were wrapping up there weekly on air show that cool Friday afternoon in October of '83. 'Fannie C', as the kids called it, was at its beginning, a school for 7th and 8th graders only. Overcrowding at Little Woods had forced the sixth grade class to move to the bigger Fannie C. Williams. That move brought the five's former sixth grade teachers, Ms. Bryant and Ms. Prell to the school. Tracey, Dominique, and Rolanda went to the teachers and asked them to put in a good word for them so they could go back on air and the two teachers agreed.

The sixth and seventh grade classes were listening to the fifteen minute program, but the eighth graders had voted against it. The girls knew earning the eight graders' approval that year would be huge because when they got to high school, the eighth graders would be sophomores and could maybe put in a good word; they were already thinking ahead. That was Tracey, Dominique and Rolanda's goal to accomplish before spring break, to earn the eighth grade class's approval. Lubby and Brianna sat on the gym bleachers laughing aloud as Rolanda continued to speak on this cool fall day in October of 1983.

"This woman gone tell me that I gave her a two dollar bill! I said, 'Lady I didn't even know they even *made* two dollar bills'. So I asked her to show me the money that I had supposedly gave to her. When she couldn't produce *any* kind of two dollar bill, I knew I had her. By this time John Law rolled up."

"You called the police, Rolanda?" Tracey asked.

"No. My momma called the police when I told her I was about ta' fight this woman if she didn't give me my correct change. Let me tell ya' somethin', the Jones family don't play about they snaps," twelve year-old Rolanda stated as she popped her neck and continued to talk over the school's P.A. system. She had the sixth and seventh grade students belly's aching as she told her story. "My momma ain't gave me five dollars since 1976 and I wasn't gone let a lady, who *thought* I was dumb, take my li'l piece of change. Besides, my momma woulda skinned me alive if I would've lost that money the first day I got it."

"So, your momma was waiting in the car when you ran and told her you was about to fight this lady for ya' change right?" Dominique asked as she sniggled.

"Right. So I ran back in the store and my momma put a dime in the payphone and called the law and told 'em we was about ta' issue a homemade East Shore beat down to retrieve our funds."

Tracey was laughing heavily as she sat at the desk rocking in her seat, "This," she said as she laughed uncontrollably, "this don't have nothing to do with the subject Dominique brought up girl."

"Y'all want me ta' stop?"

The three could hear faint moans coming from classrooms lining the long hall leading to the school's library where they now broadcasted their show. When they heard the moans of disapproval, they then knew they had a good program.

"No, don't stop," Tracey said, trying to control her laughter, "keep it rolling." she added as she rolled her hands in a circular motion.

"Alright here we go! So I went back in the store 'cause I knew it was either face the wrath of Miss Charlotte Jones for letting this woman rip me off—or chance taking on this two hundred pound Aunt Jemima looking lady and I just knew my odds were better against Aunt Jemima. By the time Charlotte came in the store we was *rollin'*! My momma tagged in and we double teamed her behind, but she caught me with a good lefty. I ain't gone lie I went down. Big-heavy knocked me down and I couldn't get up— but then Charlotte Jones went ta' dishing out a homemade East Shore beat down of her own. My momma was *dealing* with this Aunt Jemima lady when John Law came in and broke up the party! Can you believe that? I mean Charlotte was handlin' business inside that convenience store and John Law brokededed it up! I mean, East Shore was in full effect ya' understand me? So, once John Law stopped the festivities, they placed me and Charlotte in the back seat of the police car right beside one another. Charlotte hugged me and asked me was I okay. I told her my eye hurt and she said, quote me now, 'don't worry about it baby, momma got her back for ya'. I knocked her big behind down and *she* couldn't get up!' unquote. So that's how I got the dotted eye, the lady didn't beat me up when I tried to steal something like the rumor going around, she tried ta' steal my change and I called her on that. Me and my momma rode together to the police station and Bri momma came down and bailed my momma out and she signed me out; now we looking forward to going to court together. Yea, me and my momma do everything together, we eat dinner together, we go shopping together, and from time to time we whip a li'l you know what together. And that's my story on how to spend quality time with your parents boys and girls." Rolanda concluded as Tracey wrapped her hand repeatedly onto the desk as she rocked back and forth in her seat whilst laughing.

Dominique was staring at Rolanda with a wide open mouth

as she couldn't believe what her friend had said.

"What's the problem?" Rolanda said as Tracey turned off the P.A. system.

"Nothing, girl. It's just, how, where you get it from I don't know, but you tell some of the craziest tales, Rolanda." Dominique stated.

"Yea, but they all true. I just add a little flavor to it you know? Girl, Charlotte ain't worrying about going ta' jail—and everybody in East shore knew my momma beat that lady behind after she snuck me. Charlotte thought the story was funny when I read it. She don't really care what people say or think, that's why I use her for a lot of my stuff." Rolanda remarked just as the school bell rung and students were let out.

Students flocked around the three and laughed and joked with them. The On Air Show was the high-light of the kids' week. They all loved the three girls' program. They met up with Brianna and Lubby and walked to their school bus. Once home they rode their bikes over to Gabriella's house which had become their routine. That night, Gabriella informed Brianna that she would have to slow her lessons down and eventually put them on hold whilst she has her baby.

"What Ben gone have a little sister or brother?" Brianna asked.

"A little sister named Samantha Holland. I just don't want you to think I was putting you off or anything." Gabriella stated as she ran her hands through Brianna's hair.

Brianna smiled at her friend and said through happy eyes, "I understand Gabriella. Hey can I come and see the baby when she's born?"

"You sure can, sweetie pie! Come on let's finish up for the day. Remember though, we still on up until Thanksgiving break and we'll pick up again at the first of April of next year okay?"

Brianna and Gabriella had become real close over the few months; they knew one another well and Brianna was somewhat saddened when her lessons ended in November, but

Gabriella would call her over to her home from time to time and they would just sit and talk. That was more than Brianna could ask as she knew Gabriella was preparing herself for her forth-coming child. The five continued hanging out with Ben and Calvin watching as Gabriella grew bigger and bigger. They had learned from Calvin one evening on January 28, 1984 that Gabriella and her family had left early that morning to give birth to her daughter.

"Aww man, we missed it! Now we gotta wait 'til she call!" Brianna stated in an aggravated tone as she and her friends sat on their bikes in front of Gabriella's home bundled up in scarves and heavy jackets as it was cold outside.

The day Gabriella had her baby, the five represented that same night for Gabriella on Jazzy's show. Jazzy shouted back at the five across the airwaves the next night and told them Gabriella was a little sick, but baby Samantha had come into the world and all was well. They fell back on Brianna's bed clapping their hands on the 29th of January, 1984.

After about a week and a half, the five hadn't heard from Gabriella; and Jazzy's radio show was running the best of series so they could not represent. They decided to ride to Gabriella's house just to see if she was home with the new-born baby. They were only planning to stop and say hello, but they were shocked to see a U-Haul truck in front of Gabriella's home. Henrietta was there as people loaded furniture onto the truck. Calvin and his brother were helping to load furniture and Brianna and the girls rode up to the truck and asked what was going on and how was Gabriella.

Henrietta looked at them with bloodshot eyes and said, "She's gone."

"Gone where? She coming back?" Brianna asked.

Henrietta broke into tears and ran inside the house with her hands over her mouth and nose as Calvin pulled the girls aside. "I'm sorry y'all, but, but somebody killed Gabriella, Sam and baby Samantha." he said.

The girls all stood shocked as Calvin explained that Henrietta was moving Ben to her home in the ninth ward. Lubby walked into the home and saw Ben sitting on the living room floor of his home staring blankly at the floor. She walked into the living room and sat beside young Ben and hugged him. The place was in total shambles; somebody had trashed the family's once immaculate home. Furniture movers had very little items to load into the U-Haul because much of the furniture was destroyed. The men were loading what they could, but most of the furniture was placed out in front the home for collection by the city dump.

Lubby looked around at the damage done to the family's place and her eyes welled up. It no longer looked like the extravagant home she and her friends had become accustomed to seeing. Lubby said nothing as she rubbed Ben's back. The nine year-old boy fell over into her lap and wept. She stayed with Ben the whole time sitting in the center of the living room floor as the movers loaded what furniture they could from the home. No one asked the two to move out of the way.

"Ben, it's time to go, baby." Henrietta said sadly about an hour and a half later after all the furniture was removed from the home.

"All my friends are right here. I don't wanna go to the ninth ward, auntie." Ben said as he lay in Lubby's lap. Tears ran down Ben's face as he spoke to his aunt and Lubby stroked his silky hair as she wept for her young friend.

"I know," Henrietta responded to her nephew, "but we can't afford two houses, baby. As hard as it is, we have to do this Ben."

Ben reluctantly got up from Lubby's lap and they both stood. He hugged her tightly and she hugged him back and said, "Come back and see us Ben."

"Give me your number so I can call you Lubby." Ben remarked lowly as he looked up at Lubby.

Lubby didn't have a phone, but she gave him Rolanda's number, who stayed the closest to her home. She walked Ben out the door and there, they both saw Henrietta standing a circle surrounded by Brianna, Rolanda, Dominique, and Tracey. They all hugged Henrietta and said their good-byes to the woman.

"Maybe after everything settles down you all will see Ben again—but we are still shocked and just need time to deal with the situation." Henrietta stated as she looked down upon the young kids.

"Will they find whoever hurt Gabriella?" Brianna asked sadly.

"I sure hope so. Just to let you know, Brianna, my sister believed that you were going to be a great singer someday. You have a gift. That's what she said to me more than once. Please don't let her death turn you away from your dreams. Gabriella was never a quitter and neither were any of her friends. She considered you girls as friends, so you can't be quitters just because she's not here, okay? She's, she's in heaven watching you, she loved you, she loved all kids." Henrietta ended as she gently nudged Ben towards his friends. "Go and say good bye son."

Ben slowly walked pass Henrietta and over to Brianna. "She not lying Bri, my momma said you were going to be a great singer one day. I believe her. Bye Bri." Ben said as he stood surrounded by the five girls and Calvin. They all looked sadly upon Ben, they really felt sorry for him. The five hugged Ben and he dapped Calvin off as he wiped the tears from his eyes and rubbed the snot from his nose and tucked his hands inside his jeans jacket, bowed his head and walked towards the U-Haul; his friends looked at him sadly.

"Ben!" Brianna called out as she took off her skull cap and ran over to the nine year-old. "This umm, this is my favorite hat. It's a Saints hat! I know they sorry and all, but I just wanted to give you something to let you know we won't forget you, Ben Holland." she said as she smiled and hugged Ben one last time and made an E with her fingers. "This E is for East Shore. You always my friend, *our* friend, okay? Don't ever forget us—because—because we won't ever forget you."

"Thanks Bri. I like the Saints. And I will never forget my friends."

"See you around Ben. Don't forget us okay? East Shore!"

Brianna stated as she held her hand in the shape of an E.

"East Shore." Ben said softly just before he hopped into the U-Haul.

The five along with Calvin watched as the truck headed up the street towards Haynes Boulevard. Just before the truck pulled forward, Ben turned to Brianna, smiled, and made an E with his right hand and mimicked the words 'East Shore' from behind the rolled up window. The six kids in turn, all made E's with their hands and said loudly, "EAST SHORE!" as they waved good-bye to Ben Holland. Ben would later lose Rolanda's number and this day, would be the last day for many years that some would ever see Ben Holland again.

The five knew Gabriella well. She was a dear friend to them all. She was kind and generous, sincere, and fun to be around. The girls couldn't fully comprehend what had happened to the woman, though; let alone the reasons why the she was killed. It all seemed like a bad dream. It was hard to believe that Gabriella was dead. Brianna and Lubby were deeply affected by what had transpired. Brianna was the closest to Gabriella and she was deeply saddened that she had lost her friend and mentor.

Lubby, who was the closest to Ben, missed her friend the moment she saw the truck ride up the street. She rode her bike up and down the street alone in an utter daze. She would stop in front of Ben's home and just stare at the house for a few minutes. She just didn't understand why someone would kill Gabriella. She also wondered how Ben would turn out. No one noticed that Brianna had slipped away. When they did, the four rode to her home where Ms. Stanford told them Brianna was not feeling well. Neither Brianna nor her friends spoke on what happened to Gabriella that day; but Brianna's mother had learned two days later when Jazzy had given Gabriella a dedication show. She then decided to do something that she hoped would make her daughter feel better.

Brianna hadn't been to school in the two days since her mother learned why she was in such a slump. She stayed in her room in her bed crying incessantly. Ms. Stanford walked into Brianna's bedroom on the third day after learning what happened to Gabriella and her family. "Hey baby," she said in a low tone to her troubled daughter. "Why, I mean, you know you could've come to me and told me what happened right?"

"What you mean, momma?" Brianna asked as she peeked from underneath her covers.

"About your tutor Gabriella and her family. You could've talk to me, Bri. You can tell me anything you hear? You're my daughter and I love you no matter what."

"Momma, why would someone want to kill that nice lady? Not only that, they killed her husband and her new baby. I'm scared."

"Scared of what, Bri?"

"If somebody could kill a nice lady like Gabriella and then kill her baby, what would they do to *me* or my *friends*? I just don't want to see no more nice people get killed. I thought only bad people get killed." Brianna said as she stared at her mother with watery eyes.

"Well, sweetie," Ms. Stanford said as her eyes welled up. She could see the fear, the sincerity, and the sense of loss in her daughter's eyes. "Sometimes bad things happen to good people."

"Why would God let that happen, momma? Gabriella wouldn't never hurt nobody. All she wanted to do was sing, and she got killed for that? Why be good if you can get killed anyway?"

"Don't think like that, Bri. You, you continue to be good at all times. From what I know, Gabriella believed in you. *I* believe in you, child. Don't stop wanting to be a singer, okay? I'm sorry about your friend, but you can't go through life scared that you're going to lose your friends. Besides, they love you too." Ms. Stanford said as she walked over and opened Brianna's bedroom door.

Tracey, Dominique, Rolanda, and Lubby rushed into the room and jumped on their friend's bed. Brianna smiled at her friends as they began to comfort her.

"We been rolling at school. girl! The eighth graders listen to

On Air now!" Dominique stated to Brianna's delight.

"Y'all accomplished y'all goal, huh?"

"Yea! We did a dedication to Gabriella and the whole school cried. That's when the eighth graders started listening!" Tracey answered.

"Here," Lubby then chimed in, "I made this for you in art class. I miss my li'l friend Ben, too, and we all miss you Bri. You should come back to school. I hope you like what I did."

Lubby had taken the pictures that they had taken the day Jazzy was over to Gabriella's house and made a beautiful, colorful collage with pictures of Brianna and Gabriella intertwined. The center piece was a picture of Brianna sitting in front of the piano beside Gabriella. Brianna loved it. She hugged Lubby and thanked her just as she heard heels clacking loudly across her mother's floor and a voice from the hallway yell out aloud, "Now I know little Bri, ain't quitting on us! Gabriella's friends aren't quitters!"

Brianna smiled a wide smile at her friends when she heard Jazzy's voice. She got up from her bed and waited for the woman to appear. Ms. Stanford and Brianna's four friends had called Jazzy on her personal line and told her of Brianna's plight. Jazzy's heart went out to the young twelve year-old and she readily agreed to visit. Jazzy remembered the five girls and she came and sat with Brianna and her friends all day. By the time she had left, Jazzy had brought Brianna back.

"I'll always be here for you girls. For some reason, I believe we have formed a bond that will benefit us all later on. Ms. Stanford, these girls are the dearest of friends and I surely hope that they turn out all right." Jazzy said as she smiled down at the girls.

"They'll be just fine, Jazzy. Just to let you know, they are just crazy about you, and you are such a nice person to take time out of your busy schedule."

"Well, kids are our future. Bri, I've been nice all my life and I'm still here after twenty-seven years. Don't be afraid, baby. What happened to Gabriella, as sad as it is, doesn't mean that it will happen to you. You live your life and remember what happened to Gabriella and use it to help you live out your dream. She put you on the path to a career in music, but it's up to you to decide if you want to do it or not. Even if Gabriella was still alive, it's your dream to live alone. So don't give up." Jazzy said before she hugged the five girls and exited Brianna's home and got into her limousine.

As Jazzy's limousine cruised slowly down the street, she thought deeply about the five's future. She never said it aloud, but she promised herself that she would never forget them. The girls watched from in front of Brianna's house as Jazzy stopped at the end of the block and handed out T-shirts to the kids on the block before leaving the neighborhood. Brianna went outside for the first time in almost a week since learning Gabriella had been killed. Eventually she returned to her old self, but she would never forget the woman who'd inspired her and became her friend unconditionally. The five would end their seventh grade school year on a high note despite their troubling experience.

Tracey, Dominique, and Rolanda's On Air Show was approved in advance of the upcoming school year because of their overwhelming success and approval by the eighth grade class. Brianna's mother had also bought her a karaoke machine. It wasn't along the level of the equipment that Gabriella had, but it was sufficient enough to allow Brianna to continue her endeavors.

The girls did call Jazzy from time to time and she was real nice to them, but eventually as the weeks went on, Jammin Jazzy began to fade into the background as the five were becoming more interested in other things and Jazzy's career had begun to rapidly accelerate; in other words, neither Jazzy nor the five had too much time for the other. The girls still listened to Jazzy's radio show, but it wasn't as much of a priority now as it had been during the girls' elementary years. Dominique and Calvin were still growing strong; and during the summer of 1984, a new style of dance and music would make the five even more popular and change the course of the girls' life forever.

CHAPTER 8

THE LATEST FAD

It was a hot and humid summer Saturday and the five had just finished studying the bible with Dominique's mother. The girls had grown curious about the afterlife when Gabriella died back in January, and they would sometimes sit in with Dominique on her studies to learn a few things about God. Mrs. Franz spoke to the kids about God's promise of a resurrection, stating that the dead would all return during Jesus Christ's Millennial Reign. The story was uplifting, but the girls' lesson was quickly pushed out of their minds the moment they all walked out of Dominique's house and heard music coming from the huge park on Curran Boulevard.

They hopped onto their bikes and let their ears guide them towards the melodic high hats and symbols. When they reached Curran, the five saw a fat man standing behind a table that was set up on the basketball court inside the park and a song they'd never heard before was blaring loudly.

"J-A-Y are the letters of his name...cutting and scratchin' are the aspects of his game...so check out the master as he cuts these jams...and look at us with the mics in our hand...then take a count...one, two three, Jam Master Jay—Run D.M.C..." Run-DMC's lyrics to their rap song titled *Jam Master Jay,* blared loudly from the park as numerous kids danced around.

Tracey and Dominique made their way over to the basketball court and saw that the man had two turntables sitting on top of a table and a huge speaker was out in front. Kids were standing in front of him watching in amazement as he moved his hands back and forth and the record began to repeat itself while others, including Lubby, Bri and Rolanda, took to the grass where Donald and Mike and other young boys and girls were dancing atop large slabs of waxed cardboard.

Dominique and Tracey looked at one another and smiled as they walked across the court and stood before the man. They instantly liked what they saw and heard and Tracey asked what he was doing.

"I'm Dee-jaying!"

"How you Dee-jay like that?" Dominique asked.

"Like what?" the twenty-year old heavy-set jehri-curled man asked in return.

"How you make the words on the song repeat they self."

The man placed his finger tips on the album and moved it back and forth and it produced that sound again. "It's called scratching, you wanna try? It's fun!"

"Who singing that song right there?" Tracey asked as Dominique stood behind the turntables.

"That's Run-DMC! Come on over! Y'all can look at my albums!" the man told Tracey as he removed his red Adidas jogging suit jacket and pulled his safari Kangol down tighter onto his head.

Tracey liked the man's style. He looked fresh in his crisp red and white Adidas T-shirt, red and white striped jogging suit pants and red and white leather Adidas sneakers. The man donned a pair of thick sunglasses and turned his attention to Dominique, who was standing behind the turntables staring at the rotating albums.

"Alright look her li'l one, what you do is lightly place your finger tips on the album and pull it back and just let it go. What's your name?"

"Dominique."

"Nahh. If you wanna be a Dee-jay you need a name. You

should call yourself Lady D."

"What you call yourself?" Dominique asked the man.

"My real name Terrence, but they call me Terrible Tee."

"Okay, I'm a call myself Lady D like you said."

"Alright Lady D, show me some skills." Terrence said as he stepped back from the turntables and let Dominique take control of his Technic 1200's.

Dominique placed her finger tips on the vinyl and gently slid her hand back and forth and the song repeated itself. *"Jam, Jam, Jam Master Jay, Master Jay..."*

The elated thirteen year-old turned to Terrence and smiled and he encouraged her to continue as he sipped a cold quart of beer. Tracey meanwhile, was looking through Terrence's albums. He had what seemed like every song ever made in her eyes. The records were all neatly stacked inside of milk crates and he had two of everything that Jazzy played on the radio along with dozens of songs that Jazzy didn't play. He had slow jams from groups like the Isley Brothers and Earth, Wind, and Fire, The Ohio Players, Champagne, and Teddy Pendergrass. Tracey was in awe over Terrence's collection. She soon pulled out a group by the name of Nucleus' twelve inch album that had a song titled *Jam on It* and placed it on the turntable Dominique wasn't using.

Terrence then stepped in and said, "Hey, that's a live jam right there. What's your name, baby girl?"

"Tracey."

"Nahh. We gone call you Trouble Tee! You look like you know your music or was that a lucky pull from the crate?"

"No man. My momma got some of them songs. I listen to her albums all the time."

"Okay. Lady D, let me show you how to fade in another song," Terrence said as he stood in front of his Gemini mixer.

Meanwhile, out in the grassy park beside the basketball court, Brianna and Rolanda stood with a group of kids in a circle watching Lubby dance with Mike, who seemed to be floating across a piece of cardboard.

"What they doing, Rolanda?" Bri asked.

"They break dancing!" Rolanda yelled over the music.

"Lubby where you learn that from?" Brianna asked.

"I been watching Donald and Mike do that! But I'm better than them watch!"

Lubby went to the center of the cardboard and began to pump her fist furiously as she slowly sunk to the ground. People thought her dance was funny, but they quickly stopped laughing when Lubby laid down on her back and began to rotate her body until her legs were twirling in the air as she spun on her back.

"What the hell she doing?" Brianna asked.

"That's a windmill! Lubby! You gone make 'em mad, girl! Stop it!" Rolanda joked just as Lubby spun out of the windmill, spun around on her back, crossed her legs, then froze and folded her arms, calling out other dancers, including Donald and Mike.

"Man, you stole our moves! You a biter!" Donald yelled.

"Don't matter, Don. You can't beat me! Come on!" Lubby said as she glided across the cardboard. "I'm calling you out, Don! Mike? Anybody! Come challenge me suckas!"

No one came forth and Lubby had taken over the piece of cardboard as Nucleus' song continued to play. Eventually, other kids joined in; but no one challenged Lubby. She was the best break dancer on the park that day. Tracey and Dominique meanwhile, were looking through Terrence's albums and found two Herbie Hancock albums and placed them on the turntables. Terrence guided the two girls as they both took turns mixing the song *Rock It*. The five spent all day at the park until Terrence began winding down. They asked him if he was coming back and he said he would be on the park every weekend until the weather got too cold.

"Can me and Dominique help you Dee-jay?" Tracey asked.

"No problem. When y'all see me just come on by and I'll let

y'all get on the tables. Might even teach y'all some of my skills!"

"You gone help us be Dee-jays like you, Terrible Tee?" Dominique asked with wide eyes.

"Yea! I'd like to see that. Besides Jazzy, I don't know no other female Dee-jays. And y'all can be like the first ones to do parties and stuff back here. Yea, that's dope! I'm a train y'all. Help y'all out so y'all can be like Terrible Tee!"

The five went home after helping Terrence load his equipment onto the bed of his blue pickup and listened to the radio by Dominique's house as Lubby showed them some of her moves. Lubby was just too good for the girls; she out-danced them all.

The rest of the summer the five went swimming almost every weekday then rode their bikes over to Calvin's neighborhood then returned to East Shore and listened to Jazzy's show over to Tracey's house and hung out with Terrence at the park on weekends. By the time the girls started eighth grade, they were the most popular girls in school. On Air was up and running, Lubby was known for her dancing abilities, and Brianna was the school's best singer. Tracey, Rolanda, and Dominique were also becoming known as the first female Dee-jays from East Shore.

CHAPTER 9

WORD IS BOND

"We want everybody to submit the final song that they will be performing for the upcoming talent show. If you forgot the date is April 23, at seven P.M. in the school's auditorium." thirteen year-old Dominique stated on a rainy day in early April of 1985.

"Also," thirteen year-old Tracey chimed in, "the show will be hosted by East Shore's own Terrible Tee, Ms. Jones, Lady D, and Trouble Tee."

"That's right," fourteen year-old Rolanda said as she took on an impromptu imitation voice of Wolf Man Jack, a popular rock and roll Dee-jay, "come on down to the talent show and see Ms. Jones, Lady Dee and Terrible Tee in the flesh! Hey, they gone be controlling the mic and playin' whatcha' sayin' all night long!" Rolanda ended as Dominique and Tracey laughed.

Rolanda was more of a personality than a Dee-jay; she wasn't too interested in playing music, she simply loved to have fun on the microphone for as long as she could, then play music. Tracey was more interested in playing music to make a crowd dance; talking on the microphone wasn't her top priority. Dominique didn't joke at all when on the microphone she loved to discuss issues and then play music. The three complimented one another well; they would make a great team if ever the opportunity presented itself.

Kids laughed as Rolanda finished her announcements for the week. "Also, I wanna send a Happy Birthday to Miss Bryant, our favorite teacher from Little Woods, and next week, I'll announce *everybody's* birthday for the month of April along with their ages, including the teachers so y'all stay tuned for that! Hey, it's gone be a hot show!" Rolanda joked again. "Just kidding, I ain't gone tell the *students'* age! Ta-Ta y'all." she ended as Tracey played the song of the week, which was a new song titled *I Wonder If I Take You Home*, by Lisa Lisa and Cult Jam. The girls' classmates prepared to head home for the weekend, whilst enjoying the music over the P.A. system. The On Air Show was the highlight of the school week during this period of time.

Rolanda, Tracey, and Dominique were steadily growing in their understanding of what they were doing on their weekly show. After Tracey and Dominique had met Terrence, they began to take lessons from the man whenever he was on the park. When winter set in the year before, Terrence brought his equipment over to Tracey's house on Saturday evenings and set it up and allowed the girls to practice in the yard. There were no strings attached to Terrence's generosity; the man simply loved to Dee-jay, and he wanted to be able to say he trained three females to become Dee-jays like him. He didn't fully understand at the time the impact he was having on the three girls' life in the beginning, but as time went on he could see how much passion the girls had for what they were doing. Terrence had taught them how to use a four channel mixer. He taught Rolanda what to say on the microphone to get the crowd hype. He taught them all to discern when to slow the music down.

"People get tired, and the couples out there wanna get close, so after thirty minutes or so, slow it down for ten or fifteen." he said to girls one winter Saturday afternoon.

Terrence also taught the girls how to scratch and mix albums; although Rolanda showed no interest, she, too, had picked up on the skill.

"Y'all got to make sure if you using two different songs that the beats match. Never do no sloppy sounds, it turn the crowd off, and make sure you know the lyrics to every song you play. Look for rare music, too. Remember, as a Dee-jay, you wanna be the first one to play the hottest song. You wanna be known for having whatever people ask to hear. Even if you don't like a song, buy it and keep it 'cause you never know who might ask to hear something."

The girls learned a lot from Terrence during the winter of 1984 and they were now putting their skills to use.

The school talent show got underway on April 23, 1985. Rolanda, Tracey, and Dominique were doing an excellent job hosting the show that night alongside Terrence; his training was paying off.

"Alright alright! Next we got comin' to the stage, the dynamic duel Donald and Mike A.K.A. Batman and Robin! I got one question, which one of 'em is Robin? 'Cause everybody know Batman the real hero! Robin just a super-hero wanna be! Robin 'bout worth as much as a faded out food stamp! Think about it, who you know wanna be Robin? And what boy you know named Robin? What's really hatning with that?" Rolanda said as the crowd laughed at her jokes.

Rolanda was dressed in a red suit with a pair of white leather shoes wearing a white top hat. Her jet-black hair was neatly pressed and flowing down to her back; she was doing a good job with her impromptu jokes that night. "For real tho' y'all, we got our homeboys Donald and Mike doing King of Rock! Tonight live from East Shore, it's RUN-D-M-C!" Rolanda screamed into her hand-held microphone as the crowd erupted for Donald and Mike.

Donald and Mike lip-synced Run-DMC's song *King of Rock*. They were good, but thirteen year-old Lubby trumped them when she did a break dance routine all by herself off George Kranz's song *Trommeltanz*, better known as *Din Daa Daa*, which was a number one hit in the breakdancing arena.

There were over twelve acts this night; Rolanda, Tracey and Dominique did an excellent job hosting and were in rare form. Terrence grew proud when Dominique and Tracey did a Dee-jay routine where they both took turns scratching to U.T.F.O.'s song *Roxanne, Roxanne.* They had the crowd in amazement as they watched the two girls stand opposite one another and had the song repeat 'Roxanne, Roxanne' over and over, then they dubbed it up letting two of the same albums play at the same time producing an echo-like effect. They both had on red Adidas suits like the one Terrence wore the day the first met the man with black fur Kangol safari caps and black Adidas tennis and sunglasses. Needless to say, Terrible Tee was proud of his protégés.

Dominique and Tracey were at the top off the board until fourteen year-old Brianna came out and sung, *Let's Hear it for the Boy* by Deniece Williams.

"My baby he don't dress fine...but I really mind...'cause what he does he does so well...makes me wanna yell...let's hear it for the boy...let's give the boy a hand...let's hear for my baby...you know you gotta understand...maybe he's no Romeo...but he's my love and one man show... Oh,oh,oh,oh, let's hear it for the boy..."

Brianna had every girl in the audience and a few teachers as well singing along with her that night. The auditorium was in a frenzy. And when she ended the song, everybody knew Brianna had already won; but they sat and had a good laugh when Rolanda came out and did a five minute comedy routine she had gotten off of Richard Pryor's album, *Live on the Sunset Strip.* She still had on her red suit and white shoes just like Richard Pryor, and she had cleaned up the curse words and rearranged some of the jokes and the crowd got a good laugh from her act. It was crafty and well prepared, like much of her gossip skits she performed in school.

The five's parents, with the exception of Lubby's mother, was on hand this night to support the children. Lubby stood by and watched as Mrs. Franz, Ms. Jones, Ms. Stanford, and Mrs. Sanchez congratulated their daughters. Brianna was waving her trophy in the air and Dominique and Tracey were steadily being complimented by both young and old on their Dee-jaying skills. Rolanda was talking loud, steadily joking; she actually believed she was Richard Pryor for at least one night of her young life.

Lubby bowed her head and walked into the bathroom and sat in a stall and cried. Rolanda saw her friend grow sad and walk away, so she followed her into the bathroom and gently pushed the stall open.

"Lubby what's wrong?"

"Everybody momma came tonight, Rolanda. I told my momma almost every day for two weeks that I was dancing and I wanted her to come and watch me. When I was leaving, she told me have fun. Her boyfriend was sitting on the couch laughing at me. Then my momma gone say 'Why *you* going? *You* ain't gone win anyway!' And then they both started laughing at me! It wasn't about winning. We all knew Bri was gone win, but I just wanted my momma to be proud of me and she didn't even bother." Lubby said as she placed her head in her lap and cried heavily and rocked her body back and forth. "Why she don't like me? What did I do that was so bad that she don't like me? She don't even like ta' be *around* me! I love my momma and I just want her to love me back! Why won't she love me back?"

Rolanda stared down at her friend and placed her hand on her shoulder and then knelt down beside her and said, "Lubby, I'm sorry for what Cynthia did. But *we* all love you."

"It's not the same. You not my momma. I don't have nobody to talk to when I have a problem. I, I have ta' figure stuff out all by myself and I don't always know what ta' do!"

Lubby had turned flush she was crying so hard inside the stall. Rolanda did what she thought was best and called her mother into the bathroom and told her of Lubby's situation.

"Lubby come on sweetheart. Let's go home."

"Ms. Jones I don't wanna go back there. I can't!"

"I know, baby. You can stay with me and Rolanda tonight. Come on. You can talk to me about anything on your mind. Now, stop crying okay? This is our little secret, okay? Nobody won't know unless you want them to. Now, dry your eyes, and let's go celebrate, you were beautiful out there. How'd you learn how to dance like that?"

"From these two boys that ride our bus." Lubby stated as she wiped her eyes.

"Too bad your mother didn't come. She's missing out on a star in the making."

"I'm not the star. Brianna gone be a star. She was the best."

"You can be a star too, Lubby!" Ms. Jones said as she rubbed Lubby's back softly.

"I can?"

Ms. Jones had to pause for a moment. She realized right away that Lubby didn't believe in herself. All this child needed was encouragement and someone to tell her she was loved. Rolanda and the rest of her friends would tell her she was loved; but Ms. Jones knew Lubby needed to hear it from an adult. Namely her mother. Since that wasn't to be, Ms. Jones decided she would fill in whenever she could.

Back in the parking lot, Tracey and Dominique were outside talking to their schoolmates when Terrence walked up to the crowd. "Hey, we gotta gig next week!"

"We?" Dominique asked.

"Yea. They having a party by Mike house next weekend and he want y'all to Dee-jay!"

"You gone bring the equipment?" Dominique asked excitedly.

"Word is bond!" Terrence answered.

"Man our first Dee-jay at a house! Tee you cool, man!" Tracey stated as she dapped Terrence.

"Ain't nothing. Just don't forget about Tee when y'all get big."

"We won't forget you when we get grown! We gone remember you!" Dominique remarked.

"No! I mean get big like famous! Never mind! I'm a see y'all next weekend about six."

The five left the school and everybody began spring break.

The whole week following the talent show, Lubby was spending nights by Rolanda's house. She would tell her mother where she was going and she would get no more than an "umm hmmm" from Cynthia as she left out the door. Ms. Jones kept a close eye on Lubby and Cynthia. She wanted to confront the woman, but she knew if the police came out and they found out about Lubby's plight, she would be taken away. She didn't want to see Lubby go to a foster home so she kept a close eye on the thirteen year-old. Lubby seemed to be happy those few days spent with Rolanda and Charlotte; she now knew what a real family should be like; she also believed that she could be something in life. Ms. Jones had prevented Lubby from having a nervous breakdown and had given her strength to continue on dealing with her troubled relationship with her mother by the end of Spring Break.

The weekend of Mike's party had arrived and everybody was enjoying the sounds being played by Tracey and Dominique. They did their *Roxanne Roxanne* routine and had the crowd jumping again. The two girls were playing *Play at Your Own Risk* by Soul Sonic Force when Gerald, Bobby, Tank and Calvin walked into the party. Gerald and his two friends were now looked up to in East Shore. The three sixteen year-olds all wore $100 Bally tennis shoes with a single dot on the back of the shoe. The leather tennis shoes they wore were a sign of status. If you had a hundred dollar pair of shoes you were considered a 'roller'. What made Gerald and his friends practically idols was the fact that they had a car and bought their own clothes. No one knew exactly what they did to make money, but everybody knew they had money at all times. The three walked in standing taller than most of the thirteen and fourteen year-olds in the party. They each had on silk Christian Dior jogging suits with white and black Bally tennis shoes and bee-bop Kangol caps that were turned backwards. Each had a 'donkey rope' gold chain draping from their neck and a diamond ear ring in the left ear that twinkled as they walked through the crowd like kings. Young teens were glad to see the three. They could now boast back in school that their party was so live that Gerald, Bobby and Tank had showed up.

Calvin, dressed the same as his brother and his brother's

friends, walked pass the huge Peavey speaker sitting at the foot of the hall facing the living room and traveled down the long hallway and entered the bedroom where Dominique was alone with Tracey and Terrence. The two girls looked Calvin over and high-fived one another.

"You lookin' all fly tonight! What's up with that, Cal?" Dominique asked as she stared at her boyfriend.

"I wanted to look good for my girlfriend. You like this? My brother bought it for me."

"It's alright." Dominique said as she shook her hand side to side.

"You tripping, girl! This fresh! Come here. I ain't seen you in two weeks."

"I know man! Your momma and daddy planned that trip to Alabama on purpose so you couldn't come to the talent show."

"Nahhh. We had ta' go visit family. Anyway can I get a hug?"

Meanwhile, back in the huge living room, Gerald and his friends walked through the dimly lit room ogling the young females that were present. Nearly every female spoke. Gerald spoke to several females and keep pushing through the crowd, but he stopped when he saw Lubby out on the floor gyrating in a black tennis skirt, white tank top and black and white sandals. His dark-brown eyes lit up as he rubbed his chin and licked his lips, scoping out the fine thirteen year-old as she danced with another boy from her school. Gerald didn't want to be rude so he waited until the song ended and asked Lubby to slow dance with him later.

"You wanna dance with me, Gerald?" Lubby asked excitedly as her heart fluttered.

"I told you I was waiting for the right time Lubby. So can I get that dance?"

"Yes, Gerald." Lubby said with a smile on her face as Gerald walked off. "Come get me when you ready!" she yelled aloud as Gerald raised a peace sign in the air.

Lubby backed against the wall and waited for a slow song. Boys from school wanted to dance with her, but she refused. She was now waiting on Gerald. Brianna was dancing with Mike and Rolanda was dancing with anybody that wanted to dance, she held the floor down while Lubby was waiting for Gerald. The party was in full swing now; everyone was loose, right up until Tracey played a slow song…

"Look at me…I have fallen so in love with you…please don't' leave…stay around…let me tell you all the things I feel…won't you please…"

When Lubby recognized the lyrics to *Let Me Be Your Angel* by Staci Lattisaw, she eagerly began searching for Gerald; but she couldn't find him. She walked through the crowd as teens danced together. She walked the entire darkened room, but when caught no sight of Gerald, she grew sad as she sunk back against the wall. She was about to cry until she felt a hand grab hers and pull her close. The thirteen year-old was trying to resist. "No I'm waitin' on Ger—"

"On me, baby?" Gerald said as he smiled down at Lubby.

Lubby stared into Gerald's dark eyes and then admired his low-cut wavy hair, neatly trimmed mustache and smooth caramel skin. He smelled good, looked good; the two walked to the center of the floor where Lubby grabbed Gerald's neck just as he grabbed her waist. The two drew close and Lubby laid her head in Gerald's chest as if she had been his woman since the beginning of time. Gerald loved the way Lubby felt against his body. She was soft, her flesh was smooth. He sniffed Lubby's stacked hair and savored the sweet aroma of her shampoo and hairspray. Her perfume was intoxicating and her body was as soft as rose petals, a well-constructed female form deserving of the utmost care and adoration. Lubby stared up at Gerald, her brown eyes filled with joy as she danced with the young teen whom she had a crush on for over two years. She let Gerald take control of her. She hugged his neck tightly as if she didn't want to ever let go. The two had become entrenched in their own world as they danced, and this by far, was the happiest day of Lubby's life.

"Lubby, you ready to be mine?" Gerald asked as the song

continued to play.

"Let me be your angel...let me be the one for you...let me be your angel...let me be the one...you believe in..."

"I been ready, Gerald." Lubby said over the music as she looked deeply into his eyes.

"You still young."

"But I'm ready to be your girlfriend. I'm not ready for sex, but I can do this." Lubby stated as she stood on her toes and pressed her lips to Gerald's and their two tongues locked briefly.

Lubby broke away and stared at Gerald, awaiting a reply as she licked her lips, savoring his taste. Gerald smiled down at Lubby and took off his donkey rope chain and placed it around her neck. Lubby's eyes lit up as she held the chain out staring at it.

"I got another one at home. That's ta' let everybody know you mine's now." Gerald stated to the dismay of other girls who felt they were more worthy of Gerald's affection.

The five friends had simultaneously slipped into young woman hood in the spring of '85 over Staci Lattisaw's song. From this point forth, they would all experience many a dilemma that would test not only their own intestinal fortitude, but their love and loyalty towards one another as they all aspire towards attaining their individual goals in life.

CHAPTER 10

ANIMOSITY

"Lubby put your chain on! You ain't gotta be scared ta' wear that donkey rope! That's why Gerald gave it to you so these other hoes can know y'all go together!" Tracey said one afternoon in October of '85 as the girls, all fourteen and in the ninth grade walked down the hallways on the second floor inside Marion Abramson Senior High.

Abramson was the only high school in Eastern New Orleans in 1985 and the eastern part of the city was experiencing rapid growth. The five's old school, Fannie C. Williams was being transformed into Sarah T. Reed High School, until then, the girls would have to attend the over-crowded high school on Read Blvd about four miles from East Shore closer to downtown New Orleans. The school was so crowded that the juniors and seniors, including Gerald, Bobby, and Tank, would go from 5:30 a.m. to 11:00 a.m. and the sophomores and freshmen would go from 11:30 a.m. to 5:00 p.m.

The five liked going to Abramson. They could sleep late in the morning and still hang out in the evenings. Buses ran frequently, so on many days, the girls would leave school and walk through Lake Forest Mall, which was right near the school and then catch the Read bus down to Hayne Boulevard where they would transfer and catch the Hayne bus home. Methodist Hospital was close by and a police-substation was directly across the street from the school. There was a Ground Pattie Junior burger joint across the street from the school where the girls often ate and hung out with other students on the days they didn't walk to the mall. There was plenty activity up and down Read Boulevard in '85.

There were also many different neighborhoods in the area. There were neighborhoods like Bunker Hill, The Checkerboard, The Goose and Skylight, all the neighborhoods, with the exception of Bunker Hill, and Skylight, were within walking distance of one another. Another section, an apartment complex called Gaslight Square, which was closest to the school, held many drug dealers. Most kids from these various neighborhoods attended Livingston Middle School back in the day and they considered Abramson High School to be their school. It wasn't meant for students in East Shore to attend in their eyes. It was in their neighborhood and they held East Shore responsible for overcrowding the school and disrupting the regular hours. Teenagers from these various 'hoods, namely the females, despised teenagers from East Shore attending their school and walking through the school as if they owned the place. Jealousy was beginning to rear its ugly head because all of the female cliques had already heard about Rolanda, Tracey, Dominique, Brianna, and Lubby from the sophomores who resided in East Shore and often attended many of the parties Tracey and Dominique Dee-jayed.

The females also knew that the five were cool with Gerald, Bobby and Tank, all of whom were super stars at Abramson. The three young men had their pick of females, anybody they wanted they got; and it ailed a lot of females from the other neighborhoods to know that the five were in tight with Gerald, Bobby and Tank, a position many of them could only dream of being in. The 'rollers' in the school, including young males from Gaslight Square, the big drug dealing set, and Bunker Hill, who had a team of hustlers themselves, and the other neighborhoods, all hung out with the five and were cool with the girls. Dominique, Tracey and Rolanda had their weekly show running, compliments of the sophomores from Little Woods, and it was well liked by both the freshman and the sophomores from the various neighborhoods outside of East Shore. Lubby was now co-captain of the junior varsity majorettes and Brianna could often be heard singing in the school's gym. The girls were broadening their horizons and becoming more popular throughout East New Orleans, in spite of the jealousy.

Most kids were reasonable and got along, but in some of these neighborhoods there was always a single group of girls looking to start trouble with the five. There were fights at the school true enough, but the people that wanted to test the five were the types that loved to keep what would become known as 'the hood wars' going strong. They lived to fight. It was their way of getting noticed at the school. The five were popular because they were cool, but these female cliques knew they could get respected if they took the five down, so verbal conflicts were common on school grounds. An incident with Lubby on this mild morning in October of 1985, however, would push things over the edge for the next two years.

"Put your chain on, girl! Fuck them hoes!" Brianna stated as the five walked along the lockers on the second floor.

"Rolanda that was a tight show y'all did Friday. Y'all doing Mike party this weekend right, Dominique?" a male student asked as the five walked up the middle of the wide corridor.

"Yea. Mike our homeboy! We gone be in full effect this Friday so long as Terrence don't back out." Dominique answered.

"That's right! We *all* gone be there if Terrence don't back out!" a female from The Checkerboard stated sarcastically.

"You ain't invited, Shantrell!" Dominique snapped.

"Yea? Well ask Gerald if I ain't invited! When they dropped me off last night? Right before he kissed me bye he invited me to the party." the 5' 130 pound red-boned curly black-haired fifteen year-old remarked.

"You lyin'!" Lubby stated as she pulled her chain from underneath her jogging suit jacket. "We was together all night after school. So I know you lyin'!"

"Anyway!" Shantrell stated as she rolled her eyes. "You might be wearing his chain and he might be buying you all them clothes and shit, but you ain't the one riding in his car and you damn sure ain't fuckin' 'nem!'"

The five burst into laughter. They couldn't believe how stupid Shantrell was making herself look.

"Girl, you getting played and I'm getting paid. If you wanna be Gerald's come catcher that's fine with me, Shantrell. But if you ain't recognize—he layin' you and payin' me!" fourteen year-old Lubby, who was dressed in a black velvet Christian Dior jogging suit and a black and white pair of Bally's, replied as she walked pass Shantrell and her group of five friends.

"Y'all ain't shit, Bri!" another girl from the group yelled aloud.

"What man? Y'all ready?" Tracey, standing 5'3" 135 pounds snapped as she dropped her back pack turned around and walked to the back of the five.

Rolanda, the tallest of the group at 5'6" 125 pounds stepped behind Tracey. Brianna, at 5'4" 120 pounds stood to the side as she dropped her bag. Lubby, the same height and weight as Brianna, was watching the scene unfold as Dominique at 5' 100 pounds dropped her bags as well. They were preparing to square off against the girls.

"Say somethin' now!" Tracey yelled aloud, getting no response. "See? Y'all be talking brave when a bitch just passing by! But every time we stop and turn around y'all hoes shut up! Whenever you ready ta' throw tha' hands Shantrell just say so! I got you! I got every last one of you hoes *in* Checkerboard!"

Tracey was never one to back down. And whenever she flexed, girls would shut up because they knew Tracey would back her words up; and if Tracey swung, then the whole five would swing. When the odds were even, girls would back down and the five knew that. Shantrell smacked her lips as she and her group walked off. The five stood strong this day; but the day of Mike's party would tip the odds in Shantrell and her crew's favor; so they thought.

"So for everybody that's invited to Mike's party tonight we ask that you have ya' invitations ready at the door." Rolanda remarked as she ended the school's announcements for the week. "Now", she continued, "word been going around that certain groups of people were excluded because of where they stay or who they were. Ta' clear that up we only got room for fifty people. The five in there off top, so that leave forty-five. Gerald, Bobby, and Tank is in there," Rolanda stated, knowing she was going to incite the girls who weren't invited, "now we down ta' forty-two. Count fifteen majorettes, eight cheerleaders, and ten Bally Boys and we down to nine. Mike and Donald leave us with seven, count Mike momma and remember the five is in there and the three Dee-jays close that out at fifty-two partying people. Fifty two! So we already over the limit if y'all can add that up. And it's invitation only so if you show up loitering, John Law gotcha' covered, we Audi 5000!" Rolanda ended as she cut off the P.A. system inside the school's library.

"Rolanda you counted us about three different times!" Dominique stated as she and Tracey laughed.

"Girl fuck them! The ones that's left out coming ta' start trouble. Anyway, we didn't have ta' justify why them messy ass chicks wasn't invited! Come on let's go to the mall! They got them new Stan Smith Adidas at Footlocker, girl, and my feet belong inside a brand new pair of red ones!" Rolanda ended as school was dismissed.

The five walked to Lake Forest Mall and began browsing through the huge one story diamond-shaped complex looking at various out-fits. They all had money this day. Lubby had gotten money from Gerald; Brianna and Rolanda's mothers had given them money and Tracey and Dominique had money from working parties in East shore with Terrence.

As the five were exiting *The Gap* clothing store, they spotted Shantrell and about nine other girls walking towards them from the opposite direction.

"There they go y'all." Lubby stated lowly as she tucked in her chain.

"What ya' tuckin' ya' shit in for, Lubby?" Shantrell yelled from the opposite direction and opposite side of the mall.

"I swear on everything I love—if Shantrell come in any our face I'm swingin'! Y'all down?" Tracey asked as she let her back pack hang low to the ground.

"It's at least eight of 'em." Brianna stated.

"I don't care if it's eighty! That hoe Shantrell beggin' for me ta' light that ass on fire!" Tracey replied as Shantrell and her group grew closer.

Shantrell and her group crossed over to the side of the mall where the five were standing just outside of the clothing store. She was planning to talk more shit to the five, but Tracey had other plans.

"Yea," Shantrell said with a wide smile on her face as she nodded her head up and down, "we gone crash y'all party and —"

Shantrell was silenced when Tracey's back pack, containing her thick English book, slammed into her face. She stumbled over to the opposite side of the mall's walkway and fell against the wall stunned and incapacitated as her crew rushed the five. Brianna reacted next and began fighting with two females as Dominique began swinging on two girls headed her way. Rolanda, who had long skinny arms, hit a girl in both eyes repeatedly, knocked her down and then joined in to help Lubby who was being jumped by the four remaining teenagers. Rolanda was beating the back of the girls' head trying to get them off Lubby. At the same time, Lubby was swinging back, but she was too out-numbered. She caught a blow to the head and fell to the floor and the four girls began stomping her as Rolanda continued swinging.

Tracey was handling her business. She warded off the two girls she was fighting and they broke and ran. Dominique was beginning to succumb to the blows she was receiving from the two females she was fighting and she was about to fall to the floor before Tracey stepped in and slammed her fist against the side of one the girls' head. The girl stumbled and grabbed her head as blood began to gush from her temple.

"She got brass knuckles! Tracey got brass knuckles!" the girl screamed as she backed away from the fight.

Dominique looked and could see that both of Tracey's hands were clad with sterling silver four-fingered sets of brass knuckles. When Tracey knocked the other girl off Dominique, she went to help Brianna.

"I got these hoes! Help Rolanda! Help Rolanda and Lubby!" Brianna said as she dealt with the two females she was fighting by dancing around and squaring off for a few seconds before she backed away and reset herself in order to engage the girls again.

No soon as Brianna said that, Rolanda was heard yelling aloud, "Come on hoes! Come on!"

Tracey stopped in her tracks and watched as Rolanda, who now had her back against the glass enclosure outside *The Gap*, fought with all four females. Lubby crawled from underneath the five girls as Rolanda continued to swing and turned around and looked on as the two girls Brianna were fighting broke and ran. Shantrell had left long before the fight had ascended to the level it was now on. The four friends started walking towards the four girls jumping Rolanda.

"I got these hoes! Don't jump in! Don't jump in!" Rolanda stated as she continued to swing.

Rolanda's face was crinkled, and her teeth were showing as she hit each of the females that tried to encompass her personal space. Rolanda's arms were just too long and she was just too quick. She was 'sticking' the four females randomly and quickly as they tried to swarm her.

"Ung! Ung! Ung! Ung! I got somethin' for each y'all hoes! Come on!" Rolanda stated as the four girls began to grow weary from Rolanda's blows.

Other teens from Abramson were on hand to witness the fight inside the mall this day and they began cheering as they watched Rolanda beat up on the four girls. Heads were rolling back and bamboo earrings were flying out of ears as Rolanda unleashed a fast, furious and unrelenting mixture of swift jabs and powerful uppercuts. The four girls tried as best they could to get at Rolanda, but she only continued to swing and knock them back until they grew tired of her blows and broke and ran.

"What's hatnin'? What's hatnin', hoes?" Rolanda asked as she bounced up and down with her fists balled and her arms spread as the four girls she was fighting ran from the crowd.

Tracey caught one of the girls in the side with her brass knuckles when she ran by and Brianna kicked one of the girls as she ran pass her. For payback, Lubby and Dominique, who were nearly knocked out of the fight, caught one female and beat her furiously across the back of her head before they let her go.

"Ung! Ung! Bitch! You wanna jump somebody?" Dominique asked in an enraged manner as she and Lubby beat the girl until she screamed for help.

Lubby and Dominique let her go and the five called the girls names before they, too, broke and ran from the mall before security could rush the scene. The girls made their way out of the mall and headed to Read Boulevard to catch the bus, but Rolanda had to pee so they went to Popeye's, which was directly across from the mall to clean up and use the bathroom.

"I handled them hoes! Bitches can't fuck with these dum-dums this skinny black bitch dropping out there!" Rolanda stated as she referred to herself.

"Girls? We kicked ass today!" Brianna stated as she checked her appearance in the bathroom mirror.

"Everybody saw that shit! We whipped ten bitches! *Ten*! The five ain't a joke!" Tracey chimed in as she washed her blood-stained hands and brass knuckles in the sink.

The five had won this day, and they would relish the event over the weeks to come as they knew their reputation had been amped up. They later went to Mike's party and had a good time with Mike and Donald acting as host. The girls bragged about what had happened at the mall and a few people who were on hand verified what they were saying. As the rap song *Friends* by Whodini blared from the huge speaker inside Mike's mother's living room, courtesy of Dominique and Tracey, the group of teens, excited about the five winning the fight at the mall began yelling, 'Go East Shore, go East Shore, go East Shore."

Tracey and Dominique had come out the room and danced with the crowd. Everyone was in a festive mood, intoxicated off the fight the girls had purportedly won that night. They reveled in what to them was a sign of strength coming from East Shore, who had to face countless enemies. They all savored the victory of the five. Gerald, Bobby and Tank were on hand as well as the majorettes and cheerleaders. This was the elite group, the strongest of the teens attending Abramson High School on 1985. They were popular, active, and daring. They were the insiders, a group to be sought after. If you weren't apart of this group, you were a nobody to them.

CHAPTER 11

GIRL TALK

It was now late January of 1986, a cold but sunny winter Saturday morning, and the five, were over to Dominique's house. They had spent the night there after Terrence, Dominique and Tracey had Dee-jayed another party in East Shore for one of the majorettes from school, their friend Tiffany. Terrence had allowed Dominique to hold onto his turntables, speaker, albums and mixer since he didn't have another party to Dee-jay that weekend. Tracey and Dominique were looking forward to practicing and perfecting their skills. They were also planning to take the money they made the night before, about $40 and head downtown to Canal Street to purchase some more albums to add to their personal collection of albums. Although Terrence owned the equipment, Dominique and Tracey were beginning to have the equipment most of the time since most parties were being held in East Shore. Terrence trusted the girls completely; and when they started buying albums and adding them to the milk crate, Terrence again grew proud of the two. He gave them two milk crates to place their albums in so they wouldn't get mixed with his. That way, if and when they split up, they would have their albums to start out with, but they all shared, Terrence more than Dominique and Tracey as he had the most possessions.

As Brianna and Dominique were awakening, they could smell biscuits. The two sat up in Dominique's bed and looked over to Lubby, who'd just walked back into the bedroom all bright-eyed and fully dressed. "Your momma got biscuits and grits in the kitchen on the stove, Dominique. She said we can eat whenever we ready. I had just put some plates and glasses on the table."

"What ya' doing up so early girl?" Brianna asked.

"I set the table, and then I was looking for Dominique camera so I can take a picture of these two." Lubby replied as she pointed to Tracey and Rolanda, who were asleep on the carpeted floor at the foot of Dominique's bed.

Tracey was lying on her back snoring and Rolanda was laying cross-ways to her body. Brianna, Lubby and Dominique sniggled as they watched Rolanda lay on her back with her feet propped up on Tracey's 34d breasts.

"Remember Rolanda said her feet was hurting from dancing all night when we got in last night?" Lubby asked lowly.

"Yea. Why?" Brianna asked with a puzzled look on her face.

"She using Tracey titties for pillows—and she doing it on purpose. Every time Tracey turn on her side, Rolanda pull her back over watch." Lubby answered as she held back her laugh by covering her mouth.

A few minutes later, Tracey snorted then coughed and rolled on her side facing away from Rolanda. The three sat quietly as they watched Rolanda get up sleepily and pull Tracey back, "Keep your ass still shit!" Rolanda said as she plopped her feet back up on Tracey's chest.

The three laughed lowly and then went into the kitchen to eat.

"Girl Tracey gone whip that ass when she see them funky feet in her face." Brianna stated as the three fixed plates for themselves. As they sat and ate, the girls heard Dominique's father's truck pulling up. She jumped up and ran towards her father when she heard him come through the door.

"What's all this stereo equipment? Y'all broke in somebody house?" Stanley asked jokingly.

"No dad, that's Terrence stuff you know that. Hey can I have twenty dollars to buy some more albums?"

"Twenty dollars for albums?" Stanley asked as he rubbed his beard. "Albums, albums, albums. That's all you and Tracey ever buy. How many you have now?"

"About fifty."

"Nice collection. I remember when you first wanted to be a Dee-jay, Dominique. I have to admit, I was skeptical at first 'cause kids now-a-days change their minds every week, but you for real about this aren't you?"

"Yes, dad. I really want to be a Dee-jay someday on the radio."

"I hear ya' sugar cone, and I believe in you one hundred percent!" Stanley said as he reached for his wallet and handed his daughter a crisp twenty dollar bill.

Brianna watched as Lubby bowed her head and grew sad. She, like the rest of her friends and friends' parents now knew Lubby wished she had real parents; and moments like these, which took place often inside of Dominique, Tracey, Brianna, and Rolanda's homes, often made Lubby feel left out.

Mr. Franz was well aware of Lubby's plight and he quickly thought of a way to enliven her spirit.

"Hey Lubby, my wife tell me you light the floor up at halftime with the majorettes. I'm a have ta' come see you dance."

"Yea, I'm alright."

"Alright? They tell me you choreograph some of the routines! That's a tad bit better than alright! I bet you make Debbie Allen look like an amateur!"

"That's my favorite dancer!" Lubby said as her eyes lit up.

"Well, she need ta' come down to Tad Gormley Stadium during the football season or catch you at the gym for basketball season and check you out and learn some things. I know my daughter gone set this equipment up later, how 'bout putting on a show for everybody later on?"

"For real?" Lubby asked as her eyes grew wider and she began to smile. "Y'all wanna see me dance?" she asked as she looked around at her friends, who were all smiling brightly and nodding to say yes.

"I wanna see what the great Lubby Williams can do! But ya' know you can't out dance this old school brother right here, right?" Mr. Franz stated as he began to do 'The Swim' causing the girls to burst into laughter.

"That's an old dance! I been learned that one." Lubby stated through laughter as she got up and went and danced beside Mister Franz in the living room.

Dominique began pounding a rhythmic drum pattern on the kitchen table as Brianna began clapping in rhythm, the two of them providing a quick impromptu dance pattern that allowed Mister Franz and Lubby to dance in harmony.

Misses Franz emerged from her bedroom at that moment and stood at the end of the hall watching with a wide smile planted across her face. "Come on Antoinette! Remember how we used to dance together back in the day? Come on over here and show Lubby how we used to do the swim in junior high." Stanley said as he stretched out his right hand to welcome his wife.

Misses Franz, smiled and nodded to say no. She had grown shy at that moment.

"Come on Misses Franz!" Lubby stated as she began clapping in rhythm.

As Dominique continued to pound the table, Brianna and Lubby began urging Misses Franz to dance by clapping and repeatedly saying, "Dance! Dance! Dance!"

Soon everybody was calling for Misses Franz to dance. She placed her hands on her hips, bowed her head and slowly began to move her arms as if she was swimming. Dominique and her friends, along with Mister Franz, cheered Misses Franz on. She was soon rocking her hips slightly as she burst into laughter. "I haven't danced this dance in years!" she exclaimed joyfully as she joined her husband and Lubby in the center of the living room.

Before long everybody was dancing. Dominique asked her parents if they wanted her to set up the turntables but they declined.

"We're gonna finish this dance contest later on tonight," Stanley said. "Lubby you pretty good, sweetie. Now, make sure you on point again next time, 'cause you gone have ta' out dance the dance master later on this evening." he ended as he smiled at Lubby.

"I'm a do something bad for ya', Mr. Franz." Lubby replied before she went and sat back at the kitchen table to finish having breakfast with Brianna and Dominique as Mister and Misses Franz headed towards their bedroom.

After finishing breakfast, Dominique, Brianna and Lubby went and peeked in on Rolanda and Tracey, figuring they were both up by now, especially after all the noise that was made only minutes earlier. They entered the bedroom and saw Tracey lying across Dominique's bed on her stomach with a huge, black rubber spider dangling from a string in her left hand. She looked back and placed a finger over her mouth as the three peeked over the bed and watched as she lowered the spider to Rolanda's face. Rolanda brushed it away and Tracey lowered it again. The four were sniggling as they watched Rolanda ward of the intruder that was disrupting her sleep. "What the," Rolanda began to speak sleepily as she slowly opened her eyes whilst brushing the spider from her face. "Ohhh shit! Oh shit! Get it off! Get it off!" Rolanda screamed as she got up and danced around in the corner.

Tracey had tied the spider to Rolanda's night gown and she was frantically trying to get the spider off her body. The four burst into laughter as Rolanda fell backwards into Dominique's closet as she screamed loudly. When Rolanda realized the spider was a fake, she got up and pulled it off her night gown and threw it at Tracey. "Why you playing girl?"

"My titties ain't no got damn pillows! Thought I wasn't gone feel your big elephant feet on my chest?"

"That's different. You coulda gave me a heart attack with

that spider."

"Your big elephant feet coulda suffocated me! Weighing down my chest!"

"Please! Them big bazookas could hold up a brick building." Rolanda snapped.

"Elephant feet!"

"Cannon chest! Bam! Bam!" Rolanda mocked. Tracey threw a pillow at her and an all-out pillow fight ensued between the five friends.

After joyous laughter and horseplay, the girls headed back to the kitchen to finish breakfast. When they walked pass Dominique's parents' room they heard moaning.

"Ohhh Stanley! Stanley! Yes sweet Jesus! Oh, oh, oh, oh, don't stop, don't ever stop!"

"Stanley in there laying the law down!" Tracey whispered as she placed her ear to the door.

"Tracey come on!" Dominique grumbled.

"Shhh!" Tracey said as she continued to listen.

"Ohhh! Baby it's good! So good!" Mrs. Franz moaned, exciting Tracey and the rest of the girls, minus Dominique, to high heaven.

Everybody except Dominique sniggled; she was embarrassed. Something in Tracey's body, however, began to tingle. She knew Dominique wanted them all to walk away from the door, but she just had to listen in at least for a few more seconds. She placed her ear back to the door and could hear the two grown-ups moaning.

"Sex must feel damn good!" Tracey whispered to her friends.

"It's the bomb!" fourteen year-old Brianna whispered back as her friends turned and looked at her with wide eyes. "I'm not saying—I'm just saying. I mean that's what I heard. That's what they say, that's what they be sayin' at school." Briana remarked as her four friends rolled their eyes at her before they walked away from the door.

"So you the first one out the group, huh, Bri?" Rolanda asked.

"Don't tell nobody either!"

"Who it was?" Lubby asked.

"Mike."

"Mike!" Brianna's friends said in unison.

"Yea, it only happened once. He used ta' finger bang me all the time."

"Where?" Tracey asked lowly.

"In my pu—"

"I know where, Bri. I mean where at?" Tracey asked.

"Oh. Right. In the cat walk not too far from the school bus stop. Somebody threw a sofa away back there behind those two empty houses. I don't know what happened, but after I started my period, right before it come down I get hot. I was touching myself one night and my body just started tingling."

Tracey could relate to the tingling because she was now tingling after listening in on Dominique's parents.

"What else?" Tracey asked inquisitively.

"I started doing it like every day 'cause it felt good. You got a li'l fleshy knob down there and when you rub it, awww, girl! What a feeling!" Brianna remarked as she closed her eyes and sighed.

"That's your clitoris." Lubby stated.

"Hey, we know what that thang is we got down there. If you touch it it feel good, though. Bri?" Tracey then asked.

"Please! I was addicted! After a while I began fantasizing what it'll feel like if a boy touched it. I knew Mike wouldn't tell, so I just asked him to touch me. He did, and then he put his finger inside and I swear I saw lightning when that tingling came back, it's called an orgasm."

"It can't be all that." Dominique chimed in.

"Speak for yourself. I know. I just got tired of the finger and one day right before Christmas break I got a condom from the school nurse and that night I told Mike ta' put his penis inside me. He said he never done it before. I told him it was my first time too. We broke each other virgin in that catwalk on the sofa and that was it."

Dominique didn't want to lose her virginity the way Brianna did. She wanted her first time to be special; in a warm bed with soft music playing. She was glad she was going with Calvin who she knew wouldn't take her in an alley way. Still, Dominique didn't pass judgment on Brianna; she only wished her friend had waited a little longer like she was planning on doing. As Dominique was reflecting on how Brianna had lost her virginity, Tracey asked Brianna did she like how it felt.

"I wish I had bought a whole box of those things, Tracey. But I'm cool now. I'm just gone wait on the right person that's worthy of me." Brianna replied as Dominique grabbed her arm and squeezed it and smiled. She was glad Brianna made that decision. She was also glad Brianna had used a condom as there were a few girls at Abramson, some their age, who were either pregnant or who already had babies and they seemed to be ashamed and unhappy with themselves.

"I wanna wait 'til I'm married." Lubby said. "Gerald said he gone wait on me. I hope he ain't lying 'cause I like him a lot."

"Gerald cool, Lubby. Y'all gone be together for a long time. I wanna be your maid of honor when y'all get married." Brianna told her.

"No! That's my spot! Lubby already told me I was gone be the maid-of-honor!" Rolanda snapped before she stuck out her tongue at Bri.

"Girl, that's years from now, anyway you might have a boxing match that night. Rolanda 'Sugar Ray Leonard' Jones." Brianna replied as she laughed.

"Well, I ain't really been thinking about sex, but I'm like you Bri—when the moment is right there it go." Rolanda stated.

"I think I wanna wait too, like Lubby, y'all know Calvin gone be my husband right? And he already said he wanted to wait until he married; and I'm gone wait as well. So that means Calvin will be my first."

Brianna smiled at Dominique and said, "Calvin will make a good husband for you, Dominique. He smart, funny at times, and he hip to the streets in spite of being a momma's boy. I wanna be the maid of honor!"

"That'll be live! If me and Lubby get married on the same day! Then Rolanda can be there for Lubby, and you and Tracey can be my maid of honor!" Dominique stated excitedly.

"Yea, that's bad right there! A double wedding!" Tracey stated as Dominique's mother entered the kitchen and the five girls sniggled to themselves.

"What are you girls giggling about now?"

"Nothing important momma. Just something that happened at the party last night."

"I'm not in agreement with you Dee-jaying all those parties, Dominique. But your father supports you and if it's good enough for Stanley, then it's good enough for me. I just want you to be careful. I love you and it would hurt me if something ever happened to you at one those soirees."

"Swor-what?" Lubby then asked as Rolanda began looking around from her seat in the kitchen.

"What are you looking for Rolanda?" Mrs. Franz asked.

"A pen and paper. Lubby gone wanna write that down."

"A soirée is just another word that means a 'get-together', Lubby."

"Ohh okay, Misses Franz. I don't need pen and paper for that. I thought it was gonna be the proverbial long and drawn out overstated definition that only further perpetuates the sometimes lackadaisical effort on my part to broaden my understanding of the English vocabulary." Lubby replied as she smiled at Rolanda, leaned forward and rested her elbows on the table.

"That is just down right exquisite the way you avowed the use of your vocabulary, Lubby," Rolanda replied as she sat back in the chair and crossed her legs. "But once you have mastered the English language you must come to the understanding that the English vocabulary is more than just strumming together a few eight, ten, or twelve letter words to make up the proverbial long and drawn out overstated annotations that are only meant to perplex people in society who can't fully comprehend or retort the statements that are being spoken in their presence," she ended as she grabbed a pen and paper from Mrs. Franz's breakfast rack and handed it to Lubby.

Lubby took the pen and paper and said, "Anno, anno-what?"

"Annotation, Lubby. That means comment, or comments." Rolanda answered as Brianna, Dominique and Tracey burst into laughter.

"One of these days I'm a make you write down something I say watch!" Lubby said as she smiled at Rolanda.

Word play was something Rolanda and Lubby would get into from time to time. It was friendly competition that heightened both girls' vocabulary; but Lubby always came out on the losing end. Rolanda told her that it would be nearly impossible for her to win because she wrote weekly street reports that kept her skills sharp. Still, Lubby promised herself that one day she would stump Rolanda and have her reach for pad and pen.

The five girls and Mrs. Franz sat and talked in the kitchen, but it wasn't too long before Dominique's friends were sniggling again as they stared at Mrs. Franz. They just couldn't get the image of what they heard out of their heads.

"Momma, can we study so we can get ready to go downtown?" Dominique asked as she was growing weary of the sniggling coming from her four friends.

"Sure thing, baby. Give me about an hour. Me and your father have to umm, we have to talk about something." Mrs. Franz said as she blushed and got up and pranced to her bedroom door and closed it and locked it.

"They 'bouta do it again!" Tracey quipped as she hopped from her seat.

Dominique grabbed her by her t-shirt and said, "No! No more eavesdropping Tracey."

"Alright, alright. But sex gotta feel good because your momma passed up a bible study to do it!" Tracey stated through laughter as the girls began to set up the equipment before their bible study.

Later that afternoon, after the girls had studied the bible with Dominique's mother, they rode the bus to Canal Street. The girls, with the exception of Dominique, laughed about the fact that they could barely keep their composure as they sat at the table with images of Dominique's parents having sex in the bedroom running through their minds. It was a hard study for the group and they were glad when it was over. No one was happier than Dominique.

The five made it to Canal Street and entered *New Age* record shop and began perusing through the wide assortment of albums. Tracey and Dominique came out with ten new albums to add to their collection. As they walked down Canal Street towards the river, they saw a group of girls they knew from school standing in front of Footlocker on the corner of Bourbon and Canal Streets.

"Looka Brianna 'nem walking like they some beauty queens. Buncha stuck-up bitches'!" one girl, a caramel-skinned pretty brown eyed fifteen year-old named Daphne said loud enough for the five to hear.

The five merely laughed loudly as they passed the group of about seven girls.

"Yes indeed. Jealousy is just running wild out ta' Abramson! We got 'em jealous now home girls!" Brianna chided as she eyed Daphne and kept walking along with her friends.

"Say it to my face bitch!" Daphne remarked.

Just then, Tracey, tired of all the talking, immediately began to swing on Daphne. She had reacted to what Daphne had said and a fight ensued. Dominique was again fighting two females, knocking one down quickly with a strike to her mouth, and Lubby had taken off her chain and was whipping the female she was fighting across her back. People scattered away from the scene as they watched the girls brawl.

Rolanda had her back to the entrance way of Footlocker. People inside the store watched the scene as Rolanda knocked one girl down and then began punching the other two females furiously. Rolanda had a set of hands on her; and when she fought, her heart was just as ferocious as the blows she dished out. Not many people could deal with Rolanda's fist expertise.

Brianna was a scrappy somebody with the gift of prowess. She had an uncanny ability to be able to sneak through a gang fight undetected and attack swiftly. She was holding the stack of albums her girls had just bought and was using them to whack Daphne and her friends across the head as she popped in and out of the ruckus.

Dominique could hold her own, but she tired easily, especially when fighting two or more opponents. Whenever the odds were even, however, the feisty female could ward off her opponent, just as she had done this day.

Lubby would do whatever it took to survive a fight. Gouging eyes, ripping out earrings, biting, whatever it took to keep somebody off her ass, Lubby would do it. Just as she had done with the chain she'd turned into a metal whip.

Everybody thought Tracey was crazy when she fought. She often used weapons, namely her brass knuckles. Tracey would often draw blood when she fought; but she would also stand toe-to-toe, which would be a battle that would unfold on this day between Tracey and Daphne.

The girls separated eventually, and the five stood in the middle of Bourbon Street taunting the seven girls as they stood beside Footlocker. Lubby wrapped her chain around her right hand and Tracey went into her pockets and grabbed her brass knuckles.

"Umm, this ain't the Checkerboard y'all bitches fighting!" Daphne said as she pulled out a switchblade.

"Tracey, she got a knife come on let it go!" Dominique stated.

"Fuck that! Bring it bitch!" Tracey said to Daphne.

"Put the knuckles down!"

"Put the knife down hoe!" Tracey answered as she threw up her guards preparing to take Daphne on one on one.

Daphne sat the switchblade down and Tracey handed her brass knuckles to Lubby and the two squared off. The 5'6" 125 pound Daphne couldn't handle the blows coming from Tracey Sanchez. She knocked Daphne to her knees in under a minute. Lubby saw one of the girls go for Daphne's knife and she grabbed her, but another girl picked the knife up. Lubby used the girl for a shield until she was able to get away. At that moment, another female pulled a chrome .38 revolver and aimed it at Brianna and she, too, broke and ran along with the rest of the five.

Brianna was looking back as the girl pointed the gun at the five. The female then lowered the gun and began shouting, "That's right run bitches! *Bunker Hill* run this motherfucka! Rolanda! Report this shit right here on your street report next Friday ya' coward bitch you!" she ended as Daphne and her crew broke and ran in another direction.

The five entered into the French Quarters and mixed in with the crowd before they began heading for the bus stop.

"Man them bitches from Bunker Hill packing iron! We can't get caught slipping like that no more!" Brianna said, nearly out of breath as the five ran towards the bus stop. *"One of us coulda died today!"* she thought to herself as she and her girls made it to bus stop just in time and rode home in silence, each of them, especially Bri, knowing they was lucky to come away unharmed.

The girls had a private party with Dominique's parents later that night and Lubby got to do her dance routine in imitation of Debbie Allen. She was so proud of herself that she couldn't stop talking the whole night. It was the happiest her four friends had seen her since the day Gerald had given her that donkey rope. The five then spent Saturday night by Dominique's house again and they sat up and watched *Morgus the Magnificent*, a popular horror movie TV show host, and the movie *Friday the 13th*. The movie came out in 1980, but the girls had never seen it before. They were all quiet as they watched someone slaughter innocent teenagers who were camping at a lake.

"Girl, don't go in there! Don't—oh lord! She know the man in the room and she gone walk right in there?" Rolanda said as she sat with her feet in the chair.

"You don't know that, Rolanda. If she knew the killer was in there she wouldn't go in there." Lubby stated as she sat on her knees in front the floor model TV eating a popcorn ball.

"You can't hear the music, Lubby? Every time they do the li'l *'chere, chere, chere'*—he coming to chop somebody head off!" Rolanda snapped.

"We can hear the music but they can't, girl!" Brianna stated as she stared at the screen.

"Oooh! She bouta get her head chopped off!" Tracey squirmed as she grabbed a pillow and covered her face slightly as she watched the scene unfold.

Dominique was on the phone with Calvin as she lay back on the living room floor talking sweet talk. "Hold up this lady 'bouta get killed right quick!" she said as she sat up and watched the scene.

Brianna, Rolanda, Lubby, and Tracey were yelling at the screen trying to tell the woman not walk into the room. They all screamed when a dead body fell onto the screen and the four girls got up and ran around the room. Lubby dropped her popcorn ball onto the carpet as she got up.

"I told ya'!" Rolanda said as she yelled at the lady on the TV as she was being murdered. "When ya' hear the music run! What the hell y'all doin' out there in them woods anyway?" she yelled at the screen. "My, my nerves getting bad! And how the hell he just pop up like that? She left him way down by the lake!"

"It's just a movie, girl!" Dominique said as she fell back and began chatting again with Calvin.

"You can say what ya' wanna say, but this here movie right here gone have me scared in the daytime! Ohhh lord! I'm coming down with yellow fever!" Rolanda said as the five burst into laughter reminiscing back to the day they got busted for cheating at Little Woods.

After the movie, the girls all turned in for the night. Neither would admit it, but they were all scared having watched the movie. They talked for all while until each of them fell asleep. That became a contest as no one wanted to be the last person awoke, because in their eyes, you would be the first one killed. They all hurried themselves to sleep and returned to their respective homes the next morning.

CHAPTER 12

AIN'T NO LOVE

It was the Tuesday after the girls' fight on Bourbon Street and weekend spent by Dominique's house, the date was January 28, 1986 and the sophomores and freshmen were all sitting in their first period class. Teachers had decided not to issue assignments during the first period to allow the students to watch the Space Shuttle Challenger lift-off. The teachers were all in a real good mood this day because Sharon Crista McAuliffe was to be the first school teacher to fly into space and she had made every teacher in America proud. They all wished they could be in her shoes.

"Students! Calm down and watch the countdown, please! This is history in the making!" the male teacher yelled over the loud-talking pupils in his Physics class.

Daphne, Rolanda and Brianna were in the same Physics class for first period and the atmosphere was thick. Brianna and Rolanda could feel the tension; but the both of them were keenly interested in the lift-off, although for different reasons that were keenly important to them. Rolanda was going to do an essay for her English class on her views of the importance of having a teacher in space. Brianna was interested because her mother worked for N.A.S.A./Michoud, the facility that built the huge, orange center fuel tanks for the shuttles. Another student's mother, a white female named Kathy, worked at Michoud as well and she was interested in the takeoff for the same reasons as Brianna. The two of them were talking about the jobs their mothers were doing and had done in the past. Many students in the school had parents that worked at the huge facility, and that's what most of the conversation was about this day.

The teacher spoke loudly again, trying to silence the class which prompted Brianna to say aloud, "Hey, hey, hey! Y'all need ta' close it shut! A lotta people in this school parents helped build that big orange tank right there under the shuttle! It's called a center fuel tank, and it's important to getting the astronauts into space because it provides the energy needed for the thrust." Brianna said proudly.

"Nobody don't care about that!" Daphne yelled at Brianna over the rest of the loud talking students.

"See? That's your ignorance comin' to the forefront. I'm not even gone entertain you today!" Brianna replied as she turned back towards the TV.

The five had exchanged verbal assaults with Daphne and her friends on Monday. Daphne and her crew were bragging about what had taken place on Canal Street, but the five told everybody that the only reason they ran was because one of Daphne's friends had a gun. People then knew Daphne and her crew didn't fight fair. The five were already out-numbered and someone still pulled out a gun and that just didn't sit right with many students. Fighting was common, but Daphne was going to the extreme. Tracey had beaten her fair and square, but Daphne was still pushing the issue. The five had no further intentions of fighting with Daphne and her friends because they knew their clique had a gun and it may very well get used if the opportunity presented itself. The five would readily fight, but getting shot and killed was just too high a price to pay over jealousy. It was fair to say that the five were a little scared of Daphne and her crew because of the fact that they had a gun in their possession. If they were ever caught in the mall or on Canal Street, the next time, the weapon might actually get used and none of the five wanted to be killed.

"Nobody ain't jealous of y'all!" Daphne stated as students laughed.

"She said you are ignorant, not jealous. *You* said the word jealous. And don't lie; you are jealous that's why you keeping all this mess going, 'cause you jealous." Rolanda remarked on behalf of Brianna.

"Man, nobody don't care about *you*, this *school*, or no teacher on the space shuttle!" Daphne stated as she sat back in her chair.

"You should care!" Rolanda replied. "That could be you up there one day making history!" she added as the teacher turned the volume up on the TV.

"I be higher than the space shuttle every day! What I wanna go in space for? Anyway, why you care what I do? I ain't ya' friend! You and Brianna *know* we ain't cool so y'all need ta' shut up talking to me!" Daphne replied as the class grew silent.

"Just stupid, man." Rolanda said as she shook her head and continued writing her report.

"Yea, you keep writing and make sure you tell what happened on Canal and Bourbon."

"How you sound? You know that ain't ta' be told! Man I'm so tired of this jealousy stuff I just wanna run away."

"Like you did on Saturday past?" Daphne snapped with a smirk.

"Like Tracey dropped you in front of Footlocker? On Saturday past!" Rolanda snapped back.

"Payback's a you know what!" Daphne ended as she got up and moved away from Rolanda and Brianna.

The young teens growing up in New Orleans East in the late eighties were bold and brash. They fought each other over the simplest things and would act as if was just another day in the streets. Fights were common, most, like Shantrell and her crew would accept when they were beaten and leave it at that. Some, like Daphne and her crew would keep a battle going for days and weeks. The five knew they had to get Daphne to squash the matter, or this scenario would continue until someone was seriously hurt. A lot of people in the school fought, but Daphne and her crew had taken the game to another level when they produced that gun. The five could not let that get pass them. They knew Daphne would not bring the gun to school so they were planning to attempt to squash the matter this day before things got out of hand, but a situation would transpire that would change the girl's plans and have serious repercussions for the five *and* Daphne's crew.

"Yayyyy! Look what our mommas did, Kathy!" Brianna said as she high-fived her classmate and watched the Space Shuttle *Challenger* lift off into the sky.

"They on their way, Brianna." the teacher said proudly as Brianna and Kathy looked back at him with proud eyes. "Now when they get there, Sharon's gonna give classes from space and we all are going to be able to watch as she—broadcasts—from—oh my God! Sweet Jesus no!" the teacher said in shock as his mouth widened and he took off his eye-glasses.

Brianna and Kathy turned back to the screen and Rolanda had to do a double take as she watched the shuttle plummet back to Earth.

"Ohhh nooo!" Lubby and Tracey, who were sitting in English class stated at the same time.

"Damn they blew up!" a student in Dominique's History class yelled out in shock.

Dominique looked at the screen in utter confusion; she had seen the whole thing unfold before her eyes, but she couldn't believe what she had just witnessed. *"Did that really happen?"* she asked herself.

The teachers in the school went into a frenzy. They were running to each other's classes hoping that what they had seen on their TV would be different in another's class. Once the realization set in that the Space Shuttle Challenger was lost, all classes were canceled an hour later and kids were sent home early.

"You want me to be a part of that?" Daphne asked as the students prepared to leave.

"Shut up Daphne!" the entire Physics class said in unison as they walked out the door in a single file somber line.

"Man y'all don't run me!" Daphne remarked in a slightly embarrassed tone.

The five met up and waited about thirty minutes for their bus to come back to the school and pick them up. It was during that time that Daphne and her crew approached the five. "Yea, we ain't forget what happened Saturday bitches!"

Brianna, who was mad because she knew her mother's job was at risk, got up in Daphne's face and told her to respect what had just happened to Crista McAuliffe and the rest of the astronauts.

"Fuck you bitch!" Daphne yelled as she shoved Brianna backwards. A scuffle ensued between the two, but it was broken up quickly by other students. "People just died on live TV and you still with that shit?" a sophomore majorette stated to Daphne.

"Bitch please! Nobody don't give a fuck about a got damn rocket!"

"You sad Daphne." the student said as she and the five broke away. "You sad, girl."

"Another time Daphne. We gone talk another time." Brianna said as she walked backwards behind her four friends staring at Daphne.

"Yea, this shit ain't over, Bri. Fuck talking! I got you!"

The five went home sad that day. They sat over to Brianna's house at the kitchen table awaiting Brianna's mother's arrival. Ms. Stanford came through the door with tears in her eyes.

"Momma, you okay?"

"I'm not okay! They gone try and blame us for the explosion. I can lose my job baby! What I'm gone do Jesus?"

"Momma, don't cry." Brianna said as her eyes welled up. "Sometimes bad things happen to good people." she then said softly.

Brianna's mother chuckled. Her daughter had said the very same thing she said to her almost two years to the day. "You right sweetie!" The woman said as she perked up. "We did nothing wrong. Hey, it's early, I'm hungry, y'all girls wanna go to Pizza Hut!" the five all said yes and soon they were on their way to the pizza parlor.

The following Friday after the shuttle disaster Dominique, Tracey, and Rolanda did a dedication show complete with video footage of N.A.S.A.'s history from the landing on the moon up until the present time. It played on every TV monitor in the school. Jon Bon Jovi's song *Wanted Dead or Alive* played in the background as footage ran. It ended with a picture of the seven astronauts that perished and a picture of the American flag waving in the background. Students, and especially the teachers, were greatly moved by the video and they congratulated the three on their efforts.

It had been a good day for the five; and as school ended students walked with the girls as they sang the chorus to Bon Jovi's song.

"I'm a cowboy...on a steel horse I ride...and I'm wanted... wanted...dead or alive...I'm a cowboy...I got my knife on my side...and I'm wanted...wanted...dead or alive..."

It was a sight to behold as scores of students, black, white and others, sang as they walked out of the main building, some crying, replaying the image of the shuttle exploding in mid-air. As the five were walking to their bus, Daphne and her crew approached.

"What's up now bitches? Nobody don't give a fuck about that video!" she said as she pulled her switchblade.

The five scattered as Daphne and six other girls began chasing them through the school parking lot. Tracey, who seemed to be the main target, was attempting to run back into the building, but she was caught by Daphne and two other girls. A crowd surrounded the four as Tracey defended herself. She was reaching into her leather trench coat trying to grab her brass knuckles as she took blows from Daphne and her two friends.

Rolanda, Brianna, Lubby, and Dominique ran back towards Tracey, each with a girl from Daphne's crew trailing behind. They fought through the crowd taking blows to the back of the head from the girls as they made their way towards their friend who was in serious need of help.

"Tracey! Tracey!" Dominique yelled aloud the moment she saw her friend struggling to remain upright as she fought with Daphne and two other girls.

Tracey was now on the grass in front of the main building swinging on Daphne. "Y'all gotta jump! That's the only way y'all can fuck with us! Y'all gotta jump!" Tracey said as she fought with the three girls.

Daphne lashed out at Tracey's face with her knife, but she blocked it with her arm. She received a slicing gash to her left arm that ripped through her leather trench coat and sliced her forearm open and she screamed out in pain. Tracey grabbed her arm and leaned forward, her head to the ground as she watched her blood run through her torn coat and her fingers and drip into the grass. She was attempting to turn and run away, but Daphne grabbed her by her hair and raised her arm and was prepared to stab Tracey in the face.

"Come on Daphne put the knife down, you already won!" Tracey stated in fear as Daphne grabbed hold.

The crowd looked on in shock as Tracey's four friends burst through; there was mass frenzy and scores of bodies yelling aloud for Daphne not to stab Tracey.

"Don't stab me again! Heeellllppp!" Tracey yelled as Daphne grew intoxicated off her plea for mercy.

"Ain't no love out ta' this bitch! Fuck you!" Daphne yelled aloud over the screaming crowd.

Daphne raised the knife into the air in an attempt to stab Tracey just as two gunshots rang out. Students scattered and Tracey fell back into the grass, quickly got up and began running towards the hospital screaming with blood dripping profusely from her lacerated arm. Daphne lay on the grass clutching her side screaming in pain.

Tracey's four friends ran up beside her and screamed for help as they ran side by side with her to the hospital. They didn't know what to do to help Tracey except run with her.

"I gotta get to the hospital! I'm bleedin' bad y'all!" Tracey cried as she ran down the long driveway leading to Methodist Hospital. As the five were running, Tracey now out in front, the police pulled up alongside of them. They saw the shape Tracey was in and they placed her in the backseat. Her friends all piled into the car and rode to Methodist Hospital where Tracey was ushered into the emergency room for surgery on her lacerated arm.

At the tender age of fourteen, Tracey Sanchez was sliced in her left arm and nearly stabbed to death in front of Marion Abramson Senior High. She would recover from her wounds, although she would have a four inch scar on her left forearm to forever remind her of the day she'd nearly lost her life.

Daphne Raymond had nearly lost her life as well. She, however, was later charged with aggravated assault. A great majority of students had witnessed the event, but because of all the chaos, no one had actually seen who had shot Daphne; besides, most of the students felt Daphne got exactly what she deserved that day. She just simply would not let the situation between she and the five defuse itself; and on top of that, she was about to murder Tracey in cold blood over nothing.

After Tracey came out of surgery four hours later, her four friends were waiting for her. The doctors said she would have to spend the night so sadly, they would ride home with Dominique's mother. Dominique's mother sat with Tracey's mother, Maria for a while before she left. She repeatedly told Maria how sorry she was for what had happened to Tracey. "These neighborhood wars are going to destroy our daughters." Maria said as she cried and held onto her son. "Your sister will be just fine." she said lovingly as she wiped the tears from his face.

"Your daughter did nothing wrong, Maria. And even if she did, she didn't deserve to end up in the predicament she's in. But thank Jehovah that she's alive." Mrs. Franz stated.

"Who's Jehovah?"

"That's God's name."

"God has a *name*?" Maria asked in a surprised manner.

"Yes! Your daughter knows his name. And I'm sure she called on him when she was in her most vulnerable time of her life. Jehovah heard her, and he saved her." Mrs. Franz said as she handed Maria a brochure titled *God Has a Name*.

Maria took the brochure and sat back and began to read it as Mrs. Franz took the four with her and they rode back to East Shore. During the ride home, Mrs. Franz questioned the girls repeatedly about what happened and they told her that some girls had jumped Tracey and she was stabbed and somebody shot the girl who had stabbed Tracey. Mrs. Franz wondered who could do such a thing. When they got back to their neighborhood that night, the four friends exited the car and saw Gerald waiting in front of Rolanda's house for Lubby. Cynthia had run him off when he parked in front of her door. The four girls walked over to Gerald's car as Gerald exited his 1984 light-grey four door delta eighty-eight on chrome Tru rims and vogue tires and walked over to the girls and asked how Tracey was doing, and Rolanda told him she was fine.

"What happened with Daphne?" Gerald then asked as the cold wind blew swiftly.

"Somebody shot her, but we don't know who did it." Dominique stated sadly.

Gerald looked at the girls with a look of disbelief on his face.

"We don't." Lubby stated lowly. "My girl almost got killed today. God that woulda hurt. I don't wanna fight no more. Not if it's gone end like this." Lubby ended.

"I feel ya', Lubby—but if the police question y'all? They gone wanna check y'all hands for gunshot residue. If one of y'all *did* shoot Daphne, you need to get rid of that gun and rub dog shit all over your hands ta' cover that shit up. I'm just letting y'all know, you know? 'Cause when Tracey and Daphne come through it's a good chance the police gone ask what happened, and if Daphne say one of y'all shot her, they coming. And they gone check for gunshot residue. Dog shit gone help hide the residue."

Gerald then kissed Lubby and told her he, Bobby, and Tank were going shopping and he would see her the next evening.

The four friends then stood in front of Rolanda's house and talked about what happened earlier that day. They just didn't feel the same. They were missing a part of their personality and they would not be right until Tracey was back home.

As the four friends stood in the cold air chatting, Dominique, Rolanda and Lubby noticed Brianna kept looking around in the numerous yards within her eyesight. She walked up and down the sidewalk and stopped suddenly in front of Lubby's yard and ran and knelt in the grass. The three walked over to Brianna and noticed she was rubbing dog feces all over her hands as she cried in the cold night air.

"Bri!" Dominique whispered in surprise as she ran and knelt down beside her friend.

"I, I got that gun from Mike Sunday night and I, I, I carried that gun with me every day this week. I was scared ever since Daphne pulled that gun on Canal Street. I wasn't gone let them hurt us! We not bad people! Gabriella wasn't bad either, but she still died anyway! I wasn't gone let that happen to us!" Brianna said as she cried and rubbed her hands furiously, covering them in feces. "*I* shot that girl! Now I might go to jail for this shit! But at least Tracey still alive!"

Brianna was feeling guilty having shot someone. She also realized she could have killed Daphne this day. She bent forward and vomited in the grass, sickened by the thought.

Lubby saw right away that Brianna was feeling guilty and she felt her friend's pain. She knelt in the grass and rubbed Brianna's back and tried to console her. "You not going to jail, Bri. Daphne made you do that, right or wrong. Tracey needed you. She was calling for help. She begged Daphne not to kill her and Daphne told her 'fuck you'. She was gone kill Tracey today. You wasn't wrong," Lubby stated softly.

"I know. But why I still feel sorry for Daphne?" Briana asked.

"Because it never shoulda went this far." Dominique answered.

Dominique knew her parents would be pissed if she were to

get arrested with her friends. Her life, just like that of her friends, would be forever changed. Dominique also knew, just like Lubby, that Brianna was having a guilty conscience. She didn't want for none of her friends to go to jail, let alone she. She then tried to console Brianna by assuring her that it wasn't her fault. "Daphne was just, just, she wouldn't stop, Brianna! Lubby right, and if you go to jail, fuck it man, we all going to jail, right girls?" Dominique said as she rubbed her hands together.

Lubby was thinking about how Brianna had always given her clothes and even shared her money with her from time to time. She wasn't going to let Brianna go at it alone. "Yea. I'll go to jail with you, Bri." she said as Rolanda nodded her head in agreement.

Rolanda knew right away that neither Daphne nor Tracey would talk. If anything, they would probably get into it again. Rolanda knew Tracey, so as long as Daphne was around, would always be on guard. She couldn't picture the girls fighting over nothing though. All because they resided in different neighborhoods? The entire scenario was foolish to Rolanda and she couldn't imagine going to jail for nothing. "We not going to jail, Bri." Rolanda stated matter-of-factly, then added, "None of us! I, I just don't—I can't *imagine* you or any of us going to jail. We need to think. What you did with the gun?" she asked as she knelt in the grass.

"It's in my pocket."

"Bri! You rode inside a police car and stood in that hospital with that gun? You coulda got caught! We gotta get rid of that gun!" Dominique whispered as she dug her hands into the grass.

"Let's call Bobby and Tank. Gerald on his way over there by they house; they can come back and move it for us." Lubby stated as she rubbed her hands together.

"I know the number. I'm a call over there and tell Bobby." Rolanda said as she walked quickly into her house and called Bobby and told him in code that she needed him and Tank to ditch a gun.

145

Bobby and Tank told Rolanda they would stop by and get rid of the gun before they went 'shopping' and the four friends eagerly waited for the three older teens to return. The three young males couldn't wait to find out who shot Daphne, but when they got there, the four fourteen year-olds all had the smell of feces on their hands as they handed a brown paper bag to Tank. All four girls had their hands on the bag as well.

"Now," Tank said as he stared at the bag containing the gun whilst wrinkling his face at the smell of the feces, "I know damn well all four y'all didn't squeeze this fuckin' trigga! So who done it?" Tank asked, his six gold teeth shining in the moonlight as he placed a skull cap onto his jehri-curled hair.

"We all did it!" the four replied in unison.

"Hell yea! Y'all rocking like that?" Bobby asked from the backseat.

"That's tight! That's tight! We don't need ta' know who dunnit, so long as we know somebody out the crew represented for Tracey. Look, we gone take this gun and dump it in the lake. We headed out ta' Slidell anyway, we got y'all." Gerald stated as he sat behind the wheel of the light grey car.

"How y'all goin' shopping and it's after eleven?" Rolanda asked.

"Ahh, that's our secret! Y'all got a secret, and now we got a secret. So long as we keeping secrets everything alright, right?" Bobby replied from the backseat.

"Hmm…going shopping, huh? I don't know that one yet," Rolanda replied. "Yea, we cool, Bobby. Thanks Gerald. Tank, good-looking." she ended as she watched the car slowly pull off from the curb, its tail lights disappearing into the darkness as the car rounded the curve.

The four were anxiously awaiting the police's arrival the next day; prepared to tell their story. Their plan was to state to the law that they knew nothing; answer no questions and say that they knew nothing. The police never came, however, and the girls were relieved when Tracey came home a few days later. She returned to school a week later.

Daphne never told what she knew about the incident at the school. She was expelled from the school system and later moved to Florida. The neighborhood wars were coming to an end for the female cliques in eastern New Orleans; and as the school year ended in June of 1986, the five were once again back on track, but they would never forget the day that one of them had almost perished. They now had another secret to keep to themselves and they did so without regret. It should have been a turning point for the young girls, but in spite of all that had happened, the fighting, the stabbing, and eventually the shooting, the five still hadn't learned their lesson.

CHAPTER 13

GETTIN' THERE'S

It was a week after Lubby's fifteenth birthday; late August of 1986. Lubby had a huge party at Rolanda's house the week before that was Dee-jayed by Dominique and Tracey because Cynthia downright refused to have any dealings with Lubby or any of her friends. The five were all fifteen now and had spent most summer days watching movies, going swimming at Lincoln Beach and listening to Jazzy's show, something they hadn't done in a long time. They had also begun hanging with eighteen year-olds Bobby, Tank, and Gerald a little more ever since the three had ditched the gun for them the day Tracey was stabbed, but on this day, hormones were raging for several members of the five.

Rolanda cracked her front door on this muggy summer morning and peeked around the neighborhood to see if anyone was outside. When she believed no one was watching, she pranced to the mailbox.

"I told you," Dominique said lowly, as she and Lubby watched Rolanda from Dominique's bedroom window.

Rolanda was dressed in a red silk headscarf, a long black silk robe and a red pair of Daniel Greene slippers and had on a big pair of dark sunshades. She stepped quickly to the mailbox and retrieved its contents, scanned them real quick and tucked them under her armpit and walked quickly back to her house. As she did so, she looked back over her shoulders peeking over the top of her shades, swinging her head left to right to make sure no one was watching.

"Every other week around this time of day she come out and check the mailbox. She been doing it all summer. What the hell she got going on like that?" Dominique asked Lubby. "And why the hell she wearing those big ass blue blockers?" she added as the two girls laughed from behind Dominique's bedroom window.

"I don't know, but that is strange. You wanna go over there?" Lubby asked.

"Nahh, let's go by Tracey first."

Lubby and Dominique walked over to Tracey's house and knocked on the door and Tracey's little brother Marcus opened it.

"What up Marc? Where Tracey?" Dominique asked.

"She gone. She left early this morning with Brianna."

Lubby and Dominique looked at one another and wondered what was going on. Their three friends all seemed to be preoccupied on this day. They decided to walk through the neighborhood to see if they could find Brianna and Tracey and then return to Rolanda's house. They walked up the catwalk leading to Curran Street where they saw Tracey quickly disappear in between the two old houses that the alleyway ran alongside of; Tracey didn't see the two so they walked into the alleyway and stepped in between the houses. An old sofa was alongside the empty house on the left that was blocked in the front and on the right side by a wooden fence. The empty house was directly behind that house and a wooden fence blocked its view on the right. The only way you could see the sofa was to turn in between the two houses, walk to the end of the houses and look to your left.

Lubby and Dominique were walking towards the sofa between the two houses when Tracey heard them. She quickly jetted out from beside the house smiling. Tracey's smile dropped when she saw her two friends. "What the fuck y'all doin here?" she asked as she looked at her watch and saw that it was almost ten 'o' clock in the morning. Tracey was dressed in a short loose fitting mini-skirt and small tank top with a pair of sandals.

"We was gone ask you the same thing!" Dominique stated as she eyed Tracey's skimpy outfit.

"I'm tryna get mine!"

"Tracey! Not in the alley like Bri!" Dominique whispered.

"I ain't fuckin' or finger bangin'!"

"Then what?" Lubby asked as the three heard footsteps coming from the direction of Curran Street.

"Go over there! Go 'head! And shut up!" Tracey whispered as she ushered Dominique and Lubby towards the other abandoned house before quickly running over to the couch where she plopped down and crossed her thick caramel thighs, pretending that she had been waiting there the whole time.

Dominique and Lubby sat inside the empty house across from the house Tracey was sitting on side of; they peeked out the window just as 'White Boy Mike' came into view. 'White Boy Mike' was new to the neighborhood. The teens in the neighborhood called him 'White Boy Mike' to distinguish him from Black Mike that hung with Donald. 'White Boy Mike' wasn't all that cute; he had a bad case of acne, long sideburns, red hair and a thin red mustache. He was also shorter than most of the girls in the neighborhood and they often mocked him about his height. They also called him a 'geek' or 'nerd'. For anybody, especially the voluptuous and pretty Tracey Sanchez to be seen with 'White Boy Mike', it would greatly damage her reputation; but he was the only one willing to do as Tracey pleased.

Lubby and Dominique looked at one another in shock as they knelt underneath the bedroom window and listened to Tracey and 'White Boy Mike' talk.

"You ready?" Tracey asked.

"You?"

"I came didn't I?" Tracey responded.

"No, not yet, girl. Let me see it."

Lubby and Dominique watched as Tracey raised her mini-skirt to reveal that she had no panties on. The two then turned and looked at one another in shock. They peeked back in time to see Tracey sit on the sofa, spread her legs and pull up her skirt and raise her thick legs in the air as 'White Boy Mike' sunk to his knees. Both girls turned around and sat down again. Dominique gasped and Lubby sat covering her mouth as she widened her eyes and looked at Dominique.

"He was puttin' his mouth down there!" Lubby then whispered in surprise. "I ain't know he do that! I thought he was a nerd!"

"'White Boy Mike'?" Dominique stated lowly in disbelief as the two sat and listened to the smacking sounds coming from across the way.

"Ooohh, Mike! That feels so fuckin' good! Don't ssstop! Don't ever ssstop!" Tracey moaned as Lubby and Dominique sat and stared at one another with wide eyes.

"She sound like your momma!" Lubby whispered.

"Shut up!" Dominique whispered back.

Lubby peeked again and this time she saw Tracey with her legs raised and both hands on either side of 'Mike's' head as she humped his face until she shuddered and froze. "Ohhh shit white boy! Yesss indeed, oh that's so damn good." Tracey moaned lowly as she ground her vagina against Mike's face until she was fully satisfied.

Tracey's body was trembling as she lowered her legs and gently pushed Mike's head away from her sex. Mike then stood up and wiped his mouth and looked around as he unzipped his pants and pulled out his stiff rod.

Dominique and Lubby both watched as Tracey grabbed Mike's member and stood behind him and flicked her tongue along his neck and earlobe as she began to jerk his member. Tracey was startled by the teen's girth, but she quickly grabbed a firm hold and stroked his member. "You got a big dick Mike, pretty one too—but if you tell anybody I did this—I swear I'll tell everybody you ate my pussy until I came in your mouth." Tracey whispered into his ear.

"This our secret Tracey. Damn that shit feels good!" Mike moaned as he closed his eyes and enjoyed Tracey's soft, slow stroking hands.

It didn't take long for Mike to shoot semen onto the brick wall of the house and all over Tracey's hand. The two straightened themselves and Mike quickly took off as Tracey told him to call her if he wanted to do it again. She then plopped back down onto the sofa and sighed as she eyed Lubby and Dominique walking her way. Tracey wiped Mike's semen from her hands onto the side of the sofa as Lubby and Dominique approached.

"You let him put his mouth down there!" Dominique stated.

"And the problem would beeeee?"

"It's White Boy Mike!"

"I don't give a rat fat ass who it was! I ain't never felt nothing like that! I been trying all summer to get one of these li'l boys back here to do that shit, and trust, it was worth the effort! God I feel *fuckin' good*!" Tracey said as she kicked her legs in the air. "And don't tell nobody I did that with that ugly motherfucka! I only let him do it 'cause he the only one that said he would eat my pussy for me."

"He did it right?" Lubby asked as Dominique turned towards her in surprise.

"I'm not sayin'—I'm just sayin'! What I mean is, umm," Lubby said lowly as Dominique folded her arms and bounced her hips as she stared at her, not believing what Lubby was attempting to say. "Why you trying to make us feel guilty about sex? I ain't shame! Gerald do me all the time, too, Dominique! And Tracey right—it do feel good. But don't tell Gerald I told you. And that's, that's all we doing, for real." Lubby stated as Dominique bowed her head and shook it from side to side.

"Girl, you the only one ain't doin' nothin! I know you waitin' on Calvin but a li'l tongue love ain't gone hurt nothin'.

It's not real sex and you can still have an orgasm. Damn that shit feel good. It's, it's like a drug! A good drug!" Tracey said as she got up from the sofa and the three walked out of the alleyway towards Curran Street.

Once there, they saw Brianna walking up the sidewalk coming from Black Mike's house with a big smile draped across her face. "Tracey," she asked when she got close to her three friends, "Mike did it for you?"

"Yes! And oh-my-God! Like the Toyota commercial say 'Oh what a feeling'!" Tracey said as she, Lubby, and Brianna burst into laughter. "Shh! Shh! Miss Thang right here not getting hers so let's not brag and boast in front of Dominique, y'all." she then said through laughter.

"I thought you was gone wait on the right one that's worthy Bri." Dominique inquired.

"Black Mike is the right one! Right now! Anyway I got plenty of protection!" Brianna said as she waved a roll of condoms in Dominique's face. "When you marry Calvin, you gone slap yourself for waitin' so long watch!"

"Me and Rolanda the only two left I guess. Man, y'all got me wondering. I mean, y'all three make it seem like it's cool—but I know Calvin ain't with that and I don't wanna go behind his back."

"Rolanda ain't ready either, but she still do her thang!" Brianna stated.

"How?" Dominique asked.

"She rock her boat. Everybody rock they boat!"

"What's that?" Dominique asked as her three friends burst into laughter.

"We talked about this already, Dominique! Damn! You don't know much of nothing! Masturbate! Touch that button down there! Do that one time and you gone have a whole new outlook!" Brianna stated as the girls walked towards Rolanda's house and knocked on the door.

"Who the hell is it?" Rolanda yelled suddenly before she

cracked the door and saw her four friends.

"Oh! What's hatnin' y'all? Umm, umm, come back in 'bouta hour if ya' can. I'm—I'm relaxing."

"They came?" Tracey asked.

"Yea! Now let me do the same! Come back later heifers!"

"Dominique want one." Tracey stated.

Rolanda quickly closed the door and came back a minute later and handed Dominique a *Hustler* magazine before she quickly shut the door and locked it. Dominique looked at the cover and widened her eyes as she quickly hid the book from sight.

"Who gone see that?" Tracey asked as she burst into laughter.

"What I'm gone do with this magazine?"

"We can't tell you, you'll figure it out. Just look at it tonight. Come on, let's go by your house and practice on the turntables while your momma gone to the Kingdom Hall." Tracey said as the girls began heading towards Dominique's house. "I need ta' clean up, but I feel like going commando this day! White Boy Mike got my li'l cooty coo feelin' great!" she ended as the girls walked to Dominique's house.

Dominique placed the magazine in her drawer and returned to the living room and powered up the equipment and the girls sat and jammed for a while before Rolanda came over. Once the five were together, Dominique grabbed her Whodini album and cued up *The Freaks Come out at Night* as she and her friends began laughing.

"She tryna play us y'all!" Tracey stated as she waited for the song to end.

When the song went off, Tracey got on the turntables and played Madonna's song titled *Like a Virgin,* in order to mock Dominique. The five all laughed as they made fun of one another playing various songs and dancing with one another. They played the music until Mrs. Franz came home in the late afternoon. They then hung out in the neighborhood and decided to walk to Lincoln Beach for a swim. As they crossed the levee, they saw Donald and Black Mike throwing railroad rocks at a snow white, wounded pit bull puppy lying beside the tracks.

"Heyyy, don't do that!" Lubby yelled aloud in anger as she ran down the levee and knocked the rocks from Donald and Mike's hand.

"He 'bouta die anyway!" Donald said.

"He ain't gone die if y'all don't throw rocks at him like that!" Lubby remarked.

Lubby could see that the puppy had a broken leg. "He musta been hit by a train y'all." she said to her girlfriends as she knelt beside the howling animal and rubbed his side gently. "I'm a take him home and save him."

"Man, we was going swimming! Leave him there and we'll get 'em on the way out." Rolanda said.

"No! Donald and Mike gone kill 'em. He might get hit by another train too! You lucky to be alive pretty puppy!" Lubby stated as she picked the puppy up and began to tote it up the levee; her friends followed close behind as Donald and Mike cussed at them.

"Shut the fuck up punks!" Tracey retorted as Donald and Mike began walking down the pathway towards Lincoln Beach.

"He gone be dead in a week!" Donald yelled as the five disappeared across the levee headed back to East Shore.

"He all white like a kilo of cocaine. We should call him Kilo." Brianna quipped as the five walked.

"I was thinking about Lucky." Lubby replied.

"Lucky!" her four friends said at the same time.

"Girl that's a snow white, red-nosed pit-bull, he can't have a punk ass name like Lucky!" Tracey stated.

"You right, Tracey. I can't name him Lucky. We can call him Kilo, that's live right there, thanks Bri. He gone be pretty when he grow up too." Lubby ended.

"Oh lord. Now we gone have another mouth to feed!" Rolanda stated as the girls walked back to the neighborhood. "Damn I bet that water woulda felt good today!" she ended as the girls walked back towards Emory Road.

Lubby took the puppy home and placed it into her room. Her mother was still at work so she knew she had time to try and help the puppy and hide it before Cynthia returned. Her friends stood in her bedroom watching as she placed the dog on a blanket and wrapped his leg with a torn sheet and two pieces of wood she had broken off of a wooden hanger.

"Cynthia gone blow her top when she see that dog." Tracey said.

"I know," Lubby said to Tracey as she rubbed the howling dog, "but just once can she let me show her what I can do?" she asked as she stared at the dog sadly.

"You can show me, Lubby. I believe you can help Kilo." Brianna said as Lubby turned and smiled at her.

"I am gone help Kilo watch! When I'm done, we gonna run on top the levee! Remember that Bri. Watch I fix him." Lubby ended as she rubbed the dog's side.

"Lubby, if Kilo die, you still gone think he was lucky to be alive?" Rolanda asked.

"Leave her alone! That's her new pet." Brianna stated in support of Lubby.

"Man, his leg all broke, he bark all the time, Cynthia gone hate him on sight—and he got Lubby playing doctor—I'm gone miss that damn dog!" Rolanda stated as Dominique, Tracey, and even Brianna snickered.

"Y'all laugh, but this a pretty puppy and I'm gone fix him watch! And I'm a teach him to be mean to you for saying he gonna die Rolanda. Look at her face Kilo. When you get well, bark every time you see her!" Lubby said as she smiled at her friends and told them she would see them later on in the night.

The five separated that afternoon and everyone besides

Lubby, who was tending to her new friend, took long naps. Dominique had awakened about eleven that night, having missed the whole day. She went into her drawer to retrieve clothes to take a shower and came across the magazine she had gotten from Rolanda early that morning. She picked up the magazine and pulled the plastic cover off and slowly flipped through the pages. She covered her mouth and sat it on the dresser and stepped back, having become dismayed over the explicit images inside the magazine. Men were having sex with women, women were with women, and some women were by themselves touching there private parts. Dominique looked around as if someone else was in her room. She then picked up the book and turned the pages slowly. A man had his face in between a woman's legs. Dominique stared at the picture; it was the very thing she had witnessed Tracey receiving that morning. The woman had a sheer look of ecstasy on her face.

"It's like a drug, a good drug! Everybody do it! Do that one time and you gone have a whole new outlook!"

Dominique could hear her friends' comments in her head. She knew she didn't want to cheat on Calvin, and from what she had heard repeatedly, masturbation was not cheating. Her body was beginning to heat up; she had beads of sweat on her forehead as she flipped through the pages. She was already half undressed so she slid off her panties, turned her bedroom light off and turned her lamp on and lay in her bed with the magazine. Her hand slowly crept to her private area and she tentatively touched herself. She was scared at first, but when she firmly touched her clitoris she moaned loudly.

"Dominique, you okay in there?" Mrs. Franz asked from her bedroom.

"Yea momma! I'm fine!"

Dominique continued to flip the pages came across a story in the magazine about a woman masturbating herself to orgasm in the shower. She sat up and read the story and nearly came without touching herself. Her eyes were watery as she rushed to the bathroom to try and repeat on her own body what she had just read. She executed the technique to perfection and had slipped in the shower as her body convulsed in intense pleasure.

"Dominique what are you doing in there, child? You okay?" Mrs. Franz now yelled from the living room as she read a *Watchtower* magazine.

"I dropped the soap, momma! Don't, don't worry, I'm fine— Hey momma!" Dominique then yelled from the floor of the tub.

"Yes, child?"

Dominique began to laugh; she was tickled to high heaven as she gained her composure and blurted out, "Help me! I've fallen—and I can't get up!"

Mrs. Franz yelled aloud and burst into laughter.

The saying, *"I've fallen and I can't get up",* was from an old *Life Alert* commercial that showed an old lady laid out on the floor calling out for help with her emergency tag. It was a funny saying during the time and people often used the saying whenever the moment presented itself. Dominique couldn't resist. She and her mother laughed a good while before Dominique calmed down and focused on what she had just done in the shower. The water flowed onto her body as she lay there trying to regain her composure. Her vision was blurry and she was nearly out of breath, but she felt fantastic. She then laughed aloud again as she touched herself once more, *"Bri was right, that do feel good!"* she said to herself as she exited the tub and dried off her petite brown-skinned body and rushed into her bedroom and locked the door. She wanted to masturbate again, and again, and again and she did, until three in the morning.

The next day, Dominique snuck over to Rolanda's house early that morning. She had on a light green pants pajama set, a white silk robe and light green Daniel Greene slippers. The magazine she had the night before was tucked under her arms as she walked briskly over to Rolanda's house and knocked on the door.

"Who the hell is it?"

"Dominique."

Rolanda opened her door and quickly looked around the neighborhood before speaking, "What heifer? What?" she asked as she looked down at Dominique.

"Umm, umm, I'm through with this."

"You finish? Already? What? You want another one now?"

"How you get those?"

Rolanda showed Dominique the order form in the magazine and said, "You lie about your name and age and send a money order and they gone hook you up."

"My momma and daddy would kill me!"

"Well, you wanna go half and just send them here?"

"Yea. That'll work right there."

"Alright, bring your money and we'll hook it up," Rolanda said as she went to close the door.

"Rolanda!"

"What girl? I'm—I'm relaxing right now!"

"I, I wanna relax too. I need another one!"

Rolanda placed her head behind her door and laughed silently. Her body heaved as she did so. *"She coming over here like a damn crack head!"* she thought to herself as she sniggled.

Rolanda came back to the door trying to maintain her composure as she invited Dominique in to view her collection. They went into Rolanda's room and Dominique saw that Rolanda had a wide assortment, *Play Girl*, *Swank*, *Hustler*, and *Penthouse*. Rolanda also had books containing explicit stories as well. Dominique stared wide eyed at the magazines and picked up three that she thought would interest her.

"That's all you need?" Rolanda asked.

"Yea. I'm a bring the money after I get through, after I get through—"

"Relaxing?" Rolanda said as she smiled down at Dominique.

"Yea—relaxing."

"Okay you do that. Go relax, and let me do the same alright?" Rolanda whispered calmly as she ushered Dominique to the front door. "You want the blue blockers?" she then asked jokingly.

"Girl you stupid! Our secret?"

"You know how 'the five' roll. We always together as one. Don't worry about it. Anyway, it's harmless, and it feels—"

"So damn good!" Dominique sighed as she finished Rolanda's sentence, took the blue blockers and covered her eyes, tucked the magazines under her arms and quickly walked back to her home. She looked over her shoulders, peeking over the top of the sunshades as she twisted her head from left to right as she made her way back to her home.

"See that Kilo?" Lubby said as she looked out her window at Dominique whilst holding her puppy, "everybody gettin' there's!" she ended as she fell back onto her bed and laughed heartily.

CHAPTER 14

STAR CHILDREN

"On Air is we! And Rolanda, Dominique and Tracey is bringin' it to ya' Abramson!" Rolanda yelled over the school's P.A. system.

It was now October of 1986 and the girls' sophomore year was well under way. It was a Friday, and the following Saturday was the school's homecoming and the three girls were trying to get the ninth and tenth graders pumped up.

"Well," Rolanda said, "last year we got trounced by Carver High at the Jamboree and lucky for us, we got 'em on homecoming Saturday. Now, we got two new starters holding down the cornerback position, so we know good and well, they ain't gone take us deep like they did last year! We got Gerald and Bobby holding down the drum major position alongside Thaddeus Russell, A.K.A. Tank, and we got the Star Child, Brianna Stanford singing with the band! Lubby Williams choreographed the dance routine and that's an automatic win for the majorettes *and* the band, so we know we ain't gone get blown out at halftime, okay?" Rolanda ended as she rolled her neck and snapped her fingers.

"That's on the serious tip friends," Dominique chimed in, "and remember, we got somethin' special lined up to throw back at Carver for doing the Ninth Ward Shuffle on us last year. This the one we been waiting on so we encouraging everybody, tell ya' friends at other schools, tell ya' momma, tell ya' cousins, tell everybody that the Abramson Commodores gone take the halftime show tomorrow with the best performance in high school history! And remember to call in tonight and represent with Jazzy! Let's blow the lines up and put Abramson on the map!" Dominique ended as Tracey cued up *We are the Champions* by *Queen* and the classes began to get excited as the girls ended their show and school began to let out for the weekend.

The following Saturday evening, Lubby, dressed in her burgundy high school jumpsuit, called out to her mother. She had her brown hair stacked and her brown eyes were full of joy as she ran to her mother's room holding her majorette uniform. "Momma, Miss Jones said she was gone—" Lubby's voice faded off when she saw her mother lying across the bed with her eyes closed. "Momma!" she screamed aloud as she ran and shook her mother.

"What, bitch? What?" Mrs. Williams mumbled as she stirred from her slumber.

"Momma!" Lubby said as she hugged her mother, "I thought you, I thought you was dead!" Lubby ended as her eyes welled up.

"Sometimes I wish I was!" Mrs. Williams said as she got up and walked out of her room.

"What's that supposed to mean?"

"Just what I said!"

"You need ta' get out some, momma. Stop waitin' on all these different men ta'—" Lubby then caught herself so she wouldn't upset her mother, but it was too late.

"To what? Come and fuck me so I can keep the lights on in this mutherfucka? So I can keep food in this raggedly ass hovel for your ungrateful tail?"

"Momma, please? Don't be mad at me! I'm sorry! Don't be mad!" Lubby said as she cried and walked towards her mother in an attempt to hug her, something the two hadn't done in years.

"Don't touch me! Don't you fuckin' touch me!" Cynthia

yelled as she pushed Lubby away from her.

Lubby placed her hands over her face as her mother stared at her with cold eyes. "You a soft ass bitch," Cynthia hissed. "Sometimes I wish you were never born!"

"Momma, you don't mean that!" Lubby said through tears as she tugged her mother's arm to pull her back. "You said you was comin' tonight ta' watch me dance now come on, momma! Please?" Lubby pleaded.

When Cynthia shook her head pitifully and walked off, Lubby fell to the floor and screamed aloud. "Why you don't like me? Momma?" she cried aloud as she sat on the floor inside the living room. "Momma? I said why you don't like me?"

Fifteen year-old Lubby Williams cried for her mother repeatedly until she heard her slam her bedroom door shut and lock it; she then knew Cynthia wasn't coming to watch her perform that night and it had crushed her to the core. She lay on her back in the living room with her hands over face, crying her heart out on the carpeted floor until she heard the doorbell ring, which made her sit up and wipe her face with her sweat shirt. She grabbed her uniform and met Rolanda at the door.

Rolanda was holding Kilo in her arms. The puppy still had the bandages on his leg and couldn't walk so Rolanda, who was keeping the puppy at her house because Cynthia had thrown the dog out two days after Lubby found him, was planning on bringing it to the game.

"Girl! Everybody waiting ta' see y'all dance ta' night! We gone kick Carver ass! Come on, Lubby! Lubby? Lubby, you okay?"

Lubby quickly thought about the many people that loved to see her dance routines. "Yea," she answered as she smiled and grabbed Kilo, "come on so y'all can watch us dance!" she ended through a smile.

Lubby had placed the confrontation between her and her mother behind her and walked over to Rolanda's house to leave for the game. The entire neighborhood seemed to be leaving at the same time. Lubby saw Brianna and her mother leaving, she saw Dominique and Tracey's family leaving also. They followed each other to the game. Lubby was excited for all the support that was being shown; the only person missing was Cynthia; but Lubby was happy that her friends and her friends' parents were there to pick up the slack.

Just before Abramson's halftime show was to begin, Brianna went and sat on a wooden bench in the girl's locker room inside Tad Gormley Stadium all by her lonesome and stared at the collage that contained mixed photos of her and Gabriella; the same collage Lubby had made for her shortly after Gabriella was killed back in January of 1984. Brianna kept that collage on her nightstand always and would often talk to her deceased friend, asking her to watch over her and help her improve in her singing. Now, nearly three years later, the collage had more meaning than ever. Brianna stared at the picture intensely, looking deep into the eyes of a smiling Gabriella before she closed her eyes and said a silent prayer.

"God, I believe you exist. I also believe in angels. If you can, please ask Gabriella to lend me her voice for just one night. Tell her this Brianna asking for a favor. And tell her I said thank you for inspiring me. Amen."

Brianna, dressed in a white silk pant suit with a pair of burgundy knee-high boots, and wearing a burgundy silk trench coat, sat quietly and reflected on the event about to unfold in mere minutes. This was no middle school talent show. She wouldn't be singing in front of her friends with her karaoke machine, nor would she be singing inside the high school gym —this was big time. Thousands of people were on hand to witness one of New Orleans' most storied rivalries. Carver had a band that was beyond compare. They'd won many band battles. Abramson High School had been getting dominated by Carver for years during the halftime show, but this year, this year the entire school felt it would be different because of two rising stars—Brianna Stanford and Lubby Williams. Bri had a lot of pressure on her, but when one of the majorettes poked her head in and asked was she ready, Bri stood up, sat the collage inside her locker, closed it gently and calmly walked out of the locker room into the tunnel leading to the field.

The band instructor stood before the band, all dressed in burgundy, and white, and let Brianna take the lead. The majorettes, wearing glittery burgundy uniforms and white knee-high boots, and the cheerleaders, wearing white short skirts trimmed in burgundy and white leather sneakers, were out front being led by Lubby. When the band instructor blew his whistle, the entire group of over two hundred band members, cheerleaders, flag twirlers and the highly esteemed majorettes, began marching down the tunnel towards the open field with their hands in the air and rocking to and fro.

When Abramson emerged from the tunnel, students and Alumni from Abramson erupted in cheers. The band section began pounding a tune and the cheerleaders ran ahead and began back-flipping and cartwheeling onto the field as the flag twirlers ran from one end of the field to the other. Lubby and the rest of the majorettes began rocking their hips as they skipped two times to the left, two times to the right and began walking backwards as they faced Brianna, who was being followed by the band, as they egged them forward by motioning them with their hands.

"What are the Commodores up to this year people?" the sound tech quipped from his booth over-looking the football field.

This was it for Bri, she had to come correct. She clicked on the cordless microphone, paused just below the center of the field, bent forward and said, *"Well you can tell everyone I'm a down disgrace...drag my name all over the place I don't care anymore..."*

Carver's side went quiet—they had been caught off guard. Abramson's side, however, was in an uproar. The band's drum section was on point with the drum line to Genesis's song, *I Don't Care Anymore*, as Bri, now full of confidence, raised her head and trotted towards the center of field and took her place before the majorettes.

"You can tell everybody about the state I'm in...you won't catch me cryin' 'cause I just can't win I don't care anymore...I don't care anymore...I don't care...what you say...I don't play the same games...that you play..."

The halftime show was now in full swing, and Brianna was soon singing to the top of her lungs, both sounding and looking like a bona fide star, while the majorettes did dances never-before-seen, courtesy of Lubby.

Carver had performed earlier, but when they heard Brianna and saw the majorettes performing on the fifty yard line as the high school band played the instrumental to Genesis's song, they knew they ran the serious chance of being beaten this night and were now running the risk of having the three foot oak wood and gold trophy that went to the winner of the halftime show taken away. Carver and Abramson were serious band rivals and both savored winning the trophy. As Brianna sang, and the majorettes and cheerleaders performed Lubby's routine, the chance of Carver taking the trophy again this year looked real slim.

When Brianna ended the song, Carver felt as if they still had a chance, but Abramson wasn't through just yet. When Brianna ended her song, the band took center field and the majorettes and cheerleaders stood on either side of them as a table with two turntables was quickly brought to the center of the field in front of the band. Four microphones were quickly set up and wires were run from the field to the sideline.

It was quiet for a minute as hundreds of high school kids, Alumni, football fans and news crews watched as three girls, who happened to be Tracey, Dominique and Rolanda, dressed in hooded burgundy jumpsuits ran onto the field. Tracey ran and stood behind the turntables and began to scratch on the vinyl rotators as the crowd cheered. For Dominique and Rolanda, a microphone and two large bass drums were placed in front of them.

"They don't know what they doing! They can't know what they doing!" the sound tech yelled aloud just as Abramson fell into their second routine. "That Genesis song was off the Richter scale! But this? I...I don't know fans!"

Dominique and Rolanda began pounding the bass drums and creating a melodic drum line as Tank, Bobby and Gerald took center field in front of the band and began spitting lyrics as they gyrated their hips towards Carver's side of the field...

"Some say it's a art some say it's a shame...you would give me your body before your name... well I'm a giga high...I'm a gigolo...I'm a giga wherever it can go...so later on don't act like you don't know...when I pick out the freak in the front row..."

Whodini's song titled *I'm a Hoe* was being sung by Tank, Bobby and Gerald this night and the crowd on Abramson's side went wild as the band, being led by Dominique and Rolanda on the bass drums, played the instrumental. The five's parents were in the bleachers with Kilo, the canine barking loudly as he seemed to be enjoying the routine as much as the humans.

"The Abramson Commodores have come back with a vengeance this year!" the sound tech yelled, getting the crowd even more excited.

The song had no curse words except for the chorus, and when the chorus came, the tuba section took over and the crowd was floored. The band may not have been able to sing the chorus, but the students from Abramson, and even some of the people on Carver's side began singing along with the tubas..."'*Cause I'm a hoe, you know I'm a hoe...I rock three different freaks after every show... 'Cause I'm a hoe, you know I'm a hoe...How do ya' know because I told you so...*"

At the same time, the majorettes leaned forward and began swinging their arms, doing a dance called *The Whop*. They then placed their hands atop their knees and began bouncing their rear ends up and down in an in sync and swift motion.

"Ohhh nooo! Not the Lubby Dance! They told me 'bout it and here it is before your very eyes! They P-Poppin' on y'all Carver! Huh! How ya' love that?" the sound tech yelled aloud, instigating as the entire marching band slowly sunk to the ground and brought it back up during the chorus.

Fifteen year-old Lubby Williams was amongst the first in the South to institute a dance that would become known as *The Pussy-Pop*. She was all smiles on this night as she brought her new dance into fruition. She stared up at the masses of people as she danced her routine. She could see females from

Abramson, and even from Carver up in the bleachers doing her dance. The fifteen year-old was overjoyed to see the crowd had liked what she had choreographed for the band and it would become one of the happiest days of her life.

Needless to say, Abramson won the battle of the bands overwhelmingly and walked away with the trophy. The majorettes and cheerleaders from Carver High School ran over and congratulated the majorettes and cheerleaders from Abramson as they asked who Lubby was. When they found Lubby, the sophomore majorettes from Carver walked over to her and promised to redeem themselves the next time the schools played. They joked for a minute before returning to their respective locales inside the stadium.

Although intense, the competition between the two schools was nothing more than a friendly rivalry. There were no hard feelings between the two schools. Abramson lost the football game, but everybody knew that it was all about the battle of the bands, and on this night, thanks to the collective efforts of the entire school, namely the five, along with Tank, Bobby and Gerald, Abramson had won the battle of the bands. Lubby got her props from nearly every Alumni and student on this night. She had forgotten about what happened with her mother as well.

Once they were changed into their street clothes, the five told their parents they were going to a haunted house with Bobby, Gerald, Calvin and Tank. Kilo was taken home with Charlotte and the five split up and rode with Tank and Gerald and went to an old slaughterhouse in Harahan, just outside of New Orleans, underneath the Huey P. Long Bridge to enjoy the haunted house.

When the gang arrived at the haunted house they saw a long line. Nearly an hour had gone by before they got to the ticket booth where they were told that the admission price was ten dollars.

"Ten whole dollars?" Tank asked aloud. "What kinda haunted house is this?"

"One like you've never seen young man!" the attendant

replied with a smile on her face.

"Yea? Well for ten dollars, I better get the living daylights scared outta me!" Bobby stated.

"Man, I been in three haunted houses and they all damn near put me ta' sleep." Gerald chimed in.

"I ain't never been scared of no haunted house! Nightmare on Elm Street, Friday the 13th, Halloween, whatever it's all the same!" Dominique said as Calvin paid his and hers way into the building.

"The five gone wreck shop! Watch we come out laughing at this weak ass haunted house!" Tracey remarked as she walked in.

"I just want y'all to know, when the horror start, just remember, I think y'all some nice white people and I'm only here because they made me come." Rolanda said as she smiled at the lady.

"Stop kissin' ass Rolanda! Anyway I got you! Tank ain't never scared ya' heard me?" Tank said confidently.

The attendant stuck her head out of her booth after hearing Tank's proclamation and said, "I tell you what, young man—if neither of you are not scared when you come out, I'll pay each of you out my own pocketbook!"

"You on! You might as well get ninety dollars together cause the kid ain't scared of nothing!" Tank ended as the nine friends walked into the slaughter house.

When the group entered the haunted house, the attendant grabbed her C.B. radio and notified employees inside. "We got a bunch talkin' shit boys," she said with a cackle. "Give 'em the royal treatment will ya' please?"

Immediately things had gotten out of control. Doors were shut and locked and the nine was split up. Lubby, Gerald, Dominique, Calvin and Tracey found themselves locked in an old, foul-smelling meat freezer with dead bodies hanging on hooks.

Gerald curled his lips up at the sight and said, "Man, I seen this shit before. They gone start moving watch."

The people didn't move as the five walked through the freezer, however; they merely swung from the hooks slowly, causing the group to become somewhat unnerved. A door then opened on the opposite end of the freezer and a man with a hockey mask on toting a chainsaw came into view as the lights went dim. Macabre music from an organ started to play as the man slowly approached the five as he flailed about wildly with the chainsaw trying to start it.

"Okay, we just gone go right back out this door back here!" Gerald said calmly as he turned and reached for the handle.

The door was now locked, however, and the man with the chainsaw fired up the motor and began slicing the bodies that hung on the meat hook and they began to scream and flail about violently. The five could see blood spurting from the bodies that hung on the hook and they all grew terrified.

"Ohh shit the door locked! We stuck in this bitch! Run motherfuckas!" Gerald yelled as he broke out and ran inside the freezer and everybody with him scattered throughout the room.

The five all separated as they screamed aloud. Dominique and Tracey had made their way to the door where the man was standing previously and exited the freezer. The door was locked behind them and they now found themselves in a long hall that held numerous picture frames on the girls' right side. Dominique and Tracey quickly grabbed hold of another, afraid to move out of sheer fear.

Lubby, Gerald and Calvin, meanwhile, had found another exit inside the freezer and they ran through it screaming only to find themselves in a room that held a large net-covered-aquarium filled with live cockroaches.

Lubby froze on the spot and whispered, "Don't nobody say nothing! You gone set 'em off if you do!"

The three tiptoed through the room and entered another door and found themselves in what appeared to be an asylum. They stared down the long hall and took baby steps forward, when they did, the lights came on and to their left they saw two people standing behind a plexi-glass enclosure with their arms cut off staring at them just as two men in bloody surgical uniforms holding hacksaws opened the double doors and stood at the opposite end of the hall. Lubby opened the door to the room with the cockroaches and saw that the aquarium had been pushed up against the entrance. She was staring at hundreds of live cockroaches. She screamed and closed the door and the two men began running towards her, Gerald and Calvin. This wasn't to be expected by a long shot. Everybody was getting the living daylights scared out of them inside this haunted house. Gerald was trying to unlock the door to get inside the room with the two armless people but it was locked.

"Open the door! Open the fuckin' door!" Gerald yelled as he and Calvin began to kick the door furiously.

"Hurry up, Gee! They gettin' closer!" Calvin yelled.

"They ain't got no arms! How they gone open that door? With they feet?" Lubby asked as she began to cry. "Ohhh, lord...we bouta be dead!"

The three backed into a corner screaming aloud as the men approached them. They were huddled together looking away from the men and when one of the men touched Gerald, he began swinging his fist hysterically. The two men backed away and the lights came on and the two men with the hacksaws began laughing right along with the men standing behind the plexi-glass window.

"Fuck you!" Gerald screamed aloud.

Brianna, Bobby, Tank and Rolanda had problems of their own to deal with. The four were inside a kitchen trying desperately to kick the door down to get out the house. The lights went out and flames shot up from the stove. As the flames shot into the air they could see flashes of four men with machetes dressed in white blood-stained chef uniforms walking their way with evil grins on their faces. The flames went out and the four screamed for the door to open. When the flames shot up again, the four men were closer to the group. The flames went out again and the four knew what was next, the men would be right in their faces with those machetes. They all broke from the door and began knocking over pots and pans screaming loudly.

"Turn the lights on! Turn on the fuckin' lights!" Bobby yelled as he stumbled to the ground. "Who the fuck grabbing my ankles and shit? Get off me Tank!"

The lights came on and the four men laughed aloud.

"Scared yet?" one of the men asked.

"Fuck you!" Tank screamed aloud as he dashed out the kitchen. Brianna, Bobby and Tank, needless to say, were on his heels.

Dominique and Tracey were now making their way down the hall and things were just too quiet. They knew something was afoul. The chaos started when the people in the pictures started reaching for them and moaning like zombies as blood trickled out of the corners of their eyes and mouths. The two yelled and ran to the end of the hall and looked to their right only to see a lady about eight feet tall with long arms walking their way quickly. They ran the opposite way and found themselves staring out a window that was nailed shut.

Tracey looked back and saw the wild woman walking her way. "Ooohh! That bitch comin'! Fuck this man! This shit ain't funny no more!" she stated in fear.

Tracey looked around and found a chair and broke the glass pane. People outside the haunted house heard the glass shattering and looked around and began laughing when they saw and heard her trying to escape through the window while screaming for help and crying for her mother. She was halfway out the house when the woman grabbed her and began laughing as the lights came on.

"Fuck you lady!" Tracey screamed aloud as she ran towards the exit.

All the friends with the exception of Dominique were now outside the house. The people that owned the haunted house had to actually go in and search for the fifteen year-old. She was found huddled in a closet shivering in utter fear. She wasn't blinking and she couldn't speak until she was outside the house. Out of breath and a little shook up, the nine made their way out the gate. They hadn't even been through the entire house; the people that owned the house had to stop the show early to let the nine friends out, much to the attendant's delight.

"You want your money back?" she asked Tank as she laughed aloud.

"Nahh, you got me! Next time I'm bringing my fuckin' pistol! Y'all wrong for that shit!" Tank replied as the group hopped into the two cars and rode back to East Shore.

"Hey Tank," Rolanda said as she rode in the car with him, Brianna, Bobby, and Tracey, "let me hold your gun ta' night. I'm scared as shit I ain't gone even lie!" she snapped as they all burst into laughter.

"Man, y'all was screaming like girls! They ain't have me fooled at all. I knew they was playing!" Brianna stated.

"That was Bobby screaming like a li'l hoe!" Tank replied.

"Bobby? Nigga you was all on the floor grabbing my ankles and shit! And Bri—check ya' drawls too motherfucka! 'Cause I smell shit comin' from your direction." Bobby remarked.

"Boy, please! They ain't—well maybe I was a li'l bit scared, but I ain't doo-doo my drawls, brer! Come on, man!" Brianna stated.

"Shiit! We all was screaming like some bitches! But I knew they was playing!" Tracey stated as she looked out the back window.

Tank peered over the backseat at Tracey and said, "You lyin' your ass off! I heard you was 'bouta jump out the window and was calling for Maria!"

Tracey bowed her head and laughed lowly. "Man fuck that," she then said, "they was tight, but a bitch wasn't scared! I was just tryna make them think they was doing a good job scaring us!"

"Them white folks got some sick shit going on, man! I ain't

never been to a house like that. Y'all wanna go back again for Halloween?" Tank asked.

"Nah, I'm a be busy." "I got school the next day!" "We doin' a party that night!" "Lubby puppy gone be sick!" "That's trick or treat night anyway so it's a no go for me." Rolanda, Tracey, and Brianna said randomly as they didn't want any part of that haunted house ever again.

"Scary asses!" Bobby said as he dapped Tank off and lit up a joint as the group jumped onto Interstate-10 and headed back towards East Shore.

A similar scenario played out in Gerald's car as well. The teens all pretended they weren't scared, but they were all shook over what happened inside the haunted house this night. Lubby slept by Rolanda's house; they kept the light on in the bedroom. Dominique and Brianna both slept with their mothers, and Tracey slept in the living room of her mother's home with the lamp *and* the TV on.

****

It was a week after the haunted house adventure and Tracey was finishing up in the alleyway with White Boy Mike, having had her pussy eaten to orgasm once again by the love-struck young man as he'd done many times before. She pulled up her sweat pants and wiped her hands free of Mike's semen with rubbing alcohol and placed the bottle back inside the wall of the abandoned house having given him another world-class hand job.

"You gone call me ta' night, Mike?" Tracey asked as she straightened her clothes.

"You know I am Tracey. I know you don't won't nobody to know about us, but I like you, a lot."

"Just call me alright? And remember—"

"I know, it's our secret Tracey." Mike said somberly as he walked off, feeling somewhat played over the experience.

Tracey waited in the alleyway until Mike disappeared and walked out on Curran Street and waited for Brianna to leave Black Mike's house and the two walked over to Rolanda's house and knocked on the door.

Rolanda opened a minute later. "What's up heifers?" she asked as she let her friends in.

"Just got through face-humping my secret lover, you heard me?" Tracey answered in an enthusiastic manner as she plopped down on the sofa.

"Girl, that white boy gone make you fall in love with 'em watch." Rolanda replied as she held the door open.

"Please! He just got a tongue that won't quit! That's all!"

"Alright, wait and see. And when Tracey Sanchez announces to the world that she in love with nerdy White Boy Mike they gone laugh harder than a Richard Pryor stand-up routine." Rolanda ended as Lubby ran from the back of the house and out the front door.

"What the hell wrong with you?" Brianna asked towards Lubby.

"I'm 'bouta run on the levee!"

"With who? Gerald?"

"No! When you ever seen him jog?" Lubby replied as she whistled.

Brianna and Tracey looked on in wonderment and were pleasantly surprised when Kilo ran from Rolanda's bedroom and out the front door.

"Lubby! You fixed him!" Brianna stated as her eyes grew wide and she smiled and walked over and rubbed the puppy, who was barking and jumping at Lubby's side, his tail wagging furiously.

"I told you, Bri! You like him? Look, he all well!" Lubby said as she knelt down and rubbed Kilo right along with Brianna.

Brianna hugged Lubby, congratulated her and looked into her eyes and said proudly, "Lubby, you kept your word. I guess we all gone run the levee today, right girls?"

"Yea, that's cool! He a cute li'l puppy too!" Tracey added.

"Let's go get Dominique and hit the levee."

As the five were walking to the levee, Brianna pulled Tracey to the back of the group once they got inside the alleyway leading to Curran Boulevard and said, "Hey, Tracey, when you met me coming from Mike house? Right before I left he umm, he showed me a plastic bag with a bunch of rocks in it."

"Black Mike got crack?" Tracey asked in a shocked tone of voice.

"Yea. He said he want me to help him sell it with him and he gone pay me four hundred a week."

"Bri! Crack cocaine? You can go to jail for that, girl!"

"I know. But I had found out early in the week that my momma got laid off from her job."

"Nooo! Because of the space shuttle thing?"

"Yea. She got a lump sum and she gone be straight 'til they get back on line—but I'm not gone have the clothes, the medallions, earrings, and shoes, Tracey. I got used ta' that shit you know? I'm always fresh—but when my momma told me that we was gone have ta' get my winter wardrobe from K-Mart, I was stunned. I can't go out like that, Tracey. Mike said all I have ta' do is help him sell this and in a week and I could make four hundred dollars. I think I'm gone do it."

"Okay. But why you tellin' me, Bri?"

"'Cause out us five? You the one that I believe would go in that water for either of us with no questions asked. I'm not sayin' somethin' gone happen—but just help me watch Donald."

"What's up with Donald?"

"It's like this—Mike cool, but Donald startin' ta' trip. He got money a couple of months back from when he almost got hit by that train back in '83. He told Rolanda not ta' speak on it, but they got like thirty g's. He gave Black Mike twelve hundred ta' buy an ounce back in August. Now Dee and his people broke and Mike got all the money and Donald gettin' jealous of me and Mike 'cause he know we fuckin' around. He done tried ta' have sex with me a time or two and even dissed Mike behind his back sayin' he fronted Mike some dope—but me and Mike know what's up—he jealous of Mike and he wanna fuck me. If I jump in this game with Mike? That's just gone take the jealousy to a whole other level and I just wanna put somebody up on Donald."

"Dee really been trippin' lately. He ask *me* for some pussy! He run his mouth too much, though. Not that I would fuck him? But I didn't believe he came at me like he did 'cause he know me and him don't get down like that. Donald and Mike supposed to be *boys*! And he player hatin' like that on *Mike*? Fuck wrong with Donald?" Tracey asked as the two walked slowly up the alleyway.

"I don't know if Donald smoking the crack or what—but I just got a funny feeling about that dude. Anyway I'm taking Mike up on his offer," fifteen year-old Brianna said as she raised her sweat shirt and revealed a Ziploc bag full of rocks and a chrome .380 pistol.

Tracey eyed what she knew to be a drug dealer's starter kit, dapped her girl and said, "Whatever, Bri. I'm with ya' not against ya'."

"I'm a meet y'all on the levee. Let me go drop this off at my house." Brianna ended as she walked away.

CHAPTER 15

DUMB DONALD

"Three hundred!" Brianna called out as she stood behind one of the abandoned houses inside the alleyway.

It was a steamy hot summer evening in August of 1987 and 16 year-old Brianna and 17 year-old Black Mike was making money hand over fist. The five had all passed from the tenth to eleventh grade and were looking forward to the new school year as they would be attending a newly remodeled Fannie C. Williams Middle school that was renamed Sarah T. Reed High School. Brianna and Mike had been hustling the streets of East Shore since October of '86 and had amassed a good bit of clientele over that period of time. Brianna did well hiding her illegal activity. She kept most of her clothes by Tracey's house and only brought a few items home from time to time.

All four of Brianna's friends participated in concealing her illegal activities. After all, they were home girls—and right or wrong they all stuck together. Brianna's four friends would sometimes walk down the now heavily traveled crack-infested alleyway and peek in on Brianna to see if she was all right. Brianna would often break away and talk to her friends, but Mike would quickly call her back. Brianna was on top. She was making money and could now support herself; she could buy the things she was used to having, the very things her mother had spoiled her with when she was younger. She would buy groceries from time to time and tell her mother she bought some food stamps for cash with money that Tracey had given her. She would often treat her friends to Pizza Hut and McDonald's. Brianna didn't change when she started making money. She was real generous with her friends, a quality she had always possessed; and on this day in August of '87, Brianna would once again show love.

As Brianna's four friends hung with her in the busy alleyway, watching as she sold twenty dollar pieces of crack cocaine, Terrence and another young man had walked up onto the set with three baskets full of stereo equipment and seven milk crates full of albums. Dominique and Tracey's eyes grew wide when they saw Terrence, dressed in rags, with a scraggly beard, and wheeling the equipment towards Brianna and Mike. Mike, sporting a high-top fade with six gold teeth, standing 5'10" 155 pounds, ogled the equipment as it was wheeled in front of him by the now slender 28 year-old Terrence.

"Say, say Mike, brer! Gimmie me five hundred and you can have all this shit! The turntables, the albums, the mixers, speakers everything!"

"Terrence!" Dominique and Tracey screamed as Mike and Brianna's lookouts ushered people who'd just bought their crack from the alleyway as they knew a major transaction was about to take place.

Brianna shushed her friends and whispered in Mike's ear.

"Oh yea? That's what they was throwing down with back in the day?" Mike asked within earshot of Dominique and Tracey. "Go on and get that, Bri! You know how ta' run it!" Mike said as he stepped back and let Brianna handle her business.

"Man," Brianna said as she turned to Terrence, "I got like fifty dollar's worth of product! That's all!"

"Fifty? I'm asking five hundred, Bri! And this shit worth way more than five hundred! Two Technic 1200's? A brand, a brand new four channel Newmark mixer? Two fifteen inch Peavy speakers with the receiver and the amp? A microphone and all these records?"

"I feel ya'. I feel ya. But like I say, I got fifty. I might be able ta' work something—but you gone have ta' come up off that five. I got enough paper ta' by that shit ten times over! One hundred dollars." Brianna then said.

"Four hundred!" Terrence said.

"Three hundred." Brianna replied nonchalantly as she bumped her fists together and looked towards the sky.

"Three fifty!" Terrence requested in a desperate manner.

"Two hundred! And I ain't goin' no higher homeboy!" Brianna said as she stared Terrence down.

"Three hundred!" Terrence pleaded. "Come on, Bri. Don't play me like that."

"See! Now we back at fifty! I told you I wasn't going no higher than two hund—"

"Mike. Talk to your girl, man. Come on! Help a nigga out!"

"That's you and her business, brer! I mean, you heard what she said. Better jump on it." Mike said as he tucked his hands inside his jogging suit pant pockets and looked away, barely able to withhold his laughter.

"Fuck it man, give me the two hundred, Bri! That's all you can do?"

"That's it brer. Like I say, I can buy that ten more times. So what's up?"

"Give me the two hundred! But y'all some cold soldiers back here in East Shore." Terrence said as he wheeled the equipment over to Brianna.

"Here, brer," Brianna said as she reached behind her backside. "Take these ten dubs and give my home girls they shit! Don't worry 'bout it Tee, this a good deal for ya' brer!" she added as she dropped ten pieces of twenty dollar crack cocaine into Terrence's hand.

Terrence took the product and walked from the side of the house and stared at Dominique and Tracey, knowing they were disappointed in him.

"I'm sorry Lady D and Terrible Tee. I still think y'all the shit, though. Don't be like me—don't ever give up on your dream." Terrence said in a sad tone of voice as he walked away with his head down in shame.

"Forget a Lady Dee! Nobody never called me that shit anyway! I'm gone always be Dominique!"

"For real, man. Terrence had us believing that shit. Terrible Tee? I'm Tracey Sanchez 'til the end." Tracey stated as she watched Terrence walk off into the evening sun.

"And what's the lesson for today boys and girls? Just say no to drugs!" Rolanda remarked.

"I'll say no!" Mike said as he pulled out a joint. He then placed the joint to his lips and before he lit it, he said "No!" And then he fired up the joint as everyone in the alleyway burst into laughter.

Tracey and Dominique brought the equipment over to Tracey's house and would keep it there for the time being. The following week they used the equipment to throw a huge block party for Lubby's sixteenth birthday. They also continued to Dee-jay parties throughout East Shore. They were grateful for what Brianna had done and offered to pay her back, but Brianna would hear nothing of it; she was glad her friends now had full possession of all the equipment they had ever wanted and were putting it to good use.

****

As the school year rolled in, the five were now in the eleventh grade at Sarah T. Reed High School in Michoud. They were ever popular and they were going through the school year without any hang-ups. The On Air program was in full swing and had expanded. Tracey, Dominique and Rolanda were now on every day during the last ten minutes of school instead of their usual once-per week fifteen minute Friday show. Students loved to hear the girls talk, especially Rolanda because she was funny to them.

The girls were finishing up a Wednesday program in late December of '87 preparing for Christmas break as Dominique announced that she and Tracey were throwing a New Year's Eve party over to Tracey's house. Students were eager for the girls to throw another party since they hadn't thrown one on their block since August for Lubby's birthday; although they had Dee-jayed many a house party throughout East Shore. The five stayed on the liveliest block in the neighborhood and even though it would be cold out, everyone was planning on attending the block party on New Year's Eve.

"Well, that's all the info on the upcoming bash people. Rolanda you got anything from the streets?" Dominique asked.

"I sure do! Now, you know I'm all for spending quality time with your peeps. Check this out, a mother and daughter burst into Liberty bank on Gentilly Boulevard. You know the one right there by Dillard University? And let two bullets fly into the air. 'This is a bleeping stick-up!' the mother said as she hopped onto the counter and slid her big behind over the counter and ordered the tellers to put the money in the bag. Why that's hatnin', her daughter was beating the security guard silly. The two then fled the bank with sacks of loot—but once inside the get-a-away car a red dye pack exploded. The mother thought she was shot because the red dye had gotten all over her shirt. She hopped out the car and fell down dead on the spot! She caught a heart attack and dieded right there outside the bank. Her daughter hopped out the car while New Orleans' finest was pulling up and she tried to fight with the law. So— she fought the law—and of course—the law won. Now, I left out one key element—mother was 93 and her daughter was 76! The daughter looking at fifteen years for armed robbery and for her, that could be a death sentence. But I'm still stuck on the security guard. How the hell a twenty-seven year old man get beat up by a seventy-six year-old lady? I mean what kind of— either he was real nice—or he was a you know what 'cause nobody, ain't nobody laying hands on this sister! Especially no seventy-six year-old lady. Look here, I don't care how old or young the li'l hussy might be! She lay hands on me, she gettin' dealt with, that's real! Oh yea, the old man that stays behind the school lost his mule the other day, but he found it."

"Oh no! Was the donkey okay?" Tracey asked.

"That's your question?" Dominique asked.

"What? I wanna know if the donkey all right."

"What about the elderly mother and daughter that robbed the bank? Shouldn't we address that over a lost donkey?"

"Girl," Tracey said, "they shoulda been sittin' they old—never mind." Tracey said as she sniggled. "Rolanda, how the donkey doing?"

"Child that ass is dead! Been dead for days before his owner found him. I'm a miss that ass because he used to help keep the grass on the softball field low, not ta' mention well fertilized. Well I guess that's what happen to people who fail watch their ass!" Rolanda ended as Dominique shook her head in disbelief while Tracey sniggled to herself.

Rolanda only reported that story so she could say the word 'ass' over the P.A. system and Tracey had only perpetuated the matter by asking about the donkey. The girls were clever when on air and could say things that would get other people in trouble. They wanted to test the teachers, and the donkey story, which was actually true, allowed them to cuss on air for the first time and get away with it.

****

New Year's Eve arrived and the party was in full swing out in front of Maria's house. Dominique, dressed in Adidas tennis, baggy jeans, a hooded sweater with her hair flowing down her back was on the turntables working her *Run-DMC Peter Piper* mix. The party-goers yelled aloud when she made the record repeatedly quote 'there it is'. Everybody knew that mix, but Dominique and Tracey had it down to a science. The crowd was awed when Tracey took over and did the same mix —only she had her back to the turntables as she did so. Tracey worked the 1200's with her back turned to the tables as she mixed the song and the crowd was going crazy.

Dominique and Tracey were All-Star Dee-jays, the best East Shore had seen. As Dominique and Tracey were working the turntables, Rolanda and Lubby held down the crowd out on the dance floor with Gerald, Bobby, and Tank. Calvin stood beside Dominique sipping a soda and watched as Brianna stepped out the door all by herself into the cold night air.

An hour later, it was nearing mid-night. The TV was turned

on and the crowd was gathering to watch the ball drop in New York on Dick Clark's show. Brianna's friends began searching for her. They called her name repeatedly until Calvin said she had left an hour ago.

"Where she went?" Dominique asked.

"I don't know. She just walked out." Calvin responded.

"She might be by Mike house. Me and Lubby gone go get her. Come on Lubby! We goin' get Bri!" Rolanda stated as she and Lubby headed for the front door.

The girls walked out into the clear cold night, bundling up in their hooded bomber jackets as they walked towards the alleyway leading towards Curran. They were hearing gunshots as they did so.

"Damn they celebrating early as fuck! It's only10:40." Rolanda stated as she and Lubby continued walking over to Mike's house.

When the girls made it over to Mike's house, they saw that his front door was wide open so they walked up and poked their heads in.

"Hey Mike you and Bri missing a live ass party man, y'all need ta'—" Rolanda stopped mid-sentence when she saw Mike lying on the living room floor with blood spurting out his chest onto the carpet. He had been shot just moments before Rolanda and Lubby arrived on the scene. The bullet wounds riddled his torso and left him gasping for air as he bled profusely from his chest wounds. Lubby and Rolanda ran from the house screaming and entered the alleyway and made a beeline back towards Tracey's house.

"Lubby!" a voice called out weakly from behind one of the abandoned houses in the alleyway.

Lubby paused and said, "Rolanda wait. Somebody called my name."

"That might be the damn killers, Lubby! Girl come on! We gotta call the ambulance and the fuckin' police for Mike." Rolanda said as she took off running again.

"Lubby!" the voice called out again.

Lubby began to follow Rolanda, but she just knew she heard her name again. She turned around and ran back into the alley where she heard moaning and she began to slowly walk in between the two abandoned houses looking down to the ground. The moon was casting a silver shadow onto the grass as she searched around for the person calling her name.

Rolanda, meanwhile, had continued on running back to Tracey's house believing that Lubby was still behind her.

Lubby slowly walked to the back of the houses and looked to her left. There, she saw Brianna lying on the ground next to the old couch. She screamed when she saw her friend and knelt down beside her and grabbed her hands. "Bri! What happened?"

Brianna's face was badly bruised, her left eye was bleeding, and her jaw was swollen shut. The sixteen year-old had suffered a serious beating and she was grimacing in pain as she held on to Lubby's hands.

"Lubby, please, call the ambulance." she whispered through a clasped jaw.

"Who did this to you?" Lubby asked as her eyes welled up. "Bri! Bri!" Lubby screamed as she heard footsteps approaching.

Lubby got up and looked out towards the alleyway and saw party-goers running to Mike's house. "Help us! It's Bri!" she screamed to the running crowd as she ran back to Brianna's side once more.

Dominique, Rolanda, and Tracey, recognizing Lubby's voice, ran behind the house and they, too, screamed when they saw Lubby holding onto Brianna.

"I think she dying!" Lubby cried as she looked up into the moonlit darkness at her friends.

Tracey knelt down beside Brianna and wept for her friend. "Bri," she said in a low tone as she cried softly for her battered friend, "Not my girl! Jehovah please!" Tracey pleaded as she sat back on her heels and held Brianna's hand.

Brianna's mother was called to the scene and she wept for her daughter behind the house as she knelt beside her. Ms. Stanford was a calming influence for Brianna. She grabbed hold of her mother's hand and Tracey's hand as well and she waited in silence as the crowd of teenaged party-goers ran back and forth between Mike's house and the abandoned house where Brianna lay. The ambulance arrived and carried Brianna to Charity hospital as New Year's 1988 slowly rolled in amongst the many gunshots that were being blasted into the air that night.

The four friends sat in the waiting room with their mothers, with the exception of Lubby's mother, who could care less about her own daughter much less someone else's. They were relieved when the doctors told them that Brianna would recover from her ordeal completely. Her bruises, although serious, would heal. The most severe injury Brianna had was a broken jaw; her mouth would be wired shut for a couple of months or so and she wouldn't be able to speak during that period of time. The group spent the whole night in the waiting room and went in and saw Brianna briefly the next morning.

Brianna was writing a note when her friends walked into the room the following morning. She was crying as she did so. She hugged her mother and heaved into her chest when she was done writing.

"You know who did this to you, baby?" Ms. Stanford asked compassionately.

Brianna shook her head to say no.

"God, he's still out there!" Ms. Stanford remarked.

"Umm, Mike, Black Mike, he, he died in surgery last night, Bri." Tracey said.

Brianna shook her head slightly and closed her eyes.

"Brianna what happened?" her mother asked again.

Brianna shrugged her shoulders to say she didn't know. She then fell back to her bed and grieved over her friend Mike, a person she'd known since elementary school and had grown to really adore.

"We better let Bri and her mother talk. Come on, Charlotte, let's get these kids home. I'm sure they are tired, they been up all night. Come on girls, Brianna's gonna be just fine in a few days." Mrs. Franz remarked as the group walked slowly out the room, leaving Brianna and her mother alone.

Brianna tapped the bed and handed Tracey a letter when she turned around and looked at her. Brianna's mother reached for the sheet of paper, but Brianna wouldn't let her mother look at it.

"Okay sweetie, I won't peek at it." the woman said. Ms. Stanford was just glad her daughter had survived and had not suffered the fate of Black Mike. She never realized that Brianna had ulterior motives for handing Tracey the letter without letting her read it first.

As she was leaving the room, Tracey read the letter. *"We gotta punish Donald when I get out. He did this to me."* was all it said. Tracey tore up the letter and went into the bathroom and flushed it down the toilet. When she came out of the bathroom she saw Donald talking to Dominique, Lubby, and Rolanda, so she quickly walked over.

"What's up Tracey? Brianna all right?" Donald asked.

"Yea man, she just a li'l shook up. But she gone be all right. What happened with Mike, man?" Tracey asked calmly, pretending not to know what Donald had done.

"Shiit! I don't know, man. Last time I talked to Mike he say he was waiting on Bri ta' bring a package and then he was going to the party. I heard the gunshots, but I thought it was just some dudes celebrating New Year's."

As believable as he sounded, Tracey knew Donald was lying. Brianna had her suspicions about Donald and she and Tracey had talked about it over a year earlier. Tracey knew she had to wait on Brianna to get the full story, so she continued to mislead Donald by feigning ignorant about his deviousness towards his childhood friends.

Donald was now under the belief that no one knew what he had done. Tracey watched as he went in to see Brianna and she soon followed. When she walked in, Donald was asking Brianna did she know who had hurt her.

"No man, he had a ski mask on and it was dark outside. I just don't know Dee." Brianna wrote on a note pad as she shook her head sadly.

Brianna couldn't believe Donald had the nerve to actually come and visit her after what he had done to her. She was glad her mother and Tracey were still present as she believed in her heart the seventeen year-old would have choked her to death once he realized she couldn't utter a sound.

"I'm sorry that happened to you, Bri. And if I find out who did it, they gone wish the police had caught him." Donald ended as Brianna reached out and shook his hand and wrote thank you on her note pad as her mother looked on in silence.

"Donald," Ms. Stanford said, "it's not worth goin' ta' jail over. Let the police find out who hurt my daughter."

"You might be right Ms. Stanford. I don't wanna get into trouble, but Bri my girl. Whatever happen out there happen. See ya back in the 'hood, Bri."

Brianna nodded her head and Donald turned and walked out the door. She then cut her eyes at Tracey and shook her head; both sixteen year-olds were on the same page at that moment and knew what the deal was—and when Brianna was able, she would give seventeen year-old Donald his just due.

CHAPTER 16

JUSTIFIABLE BEHAVIOR

It was now early March of '88 and the five were walking along the levee on a Monday after school had let out. Kilo was walking ahead of the five wagging his tail and breaking into a quick sprint every now and then in a seemingly grateful mood for having been saved. The five all loved Kilo, he was all of the girls' pet; they all took good care of the dog who'd become a part of their circle. Kilo knew things about the five that not even their mothers knew and he would no doubt keep whatever information that whizzed across his ears a secret for all times. The girls watched as he sprinted across the top of the levee well ahead of them and stood in the center of the pathway atop the hill and began barking fiercely at a jogger approaching the group. Lubby stuck two fingers in her mouth and whistled and then yelled, "Heel!"

Kilo immediately turned and trotted back towards the girls, but he still managed to growl at the man as he tentatively eased by the girls and resumed jogging.

Brianna, now seventeen, had just gotten the wires removed from her jaw the weekend before and she was now back at full strength and now had some things she wanted to share with her girls. The five walked down the levee and crossed the railroad tracks and walked onto Lincoln Beach and out onto the pier that jutted about a hundred yards into the lake. A lone fisherman sat on the shore and he, Kilo and the five were the only ones on the beach as it was still a little cool outside, not to mention it was weekday during the school year.

As the five, dressed in an assortment of Fila jogging suits, Corniche` jeans, Bally tennis shoes, medallion earrings and the like, stood facing the lake, Brianna began to tell what she knew and believed happened the night she was nearly killed on New Year's Eve.

"Mike paged me with a code 20-10. That mean bring ten flipper twenty dollar rocks," she began.

"What's a flipper?" sixteen year-old Dominique asked.

"That's twenty dollar pieces of crack that you can cut in half and make a twenty dollar profit." Tracey answered.

"Right, Tracey," Brianna said, and then continued. "I mean, Mike was only asking for two hundred. I stepped out from the party to handle that right quick, but then he paged me right back, with a code 20-100—that meant bring two-thousand worth. I was like, 'it's almost midnight, why Mike doing this shit now'? Since I never even made it home to get the first package he asked for, I just walked straight over to Mike house to make sure he didn't make a mistake. When I passed between the two old houses in the catwalk I got grabbed from behind and drug behind the house with the couch behind it. Dee beat me bad."

"How you know it was Donald?" seventeen year-old Rolanda asked.

"Donald had a mask on true enough, but him and Mike was the only ones that knew I carried rocks in the back of my trench coat. He went straight for it when he knocked me down. When he didn't find the rocks, he beat me with the pistol. Then he aimed the gun at my head but it musta jammed or somethin'. He took off and left me on the ground when the gun jammed and I passed out."

"So he went after you first?" sixteen year-old Tracey asked.

"Yea. I'm thinking Donald called Mike and had him think he was buying a package so Mike can call me. Donald knew I would walk through the alleyway so he waited thinking I had two-thousand worth the crack on me. When he found none and the gun jammed, he went over to Mike's house. I'm guessing right now 'cause I heard gun shots a few minutes after he left. That's what woke me up. He came back with a knife, but when he heard Rolanda and Lubby running through the catwalk and I called out for Lubby, he hopped the fence and disappeared. Man, I came that close to dying." Brianna said somberly as her eyes welled up and she stared out at the lake, the evening sun coloring the water a bright orange. "That nigga Donald was gone kill me that night!" the seventeen year-old said in disbelief as she covered the lower portion of her face with hands and heaved.

The five left the lake and began walking through the streets of East Shore along Curran Boulevard as Brianna and Tracey talked about getting back at Mike. Rolanda, Dominique and Lubby uttered not a word of protest as they listened to Tracey describe how she and Donald were hooking up in the old house after dark. Tracey had finally let Donald finger bang her in the old house where Brianna was beaten. He'd been lusting after Tracey for a long time and she finally conceded a month after Brianna was beaten. Donald was so blinded by lust he couldn't recognize the fact that he was becoming the pawn in a game of revenge being played out by Brianna and Tracey and was just a couple of days away from getting his just due.

That following Thursday, Tracey was home with Dominique practicing her mixes when her phone rung.

"Hello?"

"What's up sexy, can I get that out you ta' night?" Donald asked, his voice emanating excitement.

"Yea, I told you that yesterday, boy. Meet me 'bout ten ta' night."

"Alright. I got condoms, too, ya' heard me?"

"Good, 'cause I ain't for getting' pregnant, Dee." Tracey said before she hung up the phone.

"What you up to?" Dominique asked.

Tracey looked at Dominique and shifted her weight as she placed her hands on her hips. She never gave a reply as she stared at Dominique with wide eyes before she rolled them and turned away.

Dominique removed the headphones, brushed her hair from her face and said, "Tracey, please, this is gettin' deep with you and Bri. Y'all need ta' be careful. I don't wanna see y'all go to jail."

"I know. You think I ain't scared Dominique? What if Donald know we know? But Bri saved my life when I was about to be killed, I owe her. That's our girl. Just think if Donald woulda pulled that shit off, how would you feel then?"

"The same way you feel right now Tracey." Dominique replied.

It was a no-brainer. Dominique knew and understood why Brianna and Tracey were doing what they were doing; but still, she was worried about her friends. Dominique then left Tracey's house and visited with Rolanda and Lubby. Tracey sat in her room all alone and contemplated what she was about to do. She was scared beyond words, but she dare not back out on Brianna.

Brianna meanwhile, was sitting in her bedroom staring at Gabriella's collage as she slid a clip into her pistol, knowing full-well her friend would not be in agreement with what she preparing to do if she were still alive. She then thought about the day she decided to jump into the game and remembered how she thought of all the things that could go wrong when she made the decision. She knew it may have come to this someday, but she never counted on having to shoot someone she considered a friend. Donald really was cool back in the day. Bri smiled as she reflected on the day she, Donald, Mike and Tracey had gotten busted for sneaking away to the candy store. She thought about all the fun she and her girls had with Mike and Donald at Lincoln Beach, and parties her girls had Dee-jayed for him. All those things were the ingredients of a true friendship; at least that's how Bri saw it, but it was now obvious that friendship meant nothing when it came to the game, and especially when it came to Donald. Brianna then thought about the juxtaposition she was going to put her girls in and she grew angry and began to blame Donald because she knew full well that she and her girls were all either going along with, or participating in a potential act of homicide. Seventeen year-old Brianna Stanford brushed feelings of guilt aside and told herself that this is what needed to be done in order to even the score just as her phone began to ring.

"Hello?"

"I'm on way over there. You ready?"

"Wait five minutes and then come." Brianna replied.

Five minutes later, Tracey walked over to the abandoned house and stood in the alleyway and waited anxiously for Donald to show. When she saw him approaching, she walked into the house and stood in the center of the dilapidated kitchen and Donald crept in behind her. He immediately eyed Tracey's thick thighs, her stacked hair and pouty lips and succulent-looking breasts as he walked over and grabbed her around her waist and palmed her soft, juicy ass while holding her close. Tracey responded by placing her arms around Donald and tongue kissing him lightly. She hated to do so, but she had to play it off to keep him unaware of what was actually about to go down. She released her grip on Donald and stepped back and raised her tennis skirt to reveal her peach-fuzz covered vagina and leaned against the counter in the kitchen facing the nearest bedroom.

"Come on, Dee. Lick my pussy for me." she said huskily.

As much as she was trying not to, Tracey was starting to get turned on by the thought of having her pussy licked. She really didn't care what male wanted to eat her, she simply loved the feel of a boy's tongue on her clitoris. She loved grabbing the back of a boy's head and grinding her pussy against his face until she came. She began to grow moist at the thought of having her vagina licked, so she rubbed herself, staring into Donald's eyes as she did so and asked him, nearly begging him to suck her pussy.

Donald unzipped his pants and let them drop to the floor and leaned in to Tracey and placed his left hand against the counter and his right hand on his penis and rubbed it against Tracey's vagina.

"Come Dee, man. Why you playing? Eat it for me!" Tracey pleaded through begging eyes.

"I been doing you for the longest. Do me first this time!"

Tracey had never gone down on any male in her life. Now Donald was asking her to give him head, which wasn't a part of the plan. She was reluctant to do so, but she didn't want to arouse suspicion. She let Donald place his hand onto the top of her head, wrinkling her stacked hair as he did so while guiding her to her knees. Tracey sunk to the floor inside the abandoned house's kitchen and stared at Donald's dick.

"Suck it bitch!" he commanded, causing Tracey to frown and gag.

The mere sight of Donald's dick had repulsed Tracey. She turned away, and for some unknown reason, she thought of Mike and the pretty dick he had between his legs. She was shaken from her thoughts by Donald and his firm hands that had grabbed her face. He rubbed his dick across her lips and said, "Open your fuckin' mouth and suck this dick, girl! You know you want it!"

"Come on," Tracey then said as she suddenly clicked when she realized although Donald felt he was in control, she had all the power, "put it in my mouth." she said seductively as she widened her jaws and stared up at Donald.

Donald eased forward and moaned when he felt the warmth of the beautiful Tracey Sanchez's, mouth surround his dick. He began pushing deeper into her throat and he grabbed either side of her head and began fucking her face as he moaned. Tracey's eyes were welling up because Donald was now gagging her. She could feel his dick hitting the back of her throat and she began making gagging sounds. As she sucked Donald's pole, she could see two shadows out the corner of her watery left eye.

Brianna was supposed to be by herself. Tracey thought.

"Ooohh, shit! Bitch I'm bouta come in your mouth! I'm gone

come in your fuckin' mouth!" Donald moaned as White Boy Mike and Brianna came into view.

Brianna also thought she was in the back of the house alone. Her eyes widened when she saw White Boy Mike and she quickly stepped past him and walked behind Tracey and pressed the barrel of her .380 to Donald's forehead. Donald, who was in a state of bliss, opened his eyes quickly when he felt the cold steel pressed against his skull. His eyes widened when he saw that it was Brianna standing behind the gun that was dotting his forehead. He was ejaculating into Tracey's mouth when Brianna pulled the trigger and his body stiffened up against the counter as the bullet penetrated his skull.

"Awww shit, he pissed in my fuckin' mouth!" Tracey said as Brianna wiped blood from her face and she pulled away from Donald's dick.

Tracey then realized it was semen when she wiped her mouth and saw a white substance on her hand. "He came in my mouth! Ohhh nooo! He came in my fuckin' mouth!" she said in disbelief as she spat onto the floor repeatedly.

Brianna fired the gun again and Donald fell from against the counter and onto the floor where she emptied three more rounds from her chrome .380 into his chest cavity.

Tracey stood up wiping her mouth on her shirt as she asked Mike what he was doing in the house.

"He said you was gone suck his dick. I told him I loved you, but he said you was a hoe and he was gone prove it to me. He was the one who beat Bri up didn't he? Y'all set him for killing Mike didn't y'all?" Mike asked.

"I knew that bitch couldn't keep his mouth shut!" Tracey said as she kicked Donald's lifeless corpse.

Brianna was sliding another clip into her gun; she was preparing to kill Mike as well for the simple fact that she didn't want to leave any witnesses besides Tracey. When Brianna pointed the gun at Mike, however, Tracey jumped in front of the barrel.

"Bri, no! He not gone say nothin'! He not gone say nothin!"

Tracey said in a desperate manner as she turned and hugged Mike. "Please, don't kill him."

Brianna lowered the gun and stared at Tracey and Mike and said not a word. The look on her face was enough, though; it was a look that told Tracey she had better be sure about what she was doing.

Tracey turned stared at Donald as he lay dying, blood spewing from his convulsing body. "We gotta go. Come on," she said. "Bri, we gotta go! Mike ain't gone say nothin!" she ended as she shoved Brianna in back and grabbed Mike by the hand and rushed out the house.

The three teens sprinted from the house and walked calmly through the alleyway and back onto Emory Road where Brianna pulled Tracey to the side. "Talk to that white bitch! If you even *think* he gone say somethin' let me know." she stated angrily as she flipped the hood up on her Sarah T. Reed sweater and walked towards her home with her hands tucked inside the sweater.

Tracey shook her head in agreement and then snuck Mike into her home. After rinsing her mouth out with dish detergent, which left a burning sensation, she apologized to Mike for sucking Donald's dick, but it was no need to do so because Mike understood why Tracey had did what she did.

"That dude hated Black Mike. I thought they was boys—but when Mike got killed I just had a feeling. He beat Bri up in the alley too didn't he?" Mike asked again as he lay behind Tracey in her bed with his arm across her waist.

"Yea. He did all that stuff. Mike, I ain't never suck a dick before in my life. I only did that for my girl so she could get revenge—but believe me—I hated doing that."

Mike went to kiss Tracey's lips, but she turned him away. "Not ta' night. Not after what we just did. Just hold me, Mike. Please?"

Tracey, for whatever reason, found herself suddenly being concerned about Mike's feelings. She frowned her face and asked herself what the hell she was doing lying in her bed snuggled up with White Boy Mike and giving a damn about his emotions. Why in the hell did she stop Brianna from killing him and then let him into her mother's home? Tracey had no answer; all she knew was that her heart and soul felt good being beside Mike on this night. She hated feeling this way, but she couldn't control her emotions. Her mind was saying no, but her heart was saying yes.

"Rolanda was right. I'm starting to really care about this boy." Tracey thought to herself as she cried and whispered Mike's name.

"I gotcha, Tracey. I gotcha', baby." Mike responded softly as he kissed the nape of Tracey's neck.

Tracey wasn't crying because of what she had done, which was Mike's belief, she was crying because she suddenly realized she was beginning to have feelings for the boy.

"Tracey, I love you." Mike said as nuzzled her neck and kissed her ear lobes.

"Just give me some time, but please, don't tell—"

"I know, this another one of our secrets, huh?" Mike said, cutting Tracey off.

Tracey didn't answer. She closed her eyes and thought about what she had just done. She had sucked dick for the first time in order for her former childhood friend to be killed by one of her best friends. It was a heavy burden indeed, and White Boy Mike, after witnessing what she had done was still willing to be with her, why did he love her so? What was so special about her to White Boy Mike that he would still want to be with her and willingly keep silent on what had just taken place? Could love be that strong? Tracey had done a terrible thing indeed; but she didn't feel bad for Donald in the least bit, and at a time when she should have been worried that she and Brianna's act of murder would be found out, Tracey found herself thinking about the reasons why she all of a sudden had feelings for a boy she told herself she would never like. She pondered those thoughts for minutes on in until she finally drifted off to sleep in Mike's arms.

The Holland Family Saga Part Four

CHAPTER 17

DISRUPTIVE YOUTHS

"And now that I...am here with you...I will never let you go...I look into your eyes...and know I know...know I know... where do broken—hearts go...can they find their way home... back to the open arms...of a love that's waiting there...and if somebody loves you...won't they always love you...I look in your eyes...and I know that you still care...for me..."

It was now Saturday morning in March of '88, two days after Brianna and Tracey had set Donald up to be killed. The five were out early this morning washing Rolanda's mother's car and just talking girl talk as they listened to Whitney Houston's song *Where Do Broken Hearts Go*. It was as if the horrible event that had unfolded two nights before had never occurred because the girls were joking, splashing water and making fun of one another and listening to Brianna sing along with Whitney Houston, rewinding the cassette in the dash repeatedly because they all loved Whitney's song just that much.

Brianna had thrown her pistol into the murky waters of Lake Ponchartrain in a part of the lake where no one dared swim as the water was too deep and too eerie looking. She and Tracey had also told their three friends what they had done and they all were sharing in the secret. Black Mike and Donald, two people they had grown up with were now dead and Brianna and Tracey were responsible for one of their deaths.

When the five were younger, playing on the school yard, swimming at the beach, and dancing on the park, they never imagined that they would have to kill or would have to keep secret the fact that someone out of the five would have to kill a childhood friend. Times were rapidly changing, however; the five were no longer the innocent school girls from back in the day. Brianna and Tracey were having sex in some form or the other, and they all used to fight on a regular basis. Tracey and Brianna both had nearly been killed and the two of them had committed an act of murder and the other three were willingly keeping it a secret. Still, the five didn't see what they were doing as a problem. They were only looking out for one another, which was something they always had done ever since they were little girls.

As the five washed Rolanda's mother's car, Mrs. Franz walked over to the house and asked to speak to Charlotte. She had a worried look on her face as she waited for Rolanda's mother. Charlotte came out of the house and the two women talked briefly and then walked over to the five.

Charlotte turned the music off in her car and told them she had bad news. Mrs. Franz stood before the girls and said, "Somebody killed that boy Donald. They found his body last night."

The five looked at one another and neither said a word. They then noticed Ms. Stanford walking down the sidewalk towards the house.

"I don't know what the hell going on—but they better find out who in the hell harming these damn children back here!" she stated angrily. "First Black Mike gets killed and my daughter get beat! Now somebody done killed that boy Donald! These damn streets I tell ya'! They ain't safe no more," she added as the three women stood and talked while the five continued to wipe Charlotte's car in complete silence whilst listening to the adults' conversation.

Soon, Tracey's mother Maria joined the group and the four women stood outside on the sidewalk and talked. Kilo began barking loudly from behind the gate on side of Rolanda's home the moment he spotted Lubby's mother walk out of her house.

Cynthia was called over to Rolanda's house by Maria at that moment so the adults could get her take on the matter. She looked a little disgusted as she walked over to the four women.

"Child she is loony." Charlotte whispered under her breath.

"Umm, hmm. Lubby is so sweet and she treats her own child like shit!" Maria whispered as she smiled and then waved at Cynthia amidst Kilo's ferocious barking. "That's a damn shame," she then said under her breath. "Not even the dog can stand her ass."

The mothers sniggled to themselves as Cynthia approached them with an aggravated look displayed upon her face.

"Heyyy, Cynthia. We was all taking about the kids to the Kingdom Hall tomorrow and we wanted to know if you wanted to come." Mrs. Franz said with a cheery smile.

"Kingdom Hall? What's that? Like a church?"

"Yes. Like a church." Charlotte said.

"No I don't want to go to your church! But you can take that little demon right there with you to church. She need saving!" Cynthia said as she pointed over to Lubby.

"Momma!" sixteen year-old Lubby said as she dropped her rag and ran into Rolanda's house, embarrassed by her mother. Kilo only continued barking at Cynthia; he wanted the bitch out from in front his gate A.S.A.P.

"Cynthia, why you do that to your child?" Charlotte asked.

"'Cause she a soft hearted mutherfucka! She's a follower! Just doing whatever! Lettin' boys have sex with her, she curse and fight all the time! And she a burden on me! I can't keep a man because of her!"

"You can't keep a man because of you! Lubby is your *child*! She didn't ask to be here! And until she can fend for herself it's your responsibility to look out for her!" Charlotte replied, unable accept the manner in which Cynthia was downing her own daughter.

"Lubby ain't shit ta' me! She got Gerald taking care of her ass! All she do is sleep in that mutherfucka! She ain't gone never be shit! I'm tired! I'm tired of Lubby ass! I can't wait till she leave! She keep wanting to make me proud? You know how she can do that? You know how she can make me proud? When she leave my house and my life I'll be the proudest woman in New Orleans!" Cynthia concluded as she stared at the four teens and their parents.

Mrs. Franz was appalled having heard Cynthia speak; but she believed sincerely that she could help the woman. "You need help Cynthia, come with us to the Kingdom—"

"I ain't going to your fuckin' church! Don't ask me that shit again! And I don't give a fuck about none of these kids back here! They *all* can die as far as I care!" Cynthia yelled to Mrs. Franz as she turned and walked away. When Cynthia went inside her home, only then did Kilo stop barking.

The four parents shook their heads in disbelief and Rolanda, Tracey, Dominique and Brianna couldn't help but to feel bad for Lubby, who had a mother that seemed to be in a mentally deranged state-of-being.

"Maybe she the one who killed those boys." Maria said.

Charlotte chuckled slightly and said, "I wouldn't put it pass her crazy behind."

"Charlotte, when we said we was going to the Kingdom Hall?" Rolanda asked her mother.

"You didn't have to say it! I'm tellin' ya' we going! We *all* going tomorrow so have ya' black tail ready!" Charlotte snapped back at her daughter.

Rolanda, Tracey, and Brianna all moaned. They had been to the Kingdom Hall with Dominique and Mrs. Franz a few times before and they thought the place was boring as all outdoors.

"Well, maybe I can get a good nap in tomorrow. Let me go check on Lubby." Rolanda told her friends as she walked into her home and consoled her friend.

The following day the five were attending the meeting at the Kingdom Hall sitting on the front row in front of their parents. The women sat behind the girls to make sure they stayed awake and paid attention to what was being said. Four of the teens were anxious for the meeting to end because they had never been more bored in their life.

Sixteen year-old Tracey began nodding, and each time she did, her mother would tap her head. *"Jesus please, forgive me —but I'm ready to go. Fast-forward."* Tracey said to herself.

Sixteen year-old Lubby was sleepy as well. She sat on the end of the row next to the middle aisle with her head straight ahead and her eyes closed and quickly drifted off to sleep. As the Elder gave his sermon, Lubby snored out loud and seventeen year-old Brianna shoved her side. Lubby opened her eyes and perched her lips as if she was awake the whole time. Sixteen year-old Dominique was taking notes and paying close attention. She had grown accustomed to attending the meetings and she had learned how to bide her time in a constructive manner.

Rolanda was nodding off to sleep on occasion, and she was repeatedly being tapped on the head by Charlotte.

"I'm woke!" Rolanda said loud enough for people around the group to hear.

"Don't say nothin! Just look straight ahead and pay attention!" Charlotte replied loudly inside the tranquil hall as people began focusing on the commotion coming from the front row.

Brianna kept twitching in her seat. She was restless. She kept crossing and uncrossing her legs, folding her arms and sighing the whole time. To keep from fidgeting around, she got up to use the bathroom. When the restless youngster stood up, Lubby, who had dozed off again, fell over into her seat and quickly bounced up.

"I cleaned my room already, momma!" Lubby said aloud as people inside the Kingdom Hall eyed the group that was becoming increasingly disruptive during the presentation.

"Excuse me ma'am we're gonna have to ask that you all remain quiet." an Elder in the hall stated lowly to Charlotte.

"What happened?"

"Remain quiet." the man whispered lowly.

"Mister, I ain't doing nothing. They got people coughing and sneezing, babies crying and you come over here—"

"Shh, shhh!" the Elder then said.

"I'm just sayin', man! You don't know me like that to be telling me ta' remain quiet! That's the front row! We tryin ta' keep 'em quiet!"

"Charlotte! That's an Elder!" Rolanda said as she looked back at her mother.

"I don't care what or who he is! He don't need to be tryin' ta' shush me up in here! We been maintaining the whole time up here. And I told *you* to shut the fu—just shut up!" Charlotte said as she popped her gum and shook her crossed legs rapidly; she too was now getting restless. "*What the hell Antoinette done got me into?*" she asked herself.

Brianna meanwhile, was walking back from the bathroom. When she made it to the front row, she tripped over Lubby's legs and fell to the floor, screaming aloud in the process.

"Bri, you all right?" Lubby asked.

"No!" Brianna said loud enough to cause the presentation to be halted for a moment. Brianna was lying on the floor trying to keep her composure, but she just couldn't do it. She laughed aloud and blurted out, "Lubby! Help me! I've fallen—and I can't get up!"

Brianna's four friends laughed aloud. Charlotte, Ms. Stanford and Maria sniggled, as did a few members of the hall. "I'm sorry y'all! I'm sorry! But I couldn't let that one slide!" Brianna said to the crowd of over 150 attendees. "Okay, man," she then said to the Elder as she got up, straightened her clothes and wiped her watery eyes and sat back down. "Okay, we ready now."

The elder shook his slightly and continued his presentation.

"He shook his head at you like you stupid or something!" Tracey told to Brianna loud enough for people around them to hear.

The two could be heard whispering as they mocked the

Elder.

"He standin' there in that tight ass brown suit looking like Bookman from Good Times. Fat behind!" Brianna remarked as she and Tracey sniggled aloud.

"Fish-eyed fool." Tracey snapped.

Rolanda was now thirsty. She had a soda in her purse and she wanted so badly to drink it so she went for it. At the same time, Lubby was dozing off again and she fell back against Brianna, who quickly stood up and let Lubby fall over once more.

"Momma, I did the dishes already!" Lubby yelled aloud, causing another scene.

Lubby's four friends laughed as the presentation was stopped again. Rolanda opened her soda at that moment, but because it had been shaken in the car, it began to fizz all over her face and silk dress. She jumped up from her seat and tried to cover the soda, but she dropped it on the floor. She chased the fizzing can around in a circle and picked it up and quickly walked to the back of the hall with the bubbling drink, leaving a trail of wasted soda on the carpet.

"I'm sorry. I'm sorry everybody. Go 'head and finish, mister. I be right back. I be back." she repeated loudly as she went to the bathroom to clean herself up.

"Umm," was all the Elder on the stage said as two more assistants walked from the back of the hall to the front of the Hall and escorted Brianna, Lubby and Tracey, who were laughing loudly, from the front row.

"What?" Tracey asked as she was removed from her seat. "I ain't do nothin', mister. Momma! Tell these people I ain't do nothin!"

Maria held her head down in shame. The daughters were supposed to be there to learn about God, instead, they were disrupting the entire meeting.

"That's it! We going outside!" Maria said in frustration as she grabbed Tracey by the arm and shoved her down the middle aisle hurriedly.

Maria began speaking Spanish as she escorted Tracey down the middle row amidst scores of on-lookers. Tracey trotted alongside her mother grimacing and trying to remove herself from her mother's grip.

"Come on, momma! Oww! Come on! You hurtin' my arm, man! You worse than the police! And speak English! You know I can't understand that shit you talking!" Tracey said aloud as a great majority of the congregation gasped aloud in surprise and shock.

Maria then stopped in the middle of the hall and slapped Tracey in the face and knocked her down to her knees. "Don't you curse in the Lord's house no damn more! Get up!" an embarrassed Maria yelled aloud as she and Tracey left the Hall.

The regular attendees felt sorry and embarrassed for the parents, whose daughters were acting very disruptive this day.

"There's no food allowed in here Miss." another Elder told Rolanda as she exited the bathroom with the can of soda.

"This isn't food. This is a can soda, mister." Rolanda said nonchalantly as she made her way back to the front row.

The man stopped Rolanda and told her she wasn't allowed to go back up front.

"Man, my momma up there!" Rolanda said and continued on.

"If you go back up front, I'll have to ask you to leave." the man said calmly.

"Charlotte! This man said I can't come back up there!" Rolanda yelled aloud from the back of the hall to the front where her mother sat.

Charlotte turned around and saw her daughter standing behind the stocky built Elder and she got up and walked down the middle aisle. "You got a problem with my daughter, mister?" she asked.

Before long, several more male members of the Kingdom Hall got up and began to escort Rolanda and Charlotte out of the medium-sized brick building. They both were fussing as they were lead to the exit.

"Y'all gotta fine way of treating people up in here!" Charlotte said.

"Tell 'em Charlotte!"

Charlotte smacked Rolanda across her face, hard and said, "And what the hell is wrong with you?"

"Momma!" Rolanda said in shock as she rubbed her right cheek.

"Momma my ass! Get on out the door! You wouldna spilled that soda we wouldn't even be gettin' kicked out the damn church!" Charlotte could be heard saying as she escorted her daughter outside into the parking lot. "And ya' better not get ta' cryin' out here today or I'll beat your muther—" the door closed before Charlotte had completed her proclamation.

The entire meeting had been thrown into disarray. Brianna and her mother then got up and left, and Lubby was allowed to sit next to Dominique and her mother and Tracey's little brother.

"I'm sorry for messing y'all meeting up Mrs. Franz." Lubby stated as Mrs. Franz wiped tears from her eyes.

Mrs. Franz had hoped that the teenagers and their parents would all benefit from a spiritual lesson this Sunday, but it just wasn't meant to be. Although they had been to the Hall before, Rolanda, Tracey, and Brianna had never acted out the way they had on this day. They simply weren't interested in what God had to say at that particular time. Lubby sat with Dominique and before long, she was sleep again. Dominique and her mother said nothing, they let Lubby sleep, at least that way, the meeting would not be disrupted any further.

When the meeting was over, thirty-five minutes behind schedule, Dominique went to talk with some of the people she knew from the hall as Lubby, Tracey's brother, and Mrs. Franz walked outside to find Charlotte and the rest of the bunch. They were sitting in Charlotte's car listening to the radio. The music was blaring and Mrs. Franz had to walk over to her friend and tell the woman to turn the volume down. Charlotte just didn't understand the do's and don'ts inside and outside of the Kingdom Hall. She did agree to a bible study with Mrs. Franz to learn more and that eased the tension that was beginning to rise on this Sunday. The adults all apologized and promised to do better the next time they came to the Hall. The five teens, however, had outside interests and serving God was the furthest thing from their minds.

CHAPTER 18

TURNING POINTS

"Well, it's been a long and interesting year friends and we come here on this last On Air show of the school year with heavy hearts. We, umm, we lost Black Mike," Dominique said and then paused. She hated to pay homage to Donald, but she knew she had to do so so as not to have people talking and becoming suspicious about who had killed the boy. "We also lost our friend Donald this school year as well. I know we all feel sorry for both losses we suffered here at Sarah T. Reed because Black Mike and Donald were two really cool dudes. We gone miss them both." she then paused for a second and continued. "We, well, I can't speak for everybody, but I want to personally thank Jehovah that Brianna pulled through and we look forward to everybody returning for their senior year. Remember, me and Tracey's birthday is coming up next month. The big bash is June 16, so come on over to Tracey's house and let's have a good time. And in the month of August is the big summer's end block party for Lubby. Until then, y'all be safe and have a good summer." Dominique ended as Tracey cued up *Going Back to Cali* by L.L.Cool J.

The school year had come to a close with the last airing of The On Air Show and the five each got into Gerald's and Tank's car and rode back to East Shore on this hot sunny day where they bar-b-cued and had a good time with Bobby, Tank and Gerald in celebration of another successful school year. Calvin came over later that day and he and Dominique walked along the levee with Kilo and talked about their plans for the future. Their last day of school was a perfect day for the five—they had kicked the summer of '88 off right.

As the weeks went on, Tracey, Dominique, Lubby and Rolanda had taken on jobs. Seventeen year-olds Rolanda, Tracey and Dominique now worked at a new grocery store called Delchamp's. Rolanda worked in the meat department, Tracey was a cashier and Dominique was placed in charge of the Health and Beauty Aides Department. Sixteen year-old Lubby, meanwhile, had obtained a job at a pet shop inside Lake Forest Shopping Center. The four of them were all doing okay.

Seventeen year-old Brianna, on the other hand, had jumped back into the drug game during the summer of '88. She was now working side by side with Bobby, Gerald, and Tank. The five had always wondered what the three twenty year olds did to make cash—this summer they had found out—but the girls didn't know the full story. Bobby, Tank and Gerald weren't small time hustlers like Black Mike used to be. They were mid-level suppliers, only they didn't purchase their cocaine. They robbed other people out of their cocaine and sold it at a lower price. That's what they meant back in the day when they said they were going 'shopping'. They would actually go out and rob other drug dealers. When they hooked up with Brianna, the plan was to give her a $4,000 package and she would keep half the cash and give them the rest. Brianna was shrewd in the way in which she conducted her business. She asked Tank for a gun and he gave her a .9mm that she now kept with her at all times. Brianna had learned her lesson after getting beaten by Donald earlier in the year which was to always carry a gun. She also had White Boy Mike working with her for extra muscle and would give him five hundred dollars every time she got paid.

It didn't take long for Mike to start reinvesting with Brianna, and before long, the two of them had the most fire crack cocaine connect in the neighborhood. East Shore was doing just fine under Brianna and Mike's reign. The five females were growing up quickly also; they were working and hanging out with Bobby, Tank, and Gerald more and more because the three young men were fun to be with. It was fair to say that the boys were easily pulling the five further and further into the streets of New Orleans.

****

It was now mid-August of '88, two days before Lubby's 17th birthday and East Shore was in full-swing. The bash Tracey and Dominique threw in June for their birthday was a huge hit and now everyone was gearing up for Lubby's block party which would undoubtedly be the place to be when the occasion arrived as everybody in East Shore and beyond knew that an East Shore block party was a party not to be missed.

Gerald, ever in love with Lubby, was sponsoring the whole thing along with Bobby and Tank. The three twenty year olds were planning to go all out for Lubby. Everyone was contributing to the cause.

"Hey, man! We need ta' get some meat and shit ta' throw on the grill at the block party day after tomorrow!" Gerald said aloud as he, Bobby and Tank cruised down Hayne Boulevard in Gerald's car.

"Nigga! It's gone be at least two hundred mutherfuckas out there! How the fuck we gone do that?" Bobby asked. His six gold teeth gleaming in the afternoon sun as the young men cruised towards East Shore.

"Shiit nigga! We got loot!" Tank snapped as he turned up the volume on N.W.A.'s song *Dopeman* and began singing the chorus as his boys joined in.

"Dopeman, dopeman...yeah that's me...dopeman, dopeman...yo' can I get a G...dopeman, dopeman...clockin' much as he can...fuck this shit who am I...the dopeman..."

"Say, brer! Don't Tracey work the register at Delchamp's?" Gerald asked over the music.

The three looked at one another and smiled slyly and then burst into laughter.

"Turn this bitch around, nigga! We going make some damn groceries today!" Tank yelled aloud through laughter.

Meanwhile, Tracey, Dominique, and Rolanda were hard at

work inside the grocery store on Read Boulevard, about a mile north of Abramson High School, and a half mile from the mall where Lubby worked. The three friends had been at work since six in the morning and it was now after two; they were ready to leave and head back to East Shore, but they weren't scheduled to get off for another hour and a half.

Rolanda was behind the deli counter slicing turkey; there were at least six other people waiting to purchase deli meat and they were growing increasingly impatient awaiting their turn. The customers didn't care about the fact that Rolanda was working by herself this day and they began to complain about the slow service.

"I've seen snails move at a quicker pace than this woman here!" an older black man, who was a regular at the meat counter said loud enough for Rolanda to hear.

Rolanda had heard all of the customer's complaints, but the last complaint by the old man had driven her over the edge. She knew who he was and she quickly turned around and looked him directly in the eyes and said, "Look man, I'm doin' tha' best I can back here all by myself slicing this damn turkey and shit! What you want this time? Bologna? Ham? What? Because you can take your turtle neck in the summertime wearing ass to the Chinese store and buy ya' li'l luncheon meat and cheese that you come and get every day! Wastin' my time for three fuckin' dollars' worth of food!" Rolanda stated as she walked into the huge refrigerator and sat down to cool off, leaving the customers wondering if she was ever coming back.

Rolanda emerged from the cooler two minutes later, and the customers would not utter another word. They waited patiently until they were able to be serviced by Rolanda that afternoon. "That's right," Rolanda said under her breath. "Don't fuck with me today 'cause I ain't the one."

Tracey, meanwhile, was on the register. She usually worked the express checkout lane, but on this day she was working the full service register. The full service register was the busiest because the cashier had the responsibility of getting items that can only be obtained from the Manager's Office. All day Tracey had been running back and forth to get liquor and cigarettes from the manager's booth and printing out money orders. She had to wait for people to tear food stamps out of their food stamp books and wait patiently with a smile while old ladies placed coupons on top off nearly every item they removed from their basket. People were challenging her on prices as well, and she had Dominique doing price checks throughout the day.

A customer asked for a pack of Kool Filter Kings and Tracey calmly walked to the manager's booth to grab the cigarettes. When she got back, however, the young man told Tracey he asked for Kool Filter King 100's.

"You didn't say one hundreds." Tracey said disgustedly.

"I'm sorry, baby girl. But I need the 100's." the young man stated. "I buy those all the time. You don't know my face by now?"

"No I don't know your face by now! I don't be paying attention to you or what you buy when you come in this place, man." Tracey snapped.

The frustrated teen came back to the register with the cigarettes and rung the man up and sent him on his way, ignoring his attempts to get her phone number. The next person then asked for a pack of Salem Lights.

"Unbelievable," Tracey sighed as she placed her hands on her hips and stared the man down. "You saw me go over there two times, brer! Why you ain't say nothing?" she asked disgustedly as she went to get the cigarettes.

When Tracey returned, she could see the next customer in line shaking his head in disgust. She knew the man, and he always had something smart to say. This day would be no different.

"Jesus just one time can I get in and get out this dump? I wish they hire people that really wanna work. That's why my daughter's going to college so she won't become a lazy citizen." the man told the woman in line behind him.

The woman widened her eyes and looked at Tracey as if to say, *"Girl you gone take that from him?"*

Tracey was about to go off on the mid-thirties, blonde-haired, blue-eyed white guy, but she noticed the man had a tube off Preparation-H in his hand. Rather than go off, she decided to embarrass his ass. Tracey took the item from the man and scanned it, but she had her hand over the bar code to prevent the item from registering properly.

"Hmm! It's not ringing up, mister. Let me get a price check." Tracey said as she turned on her microphone.

"Just give it here and I'll do it myself." the man remarked.

"Oh no! I'll be glad to do it for ya', mister." Tracey responded nicely as the two struggled with the ointment. "Let it go now!" Tracey suddenly yelled aloud, startling the customer, who suddenly released his grip.

Tracey then clicked on her microphone and slapped the man's hand away one last time and spoke rapidly as she held onto the ointment. "Dominique I need a price check on Preparation-H! That's Preparation-H Hemorrhoid Treatment for the gentleman at register five please!" she said loudly as people in her line sniggled. The customers saw and heard the entire scene play out and they felt the least bit concern about the man's privacy after the way he'd downed Tracey.

Dominique and other customers throughout the store began to laugh as well when they heard the request.

"Okay, okay. You just let the world know! Are you happy now?" the man asked in an embarrassed tone as his face turned beet red.

Dominique had seen this routine from Tracey before; the three girls were having a bad day so a little payback would be such sweet justice.

"You need a price check on the regular strength or the maximum strength Preparation-H Hemorrhoid Treatment?" Dominique asked as she stood at the end of Tracey's line trying to keep her composure.

"He got the Maximum Strength Preparation-H Hemorrhoid Treatment, Dominique!" Tracey said over the microphone as she pointed directly at the man standing at her register.

"Maximum—Strength—Preparation-H—Hemorrhoid Treatment…hemorrhoid treatment…hemorrhoid treatment…"

The words echoed through the entirety of the store as Tracey broke down her sentence loudly and clearly, bringing about more laughs, even those of the store manager.

"Price check for the hemorrhoid man at register five coming right up!" Dominique ended as she walked away whilst laughing.

The man was so embarrassed he left the line and began walking out the doors.

"Hey, where you going?" Tracey asked mockingly as the man disappeared from sight. "That's right! Don't fuck with me today! Or any other day!" she concluded in a low tone as she began to ring up the lady's items.

The lady laughed and told Tracey that was a good one.

"Girl, I can't wait till I get off today. I just need to get away you know?" she said as Bobby, Gerald, and Tank entered the medium-sized grocery store, each pushing a basket.

The three young men walked in, dressed in their Adidas jogging suits and 'Forum' Adidas tennis shoes with their baseball caps to the back, talking loud about much of nothing. They walked through the store throwing items in their basket, never looking at the price. They saw Dominique in the beauty aisle and they approached her and asked her if Tracey could cheat the register.

"Yea, what y'all up to?"

"We gettin' the stuff for Lubby block party, but we want it on discount, ya' dig?" Gerald said as he smiled at Dominique.

"Oh, okay! Y'all go back there by Rolanda! She by herself today! And I'm a let Tracey know what's up."

The three made their way to the back of the store by the meat counter where they saw Rolanda slicing meat again. She had calmed down, but she, too, was ready to go home.

"Can a nigga get some service around here?" Bobby said loudly as customers looked on in shock at the use of his language.

"Loooook motherfu—" Rolanda said slowly as she turned around waving a butcher's knife; she then noticed the three young men and her eyes lit , especially upon seeing Bobby.

Rolanda laughed and hurried to get rid of the three remaining customers and Bobby then filled her in on the scheme and she began to wrap steaks, pork chops, and sausage into white paper and mark them at $1.99. She nearly emptied the display case. The baskets were all full and the three went straight to Tracey's line. They had a basket full of meat, bags of charcoal, huge cans of baked beans, bottles of bar-b-cue sauce, bread, beer, and cases of soda. Dominique was waiting to help bag the groceries as she had filled Tracey in. By the time they were done, the young men paid only fifty-five dollars for over four hundred dollar's worth of food and drink. Gerald then slid Tracey three fifty dollar bills and the young men walked out of the grocery store with enough food to cater Lubby's party and have more than enough left over to throw another bar-b-cue.

****

The night of Lubby's block party had arrived and the party was in high gear. The crowd of teens and young adults were eating bar-b-cue and dancing in the street and talking about much of nothing as they enjoyed themselves. Tracey and Dominique were playing *Posse on Broadway*, by the rapper Sir-Mix-a lot and had the crowd bouncing. Beer was flowing, and weed was being smoked in the warm summer night's air.

Lubby was in the middle of the street doing her dance. She began to rapidly shake her arms and sink to the ground as the crowd cheered her on. The seventeen year-old was having the time of her life on her seventeenth birthday, thankful for her friends, who'd gone all out to make her day a special one.

Brianna was leaning against Tank's car, a four door black Oldsmobile '98 on chrome Tru rims. The car was clean; it had a fifth wheel and a white rag top with black tinted windows. Brianna was drinking a beer when Tank passed her a joint. She had never smoked weed before, but between all the partying, the drinking, and the loud music, she was seduced into taking her first toke of marijuana. She inhaled the weed and coughed. Tank patted her back as she bent over at the knees beside his car.

"You okay, Bri?"

Brianna looked up at Tank, her eyes now red and she began to sniggle. Tank then knew that Brianna was all right. The two of them would hang together the rest of the night. Dominique, meanwhile, was beside her home with Calvin. The two were lip-locked in a heated kiss. Kissing was Dominique's weakness; she could nearly orgasm from a kiss as her lips were real sensitive. She was trying her best to wait on Calvin for sex, but between her masturbating on a daily basis and hearing all of Tracey and Brianna's sexual escapades, she was growing ever curious about what real sex felt like. She was growing tired of touching herself, and she now wanted a male to make her feel good.

"Calvin," she said in between kisses, "I need to get some more albums from inside, come and help me." Dominique said.

The two seventeen year-olds walked to the front of Dominique's house and she unlocked the door. She called out to her mother and got no answer. Her father was home for the weekend and she figured they were locked away in their master bedroom. Dominique grabbed Calvin's hand and guided him through her darkened home towards her bedroom. Once inside, she left the lights off as she locked her door and wrapped her arms around Calvin's neck and began kissing him again.

"I thought we was coming to get some albums."

Dominique said nothing as she pulled Calvin to her bed. The 5' 115 pound petite sexy-eyed seventeen year-old was overcome with lust this night. She let her hair down and fell onto the bed, pulling Calvin on top of her and the two meshed together. Dominique spread her legs and began to grind herself against Calvin's jean-covered crotch. The feeling was incredible. Dominique moaned, and Calvin couldn't deny the pleasure his body was producing as he grew an erection. The two were dry humping, but before long, Dominique had rolled on top of Calvin and had managed to unbuckle her shorts. She then stood up and slid her shorts and panties down and kicked her tennis off. She was now ready to give up her virginity.

Calvin stared at the sexy physique that stood before him and eyed her fluffy pubic hair. He could see her pussy lips glistening as Dominique straddled him and began to unbuckle his pants, an act that had forced Calvin to jump up at that moment.

"What's wrong?" Dominique asked as she sat atop Calvin.

"I, I can't do this Dominique." Calvin stated somewhat shamed.

"What! You don't want me?"

"I do. But my momma and daddy, they gone be mad I can't —"

"Ohhh, I see. Your momma and daddy said you can kiss and touch me, but you can't make love to me."

"Every time we do that, I feel guilty—but this, this ain't right. Understand?"

"Yea. I think I do understand, Calvin. You wanna play on your own terms. Who are your parents to decide what's good and bad for us? Why can't you make up your own mind? You keep sending me mixed signals man. And, and I'm confused as to what we can and can't do." Dominique said as she now sat on her bed naked from the waist down, the music outside was faint in the distance and the moonlight was shining down onto both of their bodies.

"I think until we get married? I think we shouldn't be alone, Dominique."

Dominique was heart-broken. She was so ready for sex, but Calvin wanted to wait until they were married. She wondered how long could she hold out. And even if she did, would Calvin even be worth the wait?

"This not like in elementary school, Calvin." Dominique stated as she hopped from the bed and pulled her panties and shorts back on and sat back down on the bed to place her tennis shoes back onto her feet. "I can't promise you that I'll be a virgin if and when you decide to marry me." she said in a disappointed tone of voice as she went into the spare bedroom, sat on the bed and cried softly.

Dominique's feelings were hurt. She loved Calvin, but her hormones were raging something fierce. She wanted sex and she needed a type of relief that masturbation could longer sustain.

Kilo was in the spare room on this night. Dominique and Rolanda had taken him to get his annual shots earlier in the day and the dog was worn out from the medications. The dog lay on his side and watched Dominique, who said, "Sorry Kilo, but I can't hold out much longer."

Dominique stood up just as Kilo slowly crawled underneath the bed. She then pulled her shorts off again and lay down on the mattress inside the dark quiet room and began to pleasure herself and was done in two minutes. She cleaned herself up and returned to her bedroom and sat next to Calvin on her bed.

"Calvin, I love you man, and I want us to be together. When we graduate next year, will you marry me then?"

"Let's work towards that, Dominique. I wanna do right by you. I mean you special to me and want you to be an honest woman. It's hard for me to resist, but I have to be strong because I wanna do right by you, Dominique, please believe that."

"This is hard for me, too, Cal. But for love's sake, for our sake, I'll be strong. I take back what I said about not being a virgin when we marry. I don't want nobody but you, boy."

"You know I only need you, Dominique. My little sugar cone." Calvin said as he pressed his forehead to Dominique's and the two laughed just as Mrs. Franz opened Dominique's bedroom door.

"What are you two doing in here in the dark?"

"Just talking momma."

"Well, talk in the light!" the woman said as she turned on Dominique's light causing the three of them to squint their eyes at the sudden brightness. "God that's bright! I'm going make coffee for your father. You two want anything from the kitchen?"

"No, momma. Thanks." Dominique answered as she got up and began searching for albums to bring back to Tracey's house.

"Talk in the light. That's good advice you know." Calvin stated as Dominique looked up from her milk crates full of albums and smiled back at him.

"I think that's a message from Jehovah." Dominique replied.

"I think you're right. I think you're right." Calvin replied as he and Dominique grabbed a stack full of albums and soon rejoined Tracey behind the Dee-jay table in front of Tracey's home.

As Dominique took over the task of playing the music to keep the crowd pumped up, Tracey noticed Mike approaching and she told Dominique she had to use the bathroom. She walked into her home and went into her bedroom, closed the door and sat on her bed awaiting Mike's arrival. When Mike tapped lightly on her door, Tracey let him in and quickly locked her door and pulled down her spandex and sat on the edge of the bed as Mike knelt before her and placed his tongue to her vagina.

"Yea! You the only one who know what I like, Mike." she said in a raspy voice as she grabbed the back of Mike's head and ground her pussy against his lips and rode Mike's mouth and tongue to a quick and powerful orgasm. When they were done, Tracey and Mike rejoined the party.

It was an hour later, well after midnight and Mrs. Franz had decided to call Dominique home as she was scheduled to go to the Kingdom Hall later that morning. Mrs. Franz looked out the window and could see that there was still a large crowd of people out on the block.

"Stanley, go and get your daughter. She has to get up early tomorrow." the woman requested of her husband.

Mr. Franz got up from the couch and walked out into the muggy, warm air and headed towards the crowd. When he got there he saw Charlotte and Maria in the middle of the street dancing with Rolanda and Lubby having a good time. The man spotted his daughter behind the turntables with Tracey, Calvin, and Mike and made his way over to the four teens.

"Dominique, it's time to come home, baby." he stated over the loud music.

"Aww, dad! We was just gettin' into the party!"

"I know and understand—but we have to get up early. Come on, sugar cone. Let's go home."

Tracey could see the look of disgust on Dominique's face as she was led away by her father, but she had an idea to keep Dominique out a little longer until the party ended, however; Mr. Stanley loved to dance and he was a cool man. Tracey knew he liked old school jams, so she quickly went into the crates of albums and found *Don't Stop the Music* by Yarbrough and Peebles and put the song on.

As Mr. Franz walked pass Charlotte and Maria the song came on.

"Aww shit! They is jammin' out here tonight Maria! Come on Stanley, remember 'the bump' we used to do back in the day?" Charlotte yelled aloud as she bumped her hips against Mr. Franz.

Mr. Franz liked the song as well and for a brief moment he stopped and danced. Before long he had danced the entire song and Dominique was back behind the turntables. She and Tracey continued playing old school jams like the Dazz Band's *Whip it*, *Firecracker* by Mass Production, and *Let's Groove*, by Earth, Wind and Fire. Many of the classic Rhythm and Blues songs were in effect and the party-goers were all over the street, some dancing some, some talking and others just sitting out in the warm air vibing to the music.

Another hour had passed and Mrs. Franz was wondering where her husband and daughter were. She changed into a pair of shorts and a blouse and walked out into the night. She reached the crowd and when she spotted her husband, he was in the middle of the street dancing with Rolanda, Lubby, Maria and Charlotte to Johnny Kemp's song, *Just Got Paid* that was blasting from the speakers. Mr. Franz had a beer in his hand and he was out there trying to copy Lubby's moves without much success.

"Stanley! What are you doing?" Mrs. Franz yelled as she now stood beside her husband.

Mr. Franz stopped dancing and tried to plea bargain, "Oh, well, umm, baby, umm, see what had happen was—"

"Never mind!" Mrs. Franz said disgustedly as she went to grab Dominique.

When Dominique saw her mother, she knew she would be leaving this time. "Look like this good-bye for real this time y'all," she stated as she hugged Calvin, Tracey and Mike and walked towards her mother.

"You should've been home! I send your father down here to get you and he joins the party. Y'all two are a mess." the woman said. Mrs. Franz wasn't angry, she just wanted her daughter rested for the meeting tomorrow so she wouldn't fall asleep.

She went and grabbed her husband, but before they could leave, Tracey had played *Love's Trian* by *Confunkshun*. Tracey knew that was one of Mr. and Mrs. Franz's favorite songs and she had played with the hope that they would stay a little longer. She was trying her best to keep Dominique outside for as long as possible on this night.

"Aww sookie sookie, nah!" Mr. Franz said as he grabbed his wife's hands. "Come on! Come on! You know that's our song Antoinette! That's my jam when I'm on the road, baby! Come on!" the man said to his wife as he pulled her close.

"Stanley, come on now! We gotta go, baby! I gotta get up early."

"Just one dance. Come on! Let's close this party down, Antoinette!"

"Dance! Dance! Dance! Dance!" the whole crowd surrounding the married couple began yell as they clapped their hands as the song's lyrics came over the speakers.

"Warm night…can't sleep, too hurt, too weak gotta call her up…dial that number no one answers 'til two 'o'clock…"

As the song played on, Mrs. Franz smiled into her husband's chest as she slowly wrapped her arms around his shoulders and the crowd began clapping and whistling, "I haven't done this in years," Antoinette said as she looked into her husband's eyes, enjoying the melodic tune.

Mrs. Franz had to admit, although, her religious beliefs prevented her from partying too much, she was enjoying this moment spent with her husband. "We have to do this more often, Stanley. I love you, baby." Mrs. Franz stated as she gripped her husband tightly and became enthralled in the song.

"Sometimes heart strings can be broken…but you just have to keep on going…that's the way it goes on love's train…"

When the song ended, Mr. Franz asked Dominique to go and get that album for him and his wife. She did, and the three went home about thirty minutes later when the block party officially ended at 2a.m. Mr. and Mrs. Franz stood up all night listening to the album, dancing and talking. Dominique was up as well, admiring her mother and father's marriage to the highest degree. As she lay in her bed, she dreamt and hoped that she and Calvin would have a marriage that was as strong and loving as the one her mother and father had.

CHAPTER 19

THE BEST GAME EVER

The five's twelfth grade year had rolled in quickly and right off the bat they knew that their senior year would be a spectacular one. The On Air Show was in full swing, grades were being kept, and the girls had learned early on that Sarah T. Reed was scheduled to play Carver High School again this year. It had been two years since the former students from Abramson had last played Carver and neither the band nor Lubby had never forgotten what the Carver band students and majorettes promised, which was to win back the coveted Halftime Show Trophy, when Abramson had won the battle of the band trophy two years ago. Many of the students over to Sarah T. Reed were sophomores at Abramson the year Abramson won the battle of the bands, now they were all seniors over to Sarah T. Reed and would be facing many of the students from Carver who were on the losing end of that battle, all of whom were now seniors as well.

Lubby and her majorettes practiced for almost two months with the band leading up to the big game. Sarah T. Reed had won several battle of the bands so far this year, but trouncing Carver during halftime was the one win that was being highly sought after because it pitted the best against the best.

Brianna was scheduled to sing that night and she, too, had been practicing for the big performance. Dominique, Rolanda, and Tracey would have no part in this routine, so they would watch from the stands as their two friends tried to keep hold of the trophy held by Lubby and the majorettes for two years.

That cool Saturday night in October of '88 had finally arrived and Brianna was on lead in the center of the field with two other girls behind her singing on backup. *Just The Way You Like It* by The S.O.S. Band was the song of choice, and Brianna and her two backup singers were in rare form as they stood before Lubby and the majorettes, who danced before the band as the band played the instrumental. Two years ago, the drum line was the main focus of the show, this year, the brass instruments held center stage for Brianna as she sung...

...*"But I know better...you can't change years over night... and asking that I would never do...so here is the solution that...comes to mind...as long as I...can be your number one....you still can have your fun...whenever you need love...I will give it to you...just the way you like it..."*

Brianna, dressed in a royal blue leather pant suit with a yellow silk blouse underneath, a leather yellow B-bop cap on her head, with a pair of leather yellow knee high boots, was on fire as she sung the lyrics while the band played the instrumental to the song and copied Lubby's movements, but at a minimal because of the instruments they were holding on to.

The majorettes danced perfectly as they wowed the audience with their routine. Lubby was in the center of the group working up a sweat. She and the majorettes were doing a new dance she'd created that had them holding their arms out slightly on their sides as they gyrated their hips whilst twirling around in a slow circle. It was the way the majorettes shuffled their feet as they twirled around in a circle that had made the dance likeable; and the girls were all in tune with Brianna's singing, and the band's playing of the instrumental.

Dressed in blue and yellow, which was Sarah T. Reed's school's colors, Lubby lead the way in her royal blue majorette suit and knee-high yellow boots, and to say that the routine she'd choreographed for the band and the majorettes would become a classic would be an understatement. Everybody was in sync, and the lyrics Brianna was laying down coupled with the backup singers, was slowly causing this performance to transform into an epic routine that many would try to copy without much success because the forerunners of this performance would burn the trial they were blazing and would leave nothing but dust and ash in their wake...

...*"If you...plan on loving me for a lifetime...it doesn't matter what you do...with other girls they just can't change your mind(oh no)'cause when you're tired of them you'll come back to me...I won't let you down...you can play around...'cause you know where the best love is found...right here baby...As long as I...can be your number one..."*

Mid-way through the chorus, as Sarah T. Reed was spelling out their school's initials to close out their performance, Lubby had twisted her left ankle when it became lodged in the grass. She stumbled a bit, but immediately regained her composure and fell back into sync. Tracey, Rolanda, and Dominique all saw her stumble and they knew Lubby was hurt and wondered how she would fare. They watched as Lubby danced on, seemingly unbothered by the stumble. Her adrenaline was too high and her pride would not let her stop her routine, even if her ankle did pain her something fierce.

Carver had performed before Sarah T. Reed and they'd produced their own singer and he sung *Off on Your own Girl* by Al B. Sure as the band played the instrumental. Carver's band then played *Da Butt* by EU and they taunted Sarah T. Reed as they shook their rear ends towards Sarah T. Reed's home side bleachers before dancing off the field.

Lubby had all of that on her mind as she continued dancing through the pain. Brianna's voice was just too strong, and Lubby's choreographed routine was just too on point for the judges to vote against Sarah T. Reed. Carver felt that they should have won because they did *Da Butt*, but Sarah T. Reed had performed a whole routine off one song that was nearly worthy of its own Broadway theatrical show. Lubby Williams, who was responsible for the dance ensemble, and Brianna Stanford, who had such an alluring voice, were just that good.

Sarah T. Reed ended their performance by spelling their high school initials and taking a knee on the field, which was a victory move. A few seconds later, fireworks went off on Sarah T. Reed's side and the sound tech announced Sarah T. Reed as the winners and Lubby fell to the ground and immediately grabbed her ankle. The other majorettes, who were running to hoist the trophy, noticed her sitting on the field clutching her ankle and they ran back to her aide as so did her friends and Kilo.

Rolanda grabbed Kilo's collar and pulled the barking dog back as two of the band members picked Lubby up and placed her on their shoulders and carried her off the field as they repeatedly yelled her name.

"Kilo calm down! They ain't gone hurt Lubby!" Rolanda stated to the barking dog as she followed the crowd and cheered for Lubby.

Lubby was crying as the crowd cheered for her; she wasn't crying from the pain, she was crying because once again she was victorious. Carver had given her their best shot and she answered back with a dance routine that would leave the high school students coming behind her a hallmark to attain. Seventeen year-old Lubby Williams became a high school legend on this cool October night inside of Tad Gormley Stadium in the year of 1988.

The second half of the football game had started and as Lubby was being attended to by doctors, Rolanda, Brianna, Dominique, and Tracey watched the game from the bleachers. There was a middle linebacker for Carver who was all over the field wreaking havoc on defense and giving Sarah T. Reed's offense pure hell. The score was 20 to 14 with Carver leading, but Sarah T. Reed was going in for a score from the nine yard line. The quarter back threw a pass, but the middle linebacker intercepted it in the end zone and ran it back 106 yards for a touchdown.

Carver fans went wild as the sound tech yelled loudly and enthusiastically over the speakers, "A 106 yard interception by number fifty-one, Manuel Lawson Taylor Junior! It's a new record! It's a new record! Watch out Mean Joe Green young Manny is on his way to the NFL after he blows through the college ranks! Can anybody sayyyyy, LSU? Look out world! The Carver Rams has a star in the making!"

"Damn man! Number fifty-one killin' our team out there!" Rolanda snapped. "That's the second interception he ran back for a touch down!"

"Girl, we ain't got a chance as long as that boy Manny in the game." Dominique stated as she rubbed Kilo to stop the dog from barking.

Sarah T. Reed got the ball again and the quarter back was sacked by Manny on first down. Manny was having a career night; college scouts were on hand watching him, and even though he was only a sophomore, Manny was already being recruited by L.S.U. and Alabama universities, but one faithful play, however, would change his life forever. The quarter back ran a draw play that sent the running back straight up the middle. Manny had him in his sight, but the running back did a sweeping move to the right. Manny went after the running back, but his cleat became lodged in the turf. The highly-touted linebacker felt the cartilage in his left Achilles heel tear and he went down immediately, flipped off his helmet, and grabbed his left ankle screaming aloud in agony.

It wasn't right, but Sarah T. Reed's side began cheering when Manny went down. They immediately stopped cheering, however, when they realized he was seriously injured.

"Ohh noo! Manny got hurt!" Lubby, who had joined her friends after having her ankle wrapped, stated sadly.

"Damn man! He was kicking our ass for real! That dude was gone be good. I hope he play again! Kilo you need ta' stop barking before they rush us up outta here!" Tracey stated sadly to the barking pit-bull as the crowd watched in silence as the medics placed Manny onto a cart and wheeled him off the field. The crowd clapped as he was taken away.

Without Manny to lead the defense, Carver became dejected and they ultimately lost the game. This night would also be the last night that Manuel 'Manny' Lawson Taylor Junior would ever set foot on the field. His life had been forever changed.

When the football season ended, the five continued on in their studies and began preparing for life after high school. In just a few months they would all be young women preparing to enter the next phase of their lives.

CHAPTER 20

THE BALLER PACKAGE

It was now August of '89 and the five were all now eighteen. Lubby's birthday was this day and her friends were planning to take her out and have a small private party afterward because Tracey's mother Maria had recently been baptized as a Jehovah's Witness and she could no longer allow parties to be thrown in front of her home because of the foul language in the music, the excessive drinking and the occasional smoking of marijuana. Before she was baptized, Maria Sanchez was a fun-loving parent that allowed mischief to go on, but her views changed once she began to learn about God through studying with Mrs. Franz. Maria tried to have fun with her daughter in other ways, but Tracey wasn't really too interested in doing 'family things' such as bowling and roller skating with her mother and brother. She would much rather hang with her friends and that saddened not only Maria, but also her little brother because both of them felt that Tracey was isolating herself from her family. Tracey wasn't doing it on purpose at the time; she just respected her mother enough not to practice nor discuss in front of her mother what she knew in Maria's eyes, was now considered bad behavior.

The five all had graduated in the top percentile of the senior class earlier that year and they had benefited from their academic skills. Tracey and Rolanda had obtained scholarships to the University of New Orleans. Dominique would attend as well, although she would have to pay out of pocket. Her parents were proud of her and they promised to pay more than half, but she would have to pay the rest. Rolanda, Tracey and Dominique were still working at the grocery store where Dominique was now an assistant manager. She was put in charge of making the weekly schedules and that was the hand she fanned with during this period of time because it was easy for her to schedule herself and her two friends off at the same time quite often and they could all work together as well.

Rolanda, Tracey and Dominique were all planning on majoring in Broadcasting. Tracey and Dominique also wanted to take a minor course in Journalism at the University of New Orleans, or U.N.O. for short. Rolanda, with Broadcasting as her major, was planning on taking a minor course in Political Science. All three young women had hopes of obtaining a job in the radio industry someday and they were taking classes they knew would benefit them in their career endeavors.

Lubby was still working at the pet shop inside Lake Forest Mall where she was promoted to assistant manager a week after graduation. She had also gotten a scholarship to Southern University of New Orleans, S.U.N.O. for short and was planning on majoring in Business Administration. After working at the pet shop for almost a year, Lubby became interested in owning her own business. She loved pets and she saw how much money could be made from selling domesticated and exotic animals. She was becoming an ambitious young woman with entrepreneurial desires and had the dream of someday owning her own pet shop.

Brianna, meanwhile, was still hustling with Tank during the summer of '89. The night of Lubby's block party in August of '88, Brianna had left with Tank and the two had sex that night and had become a couple. The two of them, along with Bobby, Gerald, and White Boy Mike were now supplying East Shore and Gaslight Square with crack rock and ounces of cocaine. They were balling. Brianna, at age seventeen had even purchased a pink Suzuki sidekick jeep with chrome Daytona rims and pink and white leather interior with a thumping Alpine sound system. Brianna and her mother often engaged in heated debates over what she was doing to earn money.

Ms. Stanford feared greatly for her daughter, but Brianna was just making too much money to exit the game. She and her mother clashed often, but just over a month after she graduated high school in June of '89, things had come to a head. Brianna reflected on that day, which transpired only a couple of months earlier, as she drove her jeep down Curran Boulevard towards Mike's' trailer home on this hot August evening.

June 1989

"Brianna we need ta' talk." Ms. Stanford said as she and her daughter sat at the table eating breakfast.

Brianna sat her fork down as she said and leaned back in her chair. She knew what her mother was preparing to say, so she beat her to the draw. "Momma, I told you Tank bought me that jeep."

"You think I'm stupid, Brianna? Okay even if Thaddeus did buy you that jeep, what did you do to earn it? And how did Thaddeus pay for it?"

"You already know I'm having sex."

"So you're a high-priced hooker now?"

"No momma! Damn, man! I can't have nothin' without you thinkin' I'm doing somethin' bad!"

"It's not just the jeep, Brianna. It's the diamond earrings, the big medallions, the Gucci shoes and purses, the leather outfits. It's as if *you* work for N.A.S.A. now!"

"Just because I like nice things that don't make me a bad person, momma."

"You're right it doesn't. I know I spoiled you when you were younger; but if you think back, I always, *always* worked for the things I wanted to see you with." Ms. Stanford said as Brianna began to cry at the table.

Brianna knew her mother was right. She would tell herself over and over again that she was wrong for selling drugs; but she really didn't want a job. Bri wasn't lazy, she just learned early on from Black Mike that she could make easy money selling cocaine and she didn't have to answer to no one nor did she have to punch a time clock like her four friends had to do. To Brianna, selling drugs was if she had her own business. True enough, she was nearly killed a couple of years ago, but the operation Black Mike had was a 'Mickey Mouse outfit', as Tank often called it. Brianna had seen how Tank operated under the radar and she walked in his footsteps. She trusted Tank's judgment and felt protected at all times by the twenty-one year old gangster in which she'd fallen in love with. No matter what her mother said that day, Brianna wasn't going to stop doing what she was doing.

"I thought you wanted to sing, Brianna."

"I do momma. And when I get enough money I'm gone open my own recording studio and do my album."

"This ain't the way, baby." Ms. Stanford said as her eyes watered and she got up from her seat and walked around to Brianna's side of the table and held on to her daughter. "I'm scared for you, child. I know you're smart, but jail ain't for you. Your father died when you were four and God knows I miss that man. You're all I have, Brianna. And you mean the world to me, baby. I almost lost you once. If something were to happen again, you may not get a second chance."

"Momma, I'm eighteen. I'm grown now and it's my choice what I do with my life. I didn't want to tell you like this, but me and Tank moving in together next week."

Ms. Stanford stepped back from her daughter and her eyes welled up as she shook her head and walked slowly from the kitchen. "You've hear nothing I've said and your mind is already made up. I'm losing you to the streets." she said lowly. "Where did I go wrong, God?"

"It's not your fault momma!" Brianna shouted as her mother walked from the kitchen throwing her hands up into air as if she was defeated.

Brianna stared at the empty room for a minute before she got up and headed out the door.

****

Bri snapped back to her current state just as she pulled up in front of Mike's trailer home, forgetting about the conversation she'd had with her mother because she knew it would only distract her from her game and put her off base. She grabbed her bag and walked up to Mike's door and tapped lightly and was quickly let in. When she entered the trailer, Bri had to do a double take at the outfit White Boy Mike was sporting on this hot summer day in August of '89. Normally, Mike, although he made good money from selling drugs and had a low rider Nissan pick-up truck with the top cut off and his own trailer home and paid his own bills, he often dressed in cut up jeans and an old faded rock and roll tee shirt with worn out sneakers. But on this day, Mike had on an evergreen pair of Polo jeans, an evergreen and white striped polo shirt and a white pair of leather polo tennis shoes. He was fresh from head to toe with a neatly trimmed beard and moused up hair right down to his fresh white sneakers.

Briana eyed Mike and dapped him off and complemented him on his new clothes. When he smiled, Brianna could see the four gold teeth on the top row of his teeth. She covered her face with her hands. "Oh, Oh! Oh, Oh! You learnin'! You learnin', white boy!" she stated as she laughed.

"You see me, huh?" Mike asked as he stepped back and let Bri into his home.

Brianna walked towards the kitchen in the trailer where Mike had pots and pans set up on the table as she pulled out a kilogram of cocaine from a leather duffel bag. The two were planning on rocking up the kilo, which was stolen by Tank, Bobby and Gerald the night before. As they did so, there was another knock on the door and the two quickly grabbed their nine millimeter Berettas and stepped into the living room and asked who was there. They heard Tank's voice and Brianna opened the door as Mike returned to his duties inside the kitchen. Tank was followed by Bobby and Gerald and they, too, grew excited when they saw Mike in his new clothes. The five sat down and waited for Mike to finish cooking the cocaine so they could break it down into rocked up ounces and twenty dollar pieces.

It was taking longer than usual to cook the product so

Brianna told the boys that she had to go and pick up her friends from work.

"Here," Tank said as he threw his car keys to Brianna, knowing she was going to need the extra room for her four friends.

"What we gone ride in, Tank?" Bobby asked.

"The jeep, dog."

"It's pink!" Bobby stated as he sat at the table with a huge pile of crack cocaine in front of him.

"And?" Gerald asked as he opened packets of razor blades and small plastic baggies.

"It's fuckin' *pink*! Man that's gay! Four niggas ridin' in a pink jeep!" Bobby stated angrily.

"Man, who give a fuck what color it is? So long as we get to the damn buffet!" Tank stated as Brianna turned and walked out the door.

The gang was all planning on going to the buffet to celebrate Lubby's eighteenth birthday and Lubby's girls were planning to have a surprise party by Tank and Brianna's house which was in Chalmette, not too far from East Shore. The surprise party would become a private affair, however, because Tank didn't want anyone outside of the crew knowing where he and Brianna laid their heads at night. Tank knew Brianna and her friends wouldn't tell, and he trusted Gerald, Bobby, and White Boy Mike more than he trusted Brianna's friends. When Brianna began to make out a list of people to invite the week before, Tank pointed out to her that they had a nice home with nice things and were deep in the game.

"If people knew where we stayed, you think they wouldn't break in this mutherfucka, Bri? Maybe even do it why we home and rob and kill our ass thinking we got cocaine in this bitch. We can't let no outsiders know where we live, Bri! Come on, now! Be smart! Let's have a li'l small party with just our closest friends. Play some spades, drink, smoke, whatever, just a private affair, ya' dig?" Tank said.

Brianna reflected on what Tank said to her a week earlier as she drove his car towards the grocery store and realized he was dead on that day. It was one of the things Brianna loved about Tank—his keen, fore-sighted ability. In Brianna's eyes, Tank was not only a good hustler—he was a smart and thoughtful *man*. Unbeknownst to Brianna at the time, Tank, although he meant what he said about not allowing outsiders to find their 'duck off' as he called it, had ulterior motives about the private party.

Gerald was planning on taking Lubby's virginity on this night. He knew what to do to take Lubby's virginity and he had every intention on succeeding and had never lacked confidence. White Boy Mike, however, had gone the whole twelfth grade year trying to bed eighteen year-old Tracey Sanchez without success and he was no longer content with just eating her out and then receiving a hand job, something he had been doing for over three years.

Mike had lost his virginity to a crack head earlier that year and he would continue to pay the twenty dollars it cost to have sex with many a young girl who was hooked on the drug. That was the only way he was getting any action, but Mike wanted Tracey something awful, and Mike knew he couldn't offer Tracey $20 for a round of sex. He would blow it if he went at Tracey in that manner, and he knew that to be fact. Mike was tired of having to use condoms to get a blow job or fuck a young girl, and even an older woman to gain relief, and although he could now have just about any white girl, and a few black girls he wanted as he had grown taller and more muscular and his acne had even cleared up, Tracey Sanchez was the object of his desire and she had been so ever since he was fifteen. Only eighteen year-old Mike couldn't figure out what he was doing wrong. He expressed his concerns to Tank, Bobby, and Gerald a month earlier as they sat bagging up a kilo and a half of cocaine when the conversation the boys were having shifted in his direction.

"So what's up with you and Kitty?" Gerald asked Bobby as he tapped Tank on the leg as they sat at the table along with Mike that day back in July.

Tank and Gerald had never even seen Kitty, Bobby's

supposedly girlfriend, and they often mocked him, saying he didn't have an ole lady.

"Man, that bitch tripping today. Sayin' she on her period."

"So she ain't comin' to the lakefront?" Gerald asked.

"Nah, man."

"This like the third or fourth time in the row," Gerald remarked as he wrapped a rocked up ounce of cocaine in Saran wrap.

"I think she scared of us, Gee," Tank said as he laughed slightly. "Every time we have something and invite Kitty she got a medical issue or some shit."

"Don't talk about my baby like that, brer." Bobby said lowly as he stuffed rocks into a small baggy.

"Alright homeboy. So what's up with you and Tracey, Mike? You hit that big fine motherfucka yet?" Tank then asked.

"Man, Tracey, she, I think she playin' hard ta' get."

"Hard ta' get? She take her panties off for you all the time! Just ram ya' dick inside that mutherfuckin' pussy next time she do! When she feel that *cock*, she ain't gone *stop*!" Tank said as he laughed at the rhyme he made.

"I know that's right," Bobby said through a smile of contentment that went unbeknownst to Tank, Gerald and Mike.

"I tried, Tank," Mike said, "but she won't let me. She say she not ready. I asked Bri about it and she told me change my style. I don't know what that mean, but I been nice to Tracey ever since and that ain't workin'."

"Style? Oh, yea man! Change your style." Tank said as Mike looked at him in a confused manner.

"It's like this, Mike—you makin' all this money, got your own crib, but you dress fucked up! You all dirty and shit like a hobo. Tracey a fly girl, brer. She ain't gone let everybody know she sleeping with a dirty white boy!"

"Then why she let me do what I do to her? Eat her out all the time, I mean?"

"'Cause maybe she like it? You ever thought about that shit? She getting her pussy licked? And all she gotta give you is a *hand job*? Nigga please! Tracey comin' out on top! You just gotta step up ya' game, Mike! Dress better, brer! Do something for Tracey besides lick her down. Take her out, buy her something! Show her that you more than a fuckin' boy toy! Take charge of your ole lady because that's exactly what the fuck she is! Tracey *your* girl!" Tank said as he smiled at Mike and continued to speak. "Believe me, if Tracey wanted to have sex, she coulda been done that shit! She like *your* ugly white ass—but you ain't steppin' up! She ain't gone tell you what you need ta' do for you ta' fuck her! *You* have ta' figure it out —and I'm 'bouta' lay it out for you, brother man. We going shopping when we get through baggin' this shit up, nigga. I'm gone show you what you need ta' do to bone Tracey Sanchez. We gone get you some new clothes, some gold teeth, change that raggedly ass Jon Bon Jovi hair style and everything. You need the baller package for Tracey. You got the money to do it —and I got the skills to teach your ass. You gone be all right White Boy Mike." Tank ended.

Mike reflected on what Tank told him and took his advice, and over the next few weeks, with the help of Tank, he bought a new wardrobe and sneakers, a gold medallion with his name in it, and the day before Brianna had brought the kilogram over to his trailer, Tank had taken Mike to *First and Claiborne Dentistry* where Mike had gotten four gold teeth in the upper portion of his mouth. Now, with his new look, Mike was ready to see if this 'baller package' Tank had hipped him to was worth the effort.

The boys were nearly done bagging their product when Brianna called and told Tank that she and the girls were headed to Shoney's buffet.

"Yea, we gone be done in a minute. Look, don't tell your girls about Mike. It's a surprise for Tracey." Tank stated.

Brianna agreed and the four males quickly bagged the product, and hid it in the walls of Mike's trailer. As they walked towards Brianna's jeep, Bobby sighing the whole time, Tank patted Mike on the back. "You ready to fuck that girl

243

tonight?" he asked Mike.

"Nothing beat a failure but a try, Tank." Mike replied.

"Oh you ain't failing! You ain't gone fail nigga! You got the money green fit on, gold teeth shining, nigga ya' smelling good, all you need to do is run ya' mouth, homeboy! Lay ya' game down, Mike, and she comin' out them drawls! Believe what Tank telling ya'! Baller packages don't fail ever!" Tank said as he got behind the wheel of Brianna's jeep and the four headed towards Shoney's.

Mike was sincerely hoping Tank was right this night and was eager to put what he had learned from his friend over the past few weeks to use because he really wanted to get inside of Tracey. Would Tank's idea earn him favor? Did Tank really help out? Or did he merely waste a lot of money, time and effort on a young woman who seemingly had no interest in him what so ever? Mike pondered those questions as he rode inside the jeep towards Shoney's to meet up with the girl he loved more than life itself.

CHAPTER 21

MAN AND WOMAN

Tank, Bobby, Gerald, and Mike walked through Shoney's parking lot, Mike repeatedly asking if he was fresh, and walked into the restaurant where they saw the five already seated at a large table with Calvin inside the packed restaurant. They girls noticed Tank and his boys when they entered the waiting section and began yelling for them to join the table as they had enough seats for everybody.

When Tracey saw Mike she did a double take. *"Hmmm,"* she said to herself, *"the brothers startin' to rub off on him I see."*

Mike spoke to everybody and asked if he could sit next to Tracey and she kindly obliged.

He sat beside her and said nervously, "Hey, Trace, umm, I got you a li'l somethin'."

"What's this?"

"It's umm, it's a Phil Collins cassette tape and a bottle of Chanel perfume." Mike replied as he handed a small gift bag to Tracey. "My favorite song is on there."

"What song is that, Mike?"

Even though she had on her work uniform which consisted of a pair of black jeans and a green smock with a white shirt and sneakers, to Mike, Tracey was the most beautiful thing he had ever seen in his life. A work of art she was. Her dark eyes were sexy to him and he loved the way her hair hid a portion of her face and flowed gently to the nape of her neck. Her breasts were perfect, her skin caramel, toned and smooth, looking ever so soft to the touch. This was Mike's dream woman. He would do whatever it took to make Tracey his own.

"I like One More Night—'cause whenever we together and it's time to go, I always wish for one more night with you. To be honest, when I'm with you, I don't want it to end."

Tracey smiled. She could see Mike was stepping up and she was excited that he was getting on her level. Tracey had stopped viewing Mike as nerdy when she found out he was in the game. But he still didn't dress right and he seemed afraid to ask for what he wanted from her, even though Tracey already knew. Mike had not a clue, but Tracey cared for him; she knew she could have any man she wanted, but she was secretly waiting on Mike, and now he was coming around. For Tracey it wasn't about the money Mike was making, although it wasn't a bad asset either; she simply knew Mike loved her and that's what she wanted in a man; but she also wanted to be sure the man would stick around and just not use her for sex. She laughed to herself as she reflected on those thoughts because, after all, she had kept Mike around for that sole purpose. She made up her mind right then and there to be fair to Mike and give him a chance to step up, without the help of Tank, Bobby, and Gerald, the three people she knew were responsible for his transformation.

"Thank you, Mike." Tracey responded in a sweet voice as she leaned over and kissed his cheek, causing Mike to blush a little.

Tank saw what transpired and he smiled and kissed Brianna as he got up from the table to enjoy the buffet, happy over the way things were going for Mike.

"Hey, Tank, throw me a biscuit, homeboy!" Bobby yelled aloud.

Tank threw a biscuit to Bobby, but he threw it a little too hard. Rolanda, who was sitting next to Bobby talking to Dominique, jumped when the biscuit bounced from Bobby's hands and struck her in the face. Bobby laughed as Rolanda calmly got up and grabbed a bowl of bean soup. When she came back and sat down, she purposely spilled some of its contents into Bobby's lap.

"Ohh shit! That's hot Rolanda!" Bobby yelled as he grabbed his thigh.

"You tryna put somebody eye out with them damn brick biscuits!"

Bobby said nothing as he got from the table and grabbed a plate full of mash potatoes and fried chicken and sat back down. Everybody was expecting Bobby to do something, but he politely and quietly ate his food. When everything settled down, however, Bobby grabbed a handful of mash potatoes and rubbed it in Rolanda's face. Brianna, who was now at the food bar, saw what happened and she hurled a baked potato at Bobby and it struck him in the chest. Rolanda laughed aloud and patrons began pointing at the scene that was beginning to unfold.

Brianna, wanting to further instigate the festivities then took a cup of ranch dressing and splashed it on Tank. Tracey was laughing in her seat right up until the point in which she was hit in the back of the head with a wallop of baked macaroni flung at her by Gerald.

"Ohhh! No he didn't!" Tracey said under her breath as she got up and made her way to the buffet table. "This boy done fucked my hair up!"

Lubby then got up and grabbed a spoonful of tomato sauce and wiped it on Gerald's shirt. He stood surprised as he stared at his ruined Polo.

"Hey, y'all bouta' get us put out of here!" Dominique yelled. Seconds later, she was hit in the face with a whipped cream cupcake thrown at her by Tank.

Calvin then got up and grabbed a handful of string beans and flung them at Tank.

"Oh you tryna help ya' ole lady, huh?" Tank yelled as he grabbed slices of pound cake and began throwing them at everyone sitting at the group's table. "Food fight!" Tank yelled aloud as he began grabbing any and every item he could get his hands on and flung it at the group.

The entire group, with the exception of Dominique, rushed the food bar and began flinging food at one another. Laughter abounded amongst the friends as they splattered one another with various food items. Dominique was with the wait staff trying to restore order until she was hit in the face with a piece of cake by Rolanda, who was holding a cherry-vanilla cake in her hand while grabbing gobs of the sweet treat and just flinging it everywhere. Before long, the entire restaurant was engaged in an all-out food fight. White couples, Vietnamese, and other Black families were yelling and laughing aloud; they were ruining Shoney's thanks to the young group of friends who sat right beside the food bar and had gotten up and started the mayhem.

After about five minutes, every item on the buffet was either on the floor or stuck to someone's clothes and skin. The friends ran out the door after Tank and Gerald threw stacks of twenties at the wait staff.

"Sorry 'bout the mess, y'all!" Tank stated as he dashed out the door and jumped into his car and sped away with the rest of the group.

Later on that night, after everyone had cleaned themselves up, everybody went over to Tank and Brianna's home and continued to enjoy themselves. They played spades, listened to music and had some liquor before they all decided to go their respective ways. Calvin and Dominique left in Calvin's car. Tracey and Mike left in Brianna's jeep and Gerald and Lubby left in Tank's car. Rolanda slept in one of Brianna's spare rooms and Bobby went to visit his friend Kitty.

The crew was in a world of their own on this night. Love was in the air for most of the friends, but nowhere was that intangible warm and fuzzy emotion more pervasive than it was with Lubby and Gerald, who'd taken his woman to the downtown Marriott Hotel so the two of them could have a special night together. Lubby was impressed with the huge and luxurious suite that lay on the 46th floor. It had a huge king-sized bed, soft, thick carpet, a mini bar and a stunning view of the New Orleans skyline and the Mississippi River Bridge.

"Gerald this is amazing, baby. You did all this for me?" Lubby asked as she stared out the huge window looking down on Canal Street, where the people and cars looked like little ants moving about as she sipped a stem glass full of Dom Perignon.

"This all for you, Lubby. The view is pretty, but not as beautiful as you are, baby." Gerald answered as he walked up behind Lubby and grabbed her waist and drew her close.

Lubby smiled and closed her eyes as she sat her champagne glass down. She knew what Gerald wanted, and she was ready to give in to the man she loved. She unzipped her all-in-one dress and flinched her shoulders and the garment fell to the carpet. "Unhook me Gerald." she requested softly as she stared out at the city lights.

When her bra was removed, Lubby turned and faced Gerald. She stared him in the eyes as she stepped out of her dress and removed her shoes and panties. Gerald could only sigh and grow hard as he admired the specimen of woman that stood before him. Lubby Williams was the epitome of gorgeous. She was on the slender side, but had curves in all the right places. Her silky brown hair matched a perfect pair of pretty brown eyes as her light-skin glowed in the city lights.

"Be gentle?" she asked lowly.

Gerald took in Lubby's 5'6" 135 pound physique. He eyed her luscious pink nipples and stacked brown hair, her brown eyes, which were full of not lust, but love. He wanted her, and she wanted him. Gerald undressed himself and Lubby stared at his 5'10" 185 pound muscular frame. She reached out and touched his copper-toned skin, running her hands across his chest and gently stroking his face. Gerald grabbed Lubby's hand and she followed him willingly to the bathroom and waited patiently as he turned on the shower and evened the water's temperature. He then helped her into the shower and the two stood under the warm water hugging one another close as their bodies moistened under the warm and soothing liquid. Gerald leaned into Lubby, placed one hand against the marble shower wall and cupped her chin and drew her in for a kiss. She wrapped her arms around his neck and the two kissed passionately underneath the flowing water. Lubby couldn't help herself, she just had to feel Gerald. She reached down and clutched his throbbing member and looked him in the eyes as she stroked him softly. She had such soft hands to Gerald, who adored her every touch and slow stroke. He soon stepped back and placed one of Lubby's legs on the side of the tub and kissed his way down her body. She moaned as he licked the nape of her neck and kissed her earlobes. She grabbed the back of his head as he kissed her navel, and she gasped aloud when his tongue touched her clitoris. Lubby held his head in place with one hand as she rotated her hips slowly, closed her eyes and bit the index finger of her other hand whilst moaning as she climaxed quietly.

Gerald stood and he and Lubby cleansed one another and the two of them stepped from the shower and dried one another off. Gerald then took the lead and Lubby followed her man to the king-sized bed where he lay down her down on her back. Lubby spread herself for Gerald as he placed on a condom beside the bed.

"You don't need that for me."

"Why not? You don't want a baby right now do you?"

"I'm on the pill now, and I trust you Gerald."

Gerald removed the condom and moved in between Lubby's legs and placed his member at her entrance. She was dripping sweet nectar, her virgin pussy ripe for penetration. As Gerald leaned forward to enter paradise, Lubby stared him in the eyes and said, "Stop doing what you doing to me," as her eyes filled with tears.

"Run that by me again," Gerald replied, quoting Lubby's signature quote.

Lubby laughed lowly and said, "I know you slept with other girls before—like that girl Shantrell. Tonight, look me in the eyes and tell me you won't cheat on me no more." she said as she stared intensely into Gerald's eyes as her tears ran down the corners of her eyes.

Lubby was by no means foolish. She knew Gerald was

having sex with other females from time to time because she had found many so condom packages inside his car on numerous occasions, but said nothing because she wasn't ready for sex. Now that she was ready, she wanted to be sure that the man she loved would stop sleeping with other girls once she gave in. At this point, however, Lubby knew any man in his right mind would agree to knock his own mother out cold just to get what he wanted, but Lubby knew Gerald, maybe better than Gerald knew himself. The eighteen year-old could tell whenever Gerald was lying to her, something he rarely did, except when it came to the business he was involved in. She stared into his eyes deeply and intensely, scanning Gerald's soul as her brown eyes darted back and forth.

"Gerald, tell me you only love me and me only." Lubby whispered inside the tranquil room as Gerald lay positioned in between her thighs.

"I only want to be with you Lubby. It's you and me forever, baby."

Lubby said nothing as she continued to read Gerald's eyes, her body emanating heat from within her innermost parts. She believed Gerald, she really believed in the man. She also knew just by looking deeply into his eyes that he would do her no more wrong. Lubby believed in her heart, in her soul, that Gerald would not go behind her back with another woman from this night forth. With that in mind, she reached down and grabbed Gerald's aching member and placed it at her entrance and slid her hips up and moaned aloud as hard dick pierced her body for the first time.

"Make love to me. Please. Make love to me Gerald." Lubby panted as Gerald slid further and further into her crevice. "Ooohh Jesus, that feels, feels good. So good." Lubby sighed before she let out a raspy moan and her body convulsed under Gerald's weight. "Oh my God! God! Ohhh God!" She cried out through another orgasm.

Lubby swallowed hard, her breath now ragged and her voice a few pitches lower. She craved more, she thrust forward again and this time Gerald began a rhythm that took the both of them to new depths of pleasure that neither wanted to share with no one else. On this night, Gerald Huntley and Lubby Williams had become man and woman. The two made love repeatedly that night and Lubby enjoyed every minute of it. The way Gerald handled her, gentle at first, and then pushing her legs as far back as they would go and driving so deep into her she could feel his dick poking her spine. The way he sat her atop him and held her waist as he thrust upwards before he pulled her to him and kissed her deeply as she rocked back and forth, and when Gerald placed her on the edge of the bed and stood behind her and slow stoked her while rubbing her clitoris, Lubby squirted clear liquid all over his stomach and chest. It was a magical night that had transformed the two into totally different people; they drifted off to sleep as a happy couple in deep love.

The next morning, after another passionate round of lovemaking, Gerald had given Lubby her next birthday gift which was gold roped medallion with her name attached to it and a promise ring to put on her left forefinger. The jewelry cost Gerald $3200 dollars, and Lubby cherished it. She loved the medallion, but the promise ring was the best gift she had ever received as she now knew was going to become a wife someday.

"Baby, can I give that donkey rope to Kilo?" Lubby asked Gerald excitedly as she sat up on the bed admiring her ring.

"I don't see why not. He need a gangster collar. Them donkey ropes 'bouta play out anyway. That's a cool ass dog you got."

"That's all our dog. Kilo my bestest friend!" Lubby joked.

"And what am I?"

"My angel."

"No, Lubby, you my angel." Gerald replied as the two melted into one another's arms and slept in during the morning before checking out later that afternoon.

After they left the Marriott, Gerald had driven Tank's car back to Tank and Brianna's home in Chalmette. They saw Brianna's jeep in the yard and figured Mike and Tracey had returned Brianna's jeep; but Tracey was by Brianna's house by herself this afternoon. Lubby and Gerald exited Tank's car and they both stared one another in the eyes seriously. Lubby's eyes spoke volumes. She knew what she and Gerald had was special and Gerald was thinking the same thing. The two smiled as Lubby walked slowly around the front of the car and hugged her man. Gerald wrapped his arm around Lubby's waist and the two walked up the driveway to the modest three bedroom white wooden cottage home on the corner, the both of them realizing that they both had fallen in love last night.

Meanwhile, inside the house, Brianna had just heard the story of how Tracey had given in to Mike the night before. When Brianna asked where Mike was, Tracey told her that she had worn him out.

"He at his trailer, laid out on his back snoring, Bri! Girl, I *took* that dick from that mutherfucka last night, ya' heard me! He was calling my name, Bri! Shiit, niggas can't fuck with Tracey! I got 'em right here!" Tracey said as she held up her pinky finger. "Mike a good lover too. I think I love him, Bri. 'Cause he treat me like a queen. He told me that last night. He said I was his queen. Mike sweet!"

"Rolanda said you was gone love that dude three years ago, and now it's come to pass." Brianna said as she on her sofa with her legs tucked under her body smiling at her friend.

"I know, but I don't care no more. We good together. I just told him not to get me pregnant, and even with a condom on he said I was the best piece of pussy he ever had!" Tracey replied as Brianna burst into laughter. "For real, Bri. You know condoms take away a lot of feeling. I got a man who loves me." Tracey said proudly as Brianna got up to answer the doorbell.

Brianna let Lubby and Gerald in and she and Tracey watched as Lubby bounced through the door. They both knew what was up by the glow of Lubby's face.

"Virgin no more huh, Lubby?" Brianna asked.

Lubby just smiled and plopped down on Brianna's sofa and showed her friends her medallion and promise ring as Rolanda came out of the bedroom having just wakened. Rolanda sat down with her friends and the girls talked about the night before as Gerald went into the den to chat with Tank.

Lubby, Tracey, and Rolanda looked over at Kilo, who'd spent the night over to Bri and Tank's house, as he barked loudly. The husky pit bull went into the kitchen and retrieved his empty dog dish and it looked as if he flung it over towards the sofa. He then walked back into the kitchen and returned to the living room dragging his bag of dog food.

"Look at this here," Brianna said as she and her girls laughed aloud. "He? He look like he sayin' 'y'all bitches need to feed me'."

"That's exactly what he sayin'. That dog human I'm tellin' ya'!" Rolanda stated as she got up to fry hamburgers for everybody, including Kilo.

As the three females and Kilo prepared lunch, the girls all wondered where Dominique was at this time. They hung out by Brianna's house all day figuring Dominique was running errands, but when night fell, they still hadn't heard from neither her nor Calvin. The girls grew worried when Mrs. Franz called looking for the eighteen year-old shortly after dark. Gerald called his mother's house to see if they were together, but she hadn't seen Dominique or heard from Calvin and she, too, was getting worried about her son and his girlfriend. The next morning, no one still hadn't heard from the two; so Calvin's mother, and Mrs. Franz both put in a missing person's report for their respective child when night fell as they hadn't been seen or heard from in over two days.

Dominique's friends had an idea what was going on, and their thoughts were confirmed four days after Dominique and Calvin went missing. Dominique and Calvin knew they would have problems with their parents once they learned what they'd done, so they gathered all their friends over to Tank and Brianna's house and announced that they had eloped, having gotten married the day after Lubby's birthday. Their friends congratulated them, but at the same time, everybody knew Calvin and Dominique had rushed to get married just to have sex. They judged neither of them, but they knew things would get worse before it got better because both of their respective parents were sure to throw a monkey wrench into whatever plans the two had for their future. Calvin made his way home to tell his parents, and Dominique, after praying with her girlfriends did the same.

****

"You did what, Dominique?" Mrs. Franz asked stunned the moment her daughter broke the news.

"I got married, momma. Me and Calvin."

"I know *who* you married, child! The question is *why*? And the answer is 'because I wanted to have *sex*'!"

"We love each other, momma!"

"That may be so, but see you—I know you! You were more concerned about having sex than mapping this whole thing out."

"Momma you act like I don't—like *we* don't know what we doing."

"The two of you don't, Dominique! You and Calvin are not prepared for all the intricacies involved in a marriage! And the pleasures of sex will wear off quickly when the bills have to be paid!"

"I was thinking we can stay here until—"

"See that's mistake number one! Who said you and Calvin were going to stay *here*?" Dominique looked at her mother in shock. "That's right! You a married woman now! Now, unless Calvin's parents agree to allow you to stay at *their* home, which I seriously doubt, you have only six months to be out on your own! And no, *Calvin* will not spend a night in this house! You wanna do what married people do? You get your own place to do it in!"

"Momma? You puttin' me out?" Dominique asked through tears.

"You put yourself out Dominique." Mrs. Franz said as she began to cry. "What's gotten into you, girl?"

"I'm in love momma. Can't you understand that?"

Mrs. Franz felt sorry for her daughter, but Dominique would have to feel the full impact of her decision. The disappointed mother walked over to her daughter and the two embraced in the middle of the kitchen as Mrs. Franz looked down at her daughter and spoke softly but sternly, "If you are not out in six months, you will pay your way around here. I'm giving you time prepare yourself and to also think about *exactly* what it is you have done, Dominique Huntley. I guarantee that you will find out that marriage is more than just stripping off your clothes and making sweet love. You now have a husband to take care of, a job to keep, college to attend, and eventually, a home, complete with bills to pay. Welcome to the real world, baby." Antoinette ended as she clutched her daughter's hand tightly before letting it go and walking out of the kitchen.

Later on in the evening, Dominique and Calvin, having decided to rent a motel room for the night, were lying in bed discussing their situation. Calvin's father had nearly kicked him out of their home that very night. He had less than a month to be on his own.

"You're not going to be lying up in this home with no woman! Married or not Calvin!" Calvin's father stated angrily as his mother sat at the kitchen table crying her heart out. "Now, what you will do is pack all your belongings and be gone by the end of this month!"

"The end of the month? Dad I just started working full time!"

"And ya' married full time as well! You now have a woman to support—*man*! Not ta' mention if it wasn't for me putting in a good word at the marketing firm you wouldn't have a job! And even then, you just a mail clerk! See how ya' feel when you cash your check and find out you barely have enough for food and rent! You in the real world now! You can't come home and kick your shoes off and listen ta' Jazzy while you make sweet talk on the telephone! This here is real son!"

"I did it right and you still giving me hell! Gerald do all that dirt and you—"

"'Cause he don't do it here! Gerald never asked me to let him have a woman in this house overnight! And you asking me to let *you*—and your *wife*—live *here*! Ain't no way that's gonna happen, son! I'm giving you the same ultimatum I gave your brother! Rent due on the sixth at the latest, be somewhere so you can pay your *own* rent Calvin!"

"I ain't gotta put up with this!" Calvin snapped as he began walking towards the front door.

"You leaving now? Grab your stuff! Oh wait! You ain't pay for nothing in that room besides the radio you got in there! You doing right! Because all you have is the clothes on your back! And wherever ya' staying tonight, you need to be thinking about what you gone do to pay your own rent next month! If not, the covenant house got a room!" Calvin's father ended as he watched his son walk out of the door and get into his light grey '87 Toyota Corolla and pull away from the curb.

As the two lay in the motel bed reliving their confrontations, Dominique asked Calvin how much money he had saved.

"I don't have nothing. I spent it all in Biloxi."

"Nothing? Nothing? Calvin! We have to make a move, *soon*!"

"Well, you got six months Dominique."

"And what are you going to do?"

"I figure I can stay with Gerald."

"Lubby moving in with Gerald. Anyway he got a one bedroom, and before long they're gonna be moving out of that place."

"What about Brianna and Tank house?"

"Calvin, baby," Dominique said as she sat up and straddled her man, "we supposed to be on our own. Gerald and Lubby are man and woman, Brianna and Tank are man and woman. Tracey still at home, Rolanda still at home, and if they did have a place, *we* are man and woman. I got twelve hundred saved. We can find a place with that."

"We still need lights, water, furniture, phone, TV, food."

"We need lights, water, and food right now. The rest of the stuff will come later." Dominique retorted.

"You can't move without furniture."

"We don't have a choice! I'm not gonna be going here and there, sleeping by this person and that person just to be with you, Calvin. If we're gonna do this for real, we're gonna do it on our own, as husband and wife, because I want to do it with you, and you only. I don't want support from nobody but my husband." Dominique stated as she eased down Calvin's thighs and began to unbuckle his jeans.

Calvin's member popped out of his jeans and Dominique was prepared to go down on him, but Calvin stopped her.

"What, you want me fully undressed?" Dominique asked as she got up remove her all-in-one dress and two-inch heels.

Calvin sat up and took off his clothes and Dominique again began to drop to her knees beside the bed. She wanted Calvin's member in her mouth. She wanted to do it the night they were married, but Calvin merely took her in the missionary position.

Calvin picked Dominique up and guided her towards the bed.

"What's wrong? Let me suck it for you."

Calvin smiled at Dominique and he kissed her passionately on the lips, something that turned her on to high heaven. Before long Dominique was on her back panting in sheer delight as Calvin took her missionary style. She thrust her petite frame onto his rod, her black hair splayed across her face and her mouth agape. She was a woman possessed as Calvin bought her to orgasm. Dominique wanted more. She pulled off Calvin's member before he came and got on all fours and spread her cheeks for Calvin.

"Lick it for me Calvin!" she moaned huskily. "Lick my pussy from behind."

Dominique moaned with disappointment, then pleasure when she felt Calvin sliding into her from the rear. He held her hips tightly as he thrust back and forth at a rapid and steady pace. Dominique was a petite woman and Calvin stuffed her fully. Calvin, in turn, looked down at the pretty hairless vagina before him and lost control and ejaculated inside of Dominique. She quickly wiggled around when she felt Calvin spurting into her in an attempt to catch some of his semen on her lips and to lick him clean, but Calvin only let her grab his member with her hand and spurted a few more drops onto her chin. Dominique wiped his semen and licked fingers clean as she eyed Calvin seductively. She then went and got a warm towel and cleaned the two of them up and she lay back after cleaning her vagina thoroughly.

"Calvin, can you lick me? Please?" Dominique asked again a few minutes later. She quickly grew disappointed when she heard Calvin breathing heavy; he'd just gone to sleep on her. Dominique then rubbed herself to another orgasm before she, too, drifted off to sleep, somewhat disappointed, but satisfied just the same.

A week later, with the help of their friends, Dominique and Calvin found an apartment in Bunker Hill, not too far from Dominique's job at the grocery store. They had rented a two bedroom, one and a half bath one level apartment that had a small furnished kitchen, a small dining room and a medium-sized living room. It also had a balcony, a fire place and a washer and dryer hook-up in the hallway. It wasn't in the best neighborhood, but the rent was affordable at five hundred a month and Dominique was able to walk to work from there allowing Calvin to use the car to get to his job downtown. The place was close to a bus line as well, so if Dominique had to catch the bus to attend her classes at U.N.O., she only had to walk two blocks to the bus stop.

The newly married couple had a housewarming party two weeks later; and their friends, their parents, as well as their friends' parents, all bought gifts. Calvin's father said he had to be out by the sixth of September, and on the fifth of September, he and Dominique paid the rent to their own place and moved in on the nineteenth. It wasn't perfect, it wasn't big or lavish like Brianna's home, but it was theirs. Their friends and family had bought them a small table and four chairs, a bunch of bathroom accessories, kitchen utensils, pots and pans, and a washing machine. With the six paychecks Dominique and Calvin collected before they moved out, they were able to purchase a bedroom set, a TV and a dryer. The lights were on, the telephone was connected and the water was free. They only had to make groceries, and Dominique and her friends hooked that up the day after the party. Everything had worked out for Dominique and Calvin; they had their own place, were married, Dominique was doing good in school, and both had jobs. Their dream had come true. And by October of '89, Dominique and Calvin's friends and family had no reason to worry about the young married couple because although young and married, they seemed to be doing just fine.

CHAPTER 22

KILO'S MEMOIRS

"Alright now! Hey! Who's that on the radio? Hey! They sayin' fuck the police? Yea! Fuck the mutherfuckin' police! I like that jam right there ladies let me tell ya'! And it has as poignant message for the current generation!"

Lubby and Rolanda were headed over to Lubby's job to pick up her paycheck on a warm October afternoon in 1989. Lubby, who had moved into a new condo near City Park with Gerald, had picked Rolanda up and had stopped to check on her mother before she left East Shore. Cynthia was glad to see her daughter this day and Lubby was glad that her mother was glad to see her; she was even happier to help her mother out by giving her money to pay her bills. Gerald and Lubby were balling, making money hand over fist. Gerald was making good money hustling and he and Lubby were saving money to open her pet shop. Lubby's dream had become Gerald's dream; and because Lubby always had extra money, Cynthia was now nice to her at all times during this period of time. Her friends knew that Lubby was buying her mother's affection, but what could they say? They got along fine with their parents and Lubby had been shitted on all her life by Cynthia. The girls had talked to Lubby about the situation once and she got mad at them, ending the conversation by telling her girls if that's what it took to be close to her mother she was fine with the way things were, and anyway, they always had their had mothers in their life. Lubby's four friends, even though they hated to see her have to buy her mother's affection, had left the situation alone; although whenever Lubby went to see her mother, one or more of her friends was always there; and if they weren't around Kilo was on hand.

Lubby was ecstatic this day because she had gotten a kiss on the cheek by her mother after she had given her mother money to pay her light bill. Rolanda was mad at her for doing so; but in Lubby's mind, isn't that what children are supposed to do? Take care of their parents whenever they are able? She talked about her mother for a good while as they rode towards Calvin's parents' home. Lubby was driving Gerald's new car, which was a convertible white '88 Cadillac short dog. The car was clean with an all-white interior and gold Tru rims and vogue tires and a Sony sound system that shook the ground. Kilo sat in the back seat as the girls listened to N.W.A.'s song *Fuck Tha' Police,* a song they were getting their kicks off of because N.W.A. was saying what many people felt about the law—fuck 'em.

Kilo barked the whole ride as the two girls blasted the music. They got over to Gerald's parents' house and Rolanda quickly went in to grab a crock pot as Dominique was planning to cook red beans the following Saturday for the friends so they could hang out at her place. Dominique had classes this day so she wasn't able to pick it up. Rolanda came out with the crock pot and a thick piece of spam, courtesy of Calvin's mother, and she gave it to Kilo and the dog began chomping on the thick slice. As the two girls rode off, Rolanda rewound *Fuck Tha' Police, but* just before they got in front of Little Woods Elementary School, they were pulled over by the police.

"What the hell they want?" Lubby asked aloud.

"Shiit. Girl, we in this clean ass car, and we blastin' *Fuck tha' police*! Why you think they stopped us, Lubby?" Rolanda asked as she turned down the volume and rubbed Kilo to quiet down the barking dog.

"Alright, so long as we remain calm and don't make any sudden moves we'll be okay! Just don't reach for nothin'!"

The officer walked up to the clean car and asked for driver's license, registration, and proof of insurance and Lubby complied. He told the girls to turn the volume all the way down on the radio and choose a different song to play after they were done as well as he eyed Kilo.

"The fuck you looking at rookie?"

"Kilo be quiet!" Lubby stated as Rolanda grabbed her forehead in dismay.

"Doh! Why did you say kilo?"

"Your dog's name is Kilo," the officer asked.

Rolanda just knew they were about to be searched. A crowd began to form as spectators looked at the scene unfolding. The officer called for back-up and before long, a half dozen police cars were on hand—complete with a K-9 unit.

Kilo caught sight of the dog in the back of a squad car when an officer pulled alongside of Lubby's car.

"What the hell! You five-o, nigga?"

"Yea, ya' got a problem with that? I'm gone search ya' fuckin car, and if you so much as have a crumb of crack in there, I'm runnin' ya' in!"

"Ya' mother has ta' be real proud of you, ya' jive motherfucka! Of all the things ya' coulda been in life, ya' chose to be a fuckin cop? Ya' coulda been a blind human's guide dog, a house pet, a circus clown, anything but a cop!"

"Hey, the snacks are good!"

"I snack all damn day—but ya' don't see me picking up a fuckin badge do ya'? Ya' snitch! And speaking of snacks—I gotta piece of spam right here on the floor. If ya' so much as sniff my piece of spam I'm a fuck ya' over!"

The officer walked in between the two barking dogs and opened his door. Kilo, Lubby and Rolanda were all escorted to the front of the car and the police dog began searching the vehicle.

"That's an illegal search they performing! We got 'em by the balls girls! Even if they find somethin' they can't charge us

with nothing!"

The officers asked for Rolanda's I.D. and she had to retrieve it from the car.

"Rolanda, check and see if that loser ate my fuckin' spam while ya' back there if ya' don't mind!"

As Rolanda walked back to the front of her car with her I.D. card, the police dog hopped from the backseat and Kilo could see clearly that the dog was eating his spam. Lubby was holding Kilo by his gold donkey rope collar and she calmed him down as his barking was drawing more attention. A police officer walked over to Lubby and noticed the gold chain on the snow white pit bull. He then looked back at the fancy convertible white Cadillac and surmised that it was a dope dealer's car. He knew a lot of drug dealers owned pit bulls for fighting purposes and he asked Lubby if she had papers on Kilo.

"Papers! Pa-papers? I'm a fuckin dog! I don't need an I.D. Look I got a collar, that mean I have an owner and that should suffice. My name is Ki-my name is—Freddy Kruger—from Elm Street."

Rolanda had to again calm Kilo down, and when Lubby announced she had no papers for Kilo, the officer told her that he would have to take Kilo to the S.P.C.A.

"The S.P.C.A.? They gone turn me into a bar of soap! Never me! You heard the song rookie, Fuck Tha' Police!"

Lubby and Rolanda screamed for Kilo to come back the moment he broke away from Lubby's grip and ran off into the neighborhood with the police dog in hot pursuit. Kilo disappeared into an apartment complex and the dog followed closely. The fleeing pit bull turned into a narrow alley bordered by wooden fences, well ahead of the police dog, but he suddenly turned around and charged the German Sheppard.

"Son-of-a-bitch ya' ate my spam!"

The two dogs began fighting in the alleyway and Kilo quickly got the better of the Sheppard. He clasped his jaws around the police dog's neck and the dog howled. Kilo could hear police officers getting closer so he dragged the screaming dog three feet and let him fall from his mouth.

"Told ya' not ta' touch my fuckin' spam ya buster ass toy cop! Ya' asked for that shit!"

Kilo disappeared into the complex and ran through a hole in a chain link fence and sprinted through another neighborhood and out of sight from the officers, who were now tending to their wounded animal. After no drugs were found, the police let Rolanda and Lubby go free; although Lubby received a ticket for disturbing the peace. Lubby didn't care about the ticket; she had to find her canine friend because she knew the police would take Kilo to the pound and kill him and test him for rabies if they caught him.

As Lubby and Rolanda rode through the neighborhood searching for Kilo, Kilo was about a half-mile away on the corners of Read and Hayne Boulevard knowing full-well he had to hide out and hide out fast.

"Now, if I cross the levee and walk alongside the railroad tracks, I can hide out whilst I walk back to East Shore. Only I don't know which way is East Shore."

People blew their horns at the heavy-set, muscular, snow white pit-bull as he stood in the median part of the intersection trying to figure out which way was home amidst the swirling traffic.

"Just keep goin' mutherfuckas! Mind ya' fuckin' business! I know what hell I'm doin' over here! Anyways, I'm, I'm on neutral ground here! Ya' can't drive right here anyway! Now, the levee is behind me. I'm staring at Read which is right in front of me and Hayne is to my left and right. Which way is East Shore? Wait a minute. Read is straight ahead and it runs smack dab into interstate ten, now, the hamburger joint by Abramson school is on the left, the mall where Lubby works is on the right after we cross under interstate ten. When we get off the interstate from East Shore, we go, we go, left to get to the hamburger joint and the mall. If I face the same way the car is facing before we turn, my ass end should be pointing to East Shore.

Kilo lined himself up and faced the way he sat inside the car and turned around to look at his rear end but it had suddenly disappeared. He turned again and he still couldn't find his rear end.

"Where's my ass?" Kilo asked himself as he began running around in a circle trying to catch up with his rear end. *"Where's my fuckin' ass? I lost my ass!"*

Cars blew horns and people laughed at the dog that was running around in a circle in the median chasing his own tail.

"Whoa! Slow down big fella! Alright let's try this again. My ass is behind me. I know it's there 'cause I can feel it. Now when I do this again, I'm a just take off in the direction of my ass."

Kilo lined himself again facing Read and then faced the way he sat when he rode with Lubby to the mall and the hamburger stand and he quickly turned around in the opposite direction, ran up the levee and crossed over and walked alongside the tracks headed straight towards East Shore. He was halfway through his journey home when he found himself staring down three stray mixed breed dogs.

"Hey, excuse me fellas, it's been a long day, and I'm just tryna get back to East Shore."

"You can't cross here sonny boy!"

"Son-sonny boy? Hey look here motherfuckas, now, unless ya' prepared for a homemade East Shore beat down, I suggest you step ya' asses aside and let me through!"

The four dogs stood face to face as they growled. Kilo was in the center of his three attackers and he snapped at each one of them to keep them from biting him. He managed to get all three dogs in front of him and that's when they all began to fight. Kilo snapped at two of the dogs, forcing them back, and he quickly grabbed hold of the leader's neck and he yelped aloud. The other two dogs stood back and watched as Kilo dragged the dog three feet and let him fall from his mouth. The dog was still alive so Kilo grabbed his neck again and drug him another three feet and stood in the middle of the railroad tracks as he squeezed the life from the dog's neck. He drug the dog three more feet and let him fall from his mouth in the middle of the rail ties.

"That's the three foot rule! Now, unless ya' wanna end up like this bitch here, I suggest ya' get the fuck from 'round me."

The other two dogs scattered as Kilo charged at them before he turned and continued his trek home. When he got to Lincoln Beach, he crossed back over the levee and ran down the street that led towards Curran Boulevard. Before he got to Curran, however, Kilo noticed a mixed-chow stray walking from the opposite direction.

"Heyyy, there's a piece! Hey sweetie, ya' lookin' for some action?"

"Hey daddy, where ya' going?"

"I'm new to the neighborhood. Give me a tour 'round the world why don't ya'."

"Well come on over and getcha some, sugar!"

Kilo walked over to the dog and sniffed her as she hoisted her rear end into the air and readied herself.

"Hey, hey sweetie, just because we dogs don't mean we have ta' act like one. Let's walk over here to the woods and make ourselves comfortable."

The two dogs walked into the brush that separated East Shore from Calvin's neighborhood and went behind an old couch and the mixed-chow readied herself again for Kilo.

"That's it sweetie. Alright look here, I want ya' to stretch your paws out as far as you can and act like you reaching for something and raise ya' ass up high. Ohh yea that's it sweetie ya nice and tight. What's your name?"

"Candy. And yours?"

"Just call me Freddy. Freddy Kruger from Elm street."

The two dogs separated themselves a few minutes later and Kilo sat down exhausted.

"See ya round, Freddy Kruger from Elm Street."

"Hey you stay back here?"

"Umm hmm, come back anytime Freddy, you alright with this bitch!"

"Yea, I'll be sure ta' do that! Tell ya' friends Freddy on the market."

"Will do lover boy, will do!"

Kilo eventually made his way back to Emory Road. When he got there, he saw Lubby sitting on the hood of Gerald's car crying her heart out. He barked from down the street and Lubby quickly raised her head upon hearing his bark.

"Kilo! Kilo!" Lubby called aloud as she hopped from the car and ran and met her friend halfway with tears in her eyes. "We thought we lost you! God thank you! You all right I see! But we gotta take you back to the vet tomorrow to get you checked out."

"Good, the vet. Just in case that bitch Candy gave me somethin'! Lubby, listen, I whip that police dog's ass for touchin' my spam. That was on GP. I didn't have ta' do that, but it felt good in the process. Even more pressing, I just murked somebody and I really, really, need ta' be put back in Rolanda's yard for the night, sweetie. Come on now."

Lubby took the barking dog into Rolanda's yard and gave him a bath and fed him and she and Rolanda sat in the backyard and waited for the rest of their friends to come by. They all then sat outside that night and just talked girl talk as Kilo slept soundly. The battle weary and sex happy canine had an adventurous day and was looking forward to hitting the streets again in the near future.

As time wore on, Kilo had mated with almost a dozen stray dogs in the neighborhood. He'd figured out how to dig a hole at the back of the gate in Rolanda's yard. He also dug a hole in Rolanda's neighbor's yard and would exit two houses down as that house didn't have a gate. Kilo was having the time of his life and it seemed as if everybody was doing okay as 1990 got underway. But things were about to heat up for Kilo.

In March of 1990, Kilo was home in Rolanda's yard relaxing

as he listened to the five as they talked out in front of Rolanda's home. It was a peaceful, sunny day out and the canine was laying comfortably on his side flapping his tail on occasion while vaguely listening to the girls' conversation about their studies and what was going on in the streets when he heard someone yelling an old name he'd used months ago.

"Freddy Kruger from Elm Street? Show yourself!"

Kilo stood up at attention the exact moment he heard a bitch calling him by his alias name and began growling as he stood on all fours behind Rolanda's gate. *"What the fuck? That sound like Candy nasty ass!"*

"Freddy Kruger from Elm Street you get out here right this minute!"

The five began laughing as they eyed a mixed-chow barking at Kilo from the sidewalk with four puppies standing idly behind her.

"You been claiming every other bitch's babies in the neighborhood except mines. I was your first and you deny your kids?"

"Candy, first of all, don't ever come in front of my fuckin' house again! Second I ain't ya' babies' daddy!"

"Yes you are! You need ta' come back up front and take care of your family, Freddy Krueger from Elm Street!"

"We ain't a fuckin family! Anyway, there's a tiger striped pit bull that hangs up front and them li'l ugly bastards look just like 'em—stripes and all! You was pregnant when I met ya' ass! Get them li'l ugly motherfuckas from in front my house!"

"Girls? What the hell is this right here?" Brianna asked as she eyed the two dogs barking at one another.

It seemed as if the mixed-chow had brought her puppies around and she and Kilo were arguing. The fluffy haired golden brown mixed-chow stood on the sidewalk, with her four mixed-breed puppies standing behind her, barking at Kilo who was locked behind Rolanda's gate.

"Look like she sayin' that's his puppies, girl!" Lubby

answered as she laughed.

"I told y'all dogs can talk!" Rolanda stated.

"Get real! Dogs can't talk! She was just passing by and they started barking at each other." Dominique stated.

"I don't know Dominique," Tracey chimed in as she focused in on the barking canines. "That stray dog came straight over here like she knew exactly where she was going."

"Freddy Krueger from Elm Street come and take care of your babies!"

"Them li'l ugly motherfuckas ain't for me! Look around here! I breed full-bloodied pit bull babies, not no fluffy fucked up looking sons-of-bitches like that! Them ugly motherfuckas ain't mine and I ain't claimin' 'nem! And if ya' bring 'em back around here, I'm a snatch ya' ass outta place and kill all four them li'l ugly bastards and toss 'em in the canal back there one at a time!"

"You talk to me like that Freddy Kruger from Elm Street?"

"Stop, stop calling me Freddy Kruger from Elm Street, alright? That ain't my fuckin' name?"

"What's your name then?"

"It's Freddy ya' bitch you! We got together a time or two and had some fun and that was that! Take ya' ugly babies and get the hell off my block before I kill every last one of you mutherfuckas today!"

"You will take care of your babies one way or the other!"

"What? You gone take me to court? You takin' me to court, bitch? I'll fuck you up you do some crazy shit like that!"

"Freddy you talkin' crazy! All I'm askin' is for you to take care of what's yours!

"When hell freezes over ya' nasty bitch! Them hoes ain't none of my kin! Now take ya' four ugly fluffy ass bastards back up front and bring 'em to Tiger—ya' real baby daddy! Ya' look good together, ya' five fluffy ugly sons-of-bitches! I'm sorry I ever slept with your messy ass, Candy!"

"You gonna get it Freddy! You're gonna get it!"

"Sue me bitch!"

The mixed-chow walked off with puppies in tow and the five laughed aloud.

"Hey that shit ain't funny! What if it happened to one of you girls? I'm telling ya', them ugly mutherfuckas ain't mine!"

The girls were literally rolling on the ground laughing as Kilo barked at them. They had not a clue what transpired, they only went on what they thought they had seen. And to them, it looked as if Kilo was being stuck with some puppies that weren't his.

"Hey that shit, that shit ain't funny! That bitch brought them fluffy bastards 'round here tryin' to pin some shit, and hey," Kilo was now laughing with the five girls. *"Hey! That bitch was calling me Freddy Krueger from Elm Street! Nobody calls me Freddy Krueger from Elm street! She fell for that shit? And, and, hey! She, she brought some ugly li'l babies 'round here and tried ta' pin that shit on me!"* Kilo lost it, he barked excitedly as the girls laughed. The five, and Kilo as well, all thought the whole scenario was hilarious, but trouble loomed for Kilo.

Two weeks later, as Kilo was asleep in the backyard, Tiger, having found the holes Kilo had dug was trying to enter Kilo's yard. Kilo stopped him and Tiger turned and ran. Kilo was tired that night, but he made it a point to head up front the next morning.

School kids were awaiting their school bus when they noticed Kilo, who was well known in East Shore, running towards the brush.

"Tiger getcha ass out here!"

School kids watched as the two dogs barked at one another; they could tell a fight was in the making.

The tiger striped pit bull emerged from the brush toting a full-bloodied tan and white female pit bull puppy—Kilo's youngest daughter. Kilo grew angry.

"You won't ever breed with my fuckin' child ya' rabid bum!"

"After I kill you, I'm gonna raise this bitch and breed her until she dies. My 'ugly mutherfuckas' gone breed her as well."

The mixed-chow and her four puppies emerged from the woods and they all began barking at Kilo.

"Tell ya' what, Candy, when I kill ya' baby daddy right in front your fuckin' face, I'm gone ask you and ya' fluffy ass kids ta' get the fuck out them bushes for good. I don't care where ya' go, but ya' not welcome in East Shore after I kill this bum!"

"Get 'em Tiger!"

"Ya' bitch just gotcha killed mutherfucka!"

Kilo charged at Tiger and the two snapped at one another's neck. Tiger was a stray and the same age as Kilo, only he had bad eating habits. Eating leftover garbage that had been sitting out for days, dead rats and even his own feces at times, had him severely malnourished and at a high disadvantage to Kilo, who was a beast of a dog and was always ready and willing to fight to the finish. Tiger didn't know it, but Kilo was actually toying with him. He knew his opponent wasn't quick enough or strong enough to take on him on, so he was only wearing the underdog down until he grew tired of playing with him.

Lubby took excellent care of Kilo. His eating habits were top-notch, he took his medications and received annual shots and when it got down to it, the hard truth was that he simply had too much on Tiger. Tired of toying around, Kilo got behind Tiger and locked down on the back of his neck. The tiger striped pit bull widened his eyes and stared directly at Candy as Kilo severed his neck bone.

"Nooo, Freddy! You killing him! Stop! Please! Stop!"

Kilo tightened his grip on the dog's neck and waited until he heard the dog gasp his last breath. He then drug the dog three feet and let him fall from his mouth. Kilo then charged at Candy. The mixed-chow and her four puppies scattered through the brush into Calvin's neighborhood, never to be seen again.

"That's right run ya fluffy bitches! And if ya' come back, I'm a kill all of ya' ugly mutherfuckas! Stay outta East Shore!"

Kilo returned to his frightened daughter and gently picked her up in his mouth. He stepped over the lifeless corpse of Tiger, who lay in the middle of Curran Boulevard, and made his way back to Emory Road where he returned his daughter to her mother and went home. He made it back into the yard just as Rolanda came out with his food dish.

She saw the blood around Kilo's mouth and said, "Well, old friend, I guess you had a score to settle this morning, huh? Now we gotta take you to the vet again." Rolanda stated lovingly as she wet a towel and wiped Kilo's mouth before he began to eat.

All of the stray dogs from that day forth knew not to mess with Kilo, or any of his puppies. He would live the rest of his days known to other dogs on the streets, both young and old, as the 'King Beast' of East Shore…

****

…Thirty-seven year-old Rolanda opened her eyes, the telephone having interrupted her thoughts. She answered the phone laughing only to hear Dominique on the other end of the line.

"What's up Rolanda? I'm just calling to check on you down there in Phoenix, girlfriend. What's funny, chick?"

"Girl I was just thinking about back in the day. I was right up until you and Calvin had just got y'all own place. I was working on Kilo's Memoir, too. I was writing about the day he ran away from the police and had it out with that chow-chow and that pit-bull when you called." Rolanda said as she laughed.

"I remember that! That was funny. Strange how it happened —but funny at the same time! So what's up, sister?"

"Girl, I'm fine. Hey, guess who I saw today?"

"I know not Bobby? You got your gun with ya'?"

Dominique asked.

It sounded as if she was joking, but 37 year-old Dominique was dead serious.

"No not that 'morphadite! I saw Lil Ben today, girl. I do got my gun though—just in case I see Bobby out there somewhere." Rolanda replied.

"Lil Ben, Lil Ben," Dominique stated repeatedly. "You mean, Ben Holland who used to stay on Calvin block back in the day?" she then asked as she recalled who Rolanda was referring to.

"Umm hmm. He looking good, too, Dominique. He married and stay down here in Phoenix. He asked about Lubby. That was the first person he asked about."

"You told him?"

"No, I was gone tell Lubby tonight, though, and wait until next week to tell Ben. He invited us all down for a East Shore reunion."

"Oh okay," Dominique then said seriously. "Well, Lubby will be glad to hear that news. She and Ben was cool. To be honest, I thought Ben was dead, girl. New Orleans *was* the murder capitol of the world! And it seemed like everybody was getting shot and killed—especially when Bri was out there."

"I know. I thought Ben was dead too. Believe me, I think he contributed to some of what happened back in the day."

"What you mean?"

"Oh, I got his story, trust me. He said it's all right for me to talk about it, but I can't say that over the phone. I'm a tell you when I get back to Vegas."

"That's what's up! I can't wait to hear what he told you."

"Look, before you called," Rolanda stated as she began to chuckle, "I was thinking about Kilo. I was just thinking about what I believe he was saying that day me and Lubby got pulled over by the police and I embellished it a little bit with that chow-chow and that day he killed Tiger. I'm telling ya' Dee, this memoir I'm writing is gone be hot. I was writing some stuff down in my manuscript and adding to the story. It's just a li'l somethin' somethin' I feel would add more humanization to the memoir—but then you called and interrupted my relivinization."

"I give you the word humanization—but me and Tracey told you a while back that relivinization is not a word you heifer! Girl, you still believe that dogs can talk?"

"Sure do! I'm telling ya', Kilo knew what he was doing, Dominique. Think back to some of the things that went down back in the day and how he reacted when he was around for some of the drama. Think about it, sister."

"Kilo may have *reacted* in a manner as if he understood what was happening between us humans, but that's just instinct Rolanda."

"Instinct my ass! Kilo did what he did on *purpose*! And it started when that chow came around. Dogs have an ability to understand humans. That's my belief. I'm not pushing it upon you sister, but you can't deny some of the things that Kilo did, especially with that chow. Not to mention what happened to me and Lubby."

"I remember those things, Rolanda. And you right, Kilo was there, especially for you. That chow-chow, though? That li'l fluffy-looking dog came in front your door with those puppies that day! Girl that was some funny stuff! It did look like Kilo was gettin' stuck with some li'l ugly puppies. You might be right, but only on those scenarios."

"Umm hmm. Lubby, too, he was there for that! And don't forget he killed that pit-bull upfront. I'm telling ya' everything Kilo did seemed like he did it on purpose, Dominique."

"You may be right, Rolanda. You may be right girlfriend. I really hope Kilo's Memoirs sells really well. Anything I can add to it, just let me know."

"Thanks, Dominique. I feel good about my li'l doggy book."

"And we all support you, sister. Anyway that's where you stopped thinking about back in the day, though? When me and Cal got married?"

"Yea, y'all snuck off like two runaway slaves and what not. Girl, Antoinette had an A.P.B. out on your behind! That was funny as hell. We was on some other shit back then."

"Who you tellin'? Rolanda we was, we was," Dominique couldn't help but to laugh as she replayed some of the events leading up to her marriage as Rolanda laughed along with her. "Rolanda," Dominique said through heart-felt laughter, "get on back up here to Vegas and rejoin the show! We miss you, sweetie. You always, *always* brighten the day."

"I try. I really do try. That's why The Man keeping me her and I'm grateful for it. Dominique, I'm truly blessed. I'll be back in Vegas on Monday, but in the meantime, I'm bouta help these good white folks close this shop, head back to the hotel and relax. Remember how we use ta' relax back in the day?" Rolanda asked as she laughed.

"I remember those times! With, with the blue blockers, the robes and the Daniel Green slippers? Girl! My stomach hurt I'm laughing so hard! Lubby saw Tracey gettin' ate out by White Boy Mike that day in the catwalk? She gone turn ta' me and say, 'she sound just like your momma'! And then, then y'all got me hooked on relaxing! Forget hooked on phonics, girl I was like a damn crack head!"

Rolanda and Dominique held their phones away from their ear as they both laughed aloud. "Rolanda girl I gotta go pee! Hurry back, please!" Dominique ended as she and Rolanda hung up the phones.

Rolanda got up from her desk and walked out onto the main floor of the pet shop to prepare to close for the day. Meanwhile, Dominique was in her home back in Vegas. She laughed to herself after replaying some of the five's life's moments in her mind. She laughed for a good while, but as her thoughts continued on past her marriage, she grew somewhat sad. 1990 was a good year for the five, and so was 1991; but in 1992, things began to spiral downward for Dominique and her friends.

"Man, we thought we were so smart back then. A lot of the things we went through could've been avoided if we had paid

closer attention to ourselves and each other," the thirty-seven year-old woman thought to herself.

Dominique now all of a sudden felt she needed a drink. She went to her outdoor bar and fixed herself a White Russian and returned to her lounge seat where she sat down and began reflecting back to when she and Rolanda, along with her friend Tracey Sanchez first entered into the world of broadcasting.

"We shoulda been all right after we graduated high school. Lubby was good, Bri was good, but man, we fucked up big time."

Hearing Rolanda speak about back in the day triggered some of Dominique's memories. She sipped her White Russian and lay back in her lounge chair and closed her eyes as *she* now began to reflect on some of the events that took place back in the day with the five friends.

CHAPTER 23

THE FANTASTIC FOUR

"Jazzy you need to take a look at these ratings. Your show is now in last place. Your staff is depleted, you have amateurish and unethical Dee-jays working beside you and our sponsors are starting to pull out."

Jazzy was in a quarterly meeting with her Station Manager, Darius Pendleton, a thirty-three year-old Black man with no business sense what so ever; he also had a shady disposition to go along with his lack of business sense. Darius was hired by big-wigs back in New York to fill a position that was vacated in New Orleans. His hiring was based on the merits of his Ivy League college degree only in Jazzy's eyes because he had no knowledge of what it took to run a radio station in her opinion.

It was a cloudless, warm afternoon in September of '91 and Jazzy, who was now thirty-six years-old, hated to have meetings with Darius. The young man would talk into her 36d breasts rather than make eye contact with the full-figured, 5'8" 160 pound woman. Jazzy's eyes were thin and sexy. She was a real pleasant woman to look at and she often wore micro-braids in her hair which she often had wrapped in a headscarf and let it flow out the top of the scarf and down her back. She also had four open-faced gold teeth on the top four front teeth. She wore a lot of accessories and still had that same jovial, slow-talking voice. Jazzy was a woman that was hard to upset, but when she did get upset, it was a side of her that no one wanted to see.

Darius pushed all of Jazzy's wrong buttons, but he was her boss so she gave him a little leeway if only to keep her job, which she knew had been in jeopardy now for some time. Darius would flirt with Jazzy constantly during their meetings by dropping subtle remarks in reference to her ample breasts. He would sometimes seductively sip on a Coca-Cola and stroke the sides of the drink bottle when he was done just like he'd done a few seconds earlier. It was so cheesy to Jazzy what he was doing, but she only had to see him once or twice every month and that made it easy to deal with.

Jazzy knew her show was in threat of being taken off air; but she was refusing to let that happen. Her board operator, who'd been with her for over a decade, had grown tired of Darius's flirtatious ways and had moved to Las Vegas to work for an up and coming radio station. She had tried to convince Jazzy to go with her, but Jazzy just loved New Orleans too much to leave the city. She and her board-op talked often and Jazzy would always tell the woman that she had more work to do in New Orleans before she could even consider making a move. Jazzy knew Darius wanted her out, but she would not let the younger, less experienced Station Manager push her off the air. If Jazzy wanted out, it would be on her own terms; and as of now, Jazzy wasn't ready to leave.

"I know the ratings are low, Mister Pendleton—but umm, just give me some time. I have something working on my end to restore the show."

"Something like what?"

"An overhaul with fresh young talent and new segments. I'm aiming for new music and new features also, because, giving the changing times, I know that's what we need. The kids now-a-days are hipper, faster and smarter and it is my aim to catch up with this new generation by revamping the program to make it relevant towards the times. It's a simple strategy, but the right pieces have to be in place to make it work. All I'm asking for is a little time before you make any decisions."

"Who's going to lead the way in this new venture?"

"I am of course—but I have something in mind. It just may

take a little time."

"Time? I see. Something you don't have too much of at this present—time."

"Why must you be so difficult with me, Darius?"

Jazzy and Darius were on the fourteenth floor of the Amoco building on Poydras Street in downtown New Orleans, directly across from City Hall. The Amoco building held the radio station's studio and office staff, and numerous other businesses that were tied to the oil industry and public works offices for the city.

"I'm not being difficult, Jasmine," Darius replied. "I'm just tired of you breast-feeding this radio program. You're treating it like a suckling child when you need to just let it grow. Let it rise to the occasion and become fully erect."

Jazzy shook her head at Darius as she stared at him. "This show may have problems rising to the occasion Darius," she said as she leaned back in chair and crossed her legs, immediately spotting Darius trying to get a glimpse of what lay between her thick thighs, "but just like any other tense situation, it only needs a little coaxing, some nurturing so to speak. I remember the glory days of old and I plan on bringing those back bigger and better. I'm not aiming for fully erect status which may only excite a *small* portion of the audience— and I do emphasize the word *small*." Jazzy stated as she twirled an ink pen in her hands.

"Okay," Darius said as he laughed lowly, knowing Jasmine was making a sexual implication the same as he had done to her seconds earlier. "Well, the executives in New York speak well of you. They know of your reputation from back in the day so you're fine with them for now. They will soon ask my opinion, and when they do, if things aren't right? I'll be honest with them. I'll be honest now as a matter of fact."

"You don't have to be."

"No, I want to be. If I had it my way, you'd be working the ten till two shift. You'd just be spinning records. No conversations, no phone calls, just music, old school music, you know, the music of your heyday?"

"Let me tell ya' this Darius," Jazzy said as she stood up from her seat and leaned over the desk, "Do you have a better view now, sir?"

"Make your point," Darius replied as he turned and stared at the city skyline.

"My point is this—I really don't give a fuck how you feel about me and my style of Dee-jaying. You have no talent and a deep lack of knowledge about music and what it takes to keep the audience's attention. You sit here in this office as if you know the listeners but you are no more than a pencil pusher for the people back in New York. They sent you here for what?"

"To run this radio station!"

"You don't run nothing around here! You can't even take a *shit* without the people in New York giving you permission to do so! So don't give me that shit!"

"Don't stand there and take that tone of voice with me, Jasmine!" Darius remarked as he stood opposite Jazzy.

"I'm done with this meeting," Jazzy said as she threw her hands up and stepped away from Darius's desk. "All you ever do is make sexual overtones towards me! We never accomplish *anything* during these boring and highly unprofessional meetings!" she ended as she headed for the door to walk out of the huge, lavish office.

"Where are you going? I'm not done with you!"

"Well I'm done with your ass! Fire me today if you want! If ya' ain't, then I'm goin' find the people I know and believe can save my show! Because you have given me no help or advice over the two year period you've been here, Mister Pendleton." Jazzy said angrily as she slammed the door behind her and walked briskly towards her office, entered and slammed her door shut and locked it. She poured herself a shot of Vodka and went and sat behind her desk and began looking through her rolodex to search for an old number she had gotten years ago. Jazzy was about to take a huge gamble on her career as she knew this was her last shot. She wondered if the people she was about to gamble on were up for the challenge as she dialed a number.

****

"Tracey, remember, when you're fading into your song, do so just as Dominique is ending her expose`. You can wait until she's done if the song goes right into the vocals, but most songs have an instrumental intro so let the music play as she speaks and she'll be able to adjust to the music and end her expose` before the vocals, okay? Now, let's try it again from the top. Rolanda that was a funny bit you did and it goes well with the topic on hand. Dominique, your current events are fantastic—but Tracey, you were just a little bit off on fading the song in."

"I know Mister Stenopolis. I'm just having a hard time remembering the correct knob to turn to fade the song in." Tracey replied as she, Dominique, and Rolanda sat inside a model of a state of the art radio station which was their classroom inside the University of New Orleans broadcasting building.

The three girls and the other twelve students would each spend five hours a week inside the model, which prepared them for life inside a real radio station's studio. Dominique, Rolanda and Tracey all sat behind a huge square desk inside the studio, which was an exact replica of the day's most state-of-the art studio design. They sat up about five feet high inside the booth behind a plexi-glass window that faced the rest of the class. Broadcast students would either stand or sit as they watched other students practice their given assignments. Headphones were worn inside the model, and there were turntables set up along with high back leather chairs. The model studio was dimly lit and had paintings of Travis Smith, Papa Smurf, Charmaine Neville, and Pete Fountain, who were either popular musicians, or Dee-jays who traversed through the award-winning broadcasting program at the University.

As classes ended for the day, twenty year-olds, Dominique, Rolanda, and Tracey were preparing to exit the broadcast building and head to either work or their respective homes. Dominique had to work this night even though she was dead tired. She had taken out several loans, and had maxed out her credit cards and now the bills were running close together, even with her parents helping out by paying more than half of her tuition. Calvin was working overtime in the marketing firm's mailroom as well so he could gain more experience and began climbing the corporate ladder.

Dominique and Calvin Huntley were making ends meet, but the long grueling days were taking a heavy toll. The bills were paid, but neither had too much time for one another, and when they did, they were too tired to put forth any effort to keep the romance alive. Life had become a monotonous, endless struggle to stay afloat for Dominique and Calvin and Dominique had discovered months ago just how right her mother was. The sex did wear off, but the bills wouldn't fade. If anything, they only began to accumulate more and more, each one, more expensive than the next.

Tracey Sanchez was doing just fine. She and Mike were getting along well, and she was still at home with her mother stacking money.

Rolanda Jones was doing okay herself; she was still at home with Charlotte and had recently purchased a new Diamante and was saving money also.

Twenty year-old Lubby Williams, meanwhile, was trying to finance a newly built retail store lot on Read Boulevard to finally open that pet shop she had dreamed of doing. She was doing well in her business administration class, and was using the knowledge she was gaining to begin to make small business deals that earned extra cash. She was also lining up pet suppliers in Africa and South America to import her exotic pets.

Twenty year-old Brianna Stanford was still going strong with Tank and the two of them were still hustling. Tank had bought Brianna some recording equipment, but it was by no means professional. Brianna really did want to record an album, but she just wasn't that dedicated to doing so; she was letting her talent slip away because she and Tank were simply having too much fun and making too much money to worry about anything. The two were living well off the game, and not having to struggle, coupled with the large amounts of money and free time, which included shopping sprees and frequent trips to the hair salon and spa, was a big diversion for Brianna. She just didn't take her music all that serious during this period of time in her life.

Rolanda, Tracey and Dominique were climbing into Rolanda's car to head back to New Orleans East when Brianna, dressed in black spandex wearing a gold medallion, diamond hooped earrings, and a tennis bracelet, and Lubby, dressed in her pet shop uniform, pulled up alongside of the three in Brianna's jeep with Kilo in the backseat. Brianna was repeatedly blowing her horn and yelling aloud, "Y'all 'bouta go large! Y'all goin' large!"

"What the hell Brianna talking about?" Rolanda asked under her breath as she eyed Brianna.

Brianna hopped out of her jeep and ran up to Rolanda's car and said, "Follow me! Just follow me," before she ran and hopped back into her jeep.

Rolanda, Tracey, and Dominique, dressed in jeans and blouses with low-heeled pumps, followed Brianna off the University campus to a nearby Sports bar.

"What are we doing here, Bri? I gotta be to work in an hour." Dominique said as Rolanda pulled up alongside of Bri.

"Remember we met Jazzy by Gabriella a while back?"

"Yea, we still remember Jazzy, why?" Rolanda asked inquisitively.

"She wanna talk to y'all!" Lubby answered excitedly.

"You lyin'!" Tracey snapped.

"Come on now Tracey," Brianna said as she stared at Rolanda, Dominique, and Tracey. "You think me, Lubby and Kilo would be out here like this just to play a prank on y'all?"

"How she know where we were?" Rolanda asked as the girls went and stood beside Brianna's jeep inside the crowded Sports bar's parking lot.

"She called my momma house and my momma gave her my

number. She remembered me from when Gabriella, Sam and Samantha had gotten killed and she called my house. She remembered y'all wanted to be Dee-jays and she asked me what y'all was doing and were we still friends. I said 'lady we friends for life! They still in college and they majoring in broadcasting'. Then I told her, 'and they still wanna be Dee-jays but they don't do house parties no more'. I thought she wanted y'all to do a wedding or somethin'. Girls? She laughed, and told me what's up! She said she want y'all to work with her and I suggested she meet y'all here because it's close to the campus." Brianna ended as she looked around, excited for her friends.

"This like a dream come true for y'all if Jammin' Jazzy actually show up. I hope she ain't lyin' man, 'cause if y'all get on the radio, y'all can do my commercials when my pet shop open next year." Lubby stated.

"Lubby you got the building?" Rolanda asked excitedly.

"Not, not quite yet. Me and Gerald put a down payment on it, but we can't touch it until we have at least thirty percent invested. It's like sixty-seven thousand, we got eight into it, but we still need about fourteen more before we can get a loan to open up. Maybe another year or so, we gone get there."

"I can't wait for you to open up, girl. Let me do your promos and stuff!" Rolanda requested.

"Y'all ain't even in with Jazzy yet! Tracey can't work the knobs!" Brianna joked.

"You crazy, girl! I'm the best board operator in the south ya' heard me?"

"I know, girlfriend. I'm just playin'! Man I'm glad for y'all!" Brianna remarked as she continued looking around for a sign of Jazzy.

The girls sat and talked for a while until they spotted a white two door Cadillac El Dorado driven by Jazzy pull up in front of them. They smiled and spoke to the woman as they all stood inside the parking lot. The girls didn't jump up and down the way they did when they first met Jazzy years ago, however, they were grown women now; twenty years of age and leading very busy lives. Jazzy greeted the five girls with a quick hug and they all walked into the sports bar and took a seat at a booth and Jazzy got right to the point. "I'm not going to ask if you still listen to the show, I think I know the answer to that. We are *all* busy people. I called Brianna earlier and we had a long talk. When she told me you girls were majoring in broadcasting in college, I just knew you still had the dream—even if you no longer listened to the show. I know you haven't Dee-jayed in a while, but I'm offering you three girls an opportunity. I'm revamping my show and I'm looking for new, fresh, young, talented and ambitious females to follow in my steps. You three meet the requirements, I believe. I'm offering you a chance to work side by side with me and help me to build a bigger and better show."

"Jazzy, you serious? We always dreamed of working in radio, but I think I speak for Rolanda and Tracey as well when I say we never imagined we'd work with *you*." Dominique said as her heart thumped with anticipation.

"I never imagined it would have to come to this so quickly. I umm, I think when you're riding the wave of success you never think the wave will stop. I'm thirty-six now, not old, but I need new blood, a young vibe to pick up where I left off. Believe me, people would die for this opportunity to work with Jazzy. Before this jerk of a manager tries to change the format, I'm asking you three girls to join me as interns. The job doesn't pay anything right now, but you have an opportunity that comes along once in a lifetime. I promise you, if we change the ratings, we change our lives. Trust me on this, the rewards will come in due time, just put in the effort now." Jazzy said as she eyed the three girls.

"Well, umm, we have bills to pay Jazzy—but to get a chance to be on the radio with you is worth getting a late charge on any bill." Dominique stated as she Tracey and Rolanda got up and hugged Jazzy.

"Thank you, ladies! I never forgot you girls and I always hoped that you would've continued to pursue your dreams. We'll be a good team, and I'll help you every step of the way, I promise. You, girls," Jazzy said as she smiled a wide smile, "you girls will become my protégé's, the nineties version of Jazzy!"

The women had set up a meeting the following day inside the Amoco building where they met Darius for a brief moment. He liked the girls right away, not because he felt they were qualified, but because he thought they were sexy. He eyed the voluptuous 5'8" 150 pound Tracey with her firm breasts. He stared at Rolanda's pretty dark eyes and admired her smooth ebony skin and was impressed with her 5'10" 155 pound physique. He thought Dominique was button cute; her 5' 130 pound figure looked delectable. If Jazzy had brought in three males, Darius would have turned them away, but the thought of having such young tender flesh around was too much of a temptation for Darius to deny. Rolanda, Tracey and Dominique were 'eye candy' to the man. He approved their internship quickly.

The studio inside of WYLD was almost the same as the ones the girls used at the university. They did a practice run off air that day and the three found out they could operate the controls easily. They would practice an entire week before they went on air the following week. The day before they were to go on air, Jazzy held a meeting with her girls, and wanted to approve their first task, which was to give themselves on air persona names.

"Now, I told you girls a few days ago that you should use on air personas while on air. When this program takes off, you all will become well known to the callers. To use your real names, in my opinion, could set you all up for unsolicited phones calls at your homes, stalking and the like. So, what ya' girls got for me?"

"I know what you mean about stalking, Jazzy, but the way my love life going? I may begin stalking the stalker." Rolanda said.

"Jazzy chuckled and said, "You're using your real name, Rolanda?"

"Only the last name. I'm goin' by Misses Jones. It's sexy and goes with my segment in the last hour perfectly."

"Okay, Misses Jones. Dominique what you got?"

"Well, my middle name Marie and my mother's middle name is Chanel. I'm gone take those two names and flip them and call myself Chanel Marie."

"Chanel Marie sounds real good, Dominique. And it fits you, just like Rolanda's on air persona. Shit! I need and cool and sophisticated name like that. I should change my name," Jazzy stated.

"Nahh. You know you got the hippest name in the south," Tracey chimed in.

"Thank you, Tracey. What you come up with to call yourself?"

"I'm gone use the name Amanda Spanks."

"Amanda Spanks!" Jazzy, Dominique and Rolanda said aloud in unison.

"What the hell is an Amanda Spanks?" Jazzy asked.

"That's right! Catchy ain't it? That's what everybody gone ask. So introduce me as Amanda Spanks the Latin Soul Sister."

"Okay," Jazzy replied, somewhat unsure of Tracey's on air persona, although it did fit her hot-tempered personality quite well. "We'll, umm, we'll go with it and if a nick name arises, that's what'll it'll be. We're done. If you girls haven't any questions, I suggest you head home and get adequate rest because tomorrow, we go public with this thing and put our reputation on the line." Jazzy wanted to add the phrase "before hundreds of thousands of people", but she didn't want to unnerve the girls, besides, they knew how popular she was even if they didn't know the numbers of listeners.

As the girls exited her office, Jazzy sat in her chair wondering if the decision she had made would pay off. She'd just gambled on three young women whom she'd only met three times in life at the most, and had basically put her entire career, nearly three decades of work, into the hands of these inexperienced female wanna-be Dee-jays.

"Don't you dare let me down. Bring it like I know you can, babies." Jazzy said to herself as she watched her office door slowly close.

****

"Five, four, three, two, one, diamond...Talk to me nah...Cruising down the street...real slow...what the fellas be yellin'...Marrero...Talk to me nah...Cruising down the street... real slow...what the fellas be yellin'...Marrero..."

"I'mmm baaaacckkkk! Whoa! You know the voice! And you definitely know the station! 105.9 the super stud station that's ruling the nation! This the one and only Jammin Jazzy the diva of the den and I'm here with the certified Hot Girls Misses Jones the devil herself! Chanel Marie who's wickedly nice, and Miss Amanda Spanks the Latin Soul Sister.... And this...Is the Fantastic Fourrrrrrr!" Jazzy yelled in the microphone just as the lyricist's vocals came over the airwaves.

"Now sit back and relax so you can hear what I say...and realize it's comin' from the T-H-I-C-K... I'm like 'Digg 'em... so give me a smack I'll smack ya back...react whack to my attack and get a cardiac arrest...stop breathing...heart a stop pumpin'...rhymes still kicking crowd still jumpin'...then dig inside ya' chest to see what's blocking them arteries...and they'll find the rhymes that's departing me..."

MC Thick, a local rapper from the West Bank section of New Orleans, had a local hit song named after his city titled *Marrero*. It was the first song Tracey played the night the girls went on the air. Their lifelong dream had come to fruition on September 9, 1991 and the show had been kicked off perfectly. The song played on as Jazzy and the girls, who all sat behind a plexi-glass window that overlooked the city skyline from the corner studio on the 14th floor of the Amoco building, prepared to interview the local rapper during their weekly rap session.

The studio itself was breath-taking. It was a state of the art music lab that had the three girls sitting behind Jazzy in a staggered pattern that gradually increased in height. Dominique sat in a booth behind Jazzy about three feet above her. Rolanda's post was behind Dominique's to Dominique's right about three feet higher than Dominique's post. Tracey was in a separate booth on Dominique's left, lower than Dominique, but higher than Jazzy. Dominique, Rolanda, and Jazzy all had computer monitors atop their desks, but they were rarely being used, except to write down notes for upcoming segments. Tracey had a huge circular-shaped electronic board that covered her entire desk and her and Dominique's set of Technic 1200 turntables was on her left to be used during live mixes. Tracey controlled the songs that were played and the commercials while the show's two producers screened the phone calls.

When MC Thick's song ended, Dominique interviewed the rapper briefly. After the interview, the girls allowed callers to call in and talk to the rapper. That first night on air would set the show's format Monday thru Fridays from seven in the evening to eleven at night. The seven o'clock hour was for local artist only. The girls would select songs that were radio worthy and play them during a segment call 'Play it or Slay it'. They would play the song and then take calls on whether to keep the song in rotation or 'take a hammer to it', a scenario in which Tracey would literally take a hammer and smash the cassette or vinyl on live air.

Rolanda also did her hood news report in the seven o' clock hour and it, too, became a fan favorite. The audience, especially the listeners in New Orleans, all loved the seven o' clock hour because it was the most humorous part of the show, and it was done in true New Orleans fashion from the music, to the language.

The eight o' clock hour featured an Elite Eight countdown where national artists' songs were played. Dominique also did the top national news stories during this time slot. The Elite Eight countdown hour was the most informative part of the show and was well-received by all.

The nine 'o clock hour featured the teen issue segment where teens could call in and get advice from Jazzy and the girls. The advice was blunt and unscripted and the girls used some of their own experiences to try and detour bad behavior and unwise decisions. Many teens came to look up to Dominique,

Rolanda, and Tracey; they were instant role models.

The ten o' clock hour featured an adult topic ranging from domestic violence to sexual problems; it was often a hot discussion. Rolanda would select a hot letter written in to the Fantastic Four Show and read it over the airwaves. The lights would be dimmed and Rolanda would read the letter over the airwaves as *Me and Mrs. Jones* played lowly in the background to set the mood. The hot discussions would take the listeners inside someone's bedroom, a person's volatile relationship, or workplace romance. Whatever the topic, people just had to listen to see what juicy situation Rolanda would offer up for discussion. The callers would then call in the remainder of the hour and give their advice to the troubled adult while songs reflecting the letter were being played.

Within a month's time, Jazzy was back in the ratings. The show wasn't in first place but it was far from last. Two months later, the girls went on payroll, they were each earning six hundred and fifty dollars a week before taxes in December of 1991 and *The Fantastic Four* now owned the number two spot, right behind the local rock and roll station, and for them, it meant that they owned the urban airwaves in the south. Dominique, Rolanda and Tracey were riding high during this period of time, they were in their junior year of college, which consisted of fewer classes which gave them more time to hang out with Brianna and Lubby, who were doing well themselves as 1992 got underway, and all were looking towards the future which seemed to be getting brighter as each day passed by. Neither of the five girls, however, could have ever anticipated all the unforeseen drama that lay ahead for each and every one of them.

CHAPTER 24

THEY ALL HAVE HOPE

"Oh shit," twenty year-old Tracey hissed as she sat inside the bathroom stall inside the radio station's lobby on a rainy March evening in 1992. She looked at the positive sign on her home pregnancy test again realized her eyes weren't fooling her—she was now pregnant. Tracey had taken four tests this day and all of them had come back positive. "I told that white motherfucka not to get me pregnant!" she said under her breath, referring to her lover, 20 year-old Mike. Tracy was now furious with Mike. They'd this conversation before and she specifically told Mike not to get her pregnant.

Both Tracey and Mike had been making passionate love over the months, and Tracey had even let Mike make love to her on several occasions without using a condom. She knew the exact day she got pregnant. It happened back in January on a cold winter night. Mike had taken her from behind against the kitchen counter one night after work. The conversation with Mrs. Jones was about spontaneous sex and it had gotten the cast of The Fantastic Four Show all worked up. That night, Jazzy announced that she was going home and tear the clothes off her boyfriend and have him to take her right then and there; Rolanda, Dominique, and Tracey were planning to do the same.

Rolanda, went out with Bobby that night cold January night, the two had been seeing each other for a couple of months since he had broken up with Kitty about four months earlier.

Rolanda gave in that night and she and Bobby had become an item.

Tracey went over to Mike's house, and when he let her in, she walked into the kitchen, raised her knee high skirt, and leaned over on the counter, presenting herself to Mike. Mike began searching for the condoms, but Tracey pleaded. "Fuck a condom! Just come fuck me hard and fast! Come get this tight juicy pussy!"

Mike gladly obliged.

Tracey replayed some of the conversations she heard that night as Mike held her hips tightly and pounded her from behind. "Smack my ass! Smack it hard!" she moaned aloud as she stared back at Mike.

Tracey's sexy eyes were filled with lust, her long black hair covering half her face. Mike was moaning aloud, his trailer was rocking slightly as he was driving Tracey over the edge.

"Awww, Shit! Shit I'm bouta come!" Tracey yelled.

Mike clutched her shoulders and began to pummel Tracey's tight slit from behind at a rapid pace. Her ass jiggled violently, she pounded the kitchen counter with her fists and her eyes watered as she screamed like a woman possessed. Tracey came so hard she squirted fluid and it splashed against Mike's stomach and dripped down Tracey's thighs. Mike was still going at it; but Tracey's legs grew weak. She stood up and backed up against Mike and clasped her vaginal muscles around his hardened member and held it there as she dropped to the floor with Mike following her lead, his hardened dick never slipping out of Tracey. Mike then knelt over his woman, ripped off her dress and began to pound her from behind again until she squirted a second time yelling, "Fuck me! Fuck me, fuck me," in the process.

"I'm comin' baby! I'm comin!"

"Mike don't stop! Don't you fuckin' stop!"

"I can't, I can't hold it!"

"Come with me! Come with me!" Tracey yelled. "Slap my ass hard!"

Mike slapped Tracey's ass and she bucked and gripped his tool with her vaginal muscles just as Mike ejaculated into her vagina and the two collapsed flat on the floor. The two lay motionless, panting, sweating, kissing. Tracey could feel her juices and that of Mike's flowing from her gaping pussy as she lay underneath her man flat on her stomach. There was a sudden knock on the door amidst their recuperation so Mike grabbed his shorts and peeked out to see the police. They asked was everything okay and Mike assured them that everything was just fine.

The officer then caught a glimpse of Tracey walking by naked and smiling with an '*I just got the shit fucked outta me*' look on her face and knew what was going on. "Keep it down, man." he said as he smiled at Mike and walked off.

Tracey knew Mike had ejaculated inside her, but the passion was so intense that night, she didn't care. They had sex three more times with Mike exploding inside of Tracey each time without the use of a condom. Tracey had only realized the seriousness of what she and Mike had done the following morning. At that moment, she began to hope and pray that she wasn't pregnant.

That same night back in January, Dominique went home to Calvin. She listened to Natalie Cole's song *I Got Love on my Mind* the whole ride home. She played the song repetitiously until she reached her home feeling horny and in the mood for some serious lovemaking. She entered her apartment and stripped at the door and went into the bedroom and got in bed with Calvin, who was sleeping on his back in a pair of boxers. Dominique pulled his member out of his boxers and clutched it as her mouth watered. She had a serious oral fixation and wanted to know what it felt like to suck a man's penis. She had been fantasizing about oral sex ever since she began to read the stories in the magazines she had gotten from Rolanda when she was a teenager. The stories had aroused her curiosity and she just knew when she got married, Calvin would allow her to experiment on him. Dominique felt that she and her husband should be able to be as uninhibited as they wanted to be in their marital bed. They should be able to fulfill each other's desires so long as they were within reason and

Dominique felt that her wanting to give oral pleasure to her husband was not out of the ordinary. But Calvin, for whatever reason, would not let Dominique do it, and he wouldn't do her. She was growing ever frustrated with the situation, but she was aiming to do something about it on that night. Just as she licked her lips and lowered her head to Calvin's member, Calvin stirred awake and rolled on his side facing away from Dominique. "Damn baby, you know I gotta be ta' work at six in tha' morning! Come on now, tomorrow, we do it tomorrow." Calvin said as he began to doze back off to sleep.

"Calvin come on, man!" Dominique stated as she hit Calvin with a pillow.

"The hell wrong with you?"

"All we do is just lay down, fuck and that's it!" Dominique stated as she sat back on the bed naked. "Let's try some new stuff." she said as she smiled and reached for Calvin's dick once more.

"Dominique, I told you, I'm tired and—"

"Forget it, Calvin! Just forget it! The moment has just passed anyway!" Dominique said as she got up and went to take a shower, where she fantasized about sucking Calvin off while she masturbated herself to orgasm. She exited the shower relieved, but she still wanted to sample the real thing.

Dominique couldn't figure out why Calvin wouldn't allow her to please him; that's all she wanted to do—please her husband. And by doing so, she could satisfy her curiosity at the same time. *"Maybe I need a lover."* Dominique thought to herself as she laid beside Calvin, hugging him from behind. She quickly brushed those feelings aside, however, because she didn't want adulterous thoughts to start seeping into her mind. *"I just gotta get him to come around. Maybe I should get him drunk one night."* Dominique thought as she smiled slyly, having devised another way to get Calvin to become more passionate in the bedroom.

Dominique knew Calvin loved her; the man worked hard and treated her with the utmost respect. Sometimes, however, Dominique wanted to just get downright freaky, but Calvin just didn't want to play along and that often caused a little strife in their relationship. Through it all, Dominique loved her man; she only hoped he would someday want to experiment in the bedroom. She kissed her husband on the nape of his neck and turned the night light off and went to sleep wondering if she would ever live out her fantasy.

Dominique, Rolanda, and Tracey talked about their night the day after as they rode to work in Rolanda's Diamante, and Dominique and Tracey got to hear all the juicy details about Rolanda's first time.

"Rolanda why you waited so long? And why Bobby?" Dominique asked.

"Umm, don't be trying ta' interview me on the slick, Dominique." Rolanda said as the girls burst into laughter. "For real though, I waited because I didn't want to complicate my life you know? I wanted to get my career going first in order to be independent. When Jazzy came along that was right on time. I already had the car. Then I had been started a bank account and had some change put back. Now I was set. I have good credit, a good job, so I was like what's missing?"

"Good dick!" Dominique and Tracey stated at the same time as the three women laughed.

"That's right. I been had a li'l crush on Bobby. I like his short wavy hair and when he look at me, I melt 'cause his eyes are so pretty. I'm like 5' 10", and over six feet in heels, so it's hard ta' really find a good and available man my height or taller. Nothing against a shorter man, I just wanted a partner my height. Bobby six feet even, dark-skinned like me, and got a nice build. He been cool with Tank and Gerald and had been making a li'l paper. We got cool you know? Talking on the phone and sometimes having a quick brunch on some Saturdays. But I told not only myself, but Bobby as well, that as long as he was with Kitty, I wasn't going to agree to date him. He told me they broke up last year, I waited like a month and a half ta' see if they was gone get back together. Never happened. So I asked him out to dinner and we started dating exclusively that night. And after last night, Bobby was well worth the wait girls!"

"I heard that Rolanda." Dominique stated, "So umm, y'all using protection?"

"Stop trying to interview me, girl!"

"I'm just saying, Rolanda, because Bobby was a player back in the day and we all know that. You ever seen Kitty? How she look?" Dominique asked.

"I ain't never seen, matter of fact, *nobody* never seen Kitty in person. He showed me a picture of the li'l red-skinned chick, but that's about all. I used ta' wonder if Bobby was still sneaking seeing her behind my back, but I ain't never found no evidence of that. Me and Bobby cool. I trust him now."

"So you used to think he was still a player once upon a time?" Tracey asked Rolanda.

"You know what? I was reliving my first night and we done swung over into players and protection. Y'all li'l heifers is ruining my relivinization."

"Relivinization!" Tracey and Dominique said in unison as they laughed aloud. "That ain't a word! Lubby would eat you alive for using that counterfeit word!" Dominique said through laughter.

"It, it, well you know what I mean! Anyway, I started taking the pill to prevent pregnancy when me and Bobby started seeing one another exclusively. I told him what I expected of him, which is strict monogamy and he agreed to being with me exclusively. I just had to be in control of my body as far as pregnancy is concerned."

"Man, I just hope Mike ain't got me pregnant. A baby gone mess everything up for me right now." Tracey thought as she listened to Rolanda talk about being on the pill.

As 20 year-old Tracey came back to reality on this rainy March evening, she replayed that last thought over and over in her head. She was mad at herself for losing control, but she was even more furious with Mike because she felt he didn't respect her wishes. Tracey never even considered the fact that she asked Mike to have sex with her without using a condom. She also overlooked the fact that she said 'don't stop', and 'come with me' while they were in the heat of passion. She should have taken the blame for this one, but Tracey was dead set on letting Mike know he had gotten her pregnant against her wishes. She picked up her pregnancy tests and prepared to join Rolanda, Dominique and Jazzy for the night's show.

Meanwhile, 20 year-old Lubby was out in East Shore over to her mother's house. She and Kilo ran up the sidewalk and Lubby rang the doorbell. Cynthia didn't answer so Lubby turned the knob and saw that the door was unlocked. When she entered her mother's home she saw that the house was a mess. It smelled foul and was very hot inside because the windows were all shut tight with the curtains closed. Lubby and Kilo walked through the house and Lubby quickly spotted her mother sitting at the kitchen table in near darkness. She went to turn on the lights, but there was no power. She then checked the water and saw that it too was off.

"Momma, you ain't paying the bills?" Lubby asked of her mother.

"Bills?"

"Yea. I been giving you money for the bills and all the utilities are off."

"Utilities?"

"Momma," Lubby said softly as she eyed her mother sitting at the kitchen table in front of photo album containing pictures of her estranged husband and Lubby when she was just a baby.

"He left me." Cynthia said lowly as she stared at the man in the picture. "But till this day—I still love that man."

"He left *us* momma." Lubby said as she walked behind her mother and hugged her tightly.

"Get the hell off me!" Cynthia screamed as Kilo began to bark loudly.

"Momma, please." Lubby pleaded as she tried to reach out and hug her mother.

Cynthia kept pushing Lubby's arms away, but Lubby wouldn't have it. She rushed her mother and wrapped her arms around Cynthia and said, "Hug me back! Hug me back, momma!"

Cynthia cried and stopped fighting and raised her arms and wrapped her arms around her daughter, who cried silently. In all her years this was all Lubby ever wanted from her mother—a hug back. Something so simple, and so innocent, meant more than the world to Lubby. She was happy she'd remained persistent. The hug Lubby received was short lived, however, because Cynthia suddenly pulled her hair hard and grabbed her around the neck. Lubby grabbed at her mother just as Kilo ran up and began biting at Cynthia's legs, forcing Cynthia to let go of Lubby.

Lubby stepped back from her mother and eyed her disbelief. "Momma what's wrong with you? What did I do to make you hate me? Why you hate *me* of all people? I never did wrong by you. Daddy did! He left us both! Daddy left *us*!" she cried.

"He left because of *you*! Because of *you*, Lubby!"

"Don't say that, momma. That ain't true. If he loved you he woulda stayed." Lubby said softly as she calmed Kilo down. "He woulda stayed. I love you! I'm still here because *I* love you! Let me, umm, here let me cleanup for you momma." Lubby said as she wiped tears from her eyes and dropped to her knees and began picking up old newspapers and dirty clothes. "I'm a get your lights and water back on too, momma. You paid your mortgage?"

"No!" Cynthia snapped as she walked into her bedroom and closed the door.

"I'll do it for you, momma!" Lubby yelled as she began to clean her mother's home.

Cynthia had hugged Lubby for a brief moment this day; and the ever optimistic Lubby had decided to use that brief hug as a stepping stone to get her mother to finally accept her. Lubby had friends who loved her deeply. She had a man in her life as well. She was in college and was soon to be an entrepreneur. She had everything going for her except the approval, love, and affection she wanted from her mother, which was the one thing she wanted above all else. Lubby knew she was doing everything right in her life, but she just couldn't figure out what she was doing wrong to make her mother not like her. Lubby never realized that she was doing no wrong, however; Cynthia would always blame her for her husband walking out on her. Lubby could not come to grips with that fact. She believed that someday, someday soon, her mother would indeed love her the way a mother is supposed to love her daughter. Lubby's heart was an optimistic, forgiving, and long-suffering organ whose every beat longed for Cynthia's approval; and Lubby would not give up on her mother, no matter how long it took for that goal to be accomplished.

As The Fantastic Four was going on air, Lubby, having finished cleaning her mother's home and paying her mortgage, light, and water bills, was sitting over to 21 year-old Brianna's house listening to the show and telling her about the fight she had with her mother.

"Lubby, I know that's your momma, but baby please, let me know when you going there so I can go with you. If not me, then, then tell Rolanda, Dominique or Tracey, or Charlotte, or somebody, please. Kilo can't do it all by himself. I really think your momma needs some kind of medical help or something."

"She just get mad like that *sometimes*, Bri. Most times she don't even ack—most times she just be quiet." Lubby said as tears began to flow down her cheeks.

"That's not what you really want to say. What you want to say is that most times she don't even acknowledge you, huh, Lubby?" Brianna said as Lubby fell onto her shoulder and cried.

"Why?" Lubby questioned as she cried on Brianna's shoulder. "Why she do me like that, Bri? I keep asking her why she don't like me! I do everything for my momma! I clean her house, pay her bills—with *my* money! And she just, she just keep sayin' my daddy left because of me! But that's not true! She hurt me today. She really hurt me."

"I know she did. I know." Brianna said as the two females held one another on Brianna's sofa.

Brianna placed her chin on top of Lubby's head and cried

with her friend as she grew angry. She thought back to the day she had killed Donald, and then seriously thought about going over to Cynthia's house and blowing the woman away into the next life. No one would mind. Hell, nobody on Emory Road even liked Cynthia, who was nothing more than an ugly spot in Lubby's beautiful life. Bri understood fully the fact that Lubby's mother was causing her great anguish and distress, and as bad as she wanted to, she knew she couldn't kill her best friend's mother, besides, through all the drama, Lubby still believed that Cynthia would one day change. She still had hope.

"You want a soda or something?" Brianna asked, breaking the low sobs of sorrow emanating from Lubby.

"You got a wine cooler?"

Brianna's eyes widened. "Not you miss thang!"

"Yea, girl. My nerves are so bad right now. I just wanna drink and mellow out and listen to my girls on the radio."

"Now that sounds like a winner!" Brianna said as she got up from the couch and got three wine coolers. She poured some into a small Tupperware bowl for Kilo and she and Lubby sat back down on the sofa to listen to The Fantastic Four. Brianna looked over to Lubby as she turned the volume up on the radio and she could already see Lubby smiling in anticipation of hearing her friends.

Brianna was glad to see Lubby smiling again, and she knew the rest of the girls, without even knowing it would also help Lubby get over what had happened earlier in the day. Brianna sat back down beside her friend and the two smiled at one another and held hands excitedly when they heard Tracey's voice come on the air.

"We sittin' in the sound shop with this dude Big Rock from the fifteenth ward ya' heard me?" Tracey stated dryly.

Tracey was still upset that she was pregnant and she'd told no one as of yet. Big Rock had a song that he wanted the girls to play, but they had warned him that the song was whack. He insisted, however, on letting the people decide. On this day,

Tracey was mad at all men, but she would take it out on Big Rock as he would soon come to learn.

"Now, we serious over here in the sound shop. I'm telling y'all from jump before we get into this, we warned homeboy that his song was whack as all outdoors, but he insisted on us playing this garbage." Tracey stated sarcastically.

"First of all my (bleep) ain't whack and second of all—"

Jazzy had to scramble to bleep out the curse word. Luckily, the show was on a five second delay.

Tracey cut Big Rock off mid-sentence and spoke loud and clear. "No, first of all—don't be cursin' in this mother(bleep)ing studio! Second of all, we already got the table and the hammer set up so we can smash that whack (bleep) (bleep) when they vote on that raggedly mother(bleep)er!"

Brianna and Lubby laughed aloud at their friend as they sipped their wine coolers.

"Umm, umm, Big Rock tell us about your song, baby." Jazzy said as she passed a note back to Tracey telling her to '*shut the fuck up.*'

"Thank you, Jazzy. Well, it's called All On Me and it's about how the women in the club be all up on me, ya' dig?"

"What clubs you be at?" Tracey asked.

"Well, umm, the Toppa Line."

"You mean the Bottom Line right there on Claiborne?" Tracey asked.

"Yea, the Bottom Line. I be in Prime Time."

"Prime Time? The club on Downman Road that closed like two years ago?" Tracey asked.

"What? They closed?"

"Yea, they been closed. Look here man, we heard the song. And what you talking 'bout don't interest nobody! The beat all slow, ya' not rhyming and ya' lyin!" Tracey said as Dominique and Rolanda snickered.

Dominique turned and said, "Sister Spanks? Isn't most rap an exaggeration? I mean, do you believe that these rappers are actually killing people and sleeping with all those women like they say?"

"Who side you on theys or mine?" Tracey asked.

"Who is they?" Rolanda asked.

"Nothing! Forget about it! I'm, I'm tripping!" Tracey stated as she held the hammer tightly in her hands in anticipation of smashing Big Rock's cassette tape.

"Big Rock, I just wanna let you know that we don't always treat our guest in this manner. Some of us have issues that need to be dealt with *off air*!" Jazzy said as she twirled her chair around and made a slicing motion across her neck to silence Tracey.

Tracey rolled her eyes as Jazzy turned back to Big Rock and said, "Now, Big Rock, despite her being downright rude, Sister Spanks has a point. We listened to the song and it just doesn't fit what they are doing here on the streets of New Orleans. It's mainly bounce music down here. You familiar with Tim Smooth, Partners N Crime, T. T. Tucker and DJ Duck?" Jazzy asked.

"Yea, yea I know them cats." Big Rock responded nonchalantly.

"They heard your song?" Dominique then asked.

"Yea, they said it was aiight."

"See there? Now, 'aiight', as you say," Rolanda chimed in, "that really means it ain't *tight*! That's all we sayin' Big Rock. Maybe, before you put it out there, you should, rework it and make it, *tight*! I'm not sayin'. I'm just sayin', baby." Rolanda ended.

"Good point Misses Jones," Jazzy responded, "but I know this style of music. Big Rock is doing what they call over in Texas, 'screw music'. It's rapping is slow and the bass is 'gumbo thick' so-to-speak. But Rock I'm a be honest, the listeners here in New Orleans want bounce music, not some slow, deep-bass song talking about stuff they have no interest in. As hard as she was on ya', Sister Amanda Spanks was right."

"Let's just let the voters decide." Big Rock said as Jazzy threw her arms up and turned and nodded towards Tracey.

"Here we go! This here is the new joint from Big Rock representin' the fifteenth ward! Algiers and the Fischer Projects! He holding it down for the whole west bank! Marrero! Harvey! Westwego! Kennedy Heights where ya' at?" Tracey yelled as Big Rock's song went out across the airwaves.

When the song came on, Brianna and Lubby, who were sipping another wine cooler, choked on their drinks as they burst into laughter.

"What the hell is that?" Brianna asked.

"Girl, Tracey told him not to play that whack stuff!" Lubby added as she and Brianna, and a great majority of the young folk in New Orleans, Mississippi, and Alabama laughed at the song.

"When I walk into the club, what they is...all on me... stepping up like a gangster what they is... all on me, all on me, all on me...who got the most money and they what...all on me, all on me... who got 'em getting hotter than a sauna...all on me, all on me..."

Tracey, Rolanda, Dominique, and even Jazzy were bent over at the waist laughing as the song played.

"Get the hammer ready, Tracey! This shit going straight to the trash can!" Jazzy stated off air as the phones began to ring off the hook.

When the song ended, Jazzy began taking callers on air. "Hello caller you on with Jazzy what ya' think about All On Me by Big Rock?"

"Y'all need ta' take All On Me and break it all into pieces!" a male caller stated.

"Caller, what ya' think?" Rolanda asked another caller.

"That's all whack! Tell that boy he ain't got no skills!"

305

another male caller added.

"Go 'head caller!" Dominique stated.

"Yea, umm, Chanel Marie, who this bum thank he is? Ain't no females from the Fischer Projects all on him!" a female caller remarked.

"Go 'head, baby." Rolanda stated.

"Now Misses Jones! What the hell y'all doing up in there? Who let that phony mother(bleep)—"

Rolanda had to drop that female's call because of the foul language. Tracey then played *Where Ya' From* by another local artist by the name of Joe Blakk as the crew fielded more calls. Big Rock got one vote—from his mother.

When the hour was up, Tracey played Big Rock's song again. Big Rock thought he had gotten the audience's approval, but he was wrong. When an album was smashed Tracey would play thirty seconds of the song and then a pretend argument would start between, she, Jazzy, Dominique and Rolanda, they would mix in some of the caller's comments and a police siren would sound and the song would stop. There would be a deafening silence across the airwaves and then, "Bap! Bap! Bap!"

"What the hell you doing?" Big Rock asked.

"Something that shoulda been done a longtime ago ole buster (bleep) M.C.! You gettin' smashed by The Fantastic Four!" Tracey said as the sound of Big Rock's cassette getting smashed was heard across the airwaves.

The thousands of people listening to the show laughed as Tracey smashed the cassette tape to bits. A sound effect like a fuse was played and then there was a loud explosion followed by "That's all Folks!" from the Bugs Bunny cartoons. Big Rock was ushered from behind the plexi-glass window and escorted out of the radio station and off the premises.

When rappers bombed on the show, they didn't take it personal; the four Dee-jays gave them their honest opinion when they thought a song was whack. Still, most rappers wanted to let the people decide. If they wanted to go on make a fool out of themselves before countless numbers of people, the four Dee-jays would gladly help them. Some would come back with a hit, others, like Big Rock would just move on to another city. Every rapper in New Orleans knew that *The Fantastic Four Show* had the power to make or break them, so they had to be tight when going on air. The Dee-jays had helped many local rappers in their career endeavors, and if their song was hot, they put it into rotation and played it during the show's seven 'o' clock hour. The ladies received much love and respect for being supportive of true emcees and they compelled most rappers who were smashed to do better.

The girls ended the show and Rolanda had called Brianna to ask if she had listened in and Brianna told her she and Lubby listened to the whole program and laughed throughout. They chatted with one another for a while inside Jazzy's office before Rolanda hung up the speaker phone to prepare to drop Tracey and Dominique off at home.

Jazzy went home happy this day. She and her girls had an excellent four hour show and she was hoping for a repeat performance the following day to keep the good week going strong.

As for the five, they went to their respective homes tired but happy; but once the keys were turned to their respective domiciles, the problems they had before the show were still there. Dominique hoped this night would be different so as to remedy her marital bed woes. Tracey was hoping Mike would be home before she fell asleep so she could tell him she was pregnant; she would tell her friends the next morning. Lubby went to sleep beside Gerald that night reliving the episode she had with her mother, hoping that the situation would change between she and Cynthia. Rolanda went over to Bobby's house to wait on him, hoping he wasn't out with Kitty, something she feared the most in their relationship, and Brianna went to bed, hoping Tank was all right as he was still out hustling. The five all had fears, problems, or worries, but through it all they persevered, ever hoping for change, ever hoping that things would turn out all right.

CHAPTER 25

THE MOTIVE BEHIND THE ACT

Tracey, Rolanda, and Dominique were sitting in their broadcasting class preparing to leave the campus and head downtown to prepare for the show that evening. It was the following day after Tracey found out she was pregnant. The girls were tidying up the model studio when Tracey told Rolanda and Dominique she was expecting.

"Oh, Tracey! I'm the Godmother!" Rolanda said excitedly.

"No need! I ain't keeping it!"

"*What?*" Dominique and Rolanda said at the same time.

"You heard me! I told Mike a long time ago not to get me pregnant. What he do? He got me pregnant!"

"Hold up Tracey, now you know you my girl. We been down since back in the day, done whipped ass together and everything. We got real secrets we keep, but I really gotta question your judgment this go 'round." Rolanda stated as she sat down beside Tracey.

Tracey brushed her hair from her face and said, "I told Mike not to get me pregnant. I gotta career that's going somewhere, I'm getting a college degree, and—"

"You got a baby on the way!" Rolanda said as she cut Tracey off.

Tracey rolled her eyes and responded by saying, "And I just financed a motorcycle. I can't be tied down with a baby. Not now. Not ever!"

"Well, what are you going to do with your child?" Dominique asked as she sat down on the opposite side of Tracey inside the model studio.

"I'm giving it up."

"Girl, gimmie that baby! Don't *no* child need ta' be going to a foster home!" Rolanda snapped.

"Not a foster home, Rolanda! Mike gone get full custody when the baby's born. I'll pay him child support and all, but that will be as far as it goes. Y'all just don't understand. I don't want a baby right now." Tracey sighed.

"Tracey, girlfriend, think about what you saying and doing. A baby is a blessing." Dominique said softly.

"For you maybe. My decision is final, Dominique. The baby going with Mike—period! End of conversation! We gotta go to work." Tracey said as she got up from her seat in frustration.

Rolanda and Dominique looked over at one another as Tracey got up from her seat and walked out the class. "This is gonna be one hot mess." Rolanda said as Dominique nodded her head in agreement as the two walked out of the class and caught up with Tracey.

The whole ride to work, the three went back and forth with their debate inside Rolanda's car. Tracey gave reasons to give the baby over to Mike, stating that she would not make a good mother and never wanted a child to begin with. Dominique and Rolanda, in turn, gave reasons for Tracey to keep the baby and help Mike raise the child even if they weren't going to be together, stating that a mother's role is unfailing in rearing a child, especially a daughter, and if given enough time, Tracey would make an excellent mother because she often looked after her brother by cooking and washing and ironing his clothes. Tracey brushed her girls off and stuck to her guns, and that began to weigh heavy on Rolanda.

"Look at how sad Lubby be sometimes! She *dying* for her

momma to show her some love! And you gone do the same thing to *your* child?" Rolanda stated angrily as she drove.

"Lubby all right. She moved out her momma house and she gotta man and she making good money." Tracey replied from the backseat.

"You right. But Lubby still hurtin' because of the way Cynthia treat her and you know that, Tracey." Dominique stated.

"Y'all keep comin' down on me and tryin' ta make me feel guilty but I ain't! It's my baby and I can do whatever I wanna do with it!"

"You know what? You trippin' right now, Tracey! Callin' your baby 'it' and shit? Your ass is being real selfish! If you was right I'd tell you you was right, but you wrong! I'm your *fuckin' girl* and I'm saying it to your *face*—you fuckin' *wrong*!" Rolanda yelled at a near deafening level as she pounded the steering wheel.

Rolanda was furious because she knew how Lubby felt towards her mother. She practically had to fight to earn token love from Cynthia and Rolanda couldn't bear knowing Tracey would treat her own child the same way Lubby was being treated. "You see firsthand how that shit affects Lubby and you gone do it to *your own* flesh and blood?" Rolanda asked in disbelief as her eyes watered. Dominique rubbed Rolanda's back while Tracey said nothing as she sat in the backseat.

"Come on, Rolanda. Tracey gone come around. She's just confused and angry right now." Dominique said lowly.

"No she not, Dominique! Tracey do everything she say she gone do! And just like she said, she gone give her fuckin' child away! They got people like Lubby starving for affection from their parents and Tracey *know* that shit! You fuckin' wrong, Tracey!" Rolanda said with wet eyes as she rode into downtown.

The three stopped at a red-light and Rolanda placed her hands over her face and cried aloud as the car idled. Tracey, at that moment, jumped out of the backseat and closed Rolanda's door and leaned into the passenger window and stared at Dominique. "I'm a walk the rest of the way," she said lowly. "Rolanda, I'm, I'm sorry for hurtin' you, you my girl always, but I don't want a baby." Tracey said as her eyes welled up. "I didn't *ask* for this shit!" she added as she backed away and wiped her eyes and began walking down a crowded Carondelet Street towards the Amoco building.

"The older we get seem like the more stupid we get." Dominique said lowly as she stared at Tracey walking quickly down the sidewalk, her backpack hanging low to the ground just like her head.

"Tracey selfish, Dominique. That's my girl and I love her with all my heart—but she selfish." Rolanda said as she rode past Tracey. The two made eye contact with Tracey and she bowed her head again in shame, knowing deep down inside that she was wrong for talking about giving her unborn baby over to Mike. Tracey wouldn't waver, however, no matter how guilty she felt and no matter how wrong she knew she was because a child would only interfere in her plans—and her plans in life superseded everything—including the rearing of her own flesh and blood.

Tracey was truly indeed being selfish. Rolanda knew it, Dominique could see it, and when Lubby and Brianna caught wind of what she was planning on doing with her baby, they also came to know and see the selfishness within Tracey, who understood fully, but was unwilling to admit to the flaw she knew she possessed. And she would continue to justify her behavior by telling herself that she was right for feeling the way she felt towards her unborn child because she specifically told Mike not to get her pregnant and he'd failed to live up to his end of the bargain.

Tracey and Mike argued all week about her not wanting to keep the baby when she told him of her intentions. On a warm Friday night after the last show of the week, Mike was home smoking a blunt inside his trailer listening to *One More Night* by *Phil Collins*, thinking of Tracey, when he heard a low rumbling sound emanating outside his door in his front yard. He got up and peeked out his front window and saw Tracey exiting a motorcycle as she removed her helmet.

"When she get this bike?" Mike asked himself as he eyed Tracey in a tight-fitting pair of black leather pants, a black leather jacket and black two inch heeled boots with a thick buckle. Mike didn't approve of Tracey riding a motorcycle while pregnant, but he couldn't deny the fact that she looked all-so sexy in her outfit as she climbed off her motorcycle and walked across his yard towards his trailer.

Mike opened the door and smiled as he waited for Tracey to approach. When she walked up the stairs, he leaned forward to kiss her, but Tracey turned her head away from him. "Look," she said as she eyed Mike out the corner of her eye, "I'm only here to drop off some money so you can open a bank account for your baby."

"For *our* baby?" Mike asked as he stared at Tracey and reached out to turn her face towards his.

Tracey brushed Mike's hand away and backed down the stairs and stared at him through stern eyes, briefly admiring his effervescence, but refusing to acknowledge the spark ability she felt towards him at the same time. She had to admit, even in her fury, that Mike was indeed the total package and had come a long way in life. He was once a nerdy-looking kid, short and had bad skin. Now, he was a handsome 5'10" 175 pound muscle-toned, chisel-jawed twenty-one year old red-haired young man with nice tattoos and four gold teeth. And deep down inside, Tracey cared for Mike, but she knew he had a weakness and his weakness was standing before him with full knowledge of that fact. Tracey Sanchez knew-all-too well that Michael Fuller was weak for her; but rather than show love to a man whom she truly adored deep down inside, she would began to play a game of manipulation with him for the simple fact that she knew that with Mike, she could get away with her manipulation and force him to take care of a baby that she really didn't want to raise.

"This is your baby! I'm only helping you support it!" Tracey said as she backed down the stairs.

"I don't need your money, Tracey. What I need is for you to

be here with me and be a mother to our child."

"A mother? A mother? You trippin'! Haven't you heard me since the beginning of this week? I'm not doing that shit!"

"We need to handle this like a man and a woman."

"I am! *Here!*" Tracey said as she attempted to hand Mike two hundred dollars. Mike didn't take the money, so Tracey threw it at him and walked off.

Mike leapt down the stairs and grabbed her from behind and said, "Why you playing the role with me, Tracey? You know we can be a family!"

"I don't want a family! Let me go, mutherfucka!" Tracey yelled.

"No! You need ta' talk to me, Tracey!"

Tracey wiggled free and ran and stood beside her new motorcycle. "I told you! Nobody hearing me! This is your baby!"

Mike walked over to Tracey and calmly said, "Tracey come on now, don't be like that. Look, I quit hustling alright? Brianna coming to pick up this last package and I'm through. I'll, I'll get a job! We can be a family. Me you and the baby."

"Stupid mutherfucka." Tracey said lowly as she hopped on her motorcycle and started the bike.

"Why you doing this to yourself? It don't have ta' be like this, Tracey! You got this fuckin' motorcycle and you know you pregnant? You act like you tryna hurt yourself!" Mike told Tracey as she revved up the bike.

Mike couldn't see it, but Tracey was crying behind her helmet. The young woman was going out of her mind having to deal with a plethora of emotions being brought on by this unwanted pregnancy, her anger towards Mike, and the pressure being thrust upon her from her friends and her mother. She did not want to raise a child—it was as simple as that. And she saw no wrong in turning the baby over to its father.

"Tracey, talk to me!" Mike yelled over the motorcycle's engine. "Talk to me! Explain to me what's going on with you!"

Mike yelled, trying desperately to keep Tracey in his presence so as to ascertain answers to the motives behind her actions.

Mike's pleas of obtaining and understanding were falling on deaf ears, and once he realized that he would not be able to reach Tracey at the present time, he stopped yelling and watched with hurtful eyes as the woman he loved more than life itself backed out of his yard and sped off down the block. Tracey rode her bike towards Interstate-10 and headed east towards Slidell on a stretch of highway was a straight shot on level ground. She had to relieve a lot of pent-up frustration on this night having dealt with a long week of school and work, and a life outside the job that had become filled with constant arguing and accusations. She merged in with traffic and hit the gears on her cycle and was quickly up to 95 miles per hour and began passing cars as if they were standing still.

"I didn't ask for this shit!" Tracey screamed into the night air as she sped down the highway. She crossed the twin span bridges, which were two elevated portions of Interstate-10 that stretched 7 miles across Lake Ponchartrain towards the city of Slidell. Once there, she turned around and sped back to New Orleans, repeating the performance. This would become her routine whenever she grew frustrated.

As Tracey was relieving her stress, Mike was welcoming Brianna into his home. Brianna was supposed to pick up a quarter-kilo from Mike and drop it off in Gaslight Square by one of Tank's counterparts. Tank, Bobby, and Gerald were across the river delivering packages to other hustlers on the West Bank this night, so the drop off in Gaslight Square to one of Tank's' homeboys, nick-named Micey, had landed on Brianna.

Brianna had planned to do the drop off to Micey early in the day, but she had got caught up with Lubby listening to the *Fantastic Four Show*, and against better judgment, she went out to do what she had planned on doing earlier. By the time she dropped Lubby home at Gerald's house, it was after midnight when she reached Mike's home. When Brianna walked in, the troubled young man immediately went into a discussion about what transpired with him and Tracey; but

Brianna, who always had a listening ear, was anxious to get the night over with. Micey moved around a lot, and Brianna knew if she didn't drop off tonight, it may be a few days before she caught up with Micey again, and she and Tank had $4500 on the line.

"Mike, call me tomorrow and we gone talk. I don't mean to be rude, but I really, really, have to go." Brianna said as she hugged Mike, locked and loaded her .380 chrome pistol and made her way to her jeep. Mike sat back down on his sofa and relit his joint, praying that Tracey would change her mind about their child.

Brianna made her way into Gaslight Square, about two miles from Abramson High School and parked a block down the street from her preordained destination beside a wooded lot. She grabbed her package and walked down the quiet, lonely street leading into Gaslight Square and made her way to Micey's apartment and tapped the door lightly. Crickets creaked, and dogs barked, they seem to be the only living things outside besides Brianna.

"Who that?" Micey asked from behind the door.

"Bri, homeboy! Open up! It's dark out ta' this bitch!"

Micey, a twenty-two year-old hustler that grew up under Tank, opened the door and let Brianna in and gave her dap. Tank had been frontin' Micey for almost two years and they had a good business relationship. Brianna liked Micey; he was a funny dude at times. She walked through the living room and spoke to Micey's cousin Dave and his cousin's friend Jamal, who were sitting on the sofa playing Tecmo Bowl on a Nintendo game system, as she made her way to the kitchen. The two teenagers argued back and forth over who was the best as they passed a blunt back and forth and sipped on two forty ounces of St. Ides.

Brianna noticed two Tech-9 semi-automatics on the coffee table as she slid past the two nineteen year-olds and said, "Nice piece, Dave."

"Yea, this bitch fat huh, Bri?" Dave asked as he picked up his tech-nine.

"Yea, it's tight. But it can't fuck the .380 homeboy!"

"Three-eighty?" Dave and Jamal said at the same time as they laughed aloud.

"That's a fuckin' cap gun!" Jamal stated before he sipped his beer and continued his game as Brianna stepped into the kitchen and laid the quarter key on the table.

Micey was counting out $4500 as he stood at the table across from Brianna. "Bri, I put a order in for some rims today. Tell Tank big-headed ass I wants my shit prompy."

"Prompy? What the fuck that mean ya' dumb mutherfucka!" Dave stated as he laughed.

"It mean quick! Like how my foot gone go in your ass ya' bitch you!" Micey answered.

"I'm a tell ya' momma ya' cursin', mutherfucka!" Dave snapped back as he laughed aloud.

"Yea? Look here, when ya' get in contact with her ass? Tell her I said bring my fuckin' car back! Tell her just like that for me hear? 'Bring my fuckin car back', and she gone have some choice words for ya' real prompy like, ya' bitch you!" Micey stated as he continued counting the money and laughing at the same time.

Brianna was laughing as well as she stood across from Micey at the kitchen table. And while Dave and Jamal played their game and whilst Brianna waited for Micey to finish his count, they continued to joke around with one another.

"Eh Bri," Jamal said from the living room, "tell Tank don't bring that mutherfucka Micey a damn thang! He always—"

Jamal was cut off when the front door was kicked open and four males wearing bandannas over the lower parts of their faces rushed into the home. Dave reacted quickly and grabbed his Tech-9 and began blasting his weapon towards the doorway. The male who kicked the door in turned and ran, but he was shot in the side by Dave. Jamal grabbed his Tech-9 and began shooting wildly, but he was mowed down by an AK-47 from another one of the males as he ran into the house. Dave's gun suddenly jammed, and that allowed the three remaining men to enter the home.

Micey and Brianna were now hiding under the kitchen table witnessing the drama unfolding. The men were beating on Dave and turning over furniture in the living room. One of the men ran pass the kitchen to the back of the house, completely missing Micey and Brianna. Micey had left his gun on the kitchen counter and would be spotted the moment he moved, but he was still trying to figure out how to get the men up out his spot. Brianna, on the other hand, was scared out of her mind. She had her .380 on her, but the firepower the men possessed had her so unnerved she was afraid to pull the trigger. She was preparing to jump up and run out the back door.

"Bri gimmie your gun! Give me the gun if you ain't gone shoot!"

Brianna gave Micey her .380 and he began shooting at the three males who were manhandling Dave inside the living room as Brianna crawled from under the table and began creeping towards the back door. Micey missed the men and they quickly began firing their weapons inside the kitchen. Micey and Brianna both covered their heads as bullets riddled the table, the back door and the kitchen walls.

One of the males then ran into the kitchen after the gunfire seized. "Get the fuck up bitches," the dark-skinned husky male said as he flipped the table over, kicked Micey in the face and grabbed Brianna, who was jiggling the back door knob and screaming hysterically as she tried to escape. Another man ran into the kitchen aimed his weapon at Micey's head and ordered him into the living room beside his cousin Dave, who was kneeling on his knees beside Jamal's bloodied corpse.

"Say brer, what the fuck up, man?" Micey asked through busted lips.

"You know what this is bitch! We want the yao, the money and all the fuckin' jewels out this mutherfucka!" the man said as he forced Micey to his knees beside his cousin.

"It's on the table! Everything on the table, dog!"

"I know that ain't it, nigga! Where the rest," the man who'd run to the back of the house asked upon returning to the living room.

"That's it brer! For real!" Dave said in a panicked state.

The man holding Micey captive aimed his weapon and blasted Dave in the back of the head, killing him instantly. Micey then told him the rest of the money was in the back bedroom and the man who'd ran down the hall earlier, made his way back towards the rear of the apartment once more.

Brianna, meanwhile, was pleading for her life as she was being dragged by her hair into a bedroom where the man holding her captive began unbuckling his pants. "I'm taking that pussy before I kill yo' ass bitch!" he hissed as he threw Brianna up against the wall and began choking her.

"Please! Please, sir don't do this to me!" Brianna said through clasped teeth.

"You gone let me fuck, bitch?" the man asked calmly from behind his black bandanna as he gently tilted Brianna's chin up to look her in the eyes.

"Mister, please! Please sir!"

"What the fuck I told you about calling me sir? Fuck that! Strip and get on the fuckin' bed bitch! *Strip!*" the man yelled as he fired a bullet into the floor and shoved Brianna towards the bed like a mere rag doll.

Brianna cried as she began to pull off her jeans, shaking in utter fear.

"Yes indeed. This gone be some good ass pussy right here," the man said lowly. "Turn around bitch!" he then ordered Brianna as he shoved her forward.

Brianna was now naked from the waist down. She cried heavily, shaking in pure, unmitigated terror as she got on all fours facing away from the man. She soon felt his dick pressed up against the crack of her ass and she screamed and begged again. "Please! Please! I ain't gone say nothing! I ain't gone say nothing I promise!"

"I don't care 'bout your promises, bitch! And fuck you anyway after I take this pussy!"

"Say, brer! Say, brer! Hold up, man!!" Brianna heard Micey yell from the living room. Seconds later, two gunshots rang out. Brianna then knew she was the last survivor inside the apartment as Micey was in the process of being killed. She heard the last screams of mercy exit Micey's mouth before three more shots rang out and everything then went silent.

The man in the room rubbed his dick up and down Brianna's ass crack and was preparing to violate her and her life suddenly began flashing before her eyes. She thought of her mother and how hurt she would be when she got news that her daughter had been raped and killed. Bri never, not even for a miniscule second, thought her life would end this way. She was preparing to surrender and accept the fact that this would be her last night on Earth and was hoping the man would kill her quick when she heard the phrase, "Big O! Big O! Go help Earl," spill forth from the mouth of another man as he entered the bedroom.

"You trippin'! I'm 'bout ta' fuck this bitch!"

"Dog, we ain't got time! No time! Go help Manny with Earl! We got the shit! Go help them and let me do this bitch!"

The man stared at his counterpart for a few seconds before tucking his dick back into his jeans and running out of the room. "Kill that bitch and come on nigga!" he said as he disappeared from sight.

Brianna turned around and pleaded again as she got off the bed and dropped to her knees and begged not to be killed.

"Bri, Bri. Shhh. Shhh." the young man said lowly as he covered his mouth with one finger and fired four rounds into the mattress.

He said nothing as he stared down at Brianna, who could only stare back in uncertainty over the man's actions and motives. "Shhh. Shhh." he whispered again and fired two more shots.

The man then knelt down and stared into Brianna's eyes from behind his black bandanna and for the first time, she could see his light skin, his brown eyes, and long, silky black hair and it suddenly dawned on her: she knew him, and he knew her. They were friends back in the day. "You gotta get out this game, Bri. The next nigga might not be me, ya' feel?" the man said seriously.

"Nigga, let's go!" a voice called back from the living room.

"I'm comin', nigga! Stay put, brer, I got this hoe!"

"Gimmie your chain. I'm a tell 'em I was taking your chain off!"

Brianna handed the man her chain and he stood up and backed away slowly, never taking his eyes off her. "Everybody cool in East Shore?" he asked lowly.

"Yea, they all good. Lubby and everybody else is good." Brianna whispered nervously, hoping to God that one of the other men didn't reenter the room and trigger another episode.

"Okay," the man said lowly as he turned and walked towards the bedroom door.

"Ben," Brianna whispered from her knees as Ben Holland turned and stared at her, "thank you for saving my life."

Ben Holland raised his left hand and made an E with three of his fingers. "East Shore," he said in a low, but affectionate manner.

Brianna made an E with her hand as well, "East Shore," she whispered back gently with a look of appreciation displayed upon her face. She could see a smile appear briefly from under Ben's bandanna as he stood for another few seconds before he disappeared from sight.

Brianna exhaled when she heard car tires peeling out and quickly began dressing as she cried silently. She ran through the living room, blocking her face so as not to lay eyes on Micey, Dave, and Jamal, all whom lay dead inside the living room. The scene was a macabre sight that Brianna cared not to look at as the smell of gun powder and burnt human flesh was heavy in the air. Furniture was strewn about and the Nintendo game was still running as she exited the apartment and ran to her jeep, fled the scene and cried the whole drive home. She was still shaking when she pulled in front of her home, but was glad to see Tank had made it back. She hopped from her jeep, ran and unlocked the door to her home, entered and quickly locked it and fell to her knees up against the door and yelled out for Tank.

Twenty-four year-old Tank was a welcome sight when walked into the living room; and only then did Brianna truly feel safe.

"Bri," Tank said as he ran towards his woman. "What happened, baby?"

Brianna hugged Tank and whispered, "Some—somebody killed Micey 'nem just now."

"My dogs? Somebody killed my dogs? You was there?"

"Yes. And they—they killed them boys!"

"They killed Micey 'nem? Why they ain't kill you Bri?"

Brianna quickly thought about the reason she wasn't killed. She didn't, and she couldn't tell Tank that she knew one of the people who had killed Micey, Dave and Jamal back in the day. After all, Ben Holland didn't have to let her live. Ben wasn't even in the room when Brianna was about to be raped and killed, but she believed he cared enough to save her on the strength of the way she had treated him when his parents were killed and he was forced to move away from East Shore and she was right. Ben never forgot about his friends and despite his cold-hearted ways, he exercised mercy on an old friend and Brianna wasn't about to betray the young man.

"I, I hid in a closet. I was in the bathroom when they kicked the door in and I ran and hid in a closet under some dirty clothes. They was in and out in two minutes, Tank." Brianna said as she wiped her watery eyes.

"You don't know who dunnit?"

"Nooo. They took all the money that was on the table *and* the cocaine. That's it. I'm out the game. I can't do this shit no more, Tank."

"I wasn't gone let you go back out there anyway, Bri. I love you, baby. If I woulda lost you tonight, I wouldn't be the same man. I'm glad you still alive."

"You wanna call the police for Micey 'nem?"

"Knowing that neighborhood, they already out there, anyway, we done with that."

"You quittin' too?"

"Yea, baby. I had a brand new set of Dayton's for my boy too. We can put 'em on your jeep I guess. Look, I got beaucoup money stacked up, let's umm, let's—"

"Make music?" Brianna asked lowly as she smiled at her lover.

"Yea. Let's hustle legit."

"God, I was so scared. I never knew fear could be so powerful. I don't wanna ever feel like that again. When umm, when I saw you, I immediately felt safe. You my rock."

Tank leaned in and kissed Brianna as the two tore at one another's clothes. Brianna knew one of the males had slid his penis up and down her crack and she didn't want Tank to take her in her dirtied state. "Let's take a shower together." she suggested.

The two of them undressed and Brianna stood before Tank completely naked. He stared at her 5' 6" 135 pound curvaceous physique in pure admiration. Brianna's apple-sized breasts were throbbing and she was wet with anticipation. Tank stared on at his woman, her dark-brown skin glistening like brand new pennies, her dark eyes full of love and her dark-brown hair hanging just below her ears. Her hips were curvy and her lovely mound, covered by a small tuft of fluffy black pubic hairs was throbbing and getting moist by the second. He pressed his lips to Brianna's and then carried her to the bathroom. Brianna ran the water and as she did so, she stared at Tank's cut biceps and ripped abdomen. She ran her hands across his bald head and traced the outline of his thin beard before leaning into his chest to kiss her name, Brianna, which Tank had tattooed across his heart.

"Damn baby, you make me so hot, Tank. Clean your woman

up and make love to your baby. She needs you."

Tank kindly obliged his woman by bathing her and making sweet to love to her in the missionary position as they held hands tightly. As they lay in bed after an intense passionate love-making session, Brianna couldn't help but think where Ben Holland went wrong in life. He was such a sweet child, but he had turned into a monster. At least towards those he didn't know or care about. After witnessing what she had seen on this night, Brianna knew that as long as Ben Holland was in the game, a lot of people were not safe. She was glad she knew him once upon a time because she understood fully that their childhood friendship had saved her life.

The following day, Brianna told her friends about what happened the night before and they all were glad that it was Ben Holland who had robbed Micey and not someone else. This would be another secret the five would hold on to throughout their lives. The girls could've easily turned Ben in for killing Micey, but none of the girls besides Bri really had a connection to Micey. On top of that, Ben had saved Brianna's life, so in the five's eyes, they owed him that much at the very least. Brianna and Tank were beginning to think real hard about her recording her album and didn't want to risk going to jail. Going legit was the only reasonable option from that point forth, especially after all the things that had transpired the night Bri almost got killed.

Brianna Stanford exited the game in March of 1992 and never returned. She was beginning to change her ways, and she would watch with loving and careful eyes as her friends dealt with issues that weren't in her control, but often kept her wondering when and if they too would someday change their ways just as she had done, but if Brianna's life was of any indication, then she knew that more drama possibly lay ahead for her and her girls. What all that drama entails, however, remains to be seen.

CHAPTER 26

HATING AND CONTEMPLATING

"You need ta' get up off your big behind and decide exactly what it is you gone do with this baby, Tracey!" Maria shouted at her daughter.

Twenty-one year-old Tracey Sanchez was now over eight months pregnant. She had taken a leave of absence from work and she was now on bed rest at her mother's home. It was the first week in September of '92 and the five, all now 21 years of age, were heavily engaged in their careers and lives and now had very little time for one another. Rolanda, Tracey, and Dominique would see each other in school and at work, but that was about as far as it went. The friends were just too busy juggling relationships and careers so time spent hanging out with one another was rare. Although they talked on the phone with one another from time to time, they hadn't hung out in months, and that was something they really missed.

Rolanda's plight in life at the time was a smooth sail. She and 24 year-old Bobby were becoming closer than ever; so much so that Bobby had given her a key to his apartment which was near the University of New Orleans' Campus. Bobby didn't have a car so he would drop Rolanda off at school and continue to hustle the streets and Rolanda would ride to the radio station with Dominique, who had recently purchased a new Mazda 626 because all three girls had received a fifteen percent raise from the radio station.

Calvin and Dominique were doing well financially, but they still spent long hours apart and that is what was ailing Dominique during this period of time; but through it all, she hung in there with her husband and he was forever grateful because he knew in due time, he and his wife would be living a comfortable, secure life. Calvin believed in Dominique and was working hard to accomplish the goal the two of them had set. The man was ever proud of the life he was living and truly devoted to making him and Dominique's marriage as prosperous as possible.

Lubby at the time, was trying to get her mother some medical attention. She and Brianna had talked over the phone repeatedly about Cynthia maybe having a mental condition that needed medicating. Cynthia, however, refused to seek help because she felt she didn't have a problem. The only problem in her eyes was Lubby, who was refusing to give up on her even upon becoming a young and independent woman. Lubby had also finally gotten the money together so she could have full access to the retail location she and Gerald had purchased. She was now renovating the place and was scheduled to open her pet shop in January of 1993. Things were going real good for Lubby, and Gerald, wanting to make the love of his life an honest woman, had proposed to her on her 21st birthday back in August inside the retail space the two had bought. The five were all doing well in life despite the issues that some of them carried in one form or another.

Brianna had recorded her first song, a remake of Rene and Angela's song *You Don't Have To Cry*, but she and Tank had to setup copyright and royalty agreements and form a record label in order to bring the song to market. The Fantastic Four had dibs on the song, but Brianna and Tank were having a hard time finding a good engineer, not to mention their money was running low because neither of the two was working.

Neither Tank *nor* Brianna wanted to work. Not that they were lazy, it was just that the reality of punching a time clock was not in their blood. They were hustlers by nature; if they worked, it would be for themselves, but once the realization set in that they would lose their home and all their worldly possessions unless they resorted back to selling cocaine, something neither of the two wanted to do, 24 year-old Thaddeus 'Tank' Russell stepped up like a real man should when confronted with those issues and took a job at the Coca-Cola Bottling Plant in Harahan right alongside Mike. It was either go back to the game, or take a job to get him and Brianna where they wanted to be, and Tank made the smart choice—he let the game be and punched a time clock for the first time in his life; but it was all with the goal of getting Brianna's album out on the market.

When Mike found out Tracey was having his baby, the first thing *he* did was quit the game. Months before Tank got hired, Mike got a job at Coca-Cola and purchased a brand new GMC Safari mini-van in preparation for the daughter he was due to have. He had been working there since early April and he had used his outstanding credentials to get Tank hired.

Mike was setting himself up to support his daughter, and Tracey as well, but Tracey was still bent on giving him full custody of the baby. Mike had told Maria that he wanted to marry Tracey and raise his family, only Tracey didn't want to have anything to do with him or the baby. She was still mad at Mike for getting her pregnant and in her eyes, "destroying her life" as she often stated to Mike. The statement that Tracey repeatedly yelled at Mike is what was causing Maria to lash out at her daughter on this day in early September of 1992.

"Why not marry Mike and raise your daughter the right way?" Maria asked of her daughter.

"Because, first of all, I didn't ask to have a baby. Second—"

"No first of all, if you didn't want to get pregnant, you should've been using some form of birth control! And second, you should've never told him to come inside your freaky behind!"

"Momma!" Tracey yelled as she hopped from her bed and walked out her bedroom feeling embarrassed.

"That's right! Mike told me everything!" Maria said as she followed Tracey into the kitchen. "And you are just as responsible for bringing this baby into this world as he is."

"I never said come in me. I said come with me if you wanna know the real story! I can't believe he told you that!"

"You need to listen to how you sound, child." Maria stated lowly. "I never had *any* intentions on discovering what your sex life is all about, Tracey. But when Mike cried his heart out to me on that sofa in there a couple of months back, my heart went out to him after he went into full detail. Whatever y'all do in the bedroom is y'all's business. I don't care about that. What I *do* care about is my grandchild! I never neglected you in any form or fashion and you disown your own child before she even gets here?"

"I'm paying child support on my own initiative, momma!"

"It ain't about money, Tracey. It's about being a mother to your child." Maria said lovingly.

"I don't want this baby!" Tracey yelled aloud as Maria stared sadly at her daughter. She couldn't believe what she was seeing in Tracey. As Tracey leaned against the kitchen counter and cried aloud with her hands covering her face, she felt a warm liquid flow down her legs. "Momma, momma, my water, my water just broke!" she said in a scared tone of voice.

Maria rushed to her daughter's side as she grabbed the phone to dial the ambulance. Tracey's brother, who was listening to the argument from his bedroom, ran into the kitchen area when he heard his mother talking to the dispatchers from 911. "Marcus, Marcus, go get your sister's bag for me son, she ready to go in!"

The ambulance came and took Tracey to Methodist Hospital where she gave birth to a baby girl. "Ohh, she's an angel." a nurse said softly as the baby was brought forth. "What's her name going to be?" the woman asked Tracey.

"Angela," Tracey mumbled somewhat incoherently.

"Angel? Did you say Angel, miss?" the nurse asked.

"Yea, that's it. Angel," Tracey said as she closed her eyes.

Tracey was planning to name the baby Angela, but after

hearing the nurse say Angel, she went on and named her baby Angel, hoping it would bring the baby girl luck in life since she had no intentions on being around. Three days later, Tracy signed the birth certificate and Mike was there to sign his name as well. The baby's full name was Angel Michelle Fuller. Tracey had given Angel Mike's last name in another attempt to further separate herself from the child. After all the things that had unfolded leading up to birth of Angel, Tracey was still bent on giving her baby over to Mike. There was no bonding with the baby the four days Tracey spent at the hospital. She didn't breast feed the child and she rarely held the newborn. When she did, she acted as if it was more of a chore instead of a blessing. Her four friends had paid her a visit and the whole time they were there, Tracey only held the baby once to allow them to take a picture.

Everyone was hoping Tracey would change her mind once she had her baby, but that wasn't to be. Two weeks out of the hospital, Tracey delivered her baby girl to Mike and walked away from the man and would continue to give Mike one hundred dollars a week. Tracey had gotten her own apartment during that time, a one bedroom in Slidell and rejoined the Fantastic Four a month after she had the baby.

Everyone was disappointed in Tracey, but they let her be, hoping something would click in her mind and lead her back to the child she was beginning to neglect. Her friends went to see Angel all the time and were a big help to Mike. They all had motherly instincts and they gave the young man pointers on how to deal with the baby when she cried and he didn't know what to do. Maria and Marcus were on hand daily as well. Mike, Maria, and Marcus had formed a tight bond during the first four months of the baby's life. It was a hard struggle in the beginning once the realization sat in that Tracey wanted no part in rearing the child, but with help from friends, and especially Maria, Mike was slowly becoming an excellent father; still, he held out hope that the woman he loved would someday change her attitude towards her own flesh and blood.

In January of 1993, Lubby had opened her pet shop. She and Gerald were excited that cold winter day as they watched a small group of customers peruse the business in search of an after holiday gift. *Lubby Land Pet Shop* had various fish, iguanas, parrots, dogs and cats. There were also exotic monkeys, and snakes. Because it was just after Christmas, business was slow. Lubby knew the risks of opening up so soon after the holidays, and had anticipated the risks, but she wanted in on first quarter sales; on top of that, she knew what the pet shop in the mall where she formerly worked usually bought in in January so she took the risk. At the end of January when she checked her monthly reports, Lubby had nearly twice the amount of sales as the pet shop in the mall where she once worked. Her gamble had paid off better than expected. Lubby had chosen an excellent location on Read Boulevard with easy access. Rolanda promoted her commercials over the air daily during the show and Lubby's prices were unbeatable. She also had a certified veterinarian on the premises that rendered shots and spayed and neutered cats and dogs at a discount. Lubby Williams had become a successful entrepreneur, and despite her troubled relationship with her mother, who said her daughter wouldn't amount to anything, Lubby had indeed made something of herself at the age of twenty-one.

****

"We talking tonight friends about the growing trend of single family homes here in New Orleans and across America. I'm Chanel Marie and I would like to welcome everybody to the discussion," Dominique stated from behind her microphone inside WYLD studios the first week in February of '93 during the show's nine 'o' clock hour. "So umm, for those of you who have been raised under such trying circumstances we ask that you call in and give us your take on the matter. My opinion is it can be done because I've personally seen it happen—but it takes an extra effort and a special kind of parent in my opinion. Family has to pull together and that *one* parent has to not only be the mother, but the father as well, and vice-versa. I say that because there are so many single parents, both male and female in the world raising kids on their own, and that's a serious problem and a challenge within the Black community." Dominique ended.

"What if it's a father raising a child on his own," Jazzy chimed in as she rocked in her chair inside the studio. "A son wouldn't be too trying I don't think—*if* it's done right. But how can a male teach a female to be—a female?"

The Fantastic Four were doing a show on single parents. The reason being was that Rolanda had come across a letter from a young teen mother whose baby's father had run out on her shortly after she gave birth, leaving her to raise the baby alone. When Rolanda read the letter her heart went out to the young teen. She wanted to help, and by doing so, she hoped she could get Tracey to see the error of her ways. Rolanda and Dominique had went to Jazzy and told her of their intentions and she agreed to make the letter a topic of discussion during the nine 'o clock hour. Tracey caught on immediately and she didn't comment nearly the whole hour. She merely played songs relating to the subject and sipped hot fudge as she listened to her friends talk until Jazzy asked her a question.

"Sister Spanks, you been quiet the whole hour. What do you think about a father raising a child on his own?" Jazzy asked over the air waves.

"If the purported mother's intent was made known from the get go, I mean, if the female had no intention of keeping the baby, then the father has to decide what *he* is going to do."

"Yea, but what if, what if—I guess what I want to say is that nobody never really thinks of a *mother* abandoning a baby. So people might not believe it when it's said." Rolanda stated.

"Why not?" Tracey retorted. "If somebody say they gone do something, why wouldn't people believe them?"

"Okay, okay, point taken," Dominique chimed in, "but it's just hard for a male to raise a female. On top of that, if he finds another woman, then she will become that baby's mother. And I just wonder how the baby's biological mother would react if she saw her baby daddy with another woman raising her child."

"The baby's mother might feel relieved. At least people would stop trying to force her to be a mother—something she didn't want to be in the first place! Look, men leave women stuck with babies all the time—that's what Misses Jones letter was about anyway, right? Men do it *all the time*—but when a woman abandons a child she's the scum of the earth and I don't think that's fair. It's double standard if ya' ask me." Tracey replied in a disgusted manner, exasperated over the fact that her friends were trying to discuss her situation over the air waves in a subliminal manner.

"Well girls, Sister Spanks has a point," Jazzy said as she poured herself a cup of hot chocolate.

Jazzy knew her girls well. Even though Rolanda and Dominique were trying to subtly reach out to Tracey, the keen leader of the pack knew full well that the further Rolanda and Dominique pushed Tracey, the more resentment she would build towards her friends and her daughter. It didn't take long for Jazzy to realize on this night that Tracey would have to come around on her own. "If a woman doesn't want to raise a child," Jazzy said as she sat rocking with her eyes closed, "then she has every right to place that child into loving arms, be it the baby's father, grandmother, some other family member or a foster home. If the child's needs are being met, then no one should have a complaint about how the child is being raised. But remember this, leave the door open so if that parent does have a change of heart, he or she can step in. But on the flip side, don't think that you can be an absent parent and return to a child's life years down the road, because by then it'll be too late. Phone calls coming up next." Jazzy ended as Tracy cued up *This Lil Game we Play* by Subway and 702.

The girls finished the final hour of the show and as they exited the Amoco building, Jazzy invited them out for drinks at a lounge inside the Sheraton hotel on Canal Street in downtown New Orleans. Rolanda and Dominique agreed, but Tracey refused. She hopped onto her motorcycle and rode home to Slidell doing over 100 miles per hour the whole way.

Back inside the lounge, Jazzy, Dominique, and Rolanda were sipping apple martinis as they talked about the show. "Now ladies," Jazzy said as she stirred her drink, "I know you two are concerned about your friend and baby Angel, but Tracey gone have to see the mistakes she's making on her own. Nobody can do that for her. I can tell she's hurt that she's hurting you all and Mike as well, but she wants y'all to understand how she feels. She just didn't want a baby." Jazzy said as the three females sat inside the cozy dimly lit lounge inside a huge booth.

The club was a real casual place; carpeted, with a raised V.I.P. section where the girls sat and a medium sized stage in which a band often played. The lounge was half-full as it was a Wednesday night, and that sat well with the females as they wanted a laid back atmosphere to unwind and relax.

"I know she didn't *want* a baby, but how could Tracey do that to her child?" Rolanda asked.

"Selfishness is a shortcoming," Jazzy said as she smiled, revealing her four open faced gold teeth. "But in the eyes of a selfish person, their actions are always justified. If you haven't noticed, Tracey feels justified in what she is doing based on the statement she made to Mike early on, 'I don't want a baby'. When Mike got Tracey pregnant, all bets were off as far as she was concerned. Now, the right thing to do would've been to accept what happened and be a mother, but Tracey's not looking at it that way. You said yourself Rolanda that she means what she says, so why wouldn't she be reacting this way after what she requested didn't remain intact?"

Rolanda had no answer. Jazzy was making sense; and as wrong as it was, Tracey didn't want a baby, she said that, and she meant what she said.

"I just can't understand that. She see how Lubby act towards her mother having to fight and plea for affection. Why would she want her daughter to grow up like that?" Dominique asked Jazzy.

"She gave a clue back in the studio, but you girls must've missed it. Tracey's hoping somebody else would step up, but she seems to be forgetting one thing—if somebody steps up, then she loses Mike. Now, Mike has been there since she was what, fifteen? She loves him, and maybe seeing someone else share his joy would be a wakeup call. Hopefully that won't be ten years from now. Look, leave Tracey be. It's still early, maybe something will click in her. Just, just let her be. She knows where her daughter is and time is on her side as of right now. She'll be fine in due time." Jazzy ended.

Dominique got up to use the restroom and realized the martini had her a little tipsy. She walked slowly to the restroom and relived herself and washed her hands. As she was coming out, she stumbled and grabbed the gold railing leading back out into the lounge.

"You all right miss?" a deep male voice called out.

"Yes. Thank you. I think I had a li'l bit too much to drink," Dominique said as she focused on the figure standing before her.

"Well, I can call you a cab and get you home if you can't drive tonight."

Dominique looked up to see a handsome 5'10" bald-headed muscular dark-skinned man in a light-tan suit and black gators staring down at her.

"Wow," she exclaimed. "I mean, what did you ask me?"

"Do you need a cab?"

"Cab? Right. No, no I'm fine." Dominique replied as she released the rail and stood straight up.

"I'm Brad. I didn't mean to impose upon you, it just looked as if you were having a hard time. And if you were driving, I'd hate to see a sweet young thing like yourself not make it home to your husband."

"Ohh, he's probably," Dominique caught herself once she realized she was about to engage the man in conversation. "Yes, he's probably waiting on me."

"Lucky man." Brad responded.

"Who?" Dominique asked.

"Your husband. What his name?"

Dominique had to think because for a second or two, she had forgotten Calvin's name. "His name is Cal, Calvin."

The man standing before Dominique had her flushed. He smelled good, looked good and had a smooth, soothing voice.

She could tell he was older than she and that meant experience, something Calvin didn't have at the present time if Dominique had to tell it. There was no denying it either, she was instantly attracted to the man, but she was married and she knew nothing about the man that stood before her. She leaned back against the wall and Brad drew closer and said, "Seems like if he cared about your needs, you would be wrapped up in his arms tonight. It's cold outside. A woman like you should always be made to feel warm and secure."

Dominique was melting underneath Brad's refined charisma. *"Warm and secure,"* she thought to herself before quickly snapping back to her senses. "Brad, umm, thank you, but I'm okay. I'm a married woman."

"I'm married as well. That makes it all the more better. It's called discretion. You have a lot on the line and so do I. What's your name?"

"Dominique—but, I'm married."

"I haven't asked for nothing. I only asked do you need a cab and do you need to get back to your husband."

"No."

"No you don't need a cab, or no you don't need to get back to your husband?"

Dominique was ready to answer the latter question until her heart skipped a beat. She realized that she was actually about to engage Brad in conversation, a conversation grounded in adultery. She was being tempted and she was feeling guilty for wanting to continue talking to this attractive older man.

"I gotta go," Dominique said lowly as Brad stepped back allowing her the space she needed to escape his charm. She returned to the table and rejoined Rolanda and Jazzy and they continued to chat. Dominique, however, couldn't help but to wonder if she had let an opportunity slip away. Brad said he was married also, that meant that there would be no strings attached if she wanted to have an affair with the man. She could tell he was experienced, maybe he would be willing to let her experiment, maybe he would fulfill her sexual fantasies.

She pondered those thoughts before ordering another martini. Dominique was a married woman now contemplating an affair, and that gnawed at her inner being. She didn't want to cheat on Calvin, but no one knew of the conversation she had with Brad, maybe she could live out her fantasy just once to get it out of her system and no one would know. This is what the confused and tempted married woman thought about as she waited on her next drink.

CHAPTER 27

WHAT THE HELL

"Hey momma!" Dominique stated to her mother as she sat in her office inside the Amoco building. It was a week after her encounter with Brad inside the lounge's restroom area and Dominique found herself contemplating on whether she should go back to the lounge and wait and see if Brad would show up again. She struggled with that thought all day at school and she now sat frustrated in her office as she prepared for Wednesday night's show. Finally, tired of going back and forth with her emotions, she sought advice from her mother.

"Hey, baby! It's been a few days since we talked and even longer since you last visited. Your father will be home this weekend and we're all going out to dinner, okay?"

"That's fine, momma. Hey mom, dad is away for weeks at a time, how do you combat your, umm, you know, your, urges?"

"I know where you going, but I have my religion, and that in itself keeps me busy. Me and Charlotte hang out sometimes, and I drop in and see baby Angel from time to time. Before you know it, the time passes and your father's home. Besides, we've been married for as long as you are old and believe me, we've worn many a mattress. It is now more a matter of *time* for us than what it is *sex*."

"Momma, I never heard you talk like this." Dominique responded with a smile.

"What? Candidly? Come on now, Dominique. We both are grown women, and you're married. You know what it's like to wear out a mattress." Mrs. Franz said as she laughed over the phone.

"No, momma I don't. At the rate we going, we'll have the same mattress until we retire."

"You and Calvin having problems, baby?"

"Not outside the bed, but in the bed. We barely have sex, and when we do I lay on my back and that's it. I want to do different things, but Calvin just rolls over and goes to sleep." Dominique said in frustration. "Last week, me, Rolanda, and Jazzy, went to this lounge on Canal Street and this older guy approached me. Momma, I was tempted to talk to the man. I felt guilty afterwards, but I almost got caught up. My question to you is how do *I* combat those feelings."

"Well first, don't ever allow yourself to be put into a situation to where you can be tempted, Dominique. Second, talk to your husband and tell him exactly what you want. You told me you want to try something different and I'm assuming you're telling Calvin the same thing—that you wanna try different things. You're not being specific enough, baby. Whatever you want him to do, tell him directly. If that doesn't work, well, you can pray on it, but baby don't step out on Calvin, when he's ready to open up it'll happen. Remember, you two married young, so you are still learning, take that as a blessing, that you two can learn together I mean."

"You're right mom, I just thought—"

"You thought that when you married the sex would be fulfilling each and every time. Now you see different, Dominique. Look, I was against you and Calvin marrying in the beginning because I worried about your education and your financial situation. You two have conquered those things. If sex is the only problem you two have, then you are doing fine. Remember, both of you were virgins so it's all new, time brings about experience. Remember that child."

"Thanks mom, look, I have to finish prepping the show so I'll call you tomorrow, okay?" Dominique stated as she and her mother hung up the phones.

Dominique reflected on what her mother told her and knew she was making sense, but Dominique had already stated her wishes to Calvin and he flat out stated that he wasn't going to perform oral sex on her and she wasn't allowed to do him. Dominique didn't want to go into detail with her mother about her dilemma, but she listened to her mother's advice. She then decided to go and ask a person who had no religious ties what-so-ever—that person was Jazzy.

Dominique tapped Jazzy's office door lightly before entering and saw her sitting at her computer typing away.

Jazzy looked up and smiled. "Hey baby. What's up?" she asked cheerily.

"Hey umm, if you had a man that didn't want to go umm, go down on you, which was your fantasy, what, what would you do?" Dominique asked nervously.

Jazzy looked around the side of her computer and knew right away that Dominique was referring to her own plight. If Jazzy had to tell it, she would just find another man to fulfill her needs, but she wasn't married. And she knew she couldn't give that advice to Dominique. "Hmm, well, umm, gee, I'd look him straight in the eyes and tell him what I want."

"Did that." Dominique answered as she sat down in the chair in front of Jazzy's desk

"Oh, I see. Well, I'd nag the hell out of his ass until he gives in. Get him drunk, or better yet, whilst we doing it, I'd just grab his head and push it down there. Once he gets a taste of the pink gum drop he'll want to stay there on his own." Jazzy said as she laughed.

Dominique didn't laugh, however; she had a serious dilemma and she didn't know how to fix it.

Jazzy noticed the look of distress on her face and said, "Look Dominique, I can't tell you what to do with your man. *You* married Calvin—nobody else did. So if you love him, you'd respect his wishes. If you weren't married, I would lay the law down for you, but you *are* married and I'm not going to sit and tell you what you want to hear and be the one responsible for you ruining your marriage. Just keep asking, he'll come around."

"I'm, I'm sorry I came at you like this, Jazzy." Dominique stated as she got up from the chair in front of Jazzy's desk and headed for the door.

"Actually I'm flattered. I'm glad you see me as someone you can talk to and my door is always open, but I will not interfere in your marriage. You are a grown woman and you have the full capability to analyze, dissect, and rectify whatever problem you and Calvin are having at this present time."

Dominique thanked Jazzy and walked out of her office feeling more confused than before she'd ever decided to seek advice. She had pursued counsel from two older and more experienced women, but she wasn't feeling neither of the two's answers. She now understood that she would have to deal with the problem herself. By the time the show had ended, Dominique had come up with a way of hopefully getting what she needed from her husband. She drove home happy, believing her plan would work. When she got in, the house was quiet as Calvin was sound asleep in the living room chair with the TV running.

"*Perfect!*" Dominique thought to herself as she hurried to the shower. She cleaned herself, let her hair down and rubbed her body down with raspberry lotion and sprayed raspberry perfume lightly onto her stomach just above her neatly trimmed pubic hairs. After checking her naked physique in the mirror, Dominique knew she looked not only irresistible, but delectable—ready to eat so-to-speak. With her body smelling good, and her skin silky smooth and soft to the touch, Dominique eased into the living room and rubbed her sweet-smelling breasts all over Calvin's face. Calvin sniffed and then turned his head, mumbling inaudibly.

"Calvin," Dominique whispered. "Smell good, baby?"

Calvin mumbled as Dominique stroked his chest and worked her way down to his member. He was semi-hard, just hard enough for Dominique to flip his rod out of his boxers and stroke it softly. She had her breasts right in front Calvin's nose and eased forward just enough to feel his breath blow across her nipples. She stuck a finger into her mouth and wet both nipples and let her husband's breath blow across them and they grew hard instantly. Calvin began moaning as he was beginning to enjoy the sensations Dominique's hand was producing. She flicked her tongue across Calvin's chest, kissed his stomach as she stroked his member, and when she felt it bump underneath her chin, she breathed in real hard. Just as Dominique was about to go down on Calvin, however, he stood her up.

Dominique looked into her husband's eyes, "Calvin, let me, let me taste—"

The lustful wife was cut off as Calvin kissed her furiously on the lips, sliding his tongue deep into her warm mouth. Dominique's lips were real sensitive; she could almost orgasm just from French kissing. She was now too weak to stop Calvin. He picked her up and carried her to the bedroom and laid her down.

"Take me, Calvin!"

Calvin lay on top of Dominique and shoved his rod into her in one swift motion. She grabbed her ankles and spread herself wide and thrust up onto Calvin's rod, getting stuffed to the hilt as he pummeled her pussy at a quick and furious pace. Dominique had such a powerful orgasm, she began to cream from the constant friction of Calvin's member driving in and out of her dripping wet vagina. They had sex for nearly an hour in the missionary position and Dominique was spent by the time Calvin had ejaculated into her sopping wet vagina for the third time. Dominique didn't get to fulfill her mission on this night, which was for her and Calvin to sixty-nine, but at least for one night, she was sedated. Calvin had never taken her in that manner and she loved every second of the hard fucking she received.

"Maybe momma and Jazzy was right. When he's ready, he'll come around. We both still kind of new to this." Dominique thought to herself just before she drifted off to sleep.

Over the next few weeks Dominique tried to get an instant replay of the night Calvin had pounded her 5' 125 pound frame into complete submission, but it was to no avail. She pleaded with Calvin again several weeks later after growing frustrated over their one-position form of lovemaking, "Just do me one time and let me do you, just ta' get it out my system, baby. I'm asking. I'm always asking. I try to do everything for you and you not reciprocating." Dominique stated as her eyes welled up.

"I work, I pay all the bills, and we do make love from time to time." Calvin replied as he sat at the kitchen table eating a meatloaf that Dominique had prepared for him. That night Dominique had left the show early in an attempt to cater to and romance her husband. She prepared dinner and had strawberry candles lit and had on a red silk teddy and three inch heeled shoes. She served Calvin his food in her lingerie expecting to take their lovemaking to another level, but after the two ate, Calvin took a shower and went to bed—and that's when Dominique grew furious and the two argued.

"It ain't about the money, Cal. I have needs and they need to be met—*by you*!"

"This like a rerun! You bother me all the time with same thing Dominique and the answer still the same. I'm not doing that!" Calvin responded.

Dominique leaned back and stared at her husband and said nothing in response. She had made up her mind that she would not 'bother' Calvin with her fantasies anymore. She was hurt that he didn't even attempt to try and fulfill her desires and began to feel that she was being taken for granted. They would still make love, but where as it used to be once a week it was now once every ten days or so. Calvin just wasn't up on his game, but he had his reasons, and at the time they were unknown to Dominique.

After weeks of frustration, Dominique opted for a complete makeover, beginning to dress sexier. She bought new perfumes, new shoes, and dresses and had gotten her hair cut into a Chinese bob and had her eyebrows arched. Everyone noticed and liked her new look. Calvin complimented her, but she didn't do it for Calvin, she did it for herself; she had tried dressing sexy and waiting on her husband hand and foot, now, Dominique was doing what made her feel happy—and what made her feel happy at this point and time in her life was attention from the opposite sex.

****

It was a warm night in April of '93 when 21 year-old Dominique walked into the studio with her new look, having changed clothes after classes. She was dressed in a silk evergreen knee length skirt with a white sweater and white knee-high boots, looking and feeling sexy.

"So umm, you on the market, huh?" thirty-seven year-old Jazzy asked Dominique as she sat at her post inside the studio ten minutes before the ladies were scheduled to go on air.

"The market?" Dominique asked inquisitively.

"Yea, you know, you trying to get caught!" twenty-two year-old Rolanda said.

"Who said that?"

"Nobody ain't have ta' say it, girlfriend. Come in here wearing those sexy clothes, smelling good, new hairstyle, nails done. Come on now," twenty-one year-old Tracey said as she smiled down at Dominique from her post.

"I'm just doing *me* for a chance. I been catering to Calvin for over four years and I'm just doing a li'l somethin' for me."

"I understand! Do you Dominique! It's all about *you* girlfriend." Tracey stated.

"Yea, you *would* agree with that," Rolanda remarked as she placed her headphones onto her ears.

"What that mean, Rolanda?" Tracey asked.

"Nothing."

"No, go 'head and say it! You think I'm selfish! I told you about Angel and how I felt!"

"This ain't about your daughter."

"Mike daughter!"

"Whatever," Rolanda replied. "It's not about Angel—it's about the fact that Dominique and Calvin been together since elementary school and now they falling apart!" she said loudly. "We used ta' be fuckin' girls, and now we barely hang together! Everybody have one issue or another and when we *are* together we at each other throats. What the hell happened to us?"

"Ain't nobody falling apart, Rolanda." Dominique said as she got up and went and wrapped her arm around Rolanda's back. "Come on now, we still girls. We just got a lot ta' deal with right now."

"Hey, it's called life!" Jazzy chimed in. "You girls are just fine. Y'all ain't no different from any other group of women. When ya' got a lot of estrogen in the room, personalities collide. Each of you are your own woman and that is what makes you all special. You all are not followers. *All* of y'all are leaders so come on let's get ready for the show. Umm, since it's Thursday and y'all don't have classes tomorrow, y'all ladies wanna go have a drink after the show?" Jazzy asked.

"Yea, that's cool." the three said at random as they playfully tapped one another before they hugged one another and each apologized to the other.

"I been missing y'all." Tracey said as the three stood together talking idly.

"Me too," Rolanda said. "Oooh! They got this club in the French Quarter called the *Beaver Dam*? My English professor said we oughta go there because they got buy one get one free drink specials." Rolanda ended just as the on air light came on and the girls scrambled to their seats inside the studio.

As Jazzy did the intro, Dominique sent Rolanda a message and told her to call Brianna and Lubby so they could meet up outside the studio and they would all go to the club and have a girls' night out. Dominique could see the joy in Rolanda's eyes as she read the note; it had been months since the five hung and when Brianna and Lubby got the call from Rolanda, they too were looking forward to going out on this night.

The show ended promptly at eleven and the ladies all quickly signed out of their computers, grabbed their purses and headed for the parking lot. Jazzy watched with happy eyes as Rolanda, Tracey, and Dominique giggled like little kids inside the elevator. She could tell a night out was exactly what her protégés needed, if only to divert them from their home lives, which had become somewhat routine. School, work, home. School work, home. A night out was not only needed, it was well deserved.

"Traceyyyy!" twenty-two year-old Brianna yelled aloud as Jazzy and the girls entered the parking lot. "That's my fuckin' girl!"

"Bri!" Tracey yelled as she ran up and hugged her friend. "It's been a hot minute! What's up, sister?"

"Chillin' chillin' doing the music thang you know?"

Rolanda and Lubby hugged one another and spoke lowly.

"You and Gerald all right?"

"Yea. We getting married next year around this time. You gone be my maid of honor?" twenty-one year-old Lubby inquired.

"I'd be honored, Lubby." Rolanda said softly as Tracey and Dominique approached Lubby and gave her a long hug. It was like a small reunion in the underground parking lot. The five were glad to be together as the few months apart were hard for all of them.

The women then began making their way to the club inside the French Quarters. Tracey left her motorcycle and decided she would spend the night by Brianna's house rather than drive all the way to Slidell. They all found easy parking along Canal Street and walked down Bourbon Street through the Quarters stopping every now and then so that Jazzy, Rolanda, Tracey, and Dominique could take pictures with fans. Jazzy even invited Brianna and Lubby to join in. They would stop to look at various pictures on the walls outside of clubs and joke around with other partiers enjoying the sights and sounds of Bourbon Street. Jazzy had bought everybody a Hurricane daiquiri and by the time they made it to the club, they all had a light buzz going. The ladies entered the *Beaver Dam Club*, Jazzy leading the way, and eyed a dimly lit, burgundy carpeted medium-sized room with low ceilings. A large dance floor, which was filled to capacity, was to their right and a long cherry oak bar with a long row of barstools that were all filled was to their left. The tables were all the way to the back. Jazzy and the girls made their way through the crowd and as they got to the back nearer the tables, a waitress greeted them and sat them in a roped off section of the club. None of the five said a word as they all figured they were sitting in V.I.P. on the strength of Jazzy. The women all got comfortable at the huge cherry oak table and ordered apple martinis and the waitress whisked off to get their drinks. Janet Jackson's song *That's The Way Love Goes* played at a loud, but non-deafening level as the ladies bobbed their heads to the music and began chatting about their current life's status while enjoying the club's ambiance. They were enthralled in their conversations and drinking their martinis when the waitress who'd seated them came by several minutes later and brought a new round of drinks.

"Thank you, sweetie." Jazzy said as she smiled and sipped her apple martini.

"Don't mention it, sugar!" the younger lady said as she rubbed Jazzy's shoulder softly. This wasn't the first time the woman had touched Jazzy; she had done the very same thing when she brought the previous round of drinks. Jazzy thought that the over-touching was odd. "She a li'l too touchy feely for me! I'm a have ta' tell her ass ta' stop touching me when she come back this way. And who the fuck is she callin' sugar? Like me and her the same age or some shit!" Jazzy added as she scanned the club. "Where the hell all the men at tonight?" she then asked aloud.

"They probably home sleep because they have to work in the morning." Dominique said in reference to what Calvin's routine had become. "If it ain't work or sports, they not interested in nothing."

Rolanda and Lubby got up to dance, and before long they

had the whole dance floor jumping. "Girl, I ain't do these dances since high school!" Lubby said as she bounced her rear end up and down while sinking to the floor, doing her old dance to Tag Team's song, *Whoomp There It Is*. Rolanda joined her and a young woman quickly got behind her and started doing Lubby's dance, only she was touching Rolanda's back. Rolanda didn't pay it no mind as she was enjoying dancing with her friend. While dancing, another waitress brought Rolanda and Lubby another round of drinks.

"Tell Jazzy this my last one. I gotta open my pet shop in the morning." Lubby told the waitress before thanking her.

"Jazzy didn't send these, miss! That lovely woman over there by the bar says she thinks you are gorgeous!" the petite blonde waitress yelled into Lubby's ear over the music.

Lubby turned and looked to see a tall slender white woman with frost-white hair raise her glass and blow a kiss at her. "What the hell?" she exclaimed under her breath.

Meanwhile, Dominique had to use the restroom. She walked pass a light-skinned young black woman who smiled and blew a kiss at her before saying, "How ya' doin' short and sweet?"

"Did she just blow a kiss and call me short and sweet?" Dominique asked herself as she walked into the restroom.

Dominique entered a stall and pulled out a small can of Lysol and sprayed the seat and placed toilet paper around the top and sat gently to urinate. As she did so, she heard moans coming from the next stall.

"Ohh, baby lick that mutherfuckin' clit!" a female moaned in a raspy voice.

Dominique was a fan of oral sex. She wanted her pussy licked just much as the next woman, but she was shocked when she heard another woman's voice say aloud, "My turn girl, lick mines for me."

Dominique looked down at the floor and could see the woman's feet facing the front of the stall and she could tell a female was kneeling behind her. She knew right away what was happening when the woman began to moan. Dominique was glad that somebody was getting it done. She didn't want a woman to lick her pussy, but hey, *"whatever toots your horn"* she thought to herself. Only then did it dawn on Dominique: a woman called her 'short and sweet', hitting on her subtly. Two women were getting their freak on in a bathroom stall, and a woman was rubbing Jazzy's shoulder whenever she passed by.

"What the hell?" Dominique thought as she washed her hands.

Back out in the club, the waitress who'd escorted the ladies to their seats brought another round of drinks to their table, but Jazzy refused because she was buzzing, as were the rest of the girls. "Hey, bring the damn bill so we can pay that shit and get the hell out this weird ass club!" Jazzy yelled aloud over the music.

"Weird? Weird? She wasn't weird when you were accepting her drinks!" the blond waitress snapped.

"Who the fuck is *her*?" Jazzy asked, her buzz slowly diminishing.

"The woman at the bar with the frost-white hair and her two girlfriends."

"Girlfriends!" Jazzy, Brianna, and Tracey yelled at the same time.

"What the hell?" Jazzy then asked loudly over the music.

"Bri, I thought you was buying drinks!" Tracey snapped.

"Me? I thought Jazzy was treating!" Brianna stated.

"You gotta be kiddin' me! I thought Rolanda was ordering these drinks! She brought our asses up in here!" Jazzy stated. "Now look here, sugar," she then said to the waitress, "bring us our *bill* and tell that woman over *there* we don't swing like *that*! Thanks but no thanks and no hard feelings!"

The waitress went to get the bill and Jazzy watched the whole scene unfold. The slender blond went straight to the woman with the frost-white hair and the two talked briefly. Jazzy knew what was going down and could see the woman's angst and knew trouble lay ahead.

Just then, Dominique made her way back to the table. "Hey y'all I think this is a—"

"Gay bar?" Jazzy, Tracey, and Brianna said in unison.

"Where Lubby and Rolanda?" Dominique asked as they all looked towards the dance floor only to see Rolanda and Lubby dancing the night away with a group of women surrounding them. "Rolanda! Rolanda!" Dominique yelled aloud, but Rolanda couldn't hear over the crowd and the music.

Tracey walked through the crowd and grabbed the two and pulled them away.

"Hey! We was doin' the damn thang, Tracey! What ya' doin', girl?" Lubby asked as she bobbed slightly to the music.

"You gone dance your happy ass right into one of them bull-daggers' bed!"

"Run that by me again!" Lubby stated with wide eyes as she immediately froze on her tracks.

"Bull-dagger! Bull—*dagger*!" Tracey yelled aloud as women nearby focused in on her, Lubby, and Rolanda.

"*Bull-dagger?*" Lubby asked aloud. "They—these people gay?" she then asked lowly when she noticed the many pairs of eyes staring at her and her friends.

"What the hell kinda shit is this? Girl, I shoulda known when that damn English professor told me about this club! I figured she was gay!" Rolanda snapped.

"Well, if your *teacher* gay, and she told *you* about this place, then what she tryna say about *you* Rolanda?" Lubby asked as she, Tracey and Rolanda approached the table.

"Lubby, please, please don't do the 'can't see the forest for the trees' routine tonight. Now, you know—like we all know—ain't no candy lickers in this bunch right here!"

"I know that's real! But I'm a say this and end mine—if this bitch got something on her mind, I'm a kick some ass tonight! This shit worse than being in jail! Bitches tryna *take* some pussy!" Jazzy said as she eyed the white-haired woman and her two girlfriends approaching. "Get ready girls, when I swing everybody swing."

"You gotta problem with my gratitude, Jasmine?" the white-haired woman asked as she stepped inside the ladies' V.I.P. booth.

"Look here, this is a big mistake! We got mislead. Now, I offered ta' pay the tab and that's as far as it goes." Jazzy said as she stood up from her seat and draped her purse across her shoulder.

"It's gone go until this white bitch say otherwise! I wants what I paid for!"

Jazzy needed to do no further talking. The thirty-seven year-old woman wasn't about to entertain a group of lesbians who wanted to have sex with her and her girls. She punched the white-haired woman in the face knocking her back and Tracey and Brianna began swinging on her two friends. Tracey already had a lot of pent-up frustration so she let loose, beating the slender light-skinned female that had flirted with Dominique to the floor. Rolanda helped Brianna fight the other woman and Dominique and Lubby each had a chair and were prepared to strike anybody that tried to jump in.

BLAM! BLAM! BLAM! BLAM!

Everybody hit the floor when four gunshots rang out and the entire club fell silent.

"Now! The next time I fire this damn gun I'm gone part a bitch head like the mutherfuckin' Red Sea!" Jazzy yelled aloud as she held her .9mm high in the air. "We walking out this bitch and ner' one of you bitches *better* not move! Come on girls!"

"She like, like Jesse James in this bitch!" Tracey thought to herself in reference to Jazzy as she and her friends got up and followed Jazzy out the club.

The police met the women at the door and recognized Jazzy immediately and asked what the problem was. Jazzy explained that the women in the club were harassing them and she had to defend herself and her girls.

"This is a women's gay club you know? The name says it all,

the Beaver Dam Club," the officer said with a slight chuckle once he realized the girls had stumbled into a situation they knew nothing about.

"We know now," Jazzy said. "Rolanda, baby, next, next time, let me or one of your friends pick the club 'cause umm, this scenario here is one for the books!"

The officers issued a citation to Jazzy, but that wasn't a problem. She had an expense account and she immediately wrote a check to pay for the damages and all the drinks the girls had consumed.

"Get outta here, Jazzy. We'll handle things here and make sure you're covered." the officer said as he took the check and walked into the club.

The five mocked Rolanda as they walked up Bourbon Street. "We almost got jumped by a bunch of lesbians! Rolanda what the hell you was thinking dragging us to that place?" Tracey asked as she laughed.

"I'm a slap the hell out of that professor when I see her! We went to have a good time and she set us up for the oaky dokey." Rolanda remarked.

"Shit," Jazzy said, "you think my grown ass woulda picked up on that the time we hit the door, but I was so bent on seeing y'all have a good time it didn't register. The fuckin' Beaver Dam? And then there wasn't a single man to be found in that place!"

"Girl, that was fun! I got a li'l stress off my chest!" Tracey stated happily.

"Well, judging by the size of those big cannons you had a hella lotta stress on your chest." Rolanda said through laughter.

"You always got something smart to say."

"That's get back for mocking me. I ain't know that was a gay club. But that was some funny shit, though."

"I know, huh, Rolanda?" Brianna said.

"We ain't have fun like that in years. Remember Lubby used to have fight Shantrell almost everyday?" Dominique asked.

"Remember Daphne crazy ass?" Tracey asked as the girls walked and laughed. "Crazy bitch tried ta' kill me!"

"We used to kick ass back in the day!" Brianna stated as the girls walked along Bourbon Street with Jazzy. "And we did it again tonight! Just like old times!"

"Good thing Jazzy had that piece, though—them gay ladies wasn't gone stop." Lubby said.

"I haven't blasted ole' Nellie in years. Good thing I never leave home without it. Forget American Express, Luger Nine, baby!" Jazzy said as the girls laughed.

The ladies eventually found another club, a heterosexual club that played good music and also had a café. They sat and ate hot wings and drank some more until nearly four A.M., near bout closing down Bourbon Street and went home happy women. As the weeks went by, the group of females had made Thursday nights their girl's night out. Dominique, Lubby, Rolanda, and Tracey graduated in June of '93 and during the summer, the five began planning Lubby's wedding set for April of '94 while steadily moving forward with their lives.

CHAPTER 28

HAPPILY EVER AFTER

"Momma look! I got you a matching gown for you wear to the wedding next week." Lubby stated to her mother.

It was April of '94 and 22 year-old Lubby and 25 year-old Gerald's wedding was just a week away. For almost a year now, Lubby and her four friends had been planning her wedding. Throughout that period of time, Lubby was trying to get her mother involved, but each time Lubby tried, Cynthia negated the offer. Lubby also wanted her mother to stand in her wedding, but when Cynthia found out Rolanda was going to be the maid-of-honor, she vowed not attend the event. For months Lubby pleaded with her mother to stand in her wedding, to at least tend, and at the very least, help with the planning, but Cynthia only remained distant and obstinate. Lubby's friends didn't care whether Mrs. Williams showed up or not, but Lubby wanted her mother there on her special day. Her friends repeatedly told her to let Cynthia be and if she showed up, then fine, if not, then fine; but Lubby would hear nothing of it. She knew her friends didn't want her going by her mother's house alone so she would sneak away and try to get her mother to change her mind about not attending her wedding, and each time, Rolanda would walk over and make sure Lubby was okay.

After numerous cries and pleas from her daughter, Cynthia finally told Lubby she had nothing to wear. Lubby went out and bought her mother a five hundred dollar turquoise silk gown and a hundred dollar pair of matching shoes and a string of pearls. She'd entered her mother's home early this morning holding the items with a big smile on her face, hoping her mother would be pleased. Cynthia snatched the items from Lubby and looked them over carefully. She found the receipts to the items her daughter had purchased the day before and sat them aside and hugged Lubby, who had not a clue what her mother was up to, but was only happy that her mother had approved of what she'd done. Lubby gripped her mother's blouse and held her tightly as she cried. "Momma," was all she could say as she held onto her mother tightly and shed tears of joy.

Cynthia had her eyes closed as she listened to her daughter weep. She eased away from Lubby and went and placed the items in her room and sat on the bed and stared at the dress and reflected on her daughter's upcoming wedding and smiled proudly. When Cynthia reentered the living room, she saw Lubby laying the sofa with her eyes closed crying lightly with tears running down her cheeks, overjoyed that finally, finally, without having to force or fight, her mother was being nice to her. Lubby was expecting this moment of happiness to end when her mother entered the living room, instead, Cynthia turned on the TV and sat beside her and rubbed her side gently. Lubby reached out and grabbed her mother's hand, beginning to believe that all of her praying and pleading with her mother was beginning to pay off; she was glad she didn't listen to her friends and stood by her mother.

The following weekend arrived and Lubby's wedding day had gotten underway. The night before, her friends had thrown her a bachelorette party complete with male strippers and a huge cake. Now, the friends were all in the throes of getting dress for the wedding on this warm cloudless Saturday morning in April of '94. Rolanda and Lubby were over to Rolanda's house getting dress and were moving about in a frenzy. Hair had to be done, baths taken, pictures had to be taken—items couldn't be found. It was a busy morning for all five friends.

Brianna and Tracey were over to Brianna's mother's house getting dressed. Bri was practicing as she dressed because she was scheduled to sing *Save the Best for Last* by Vanessa Williams while Lubby walked down the aisle through the garden of a three story colonial-style mansion she'd rented in uptown New Orleans that would also host the reception. She was standing before her full length mirror in her old bedroom wearing only a bra, slip and panties admiring her physique as she sung. *"Sometimes the very thing you're looking for...is the one thing you can't see...now we're standing face to face... isn't this world a crazy place...just when I thought our time had passed...you go and save the best for last..."*

"Tracey, how that octave sound?"

"Righteous, girl. Tighten this girdle for me, Bri."

"Thanks, Tracey. I been practicing for months and I'm still more nervous than the first night I sung on the football field when we was at Abramson."

"You gone be great, Bri. You know who woulda loved this performance by you today, though?"

"Gabriella," Brianna replied as she tightened Tracey's girdle. "I still have the collage Lubby made. Remind me not to forget it before we leave because I left it in Tank's car."

"Alright. Damn!"

"What happened?"

"Gotta lose weight. My big ass can barely breathe with this thing on. Cutting off circulation and shit." Tracey said as she and Brianna laughed.

The day was turning out perfect. All the planning, the picking of colors, flowers, and dresses, the renting of the mansion, pre-wedding dinner, everything was a joyful task and event leading up to Lubby's day and now it had finally arrived.

Dominique was at her mother's house getting prepared. She was reflecting on the day Lubby had chosen her colors and the debate the girls had while walking on the levee. It was Rolanda who'd suggested, what was to Dominique, the outrageous colors of orange, yellow and white set to a tropical theme. Tracey suggested blue and gold, Sarah T. Reed's colors and Brianna had suggested lavender. The girls liked Bri's suggestion, but they all flopped on lavender when they realized that Gerald would have to wear a lavender tuxedo and may not be up for that one, especially on his wedding day. "Momma, Lubby planned a beautiful wedding. Turquoise and white. I woulda chose like a strawberry red or maybe peach though."

"Well, maybe you and Cal can have another ceremony later on. Maybe for your fifth anniversary that's comin' up later this year." Mrs. Franz replied as she did her daughter's make up. "Oh you are so beautiful, baby. I wish—"

Dominique knew what her mother was going to say so she finished the sentence by saying, "You wish I would've waited so you can do what you are doing now on my wedding day, right momma?"

"Yes I do, baby. That would have been such a fun task as you've seen while planning Lubby's wedding. But I'm proud of you anyway, Dominique. You know what I love about you and your friends is the fact that you all stand up for what you believe in. You all never let anyone influence your decisions be it right or wrong. When you married Calvin, everybody had doubts, myself included, but you two made it work. I love your fortitude."

"Thanks mom, but it's hard you know?"

"You mean with you and Calvin and the romance issue?" Mrs. Franz inquired as she sat her make-up brush down.

"Yes," Dominique replied as she checked herself in the vanity mirror and turned back to her mother. "Every now and then Calvin does something sweet, but those long hours he work are really taking a toll. Not to mention that I don't get off until after eleven at night. We go out to dinner on the weekends and sit by his parents' home when we're not here with you and dad whenever he's, in town, but I just want a little bit more excitement."

"You are just a feisty little young thing! It'll come a time sweetie when all you'll want to do is just kick back and relax. Then Calvin will be the one wanting to do the horizontal hump." Mrs. Franz stated as she and her daughter burst into laughter. "Now come on girl, we running behind with all this talk." she ended as she continued prepping her daughter.

Back over to Rolanda's house, two limousines had just pulled up in front the home. Lubby saw the cars pull up while walking out of the kitchen and she went to check on the two cars. Rolanda was curling her hair and Charlotte was on the kitchen phone with Maria, who was preparing Tracey's baby for the wedding.

"How baby Angel doing?"

"You can't hear her fussing, Charlotte? This baby here can go let me tell ya'."

"And Tracey?"

"Still stubborn as hell, child! She gone have to deal with this one though, because Angel already saying momma. I keep saying to her, 'that's right keep calling her stubborn butt! She gone come and get you'!" Maria said as she and Charlotte laughed.

"Let me jump in the shower real quick. Come on down when you ready, Maria." Charlotte said before hanging up the phone and heading towards the shower.

Everyone was preoccupied when Lubby, dressed in a pair of turquoise jean shorts and a white blouse and white sandals, slipped out of the house to check both cars. The drivers left briefly to top off the gas tanks after Lubby approved and she then decided to go and check on her mother to see how she was coming along with her preparations for the wedding. At that moment, Kilo began barking when he saw her walking towards her mother's home alone.

Lubby knocked on her mother's door and Cynthia eventually answered. She wasn't dressed at all, and to Lubby, she looked as if she wasn't even trying to get ready for the wedding when she eyed her mother standing in a black silk robe with her long mane of brown hair draping down her shoulders.

"Momma, we leaving in another hour! Why you not getting dressed?"

"I'm not going!" Cynthia said as she walked back into the living room.

"What?" Lubby asked surprised as she closed the door and shadowed her mother.

"You heard me! I'm not going!"

"Momma, I can't believe you! You ain't doing nothing around here! You can come to my wedding!"

"Now why would I want to do that? Why would I want to sit and watch you celebrate getting married, Lubby?" Cynthia snapped as she turned and placed her hands on her hips and stared her daughter down.

Lubby shook her head and stared at her mother in disappointment. "You know what," she said as she grew nearer her mother, "last week I actually believed we were making progress. I actually *fell* for that! I been falling for that all my *life*! You act nice to get what you want and then you shit on me! Rolanda 'nem was right—you don't love me! And I'm not gone cry on my wedding day over this shit!" Lubby said sadly as her eyes welled up, but she couldn't help but to cry. "You hurt me for the last time, Cynthia." she ended in a low, sad tone before running into her mother's room to retrieve the clothes and jewelry she had bought the week before.

Cynthia quickly followed. "Get the hell out my room!" she yelled loudly as she ran into her bedroom and slammed her closet doors shut. "You bought those for me and I can do whatever I want to do with those things!"

"No you can't! I want my clothes and jewelry back! I'm through being your fool, Cynthia! I want my clothes and my jewelry! You can find another fool, some old, some old stupid no good man ta' pay your bills! I can't believe you would do me like this!" Lubby yelled at her mother as she searched for her clothes without success. "Forget it man," she then said angrily as she brushed past her mother. "I'm never coming back here! All my days I been kissing your ass! *Asking* you, *begging* you to be a mother! Just to be there *one* time in my life! Everybody else been there! If it wasn't for my friends, and my husband, I'd be dead fuckin' 'round with you!" Lubby ended as she walked towards the door, leaving her mother behind in the bedroom.

Kilo was trying to escape from Rolanda's yard. He could hear the argument inside Cynthia's house and was barking fiercely as he crawled underneath the side fence and ran through the neighbor's yard and crawled under their fence and sprinted towards Lubby. Lubby was walking out of her mother's home and she never saw it coming. Cynthia ran out from her bedroom and came from behind her back with a .44 magnum and shot at her daughter from across the living room. Lubby screamed and grabbed her side and stumbled out of the doorway.

Rolanda heard the faint gunshot and her stomach churned. She dropped the curling iron and looked around in a panicked state. She then got up and ran through the house calling Lubby's name. Upon discerning the fact that Lubby was not inside the house, she called out for her mother and ran out the front door in just her robe where she eyed Lubby on the opposite side of the street wobbling down the sidewalk clutching her side.

Cynthia came out of the house and aimed her weapon again and Rolanda screamed aloud, "Lubby! Lubby," whilst running towards her friend.

Kilo had made it to the scene before Rolanda and he jumped on Cynthia and grabbed her arm and began tugging at it as Lubby slowly sunk to the ground and crawled onto the grass outside her mother's home. "Momma! Why? *Why?*" Lubby cried as she turned and looked up at her mother, who was wrestling with Kilo.

"You think you gone *marry* somebody? You the reason *my* husband left! I be damn if you live happily-ever-after, bitch!" Cynthia yelled as she switched the gun to her other hand. Kilo was trying his best to protect his master and friend, but the hand switch had slipped by the protective beast.

"Rolanda, get her away from me!" Lubby screamed as she eyed her friend running towards her. "Please, momma! Momma, please!" Lubby screamed as she crawled backwards, away from her mother.

Rolanda could hear her friend's pleas of help and she was

running as fast as she could to help her. She was calling Lubby's name aloud, telling her to get up and run. She was yelling for Kilo to kill Cynthia. The pit-bull was struggling to keep Cynthia within the grasps of his jaws, but she kicked him and broke free of his grip. Rolanda was only fifteen feet away from Lubby when she heard Lubby cry aloud, "Momma don't kill me!" as she held her hand in front of her face.

Cynthia walked over and stood over Lubby, just as Kilo grabbed her leg and began tugging again, and she fired another single shot from the .44 magnum she held in her hand. The bullet went through Lubby's right hand and landed in her face just below her right eye and she immediately fell flat on her back in the grass and went silent. Kilo quickly let go of Cynthia's leg and went and stood over Lubby as he turned and barked ferociously. The dog was actually trying to shield Lubby and protect her from further harm, willing to take bullets on Lubby's behalf.

Rolanda had frozen in her tracks and was looking on in shock after witnessing her friend lying flat on her back, having been shot by her own mother. Cynthia then aimed the gun at Kilo as the dog continued to bark ferociously. She cried as she stared at the barking dog before suddenly placing the gun into her mouth and firing the weapon one more time, taking her own life.

Rolanda covered her mouth and her heart and walked in a dreamlike, wobbly state over to Lubby. Although naked underneath her robe, Rolanda didn't care that her flesh was now exposed. She'd just witnessed the most horrifying thing ever. She stumbled over to Lubby and dropped to her knees in the grass beside her friend and gently picked her head up. "Lubby! Lubby, please get up!" she cried through tears as people began coming out of their homes to see what the commotion was about. "Somebody call 911! She shot her! Oh my Goddddd!" Rolanda cried hysterically as she rocked Lubby's body back and forth. "Lubby no!"

Brianna and Tracey could see people running down the street at a quick pace and could tell right away that something was going down. Brianna's home was too far away to hear the gunshots, but when she and Tracey stepped onto the sidewalk and saw people gathering in front of Cynthia's home, their hearts dropped.

"Lubby!" they said in unison as they ran down the block.

Dominique, who was fully dressed for the wedding, saw the people running by and she came out the door and met Tracey and Brianna and the three ran together. The nearer they grew to Cynthia's home, the clearer the three girls could hear Rolanda screaming Lubby's name.

"Lubby! Wake up! Lubby wake up!" Rolanda kept yelling through her tears.

People were trying to get close to Lubby, but Kilo would let no one outside of Rolanda get near her. He was running from side to side, drooling from the mouth and snapping violently at anybody who tried to get pass him. He stopped barking momentarily to let Tracey, Dominique, and Brianna get through, and then continued barking at everybody else, keeping them at bay. The four knelt down beside Lubby and tried to keep her calm amidst the chaos. People were screaming through their tears, running back and forth telling others to call 911 and Kilo was steadily barking. What had started out as such a beautiful day had quickly turned into a living nightmare.

The girls were all trying to comfort Lubby until help arrived. Her eyes were open and she was moving her mouth trying to speak. Rolanda and Tracey each held a hand as Dominique and Brianna knelt at her feet and rubbed her legs gently while telling her to hold on, all the while crying because they couldn't help their friend.

"Why she did this to me?" Lubby whispered to Rolanda through a bloody mouth.

"Be calm, Lubby. The ambulance is coming. You gone be all right just wait. Breathe. Come on now. Gerald 'nem waiting for you. Everybody waiting for you. You getting married today, Lubby." Rolanda said through tears as she looked her friend square in the eyes and brushed bloody hair away from her friend's face. It was then that the four saw what an ugly thing had happened to Lubby. A great portion of her face beneath her right eye was missing and her right eye looked as if it had been gouged out.

The girls could barely recognize the person before them, but they all remained calm as best they could so as not to upset Lubby, but Lubby seemed to know what bad shape she was in. She shook her head from side to side slightly and her body convulsed. She spat out blood and gasped for air, swallowing hard and breathing even harder. With her face torn from the bullet lodged in her cheek and her right eye shattered, Lubby looked up and whispered again, "Rolanda why she did this to me?"

"We love you, Lubby!" Tracey said through a face full of tears.

"Lubby, please." Brianna pleaded as she shook Lubby's legs. "Lubby don't die we love you! Don't die, Lubby!" she cried aloud as she leaned forward and placed her head in her lap. "We love you!"

Dominique began praying to herself, "*Jehovah, whatever the outcome, give us strength to deal with what we are going through today. Forgive Lubby for her sins and remember her on Judgment Day. Amen.*" Dominique sat back on her heels with her head bowed, refusing to open her eyes. She cared not to see the image of Lubby in such a horrifying state. She could only cry and hold onto to her friend's legs, feeling her pulse grow weaker and weaker. "I love you, Lubby," she cried.

Lubby looked up at the sky, took three deep gasps of air, exhaled heavily, and said, "Momma, I love you," just as she released the last breaths of her young life. The girls looked at Lubby in stunned silence as Kilo stopped barking. He seemed to sense what the four friends knew: that Lubby had just died. He walked over and lay down at Lubby's feet and began whimpering.

Rolanda was the first of the friends to break down. She fell back into the grass and grabbed her chest and screamed loudly towards the sky. It was a lurid and hauntingly agonizing scream that silenced everyone that was out there and brought whoever wasn't crying as of yet, to tears of sorrow and anger.

Tracey stared at Lubby with wide eyes. Her mouth was agape and she refused to let go of her hand. She squeezed tighter, trying to hold on to her friend as she, too, began breaking down, bowing her head and rubbing Lubby's stomach gently, crying uncontrollably.

Brianna stood up, looked at Lubby's body in disbelief and placed her hands on top her head and walked away crying; squinting her eyes in pain. She bent over and screamed aloud as Ms. Stanford ran up and hugged her from behind. Bri screamed into the warm morning air and was trying to break free of her mother's grip. All she wanted to do was just run. Just run and scream aloud and ask God why He'd taken her friend in such a tragic manner, but Ms. Stanford would not let go. Bri dropped to her knees, leaned forward and pounded the concrete and cried aloud in pain.

Dominique crawled over to Rolanda and covered her up. Rolanda sat up slightly and hugged her tightly. "Why?" Rolanda screamed. "Why this had to happen? Why this had to happen?" she asked repeatedly as she stared at her deceased friend. "Oh my God! Look what she did to her! Look what she did!" Rolanda fell back into the grass and began thrashing about and Charlotte went and covered her up along with Dominique.

Tracey then went into a rage. "You mutherfuckin' bitch!" she yelled aloud as she let go of Lubby's bloody hand and ran over to Cynthia's lifeless body and repeatedly kicked the dead woman.

Maria and Mrs. Franz had to pull Tracey away, but she fought with the women flagrantly, throwing fists of fury as she kicked at Cynthia's corpse, which lay bloodied in the doorway. Maria and Mrs. Franz were able to grab hold of Tracey and she spat at the woman as she was being dragged away. "You a evil bitch! I hope you go to hell today, bitch!" she yelled.

"Tracey! Tracey! She killed herself! She's dead now! You can't hurt her no more!" Maria said as she pulled Tracey away. "You can't hurt her no more!" she reiterated through tears.

Tracey dropped to her knees on the sidewalk in defeat and

wrapped her arms around her mother's legs, staining her clothes with Lubby's blood as she screamed into her mother's body. Maria rubbed her daughter's head softly and then knelt down beside her daughter. "I can't believe she would do this to my friend, momma! Why?" Tracey screamed. "Momma, why?" she screamed again as she continued to cry.

Gerald, Bobby, Tank, Calvin and Mike made it to the scene and they, too, broke down when they saw Lubby's body laying beneath a bloodied white sheet on her mother's front lawn that was now surrounded by yellow tape. Gerald went and sat down on the curb and the young men sat beside him as he wept. He, like everyone else, was shocked. How could a mother take her own daughter's life? On her wedding day to add insult to injury? East Shore would forever remember the day that one of its brightest, one of its sweetest residents, perished on what was supposed to be a happy day.

Lubby's death had affected the entire community and her funeral was one of the biggest East Shore had ever seen. People piled into New Baptist Church to pay respects to 22 year-old Lubby Williams, who was well-known throughout the city, mainly through her many high school choreographs. Ex-cheerleaders showed up in uniforms to honor her, and Abramson, Sarah T. Reed and Carver High School bands had gotten together to play on the park in East Shore the day before her funeral.

There was a huge choir inside the large capacity church the day of Lubby's funeral as Brianna stood before the group facing scores of visitors listening to the instrumental to *Gone Too Soon* by Michael Jackson. This was not the song Brianna had in mind to sing. Five days earlier, she was supposed to have sung *Save The Best for Last*, have a blast at Lubby's reception, and then open gifts with her and Gerald the day after. Instead of watching her friend traverse into a new life full of potential, however, Brianna was now sending her home to God. What happened to Lubby, in Brianna's eyes, was like a person taking a sip of unfermented wine. Lubby Williams was unfermented to Brianna. She was not ready; hadn't reached her full potential. Didn't ascertain all that life had in store, and she never got to fulfill all the things that she had in store for life.

What happened to Lubby Williams was the epitome of tragedy, and everybody inside the church knew it all-too-well. Her story, her life, will never be forgotten.

Rolanda sat next to her mother and lay on her shoulder and cried as Brianna began to sing lead. As she listened to the song, Rolanda stared at her friend's closed casket. The image of Lubby pleading for help and begging her mother not to kill her was an image that 23 year-old Rolanda Jones could not remove from her psyche. She cried openly, wishing she would have reacted a few more seconds earlier, thinking had she done so, maybe her friend would still be alive.

Tracey sat with her mother, her head bowed as she stared at the floor. She was wondering why of all people, why did Lubby have to die the way she did? Tracey kept opening her eyes wide as if to wake up from a nightmare, but the pain in her heart was too great. She knew that what was going on on this sad day was not a dream. Lubby was dead. Tracey watched her tears fall onto the marble floor as she listened to Brianna and the choir.

Dominique was in a state of shock. She stared at Lubby's coffin as she lay on Calvin's shoulder. She was sore with remorse, hurt from crying ever since Lubby breathed her last breath. Dominique closed her eyes as the song approached its crescendo and she replayed the good times the five all shared together. She remembered Lubby's smile, the way she treated young Ben, the day she found Kilo and how happy she was each and every time she performed in front of a crowd during high school. She remembered the last time she saw Lubby smile which was on the day she was killed.

"Born to amuse...to inspire to delight...here one day gone one night...like a sunset...dying with the rising of the moon... gone too soon...gone too soon..." Brianna ended the song with a face full of tears. She had to be helped by Tank and Gerald from the choir's stage and she broke down and screamed aloud when she walked past Lubby's coffin. The realization that Lubby was gone was felt harder than ever when she got nearer her deceased friend.

Lubby was placed into the ground and her friends went to

Charlotte's home for the repass. Neither could look over to Cynthia's old home, which was now boarded up, as the pain of that day was too fresh in their minds. The four friends took Kilo and they left the dinner and walked along the levee and talked about the good times they shared with Lubby. There was a little laughter, but mostly it was a lot of crying and group hugging because it seemed that no matter where they went that day in East Shore, everything reminded them of their friend, and knowing she wasn't coming back caused them all great distress. Moving on would be hard, but the four ladies knew if they leaned on one another, they would get through one of the most difficult times of their lives.

CHAPTER 29

PINCH HITTERS

"Just because you perform oral, can, can I say oral on the air?" twenty-three year-old Rolanda asked aloud.

"Well, if you couldn't you already said it—twice!" Jazzy responded before she sipped a cup of coffee.

It was two months after 22 year-old Lubby had passed away and all four friends were still feeling the effects of her death. In spite of their grief, however, they were slowly healing. Rolanda had taken over Lubby's pet shop because Gerald had joined the National Guard shortly after Lubby was killed. He just had to get away. The man was devastated from having lost what he could only describe as the most beautiful thing God had ever created.

The friends were all in pain after witnessing the death of their friend, but Rolanda was the most affected. She did well hiding her pain during the first few weeks; however, things were spinning out of control for Rolanda during that time. She'd moved in with Bobby three days after Lubby's funeral because just the mere sight of the house where Lubby once lived, and the exact spot where she died pained her that much. Bobby was gone from the house most nights as he was still hustling the streets, and Rolanda had plenty of time to be alone and think about her friend—and it wasn't a good thing for her. She would get off work and come home to an empty house and just sit on the sofa and cry most nights. She would drink herself silly every night, her way of coping with Lubby's death numbing the pain. She would then sleep maybe four or five hours and get up early in the morning and open Lubby's pet shop. She would leave about noon and return home and have a drink and sleep a few more hours before leaving at five in the evening to prepare for the show. Nobody knew of Rolanda's plight at the time, but when she announced she was closing the pet shop, her friends took note and paid her a visit one Saturday during the latter part of June '94. Twenty-six year-old Bobby was gone as usual, and when the girls arrived, they found Rolanda sitting on the sofa staring at the last picture she and Lubby took, which was on her wedding day as they were just beginning to get dressed.

"Rolanda, we worried about you, sister. You haven't been yourself lately." Dominique stated in a concerned tone as she sat down beside Rolanda.

"I'm, I'm cool, Dominique." Rolanda said as she wiped tears from her eyes as she stared at the picture.

"Well, why you closing the pet shop? If I may ask." Dominique inquired.

"Because," was all Rolanda said in response.

"Rolanda, look, we all feeling what happened to Lubby, but baby girl we gotta move on. As hard as it is, we gotta go forward." Brianna stated as she sat beside Rolanda.

"Hey, y'all remember how Lubby used to try and get me to grab the pen and paper?" Rolanda said as she laughed through her tears.

"Yeah." Tracey, Dominique and Brianna replied in unison.

"Girl, she swore *down* she was gone get me, but she never did." There was a long pause as Rolanda stared at the picture in her lap. "Because that bitch took her away from us!" Rolanda suddenly yelled as she jumped from the sofa and attempted to throw Lubby's picture against the wall, startling her friends in the process.

Tracey grabbed the picture from Rolanda's hand and

Rolanda dropped to the floor. Brianna knelt down hugged her from behind and held her close. "It's gone be okay. You gone be okay, sister."

"That was my fuckin' *girl*, Bri!" Rolanda cried. "Why her momma do that? Why she *did* that to our *friend*?" she asked as she looked around to her three remaining friends awaiting an answer.

None of the friends knew what to say. Dominique, Brianna, and Tracey were trying to go forth and they were succeeding in their own way, but Rolanda was having a hard time letting go of what happened to Lubby. "I can't, I can't get the image of Lubby sitting there, *begging* Cynthia not to kill her out my head. I was, I was like twenty feet away and I saw that bitch shoot Lubby in the face! In her *face*! I dream about that shit every night. Y'all wasn't there to see what I saw! To hear Lubby *beggin'* for her life! Those four words, that—one—*sentence*—'Momma don't kill me'—is the most horrible thing I have ever heard in my *life*! In *my life*! You hear me? And I can't get it out of my head! A child should never have to utter those words—ever! What a pathetic thing for a child to have to say! God Jesus why?" Rolanda asked as she clutched her fists tightly and leaned back into Brianna's breasts and cried a painful, heartfelt cry. "That was my *best* friend! Why Cynthia do that to her?"

"Nobody knows Rolanda, but we still have each other. We still here. Come on now, this ain't you sister. You always made us laugh. We just want you to be yourself again." Brianna said as she nodded towards Tracey.

Tracey got up and walked out of the house towards Dominique's car. "Somebody's been missing you Rolanda," Dominique stated as she eyed Tracey and Kilo walking back into the living room. Kilo barked happily and ran towards Rolanda, the muscular pit-bull wagging his tail rapidly and barking happily as he stood before Rolanda, who could only smile at the dog. When Kilo began to lick her tears, Rolanda let out a small laugh.

"Hey old friend." Rolanda said as she rubbed Kilo's back. "Thanks, girls. It's gone be hard without Lubby around." she said as she continued to rub Kilo, who remained still and let Rolanda pet him until her heart was content. He then knelt down beside her and laid his head into her lap and wagged his tail excitedly.

"It's hard for all of us," Tracey said, "but you know Lubby—always optimistic. Full of hope. And she never gave up. Neither should you."

"I know, Tracey," Rolanda replied. "I can and I will do this. I regret one thing though."

"What was that," Dominique asked.

"I didn't tell Lubby I love her before she died."

"I figured that was bothering you, Rolanda." Brianna said. "But you know Lubby loved you and she knew you loved her. Y'all were more close than any of us."

"We all, we all just close, Bri." Rolanda replied.

"You didn't, you didn't say it because you still had hope." Tracey said.

"What you mean?" Rolanda asked.

"Me and Dominique talked about that," Tracey said, "when we told Lubby we loved her, we knew, well we believed she was gone die. But you, you held on to the very end. Lubby knew you loved her, Rolanda. She ain't mad at you for not sayin' that."

"Thank you. I love you all. I'm gone say it and keep sayin' it. I love y'all."

The girls all hugged and stated their love for one another and then got up and took a walk with Kilo through City Park, which was near Bobby's home. Dominique, Tracey, and Brianna didn't say a word the whole time, they let Rolanda, who only wanted a listening ear, do all the talking. The girls sat at a picnic table in the park and Rolanda was finally was able to express herself fully. All the pinned up grief she was feeling was let go that day. She also decided to close the pet shop because she didn't have the time or the exact know-how to keep the place running, and her girls all agreed that closing the pet shop, for now at least, was the right thing to do; but it was Brianna's idea to have everybody chip in and pay the mortgage and the taxes on the building and that way they could one day reopen the pet shop in honor of Lubby.

By the time her friends left, Rolanda was feeling a whole lot better. She had called and asked Bobby was it okay for Kilo to stay with them and he agreed. The beloved canine was a big help to aiding Rolanda to move forward, doing things unexpectedly and bringing unmitigated joy to her life. One of the things Rolanda came to love about Kilo happened when she arrived home from work the following Monday after she'd moved him in. Kilo was sitting in the middle of the living room floor with her slippers at his feet and it tickled her. She walked over to him and said, "You miss Lubby like me too don't you? I wonder what goes on inside that head of yours because you seem to know a little too much to be just a dog."

Kilo barked happily and grabbed the slippers and walked over to the couch. Rolanda laughed and walked over and removed her shoes and placed her slippers on her feet and got up and fixed a bowl of popcorn. She turned on the TV, found a nice movie and sat down and watched TV with Kilo beside her wagging his tail playfully. The events that unfolded on that night had become Rolanda's daily routine. When she made it in from work, Kilo would be sitting in the middle of the living room waiting for her with her slippers. She would pop popcorn and watch a movie with the dog at her side, the two of them 'talking' as Rolanda had come to call her one-sided conversations with the canine. Although he couldn't answer nor understand Rolanda, to her, Kilo was a listening ear. She talked as if the dog could understand what she was saying, and never once did Kilo walk away. He was of great therapy to Rolanda. It's fair to say that without her friends and Kilo, Rolanda may have had a nervous breakdown; but thanks to her three friends and Lubby's ever loyal pit-bull, Rolanda put down the bottle, regained her focus in life, and was able to pull through one of the most trying times of her life.

After Rolanda was put back on track, Brianna began putting the final touches on the songs for her album and she was scheduled to release in March of '95. Bri was using Lubby's death as motivation to pursue her dream of becoming a professional singer. She remembered when Gabriella died, she often reflected on the situation with Black Mike and Donald, and the near death scenario with Ben Holland and his gang of thugs, and ultimately, the untimely death of one of her best friends. She knew she was lucky to be alive, and she promised herself she would not waste another opportunity. Brianna took those experiences and began writing her own songs to express her thoughts. She had also put the final touches on the first song she'd recorded—Rene and Angela's duet *You Don't have to Cry*. She would still have to wait for approval from the original artists' record label to release song, but she knew with that one song she had a hit. She was also planning to shoot a video to honor her friends. She and Tank were getting close to realizing their dream as of June of '94.

Tracey and Mike, meanwhile, still weren't on good terms in June of '94; and although Tracey steadily paid Mike $100 a week for baby Angel, she still had no intentions on becoming a part of her daughter's life. She would merely ride by Mike's trailer late at night and place a money order in his mailbox and speed off on her motorcycle. Angel, who was now two and a half years old, asked her father one night did she have a mother and it shook Mike's emotions. He bowed his head, wondering if Tracey knew or even cared how much her absence was beginning to affect her child, and told Angel that she did have a mother, but she worked all the time, which was his way of placing Tracey in good-standing because he loved her too much to ridicule her ever. Angel looked at her father sadly and asked could she see her when she gets off and Mike wiped his eyes that were beginning to water. Mike knew he and Tracey were on bad terms, but Angel had asked to see her mother and he couldn't refuse. He stayed up one Friday night, usually the night Tracey came by, and he let Angel look out the window at Tracey as she slipped an envelope into his mailbox. Angel could see a woman on a motorcycle dressed in all black stop quickly and then speed off. She couldn't see her face because the woman had on a helmet.

"Momma! Momma!" Angel called out as she patted the window. She then asked where her mother was going.

"Back to work, baby," Mike answered. "She has to go back to work."

Angel didn't ask any more questions. All she knew was that a woman wearing black was her mother and she was now looking for her. Mike would have to constantly apologize and quiet his daughter down whenever they were in public because anybody that Angel saw wearing black, the curly amber-haired bronze-skinned green-eyed little girl would ask the person if she was her mother. Tracey didn't know how much her absence was beginning to affect her daughter's life. She was busy doing her own thing. Lubby's death was subconsciously affecting the friends in various ways, for the good, like in Brianna and Rolanda's case, and also for the bad, which would become the case for Tracey and Dominique.

The incident with Rolanda happened a month ago and the incident with Tracey's daughter had taken place two weeks ago, and now on this night during the latter part of June '94, the Fantastic Four Show was on air during its last hour for the day and the hour's discussion was based on a letter read aloud by Rolanda. The letter described a woman who was refusing to go down on her husband because she viewed it as an act of submission.

"Well, seems like to me that oral, since I now know I can say that on air, seems like oral is just another form of pleasure. How can pleasuring your husband be viewed as being an act of submission?" Rolanda asked over the airwaves as the women discussed the issue.

"Well, some people have a problem submitting. I read in a magazine that people who have a problem performing orally have a problem with giving up control. They actually view giving oral as an act of submission, maybe that's this woman's problem." Tracey remarked.

"Well, Sister Spanks," Dominique chimed in, "'to submit', as this listener calls it, can also be defined as to put forth, such as effort, and it can also mean to propose or suggest. So I suggest that this woman put forth the effort and do what she needs to do to keep her husband satisfied before he gets a proposal from another woman. And know this, the opposite meaning of submit, means to withdraw. So if she loves her husband, she should, as she said, 'submit' before he withdraws from her completely and finds someone who is willing to submit!" Dominique ended matter-of-factly as Rolanda and Tracey looked at her and sniggled, both knowing full-well Dominique was upset with the woman in the letter and subtly referring to her own plight.

"Alright, Chanel Marie! You got a li'l feisty with that one sister! Let's take some phone calls on the matter. You are listening to the Fantastic Four Show on 105.9, the station that's ruling the nation." Jazzy ended as Tracey cued up *Weak* by the singing group SWV.

The show ended on this Friday night and the women were all headed home. Tracey had to stop by Mike's trailer to drop her money order, Rolanda was headed home to Bobby's house, and Jazzy was headed to her home. Dominique had plans as well, only her plans didn't involve either of her girls. She called Calvin from her office phone and told him that she and Jazzy was going out to have a drink.

"I thought you was gone order some pizza and watch a movie with me tonight." Calvin said.

"Baby, we can do that tomorrow. We both off, so we can do that then, okay? I'm just hanging with my girl for a while." Dominique ended as Calvin told her he loved her and the two hung up their phones. *"Pizza and a movie my ass! I'm gone get mine!"* Dominique said to herself as she grabbed her purse and walked out of the office.

Dominique had no intentions on meeting Jazzy; but she did plan on meeting up with Brad. Two weeks after Lubby died, Jazzy had taken Dominique, Tracey, Brianna and Rolanda back to the Sheraton lounge to help them get over Lubby's death. There she ran into Brad again. Dominique was still grieving the loss of her friend at the time, and what *she* had taken from Lubby's death was that life was not promised to anyone. You could die at any moment. She and Calvin were still having problems in the bedroom and Dominique no longer wanted to 'bother' Calvin with her desires. She and Brad had been secretly talking since the second time they had met in the lounge at the Sheraton. They then started secretly meeting once a week at a lounge inside The Double Tree Hotel, which was a high-priced hotel not too far from the Sheraton.

Dominique had learned that Brad had a well-paying job inside City Hall, operating as one of the city's Mayor's aides and campaign strategists. He was married and had two preteen kids. He and Dominique had good conversation over the phone and even better times when they met in person inside the lounge. Dominique found that she could talk about everything with Brad, from childhood high-jinks, stories in which Brad told from his time coming up as a child in the seventies that left her laughing to she nearly peed herself, to his days wearing a Jehri-curl and working as a clerk inside of city hall. Politics, the latest songs, travel, history sex, whatever Dominique and Brad discussed, the conversation was always engaging, humorous and more often than not, arousing. From time to time, while they were on air, Dominique would ask Tracey to play a certain song that she would secretly dedicate to Brad. They had a good rapport going, and on this night their clandestine affair was to attain new heights.

As Dominique headed towards her car, she thought about the conversation she and Brad had two weeks ago that led up to this night. Brad had told Dominique he had gotten something special for her a few minutes after they met inside the Double Tree Lounge. The two were engaging in light talk and waiting on their drinks when Brad handed Dominique a key and said, "Next week when we meet, I want you to go up room 4303 and wait on me. I have something special for you."

"Brad, we can't. I mean, we shouldn't do this. You married, I'm married, and we can ruin our lives. I enjoy talking to you but, you sweet and understanding, but this, I don't know." Dominique replied as she twirled the key in her hands.

Thirty-seven year-old Brad placed his arm around twenty-three year-old Dominique and slid closer and said, "I thought you said you wanted to live your fantasy. It was you who said you only live once right?" he told Dominique as the two sat inside a cozy booth in the dimly lit lounge and sipped their Vodka and orange juice. "Look, Dominique. Baby, I care for you, I'm a give you this key and if you don't want to go through with this I won't pressure you anymore. But baby, I wanna make you feel like a woman should. That's all. I can't get you out of my head, and I'd give anything to be with you for just one night. And deep down inside, I know you want to be made to feel like a woman, if only for one night. No strings are attached here. I just want to show you something special, satisfy your desire. I'm not asking you to marry me." Brad then joked as he could see in Dominique's eyes that she was going along willingly with his seduction. Brad cupped Dominique's chin in his well-maintained hands and manicured nails and she could smell the manly fragrance of his cologne on his skin. There was no denying it for Dominique, Brad moved her; he pushed all the right buttons and knew what to say. She closed her eyes and moaned softly as Brad drew nearer and whispered in her ear, "Can I make love to you?"

"Yes," Dominique responded. "Yes, I'll be there." she ended as Brad got up, paid the tab and backed away from the table, all-the-while smiled at Dominique as he blew her a kiss. Dominique was hoping Brad kissed her lips then and there, but she would have to wait. The week couldn't go by fast enough, but finally, the time had arrived. Dominique now found herself walking towards the elevators inside the Double Tree Hotel in high anticipation of what lay ahead for her and Brad.

She walked hurriedly to the elevator and rode up to the top floor where the suites were located and went to room 4303 just as Brad had instructed her to do. She slid the key in the slot and turned the knob and opened the door to a condo twice the size of the apartment she shared with Calvin. The condo featured three overly large bedrooms, a gourmet kitchen and a huge living room with a balcony that overlooked the entire skyline down Canal Street. A huge screen TV was in the living room along with a small fireplace. Dominique immediately felt comfortable and secure inside the luxurious domicile. She kicked off her shoes and ran like a little girl from the doorway to the balcony and back again. She then walked cautiously throughout the penthouse, looking at its beautiful vases and other clay artifacts. She fell upon the white velvet sofas and rolled along the plush white carpet. Her shoulder length hair was splayed over the carpet as she ran her fingers through its soft wool. She had never seen a place as beautiful as this penthouse suite. Wondering how the bathroom looked, Dominique got up from the floor and walked to the master bedroom. She stared at the oval-shaped king-sized bed as she walked into the bathroom and stood in front of a huge circular tub that could maybe seat six or seven people that was trimmed in gold and had genuine gold faucets.

Dominique was in awe of the beauty that lay before her eyes. She walked up the stairs leading to the tub and peered over into its marble insides and saw the name *BRAD* on the bottom of the tub. *"Who is this man?"* she asked herself as she continued touring the penthouse's kitchen, dining room and two spare bedrooms.

Dominique was in paradise and thoroughly impressed by Brad's tastes. She found the wet bar in the living room and poured herself a drink and began cueing up the Bose sound system that Brad had set into the walls throughout the penthouse. She found the remote and turned on the CD player and a mixed CD began to play low and mellow. She flipped through the songs until she found one she liked, *Breathe Again*, by Toni Braxton.

As the song played, Dominique walked back to the bathroom and began to draw herself a luxurious, warm bubble bath. It would take at least twenty minutes for the tub to fill so she went and stood on the balcony overlooking the city feeling like a queen. After a while, she walked back into the penthouse and into the bathroom, stripped of her cream-colored silk pant suit and removed her matching bra and panties. She walked back to the living room, her sexy body sashaying through Brad's crib like it belonged there, turned up the music, and walked sexily up the stairs leading to the tub, sat on its edge, and then gently slid into the warm water and quickly became lost in pure ecstasy, letting her head lay back against the leather pillows surrounding the huge tub with her eyes closed.

Thirty minutes had gone by, and Dominique was still soaking in the tub with her eyes closed listening to George Duke's song, *Rhyme or Reason* when a soft tap on her shoulder startled her, inciting her to scream as she sat up in the tub. She sighed in relief when she realized it was Brad. She stared at the man as he stood before her in a white silk suit and black gator shoes, holding a bottle of champagne and two glasses whilst smiling at her and licking his lips. Brad stared deeply into Dominique's dark eyes, appreciating her pouty, sexy lips and her wet, slick caramel skin that was ripe for some tender loving care in his eyes.

"Sit back down." Brad said, never releasing eye contact from Dominique.

Dominique's pussy had throbbed over the simple, yet firm manner in which Brad had spoken to her. She loved the way he commanded her; so much so, she'd grown wetter than she'd ever been in her life. She did as Brad commanded and he poured her a glass of champagne before exiting the room briefly, returning a few minutes later, to slide his now-naked muscle-toned, copper-skinned body into the tub and sitting across from Dominique as he held onto a slice of key lime pie on a silver dish. Dominique watched in intrigue as Brad took the silver fork in his hand, cut a piece of the key lime pie and slid it slowly into his mouth; never relinquishing eye contact with the most beautiful specimen of female flesh that sat across from him. Dominique sighed as the fork slid seductively from Brad's lips and back to the saucer to retrieve another piece of the pie. He took the fork and placed it to Dominique's lips and she licked the tip of the pie and then slowly pulled her head forward to engulf the length of the fork and pulled back slowly, never relinquishing eye contact with Brad. The two repeated the routine until the pie disappeared from the saucer.

Brad placed the saucer and fork on the stairs outside the tub and climbed onto his knees. Dominique could see his huge member bobbing underneath the water as he slowly approached her and she began palpating as he grew nearer. He reached for her and she opened her arms to embrace him. Brad, however, grabbed her under either side of her armpits and raised her from the water and sat her on the side of the tub. He sat back down before Dominique in between her thighs and kissed her navel softly. She placed her hands on either side of her body and widened her legs hoping to high heaven that Brad would do what Calvin never had done.

Brad again rose on his knees and ran his hands across Dominique's breasts, massaging her nipples that had become engorged with blood and aching for attention. She didn't say it aloud, but the look on her face said it all, she needed to be fulfilled. Brad was to become her fulfillment. Dominique grabbed Brad's bald head and pulled his face into hers and the two kissed hungrily, Dominique almost in tears and moaning Brad's name as she kissed him hungrily. She rubbed her hands all over his body; his back, his chest, thighs and she grabbed his throbbing member and clutched it tightly. Brad removed Dominique's hands and placed them at her side and began kissing his way down her body, feeling her tremble slightly while marveling at how soft her pubic hair felt against his nostrils. Silky smooth. She smelled of sweet fragrance as well, and when Brad opened his mouth and slid his tongue forth to taste the lovely flesh that sat before him, Dominique moaned his name and gripped him tightly, holding his head in place and not wanting him to stop ever. Lost in wanton lust, pure passion, and heartfelt desire, Dominique spread herself wide and gave a mouthful of pussy to Brad, raising herself up off the edge of the tub to make sure he engulfed all of her and got a full taste of all of her juices as she exploded into his mouth.

The two exited the tub and dried one another off and Dominique walked over to the king-sized bed and lay on her back and spread herself for Brad, who ate her to orgasm once more and slid up her body and kissed her lips passionately. She loved all that Brad was doing to her, the way he touched her, the way he sucked her clitoris while finger-fucking her gently. All the things Dominique had fantasized about oral sex was being brought to fruition and she only wanted more. Whatever Brad wanted to do, the adulterous wife was ready, able and willing. When he'd brought her off a third time with his tongue, Brad stood up and placed a condom over his throbbing member. Dominique was panting in anticipation of what was about to take place. She was a married woman, but on this night, at this moment, she belonged only to Brad.

Brad lay back in the bed beside Dominique and cupped her face in his hands and pulled her close for a passionate kiss and she moaned aloud and melted into the mattress. He hovered over Dominique and she moaned and widened her eyes and stared up at Brad as he penetrated her tight snatch with a thick dick that went on and on and on. With legs raised high in the air and a thick dick inside her pussy that only knew how to administer a good fuck, Dominique, who was being fucked like never before, called out to god and came dramatically, thrashing about and backing up from Brad's dick, but he didn't stop. Dominique was asking for a break, all the while following Brad's lead as he lay down on his back and sat her atop his dick. Another moan spilled forth as he thrust upwards, filling Dominique fully as he slapped her ass, commanding her to ride his dick harder, faster, "Do it for daddy!" he ordered.

Dominique shuddered, moaned, planted her hands firmly on Brad's chest and began rocking back and forth furiously. "Oh my god!"

"Shit feel good don't it, bitch? Who this pussy for? Who's pussy is this?"

"This your pussy, daddy! It's your pussy!" Dominique cried as she leaned forward and kissed Brad passionately. He grabbed a handful of Dominique's ass and began raising and lowering her petite body onto his stiff dick and like a woman possessed, she rode him to climax, having been taken to places she never imagined, better yet, places she never even knew existed.

By the time Brad was done fucking Dominique, her pussy lips were puffy and swollen, dripping wet and she was a hot and sticky disheveled mass of satisfied womanly flesh. The young married woman had been thoroughly fucked by not her husband, but by a man who knew how to use the pussy for his own pleasure, a man who knew how to lick it out and dick it down without any instructions or apprehension and pummeled her into submission—just the way she'd always been wanted to be taken. Brad brought out the inner slut in Dominique on this night and she loved every minute. That inner slut had lain dormant for several years, but no more. And although she was thoroughly pleased, Dominique still had one more thing she wanted to do. After a break of thirty minutes or so, she looked down to Brad's member, clutched it in her tiny hands and asked in a raspy voice, "Can I taste this?"

"Do whatever you want to do with this dick, baby."

Dominique got up and knelt before Brad and clutched his hardening rod. Her mouth watered. She eyed the uncircumcised dick in her hand and began to palpate. For so long she had fantasized about going down on a man, now she was seconds away from doing so. Dominique laid flat on her stomach and drew her face close to Brad's dick and examined it. "It's different from Calvin's. My husband is circumcised, you have foreskin around the head." Dominique said as she stroked Brad's dick, watching the purple glans disappear and reappear as she gently stroked the now rock hard penis. Dominique tentatively stuck out her tongue and moved her head forward, tasting her first dick ever. Soon she was licking and sucking on Brad's rod like a woman possessed, slurping and slobbing, rotating her head in a circular motion while stroking the shaft, becoming an instant oral technician worthy of her own banner.

With Brad, Dominique was able to be the uninhibited sexual creature she had always wanted to be. She loved the way he grabbed the back of her head and drove his dick deep into her esophagus. When he announced that he was coming, Dominique pulled away just as Brad splattered her chin and her continuously stroking hands. She moaned in satisfaction, pleased that she was able to make a man come with her mouth the first time out. Brad then laid Dominique on her back and placed on a condom and pummeled her pussy repeatedly with enough force that she could feel him nearly touching her spine. She then turned around and got on all fours and Brad entered her from behind. When he pressed his chest onto her back and rubbed her clitoris as he made slow love to her, Dominique screamed and thrust back hard, planting herself firmly on his dick as he slapped her ass repeatedly.

Dominique was a satisfied soul when the two finished two and a half hours later. She bathed herself again and dressed. *Rhyme and Reason* had circulated back into the CD player as Brad handed her a diamond bracelet with the inscription *Our*

Secret underneath. Dominique would later hide the bracelet in her room at her mother's home. She kissed Brad on the lips as the music continued to play, and no further words were spoken as Dominique turned and walked slowly out the door never looking back.

At the outset, Dominique was supposed to sleep with Brad for only one night just to get her unfulfilled desires out of her system, but she couldn't deny the fact that she needed to see him again. She pulled over to a payphone and called Brad and thanked him once more, inviting him back into her life.

"You wanna come back next week, baby?" Brad asked, all-the-while knowing the answer to his question.

"Yes. Yes I do."

"Okay then. You know how to let yourself in right?"

"Yes. Thanks Brad. It was good—real good."

"See you next week, baby. Take care of that gorgeous body for me." Brad ended as the two hung up the phones.

Dominique was now under Brad's spell. She felt secure and wanted by the man, and the thought of having someone to live out her fantasies with without none knowing sent a thrill through her body that literally made her wet down below and shook her to the core. The satiated wife took the long way home, savoring the memories of her night with Brad; the second man, the only man who had ever attempted to allow her to be herself.

"Home run, Brad." Dominique said lowly as she smiled, "Home run, baby."

CHAPTER 30

THE END RESULT

"You see...My momma scorned me...And my closest friends, oh lord, you know they warned me... They said that you're no good for me...But I just ignored it..."

En Vogue's song *Just Can't Stay Away* played inside Dominique's headphones as she sat with Tracey, Rolanda, and Jazzy during the show's eight 'o' clock hour. It was now mid-July, a month after Dominique began her affair with Brad and ironically, the females were doing a segment on reasons married people cheat. As the song played, Dominique listened intently to the song's deep, thought-provoking lyrics, realizing the lyrics were similarly describing her feelings at that particular juncture of her young life, *"Cause I didn't have time...No time to sit 'round and decide...When someone control's your mind...There's not much you can do..."*

Dominique listened deeply and reflected on her current life's status. She was a married woman involved with a married older man who made her feel emotions she'd never felt before in her life. Neither Calvin nor her friends had a clue what she was doing, and the tabooness of her secret affair was not only exciting—it was alluring. She reflected on some of the things she and Brad had done together, one thought in particular being when she asked him to allow her to sit on his face and the manner in which he obligingly responded.

Dominique, at the time, didn't care about Calvin's feelings

and all she was putting at risk. She was getting all she needed sexually from Brad and she was keeping it well hid from her friends and family. So long as no one knew, there would be no hurt feelings. That's what Dominique thought about as she was hit with a piece of paper thrown at her by Rolanda.

"What happened? What I miss?"

"Nothing. The song's about to end. You said you had some statistics." Rolanda stated as the song came to a close.

"Alright, that's the song right there sisters. Number two on the hot eight at eight, Just Can't Stay Away by En Vogue. Now, how many of us got that somebody that we just can't stay away from? Bad habits are hard to break, but if ya' callin' some good lovin' a bad habit, well sweetie that just might be a habit ya' want ta' keep!" Jazzy stated as she laughed over the airwaves.

"Eh y'all, check this out," Dominique chimed in, "fifty percent of all marriages end in divorce. The main cause of marital breakups is infidelity with financial difficulties running a close second. I wonder how many marriages could be saved if both parties compromised on certain issues concerning romance and finance. What do you ladies think?"

"Well, in order to compromise you have to give up something you really like and expect the other person to do the same. If you have a selfish individual that's unwilling to give up *anything* then compromising might not be an option." Jazzy stated as she rocked back and forth in her chair.

"So what you are saying is that the lack of compromise can set the wheels in motion for a marriage to fail, right Jazzy?" Tracey asked.

"Yes Sister Spanks," Jazzy replied. "In my opinion, two people operating as one will go much further than two people engaged in a battle of tug-of-war. Some women, because they feel taken for granted, will seek the comfort of another man. Men still want to know if they still 'got it' so to speak. To see if they can still attract the opposite sex. Most times people cheat because they are missing something in their relationship. Now, I don't condone that behavior 'cause if ya' cheating on your woman, or ya' man, then why get married? I can't understand that."

"What if a woman was seduced? Or say she was offered a large sum of money." Dominique asked.

"None of that matters," Rolanda chimed in. "Married people should be able to talk about anything. But umm, if it was like a million dollars or something and I was married? I would tell my husband that I was considering the offer."

"What if he told you not to do it?" Dominique asked.

"Hmmph! After I get through cussin' his ass out—'cause that's what he gone get—a good cussin'—I'm going collect my million! I'd be somebody's love slave for a night, sure would, for a million dollars? Sure would!" Rolanda ended as the females laughed aloud.

"Alright, alright! Let's talk about that right there. Sister Spanks clear the lines, and we gone have a li'l fun tonight. And oh yea, tonight is ladies night. Every Thursday you can catch me and the girls at Utopia's in the French Quarter. Come on out and have a drink with the Fantastic Four tonight. Now, we takin' calls on would you or would you *not* sleep with a man for a million dollars. And fellas? Would you even allow your woman to sleep with a man, or another woman, well, of course you would let her sleep with another woman if you can watch it or join in, right? That's just how most men are!" Jazzy said as the group laughed. "But seriously people, would you let your spouse sleep with a member of the opposite sex for a million dollars?" Jazzy asked then added. "I know this here, if my man tried ta' stop me from collecting a cool mill, I'd have ta' tell him, 'baby, I love ya''—but tonight you gone have ta' excuse me, because ain't no way I'm leaving a cool mill on the table'! Hey, he'll thank me in the morning! And, and I'd just have ta' let him know I did what I did... Foe the love of money!" Jazzy ended as Tracey faded in Bone Thugs in Harmony's hit song *Foe the Love of Money*.

"That's number one on the hot eight at eight! Foe the Love of Money by Bone, them boys from Cleveland holding it down off top! Ladies hit us up on the hotline! Would you sleep with a man for a million?" Dominique yelled into the microphone as the rap lyrics began blaring across the airwaves.

The girls ended the show on a high note; something they did often. Their ratings were sky-high and they were due for another substantial raise in the up-coming weeks. Dominique, Rolanda, and Tracey were at the top of their careers. They had come a long way and were now living their dream to the fullest. Everything looked good on the surface, but each of these three females either knowing or unknowingly were treading dangerous waters. Their faces were plastered on the sides of city buses and also on bill boards out near the airport. The cast of the Fantastic Four was one of the first images travelers would see when they left the airport to head into the city of New Orleans. The girls mingled with the crowd inside the packed club until the wee hours and headed home. They did their Friday show and headed out to enjoy the weekend.

Dominique was home reading a steamy romance novel Saturday afternoon when Calvin burst through the door of their apartment and grabbed her from the couch.

"Calvin, what are you doing! I'm reading!"

"Read in the car! I gotta show you something!" Calvin said excitedly.

Dominique had on a pair of 'daisy duke' jean shorts and a light blue t-shirt with a pink bandana on her head and pink Daniel Green slippers. "Calvin I can't go out like this! Where we going anyway?" Dominique asked as Calvin ignored her statements, locked the door and ushered her towards her Mazda 626.

"I gotta show you something." Calvin said again as he backed out of the parking spot and headed towards a small subdivision off Lake Forest Boulevard, not too far from Abramson high school.

Dominique looked on in wonderment trying to figure out where she was being taken on this sunny summer afternoon. Calvin turned into a new subdivision and parked in front of a neatly built, large, white stucco home. The two exited the car and Calvin walked around and pulled Dominique towards the beautiful home.

"Calvin, whose house is this?" Dominique asked as she stared at the structure.

"Just look inside and tell me what ya' think, baby." Calvin said as he and Dominique entered the home.

The house was immaculate. It had light tan marble floors to match the trimming and the wood on the vaulted ceilings. A huge kitchen with an island counter was on the right. Behind the kitchen was a nice-sized dining room. Straight ahead, was a sunken living room with a fireplace on the left wall, and an empty aquarium was straight ahead. To the right was another room that led out into a three-car garage. The two walked and stood before the living room where Calvin pointed to his right. Dominique looked and saw two huge double doors. She walked down the long hall and noticed another bedroom on her right and a huge bathroom to her left. She opened the double doors and stared at a luxurious master bedroom. Her draw dropped when she looked and saw a Jacuzzi tub sitting three feet off the ground. It was a garden tub. Stained glass separated the bathroom from the bedroom, but Dominique could tell that plants were supposed to lead up to the tub. There was another fireplace inside the bedroom as well. The opposite end of the hall held two more bedrooms on either side and another full-sized bathroom. The house was lovely at its worst.

"Calvin, it's beautiful. Tell me it's ours." Dominique said softly.

"I'm sorry baby, I can't. It's not ours." Calvin said sadly.

Dominique began to wonder why Calvin bought her to such a lovely place; her wonderment was answered when Calvin laughed and said, "It's not ours until you sign your name right her on the dotted line! Baby we bought a house!"

Dominique screamed and jumped into her husband's arms and kissed him passionately on the lips as the two stood in front of the living room.

"Calvin, I love you! I love you!" Dominique stated as she leapt from her husband's lap and signed the contracts to the home. Afterwards, she began to run around the house dancing. She soon began thinking about how she wanted her new home to be decorated as she saw so much potential in the spacious place.

"Look here, baby," Calvin said as he hugged Dominique from behind as they walked down the three stairs leading into the sunken living room. "I been working overtime for almost five years to get this place. It's cheaper than what we paying in rent and we on a twenty-year plan. Before we forty-five we gone own this place. And oh yea, I got a position in the advertising branch of the marketing firm. It's less hours, and a tad bit more money. We made it, Dominique. Hard work has just paid off for us." Calvin stated as he walked behind Dominique.

The last image Calvin saw on Dominique's face was that of a huge smile and proud eyes, but as he walked behind his wife hugging her, he couldn't see the disappointed look on his wife's face. Dominique wasn't disappointed in Calvin; to the contrary, she was disappointed in herself for what she was doing behind her husband's back. Calvin was working hard to provide a better life for him and Dominique; but Dominique was out having an affair because she felt her husband was neglecting her sexually, which he was, but Dominique now knew why Calvin was doing what he was doing the first five years of their marriage. She felt ashamed of herself, but then again, if Calvin had told her of his plans she would have understood. Dominique brushed those thoughts off. Trying to blame Calvin for her having an affair was an easy way out. She was in the wrong and she knew it. She also knew she had to give up Brad because she'd suddenly realized she had made a terrible mistake by beginning the affair.

"When can we move in, Calvin?"

"It usually takes two weeks to close the deal, plus they have a little more plumbing to do and some minor work on the landscaping so we looking at another month."

"We can use that time to purchase some new furniture. Ohh, we can have a house warming party and invite our friends over once we settle in!"

"Yea that's cool right there. Look, I ordered that aquarium from Lubby's shop the week before she was killed. That was one of the last things she did. She umm, she was gone set up a salt water tank for us, but—"

"I know. I know, Cal." Dominique said as she held her husband's hand and stared at the aquarium and reminisced about her friend. "We can still set it up. Rolanda closed the pet shop, but I still remember some of the things Lubby had in there, we'll get it done. Lubby, man, she was just so sweet." Dominique stated as she wiped her watery eyes.

"Gerald ain't been the same since that happen."

"How's he doing?"

"Okay. He be home next month after boot camp. He gone be stationed out in Belle Chase across the river so he'll be around, unless they have another war or something."

Dominique and Calvin left their home and went back to their apartment where she phoned her friends and told them the good news. They were excited and they all wanted to help decorate. The next three weekends were spent shopping for furniture and decorations with Calvin, Rolanda, Tracey, Brianna, and Mrs. Franz.

Dominique was now seeing her husband in a new light, he was her everything, but in spite of her newfound love for the man she'd married, she still hadn't told Brad of her intentions. She had met with him twice after learning that she and Calvin were to become home owners although they did not have sex and she grew nervous about ending the relationship, not sure how to break the news to Brad, who was really getting into her.

Three more weeks had gone by and Dominique and Calvin were settled into their home. Dominique and her friends, along with Mrs. Franz and Calvin's mother had done an excellent job decorating the home. Plants hung throughout, the bedrooms were all furnished as well as the dining room. Appliances ran throughout and paintings hung on walls. Dominique and Calvin were living the American dream. Both had good jobs, a home, were married, and they were happy, only Dominique had Brad hanging over her head.

Brad was wondering what was going on between he and Dominique, and Dominique swore to herself that she would cut all ties off with Brad on Wednesday. When Wednesday came around, Dominique was so glad she was on her cycle. She would no longer have to lie to Brad about the reasons why she wasn't making love to the man. She walked into the Double Tree Hotel lounge and spotted her soon-to-be ex-lover and sat next to him in a secluded booth towards the back of the lounge.

"How was work?" Brad, who was dressed in a pin-striped navy blue and white suit with a pair of black gators on his feet, asked Dominique.

"You didn't listen to the show?" the twenty-three year old petite woman replied as she removed her hair from her face.

"I couldn't. I had a meeting with the mayor. Then my wife called, she was pissed about something, but that don't matter, I'm here with you." Brad said as he leaned into Dominique to offer a kiss.

Dominique kissed him softly and backed away. "Well, you didn't hear my dedication to you then."

"What dedication?"

"Kiss and Say Goodbye by the Manhattans."

"No I missed that. What else am I missing here, Dominique?" Brad asked as he sipped his vodka and orange juice.

"Well, Brad, and you've been wonderful. You've taken me to new heights. The love-making was intense, but I realize my mistake." Dominique said as Brad ordered another round for the two of them. "Me and Calvin, we umm, we are a good team. My husband doesn't deserve to be treated like this."

"He bought you a house that's all. What's special about that? I gave you a place to stay before he even did what he did."

"Yea, but my name is on nothing you own. Anyway, you married, I'm married. I belong with my husband. I see that now."

"If he would not have bought that house, would you be

telling me these things?"

"Well, he did. And by doing so I now see that all he did, he was doing for me. That's what real love is about. We had some good times, you've shown me some things and I thank you for that, but this is where it ends, tonight it ends." Dominique stated as she sipped her drink.

"That's fine. I respect your decision. You won't have no problems from me, lady. It was a pleasure just to be with you for this short period of time. I thank you for that." Brad said as he held up his glass and the two toasted. "Come on, let's take a ride." Brad requested as he motioned for the waiter and ordered a large bottle of champagne.

"Brad I shouldn't. I have to get home."

"Come on now. It's our last night together. Let me take you for a ride through the city. No strings attached. Just my way of saying good-bye to a special friend." Brad stated as he placed two twenties onto the table and stuffed five hundred dollars into the waiters pocket. "Now, I just brought a nice bottle of champagne. I got my limousine out front with some nice sounds inside. It's a beautiful night too; let me say good-bye to you properly."

Dominique reluctantly agreed to take the ride with Brad. The two walked out of the hotel and quickly hopped into the limousine careful not to be seen. The stretched Cadillac limousine was the nicest car Dominique had ever been in. The windows were darkened, there was a mini-bar inside and when Brad selected the song *Hooks in Me* by the O'Jays Dominique smiled, grabbed a long-stemmed crystal glass and stretched her arm out to allow Brad to pour her a glass of sparkling Dom Perignon and sunk back into the soft leather seats of the limousine and listened to the music as Brad raised the partition and removed his suit jacket and loosened his tie.

Dominique had nearly forgotten how much of a good time she and Brad had when they were together. Soon there was laughter as they talked about their marriages and careers. Dominique never chatted with Calvin in this manner, it was always work, work, work. She couldn't deny that she would miss being with Brad because his conversations were always stimulating. Had they not had an intimate relationship, Dominique could see herself being platonic with Brad, he was a smart and thoughtful man that could offer up a good conversation at any given moment. Dominique had crossed the line when she slept with Brad, however; so remaining friends was not an option. She decided to enjoy her last night with the man who had made her feel like she was a real woman, a highly attractive female to be desired by all male members of the human race.

"Brad this is nice, I never been in a limousine this big before. Except when Lubby died, but you can't count a funeral as a good experience for riding in a limousine." Dominique said as Brad topped off her glass.

"See, I told you this was gone be a night to remember, baby. I just wanted to thank you for allowing me to share at least a part of your life. I'll remember you for as long as I live Dominique, you are a very special woman. Not just to me, you're special to everybody that's a part of your life at this present time. And when you're gone, I'll have the pleasure of knowing that somewhere out here in the world, I was blessed to meet one the most beautiful women to have ever graced this planet." Brad stated as he rubbed Dominique's leg, squeezed it softly and smiled at her; causing Dominique to blush slightly.

Before long they were riding across the Causeway, a twenty-four mile long bridge that spanned the width of Lake Ponchartrain from north to south that led out to the town of Covington, Louisiana. The ride across the bridge was long and romantic. Dominique was enjoying the music, and she was now getting a little tipsy from the champagne. Brad leaned into her smoothly and pressed his lips to hers. This time, Dominique didn't resist. Her mouth opened widely as she accepted Brad's probing tongue. She held onto her glass of champagne as she returned Brad's affection. Brad, who was sitting to the right of Dominique, reached out and cupped her rear end and Dominique moaned.

"Brad, Brad, I'm on my cycle. We can't."

Brad moved his hands to Dominique's breasts and cupped

them and once again, at that moment, she came under his spell and was unable to resist. She really didn't want this to happen, but she just couldn't control herself whenever she was around the man and he touched her. She slowly assisted Brad by removing her blouse and raising her bra to reveal her breasts and allowed him to suck on her hardened, darkened nipples. The two were all over each other as the limousine cruised across the Causeway, its interior hidden by the limousine's dark tinted windows. Dominique was topless on the backseat, Brad had unzipped his pants and freed his throbbing member from his slacks and placed her left hand onto his manhood.

"Stroke that dick for me, baby. Just stroke it for me till I come." Brad pleaded.

Dominique knew she couldn't have sex, but Brad was making her feel good, she only wanted to return the favor. She clutched his rock hard, thick dick, the same dick that had taken to her countless orgasms, the same dick she let slide back and forth between her lips on countless occasions. She stroked it lovingly as the two continued their oral assault on one another. Brad tasted good, he smelled good, his body felt good. Not a soul knew of their clandestine affair and tonight was the last night they were to ever be together. All of those thoughts ran through Dominique's head as she stroked Brad's dick in her tiny hands, contemplating her next move. *"Should I?"* She asked herself. *"Why not?"* she thought, *"Just one last time."* Tonight would be the culmination of their affair. If Dominique had it her way, she would strip naked and have Brad take her right then and there. Instead, she decided to do what she could never do to Calvin, she leaned down into Brad's lap and took his member into her mouth, again.

They both moaned, Dominique nearly orgasmed from having Brad's member in her mouth. After enjoying Dominique's aggressive sucking for several minutes, he removed Dominique from his member and removed his shoes and slacks and unbuttoned his shirt to allow her full access to his body. Dominique licked his chest and tweaked his nipples, she continued to stroke Brad's dick. "Take it in your mouth again and suck it hard." Brad commanded.

Dominique loved having this older man ordering her to please him. Calvin never let her know how much she was fulfilling him, but Brad always acknowledged Dominique to let her know how good she was making him feel. She slowly worked her way down to Brad's dick and rubbed it across her cheeks, moaning as she did so. "Mmm," was all she said as her lips slid over the plum-sized head.

Before long, slurping sounds could be heard coming from Dominique's mouth and she began moaning, her voice muffled by Brad's dick. The twenty-three year-old was at a loss for words as she let Brad's penis slid deep into her mouth, bumping her tonsils, the erotic and erratic sounds emanating from Brad only spurning her on further—urging her to deliver the best blow job she possibly could.

As the limousine continued traveling across the Causeway, Dominique's head bounced up and down in Brad's lap. She was now on the floor of the limousine, on her knees like a depraved whore as she sucked and licked. Brad clasped both of his hands to either side of Dominique's head and began to thrust his hips forward, his lower waist bouncing off the soft leather seats. Dominique moaned around his dick as she was blasted with a load of sperm that hit the back of her throat. She shuddered with a small orgasm as she swallowed most of what Brad had to offer. The rest ran down the corners of her mouth. She licked her lips and moved down to Brad's scrotum to lick his balls clean of semen. She then licked Brad's softening dick clean and leaned back on her heels and stared at him as she moaned in utter ecstasy. For the first time since they began their affair, Dominique had allowed Brad to orgasm into her mouth. She always sucked him to the edge and then jerked him off the rest of the way; but on this night, Dominique swallowed for the first time; it was to be her final good-bye to Brad, the culmination of a love affair that was fueled by sheer lust, selfishness, and a burning curiosity that had taken Dominique over the edge into a world she dared not share with another man ever again. She was going home, home to her husband, where she belonged.

"You like that?" she asked as she reached for her champagne glass and guzzled the remaining liquid down to remove the taste of semen from her mouth.

Her question was answered when Brad leaned forward and kissed her lips, tasting the remnants of the champagne that Dominique had guzzled. "Your mouth is pure magic, baby." Brad whispered as Dominique got up from the limousine's floor and lay into his body. She closed her eyes, reliving the experience as the limousine exited the Causeway and made a quick U-turn and headed back to New Orleans.

"Brad, I just want you to know that, that—"

"No, you don't love me. You like what we do, but you don't love me. You love Calvin. You know it, I know it. I'm always here for you though." Brad said as he lay naked from the waist down whilst holding Dominique, who was naked from the waist up.

"I wasn't about to say *love* man," Dominique said playfully, "I was going to say that tonight really is our last together." she ended as she sat up, grabbed her purse and handed Brad his hotel key.

"Okay. Well, you know where to find me right? Misses Huntley." Brad stated playfully as he threw the key aside.

"My friends and my momma would be so ashamed of me. You know, you bring out the wild side in me—but like the bracelet you gave me says, it's our secret, right?"

"Dominique, what happened between us, stays in my heart and within the memories of my mind, the same mind that will always feel a connection to your soul. I know you inside and out, literally speaking. Like I say, it's been short-lived, but these few months with you ranks high upon my life's most memorable experiences. I will never forget you. Remember, if you need me, I'm not hard to find." Brad ended as Dominique closed her eyes and took a short nap before being dropped off at the Double Tree. She kissed Brad good-bye in the limousine and the two parted ways, never to see one another again. Dominique returned home to her husband and entered their lavish four-bedroom home and showered and went to bed a relieved woman. She'd ended the affair without getting caught, had satisfied her sexual desires and now, she could focus solely on her marriage.

The following weekend after her night with Brad, Dominique's cycle had withdrawn and she and Calvin made love in their home all weekend. They 'christened' every room in the house. Calvin never noticed that during the entire weekend, Dominique was reluctant to kiss him. She'd complained of a sore throat and she didn't want Calvin to catch what she believed was a cold.

Calvin got up to prepare for work Monday morning while Dominique was in the kitchen preparing coffee and eggs, which had become their morning routine since they moved into their new home. As she prepared breakfast, Dominique kept coughing and rubbing her throat. She had a fever and her esophagus felt as if someone was holding a blow torch to it. She whispered for Calvin, because she had lost her voice, and suddenly fell to the floor, spilling the scrambled eggs and the dishes that held them.

Calvin ran into the kitchen half-dressed when he heard the dishes shatter and saw his wife lying on the kitchen floor. Shattered dishes were all around her as she clutched her neck whispering hoarsely that she could barely breathe. Calvin called 911 and the ambulance was on the scene in minutes to rush Dominique to Methodist hospital. Calvin had called Mrs. Franz and the two anxiously awaited word of Dominique's situation in the lobby of the emergency room. When the doctor came out, he stared at Calvin and Mrs. Franz. "You are Dominique's husband correct?" the doctor asked Calvin.

"Yes sir. What's going with my wife? Is she okay?"

The doctor pulled Calvin to the side and said in a low tone. "Mister Huntley, I don't know what kind of lifestyle you and your wife are leading, but there're a lot of sexually transmitted diseases that one can catch."

"Sexually transmitted diseases? What the hell you talking about, man? What kind of disease?"

"I have seen swingers come in and either partner has had a disease, but they can't figure out where they went wrong. Now —"

"What ya' mean swingers? What's this talk about disease and shit? What the *fuck* is wrong with my wife?" Calvin asked angrily.

The doctor looked Calvin in the eyes and said, "Dominique has a bacterial infection in her esophagus. Gonorrhea. Your wife contracted this disease from performing oral sex on somebody that was infected with the Niesseria gonorrhoeae, or Gonococcal bactermia, commonly known as Gonorrhea, or 'the clap'."

"You telling me my wife, my wife 'burning'?" Calvin asked in shock.

"Well," the doctor replied, "she has a bacterial infection that can only get only get worse. It has infected her esophagus and the only way for her to have contracted the disease orally is to have had performed oral sex on an infected individual. I am making a recommendation that you get tested as well Mister Huntley." the doctor concluded as he turned and walked away from Calvin, who was now being approached by two nurses who were preparing to take him to a room to be tested for Gonorrhea.

Calvin knew that Dominique had never given him oral sex before; if his wife was indeed infected with Gonorrhea then that meant that she would have—had—to—Calvin's eyes watered at the realization that his wife had stepped out on him as he sat inside a hospital room waiting to be testing. *"Tell me this is not happening. Tell me this woman didn't destroy the life we built together."* Calvin said to himself as he wondered what in the hell Dominique, the woman he loved more than anything in life, had been doing behind his back.

CHAPTER 31

SHE CAME AT A BAD TIME

Calvin stared down at his wife as she lay in her hospital bed the day after she had been rushed to the hospital. Dominique's mother had just left to allow Calvin and Dominique time to talk alone. They stared at one another in silence for a minute before Dominique spoke hoarsely. "I'm sorry, I'm so sorry Calvin."

"You're sorry? How could you do what you did to me? Do what you did to *us*? What can you possibly say to make me understand why you went out and did what you did to me."

"Nothing. I can't say anything except that I fucked up and I'll never do that again. I promise."

"You right. You will *not* do this again! At least not *to me*! When you leave this place," Calvin stated angrily as his eyes watered, "don't come home! Don't *ever* come near me!"

"Calvin, let me explain."

"What is that you're going to explain? You gone explain to me why you gave head to another man? I'm supposed to understand that shit?" Calvin asked as he looked Dominique directly in the eyes before turning away quickly. "I can't believe you, Dominique! Never, never in life, in *life* would I have thought that you—*you* off all people would do something like this!"

Dominique could not bring herself to tell Calvin the reasons she had an affair. At the time, she thought she was missing out on something. She had fantasies she wanted to live and she selfishly pursued her own desires. "I have no reason for doing what I did. Forgive me please. I, I realized what I was doing and I ended the affair almost a week ago. I promise to God, I was a little drunk that night and things got out of control."

"That's an understatement. How long has this been going on?" Calvin asked.

"Calvin please. I'm sorry. I'm really sorry. I had an affair and now I have to pay for it. Don't, don't make me relive that."

"I mean, you two were fucking as well right? How long?"

"Calvin, don't—"

"How long?"

"A few months. Don't make me do this please. I'm sorry. I swear to God I'm sorry." Dominique cried hoarsely.

"Your ass can be sorry all you want. I don't have to accept that shit! I'm just glad I don't have no disease. What you did to us—to me? What you did hurts more than anything! The same lips you use to tell me that you love me! The same lips you *kissed* me with!" Calvin said as tears ran down his cheeks.

"I can't say nothing except that I'm sorry. I feel so dirty. I'm ashamed of myself. I'm sorry. Please, say you forgive me."

Calvin stared at Dominique and turned his head away and wiped his tears. It hurt the young man to look at his wife because every time he did so, all he could image in his mind was Dominique with another man doing the deed. She had such sweet lips—they were all his—so he thought, but everything about his wife was tainted now. She was defiled in his eyes. She had given herself to another man and in the end, she had contracted a disease. If she hadn't gotten sick, would she still be having the affair? Calvin knew firsthand how sexual his wife could get. He visualized the way Dominique spread herself for him when they made love. She did what she did for him with another man. She willingly took off her clothes and had sex with another man. She gave away what was rightfully his in the eyes of the law. She made love to someone else, and for a man to have his woman, better yet his *wife* sleep with someone else is the ultimate act of betrayal. A woman's body, to the man who loves her is personal and private. Dominique allowed another man inside of her body. That was no accident. She did what she did willingly. Calvin thought about those things as he turned back to Dominique and said, "We done! You can come and get your things when you leave here. Just call me so I won't be around."

Dominique's eyes were filled with tears as she watched her husband walk slowly out of the room. "Calvin!" she called out as loudly as she could. "Calvin, please, I'm sorry!" she said hoarsely as her husband disappeared from sight.

Dominique cried the whole day. Her marriage was ruined as well as her reputation. She felt like a loose woman, a selfish, dirty whore that could not even look at herself in the mirror because every time she did so, all she could see was her mouth, which had become a 'dirty orifice' in her eyes. She couldn't blame Calvin for doing what he did, if she had the courage, she would have ripped her lips off her face completely. She was that ashamed of herself. It took her ruining her marriage to understand just how much Calvin meant to her; how could she? How could she betray the man she swore to love before God? *"Will he ever love me again?"* Dominique asked herself as she cried silently before turning away from the mirror.

Dominique friends arrived later that night and sat with her for a good while and listened as she revealed to them what had transpired. Although she knew they were all shocked, Dominique was glad her friends didn't judge her. "I can't believe myself. I was so caught up into the way Brad made me feel, I wasn't thinking straight." she told her girls.

"At least you didn't get AIDS or give anything to Calvin." Tracey said softly as she stared at her friend with sad eyes. Tracey, Rolanda, and Brianna felt so sorry for Dominique and their hearts went out to her.

"No matter how you spin it, there isn't a bright side to this situation. I fucked up big-time. For what? To satisfy a curiosity? To do things to a man that I've never even done to my husband? Oh my God! I ruined my marriage! And, and, I lost the best thing in my life!" Dominique cried aloud as her friends all stood around her and rubbed her affectionately. "Y'all must think I'm a fuckin' slut! Some kind of a perverted whore!"

"No we don't, Dominique. We not here to judge—we here to comfort." Brianna stated softly.

"As fucked up as this shit is, we all knew you and Calvin were having problems in the bedroom." Rolanda stated.

"That don't justify what I did, Rolanda. This is all my fault!"

"We with you for whatever you 'bout ta' go through girlfriend. Right or wrong, we stand beside you, Dominique. We your girls and through thick and thin, we always stand as one." Tracey said as Brianna and Rolanda nodded their heads in agreement.

Dominique was glad for her friends being there to support her. They were of great comfort. As far as her job was concerned, Jazzy had given her the week off to get herself together. Dominique told her over the phone what she had done and Jazzy frowned upon Dominique. But despite her troubles, she still told her it wouldn't affect her job. "Your personal life is your business," Jazzy said over the phone, "but had this thing gone public, it would've damaged your reputation in front of the audience. We'll keep your seat. I remember you asked me about your problem. You did what you felt you had to do, and you got caught in the process. Now you understand why I don't condone extra-marital affairs. You see how much hurt and anger it can cause?"

"Believe me, I understand fully, and I'm paying for it now. I lost my home, my husband, and put my career at risk. If I ever get a second chance, I'll never take those things for granted." Dominique stated as she sat on her bed preparing to leave the hospital.

"You still have your career, but your marriage needs some serious restoration. I hope and pray that you two get it together one day soon."

Dominique thanked Jazzy and hung up the phone and called Calvin to let him know she was on her way to retrieve her clothes. The betrayed husband was so disappointed in his wife, and hurt over her actions, he'd taken the week off from work as well. He left his home and went over to his parents' home and waited for Dominique to gather her belongings.

About an hour and a half later the door bell rung over to Calvin's parents' home. Calvin opened the door to see Dominique at the front the door. "I told you not to come near me." he said angrily.

"Calvin, please? Give me another chance? I know I fucked up, but just give another chance please?" Dominique pleaded through watery eyes.

"Why? Why Dominique? I can't even look you in the face." Calvin said as he walked into the living room.

Dominique walked in behind Calvin and hugged him from behind placing her teary face into his shoulder blades. "Baby, please, look at me. Just look at me."

Dominique could not even look at herself in the mirror for feeling so guilty, but she was begging her husband to look at her. She knew Calvin visualized her with her former lover every time he looked at her and she was hoping he would maybe get the image of her and another man out of his head upon seeing her dressed up and wearing make-up.

Calvin removed Dominique's arms and turned around and said, "All I see, all I *see* when I look at you is you with another man. I see you not as my wife anymore, but some other man's bitch. You understand? I can't deal with this shit right now! Knowing my wife sucked another—you have the nerve to come *here* and ask me to forgive your bullshit? You nothing but a diseased dick-sucker to me now!" Calvin yelled angrily as he stared down at Dominique.

Dominique covered her mouth and widened her eyes and ran into the bathroom. She had to vomit. Calvin knew what he was doing. He could've just walked away, said nothing, or just refused to let Dominique into his parents' home, but the truth was, he was trying to hurt Dominique with his words just as much as she had hurt him with her physical actions because she wanted him to feel the pain he was feeling. He still loved her, but he could no longer trust the woman and he didn't want to be hurt again. Calvin sat on the sofa and wept softly just as the door bell rung. He wiped his tears and opened the door to see a somewhat tall, tan-skinned hairy woman with jet black hair that was styled into two thick plats standing before him.

"Can I help you?" Calvin asked.

"Yes. My name is Mary Holland. I was wondering if you knew the whereabouts of Sam Holland? He lived across the street over there."

Calvin had to think for a minute before he recalled who the lady was referring to. "Sam, Sam, yeah! Gabriella and Sam!"

"Who's Gabriella?" the woman asked.

"That was Sam's wife."

"Calvin, talk to me!" Dominique yelled, running back into the living room.

Calvin was feeling a mixture of emotions at that moment. He was ready for Dominique to leave, and he had a strange woman asking about a man who had died almost ten years ago. The bewildered man only wanted complete silence and to be left alone on this day.

"I'm sorry. Did I come at a bad time?" the woman asked.

"Actually you did, but umm, Sam, his wife Gabriella and their daughter was killed in 1984. Everybody in that family dead." Calvin stated as the woman began to cry.

"Oh my God! I'm, I'm sorry for bothering you mister!"

"How are you related to Sam?" Calvin asked as the woman walked away.

"He was my brother!" the woman stated as she ran back to a convertible white Chevy Caprice. Calvin could see two black females in the backseat and a white female was driving. He watched as the car pulled away from the curb and rode down the street and out of sight before turning his attention back towards Dominique. The couple argued briefly before

Dominique, who still believed in her heart that Calvin loved her, abruptly ended the dispute, not want any more hurtful words to fly from Calvin's mouth.

"I'll be at my mother's house. I'll call, even if you only say hello and hang up when you hear my voice, I'll call—because no matter what you say or how you feel—I'll never stop loving you. And I'm not giving up on *us*. I hope you can find it in your heart to forgive me someday because I'll always be your wife. I admit, I fucked up, but baby, I promise, I'll never, never, hurt you again. I deserve what I'm getting right now." Dominique said as she fell to her knees in the center of the living room as Calvin sat a short distance away on the sofa with his head down. He briefly looked at Dominique, but turned away as it was still hard to look at her. "Please, Calvin. Please, forgive me? If not today, tomorrow, if not tomorrow, someday. Give me another chance, please, I love you." Dominique ended as she got up from the carpeted floor and walked slowly out of the house, leaving Calvin alone to cry on the couch.

Dominique went to her parents' home in East Shore and Mr. and Mrs. Franz greeted her at the door. Dominique dropped her suitcase in the foyer and leaned into her father's chest and cried heavily. "Shh, shh, it's gone be okay sweet heart."

"Dad, I ruined everything!"

Mr. Franz felt pity for his daughter. Sure, he and Mrs. Franz had had their share of troubles, as do all marriages, but what Dominique had encountered was at the very least, shameful and embarrassing for a woman to have to endure. No matter what the circumstances, however, the man would stand behind his daughter and encourage her to pursue her marriage and do all she can to save it if that is was what she really wanted to do.

Mrs. Franz, on the other hand, was disappointed in Dominique. Stanley had never cheated as far as she knew, but he had a problem with alcohol in times past. So much so he sought counseling. Now he was able to have a beer or two whenever he returned home from the road. He'd gotten control of his habit. Mrs. Franz reflected on her husband's resolve to gain control over his drinking and put it into context with

Dominique having loss control of her sexual desires to the point of stepping outside of her marriage. The disappointed mother understood the plight of temptation as she herself had been tempted many a time while Stanley was on the road, but she had resolve and willpower, something she knew her daughter was lacking at this point and time in her life. She walked into her daughter's bedroom and handed Dominique the bracelet that Brad had given her and said, "I found this while I was cleaning your room one day last month. I knew then that you were having an affair. You knew *exactly* what you were doing, Dominique. You deserve to feel what you are feeling right now."

"Momma, I never meant for this to happen. I tried to talk to Calvin and he—"

"It doesn't justify what you did Dominique. I love you more than life itself my child, but you have to wear this one. And take a look a Proverbs chapter thirty-one. Read it daily. Because you have it in you to be a very capable wife. You fell weak—but you can make it up, baby. You can make it up if you try hard enough." Mrs. Franz ended as she closed Dominique's door, leaving her alone with her thoughts. Dominique sat for a minute and stared at the bracelet in her hand. She then got up and ran to bathroom and flushed the trinket down the toilet. She was through with Brad forever, she wanted her husband back, and she set out to regain what she had lost.

****

A month after she moved back in with her mother, Dominique learned that she was pregnant. She would call every night to leave a message for Calvin before she realized she was to have Calvin's baby. When she learned she was pregnant, the calls stopped; and that made Calvin call her to find out what was going on. It was mid-September when he called Dominique for the first time since the two of them separated back in early-August. "Why you didn't call me?" he asked.

"Because I'm pregnant, and I know you won't believe me when I tell you the baby is yours."

"Did you tell anyone?"

"Not yet—but just to let you know—it is your baby. But I won't blame you if you don't want to be around us after the things I've done in the recent past."

Calvin didn't respond. He hung up the phone hoping that the baby was his, but still he wasn't sure. Dominique had repeatedly told him that she had ended the affair and she was constantly apologizing to him for her indiscretions while doing all she could within her power to regain his favor, but Calvin really wasn't trying to hear it at this particular time.

"He didn't even acknowledge the fact that I'm pregnant with his child," Dominique said to herself when she heard the dial tone. Her eyes welled up as she hung up the phone, still hoping and praying, however, that Calvin would someday change his mind and take her back...

...Thirty seven year-old Dominique was shaken from her past experiences when she heard a car pull up onto her driveway. She looked around, remembering that she was not in New Orleans in September of 1994, but tucked away in her backyard in Las Vegas in the October of 2008. The experiences she'd replayed seemed just like yesterday.

She wiped the tears from her eyes and got up and walked around the side of her house and saw 37 year-old Tracey exiting a new '08 Land Rover. "Hey girl! Check out this new ride! Clean ain't it?" Tracey asked. She then noticed the sad look displayed upon her friend's face. "What's wrong? Don't tell me you and Calvin—"

"No we fine, Tracey. Remember Ben Holland, though?" Dominique replied.

"From Calvin's block?"

"Yea."

"He dead right?" Tracey asked.

"No. Rolanda ran into him down in Phoenix. He invited us down there next weekend."

"That's why you was crying?"

"No girl." Dominique answered as she laughed half-heartedly. "I was just thinking about the day Lubby died and when me and Calvin split up. Rolanda called me and told me she was thinking about back in the day and it kinda sparked a little of my memories."

"Back in the day? Damn, Dominique. Why you wanna relive all those hurtful memories? You making yourself cry girl, replaying that stuff." Tracey stated in a concerned manner as she looked to the ground, then added, "I haven't thought about those times in a long while. You know, we shoulda seen the writing on the wall after all that, but we were still fucking up, big time!"

"I know, that's what hurts Tracey. I mean, it took all that shit for us to get it right."

"Well, girlfriend, you umm, you wanna talk?"

"No, I'm just reliving some memories, some big mistakes. You don't mind do you?"

"You gonna be okay Dominique? I mean, you need me to stick around?"

"Yea. If you don't mind, just, just come and sit with me." Dominique stated as she reached out her hand towards her friend.

Tracey grabbed hold of Dominique's hand and entered Dominique's backyard and the two walked and sat outside on the patio. Dominique folded her legs into the chair and rested her head on her knees. Tracey sat beside her friend and rubbed her back gently as Dominique cried. Tracey couldn't help but to well up as well. She knew what had transpired after Lubby's death and once Dominique and Calvin had split up. She knew it all—the good, the bad, and the downright ugly. Tracey couldn't help but to think that Dominique was reliving some of her darkest memories. She sat quietly with Dominique as *she* now began to reflect on some the events that transpired with the four remaining friends.

CHAPTER 32

IT'S NOT OVER

"For the first time on the radio, we got my girl Bree's song You Don't Have to Cry which is a remake of Rene and Angela's hit song from back in the day! Come on and turn the volume up on ya' radio and support your local talent!" Tracey yelled over the air waves.

It was now March of '95 and the Fantastic Four Show was on air promoting Bree's song. After almost three years of planning and preparations, Brianna and Tank had finally produced the first single off Brianna's upcoming debut album titled *Reflections of Bree*, and had introduced the song to the public. Bri took on the name Bree because she felt it looked better and would cut down confusion over her name whenever people looked at the CD in stores. The song was played during the seven 'o' clock hour and the audience adored the melodic soul-stirring song. Brianna was on hand inside the studio and as her friends fielded calls, all voting positively for the song, she couldn't help but feel proud of what she and Tank had put together. As various callers called in to show love for the song, Brianna thanked each and every one of them.

The song would become a hit locally and before long, it was being played all over the south east. TLC, a popular R&B female singing group, caught wind of Brianna's song while touring through the state of Louisiana and they sought her out to open up for them on their tour through the south as they promoted their latest album titled *CRAZYSEXYCOOL* and

Brianna and Tank leapt at the chance. They were scheduled to open up for the first time for the group in Jackson, Mississippi in late-March of '95. Brianna's friends were happy for her; through patience and perseverance, she had brought her dream to fruition.

The weekend of Brianna's performance had arrived and she, Tank and Mike had set out to drive up to Jackson, Mississippi. The Fantastic Four Show was a big hit in Jackson, so all week, Jazzy and the girls were pumping up Brianna's performance. TLC was performing on the campus of Jackson State University, a historically black college that produced one of the greatest running backs the world has ever seen, 'Sweetness' A.K.A. Walter Payton. The campus of Jackson State was *thee* place to be on weekends in the city of Jackson, Mississippi. It was a highly energetic, sometimes ruckus-filled college campus that held many fraternities and sororities that sported the two gang colors that dominated the scene in Jackson. The college's color was blue, and that held favor with the Folk gang members in the city. Some fraternities wore red and carried a cane, and that held favor with the Vice Lords. The gang members in Jackson often perused the campus looking for recruits or just looking for trouble.

The night Brianna was scheduled to perform, many female gang members were on hand to see TLC. A lot of people were on hand to see Brianna as well as the Fantastic Four Show had propelled her song to the tops of the charts in the south. People really liked Brianna, and they wanted to see what else she had to bring to the table. The campus was packed on this warm night in March of '95. Brianna, Tank and Mike rode onto the campus in Tank's black on black four door Oldsmobile ninety-eight and waited patiently in the long line of flashy cars cruising the campus until they reached the parking lot. They parked in V.I.P. and exited the car and walked amongst the many collegiate students. Some people recognized Brianna from the promotional flyers that students handed out earlier in the week, but for the most part she remained in anonymity. The three of them made their way to the huge stadium where they were scheduled to perform and there they met up with TLC inside the girl's locker room. T-Boz, Left Eye and Chili were very cordial towards Brianna, Tank, and Mike as they conversed.

"Bree, what happened to Jazzy and ya' girls? I thought they were going to be here." T-Boz said.

"They won't be able to make it tonight. They had a board meeting or something, but they wish us all well." Brianna answered as she was given a glass of Dom Perignon courtesy of Left Eye. "Damn, I really wanted to talk to Jazzy. I wanted her to debut this hot song we plan on pushing next month, oh well. Hey this gone be a hot show people. They loving your song, Bree." Chili remarked.

"I know. I got some more shit I'm gone bring out tonight too. I wanna thank, *we* wanna thank y'all for giving us this opportunity to showcase my talent. This is like a dream for me."

"It was dream for us in the beginning. We usually do arenas, but we really wanted to hit off on the college scene with this album so we took it to the field."

"I used to perform on the field at high school. But this is huge!"

"Don't, don't you get nervous on us sister," T-Boz joked. "We need you to hype that crowd up for us."

"I'm fine. Just nervous," Brianna joked. "I'm okay. Again, thank y'all for giving me this opportunity."

"We know talent when we see it, Bree. We just tryna help out." Left Eye stated as the ladies toasted towards a good night's performance.

****

"Alright, we know y'all been waiting, and here she is, the one you been waiting on, the south's princess! The southern sensation! Jackson state give up for BREEEE!" the MC yelled aloud as Brianna, dressed in a white silk pant suit wearing a white ¾ length silk jacket and white two inch heels, ran onto the stage and began singing an upbeat song she had recorded titled, *Southern Sensation*. The song was a mixture of rap and song, with a thick bass-line and melodic strings. The crowd of over thirty-five thousand people cheered and danced in the stands as Brianna put on a star-worthy performance in the center of the football field. She finished the song and then song her southern hit, *You don't have to Cry* and that left the audience in awe of her voice. They wanted more the upcoming star, but Brianna's time was up and before long, TLC had the audience in an uproar as they took the stage.

Brianna, Tank, and Mike walked through the crowd as TLC performed and handed out demo CD's of her song, *You don't have to Cry* and sold advanced copies of her album for $10. Bree also signed autographs and took pictures with some of her fans. It was a festive night for Brianna, and when the show ended, she, Tank, and Mike took pictures with TLC before the group boarded their tour bus. Bri and company then left Jackson State's campus and began to make their way to their hotel. They were scheduled to leave early the next morning and rejoin TLC in Memphis, Tennessee.

As they rode, Bri, Tank and Mike reflected on what had taken place. "Hey baby, you gone be large after while! We got Memphis Tuesday night and Atlanta next Friday! The song growing on the radio and we set for release in the next six weeks, we gone be large baby—*large*!" Tank said in an exuberant manner as he rode down the streets of Jackson, Mississippi.

The three were talking and dreaming of the future as Tank fired up a blunt and passed it to Mike. *Stoned Junky* by the rap duo UGK was blaring as they rode through Jackson headed towards the hotel. Brianna was counting her earnings, about $4500 dollars, as she bobbed her head to the music. The car vibrated from the heavy bass permeating from the CD as Brianna placed her money in the glove compartment, turned and looked out of the darkened tinted windows, stared at the unfamiliar surroundings and said, "Tank? Where the hell we at?"

"Shit I don't know! We just ridin'!"

"We need to ride back to the hotel and put this money up. I'm tired and hungry, too."

The three were riding down a dark four-lane road bordered by houses that sat atop a low hill that spanned the roadway. A two-foot high brick wall ran down the sidewalk in front of the houses. Many houses were dark, some had porch lights on, but most were darkened. As they descended a hill, Brianna noticed a store that was on a well-lit corner to her right.

"Bi right, Tank," Mike said from the backseat as he flicked the blunt out the window. "We need ta' get back to the hotel, brer. We high as shit! Where the fuck we at for real?"

"I ain't gotta clue where we at! I think we fuckin' lost." Tank replied as he turned down the stereo and began to focus in on his surroundings.

"There go a store right up there. Pull in and ask how we get back downtown." Brianna stated.

"Cool," said Tank, "we need another swisher sweet anyway."

The three pulled up to the corner store and exited the Oldsmobile. They quickly summed up the scene as they eyed a heavy set black male standing beside a white convertible Caprice Classic with loud music blaring from his stereo. A dark two-lane street ran down the side of the store and there was another two foot high brick wall that ran along the sidewalk in front of the houses as well. That block was also dark. Brianna surmised that they were in 'the 'hood'.

Unnerved by their surroundings, the group walked up onto the sidewalk in front the store and eyed the black male in front of the Caprice. Mike walked up to another black male and began asking for directions and a conversation ensued. The men seemed cool so Brianna walked towards the front of the store, passing a set of telephones in the process. One of the phones rung and Brianna, who was just as high as Mike and Tank, answered. "Hello?"

"Eh, who this?"

"Who this?" Brianna asked in return.

"Never mind! Just ask if Folk out there!"

"What?"

"Just ask if they got Folk out there!"

"They got Folk out here?" Brianna asked aloud.

"Yea, yea!" the black male standing in front of the Caprice yelled out as he walked up and grabbed the phone. "Thanks Folk."

Brianna smiled and walked towards the store's entrance and was greeted by a young black female and an older black woman. The three spoke as Brianna held the door open for the two women and she followed them into the store. Mike meanwhile, was still outside talking to the other black male trying to get directions back to the hotel.

Within a few minutes, Brianna had purchased the swisher sweet cigar and was now exiting the store with the two black females chatting lightly. Tank was still in the back of the store looking for some beer to purchase. As Mike took directions, and while Brianna chatted with the two females after giving them a demo of her CD, a car suddenly pulled up in front of the store and began blasting at the front of the building. Everybody scattered as gunfire erupted into the night air. Bullets ricocheted off the front of the store's brick wall and shattered windows as everybody scattered into different directions. The male talking on the phone ran back towards his car, but he was riddled with bullets. He was now lying face down on the ground, having taken several bullets to the head.

The older woman had shielded the younger woman and the two of them now lay in front the store's entrance. The older woman had a bullet wound in her back and the younger woman was clutching her screaming aloud as the gunfire continued to erupt.

Tank ran from the store amidst the gunfire searching for Brianna. He stepped over the two females in front the store's entrance, and was attempting to run his car to retrieve his gun. The gunfire was too heavy, however, so he took cover in front of the Caprice. Tank, at that moment, believed he was about to be killed. He laid flat on the ground to dodge the volley of bullets and found himself staring directly at the young man lying on the ground beside the car and grimaced at the sight of the man's trembling body. Tank was just inches away from the man's trembling corpse and could clearly see brain matter seeping from the side of the man's head. He called aloud for Brianna and Mike as the gunfire continued to erupt from a red convertible Cadillac Brougham. The attackers then quickly sped off when they saw two pimped out convertibles emerge from the street that ran beside the store leading into the neighborhood.

When the gunfire seized, Tank immediately leapt from his position and yelled out for Brianna, who was nowhere to be found. The panic-stricken man watched as the two cars pulled into the store's parking lot, believing he was about to be shot again. Instead, a female got out of each car, one ran to the downed male beside the Caprice, and the other ran to the two females lying in the doorway.

Tank saw he was in no immediate danger so he began wandering around the parking lot searching for Brianna, calling her name franticly. It was then that he heard Mike screaming aloud. Tank approached the scene where Mike was and it was there that he saw Brianna lying on the ground clutching her neck. When the gunshots first erupted, Mike and Brianna were running to attempt and hide behind a dumpster. In the process, Brianna caught a ricocheting bullet fragment in her neck. She fell onto Mike and he rolled her over and lay on top of her until the gunfire seized.

Tank stared at his woman as she lay on the ground. Blood trickled from between Bri's hands and her mouth was agape as she stared Tank square in the eyes as she lay on her back. Tank's eyes flooded with tears as he knelt beside her in stunned silence before he and Mike, who now knew the way back to hotel, made the decision to put her in the car and take her to the hospital, which was near the hotel.

Tank grabbed Brianna by the shoulders and Mike grabbed her legs and they made their way to the car. When they got to the car, however, the two young men could see that the vehicle was riddled with bullets and the back tires were flattened. They had no way to help Brianna. They laid her back on the ground and had to hold her down as she kept writhing around on the concrete.

"We gotta get some fuckin help! Call 911 on the pay phone!" Tank yelled out to Mike. "They should have the address where we at when you call in! Tell 'em where we at! Tell 'em a lotta people been shot!" he cried aloud as he held Brianna down to keep her thrashing about.

Just then, two the two cars that pulled into the parking lot were about to leave. Tank had seen the females carry the older woman to the car; he knew the woman had been shot and he knew the group of females was going to the hospital.

"Help us! Help!" Tank called out to the females just as they were about to pull away from the parking lot.

"Cuz! Put her in here! Come on man!" one of the females yelled aloud as she got out and waited for Tank and Mike to carry Brianna to her drop top.

Tank and Mike hurried Brianna to the car, placed her in the backseat and the female got behind the wheel and sped towards the hospital with Tank, Brianna, and Mike. Inside the car it was chaos. Bri was kicking and coughing up blood. She was gasping for air and had urinated in her pants. Holding her down did little to control her movements. All Tank could do was tell her to hold on.

The female driving kept looking over the backseat while speeding towards the hospital and it seemed to have suddenly dawned on her. "Y'all was at J-State tonight huh?" she asked as she sped towards the hospital.

"Yea that was us! All she was doin' was singin'! We got lost! Why they shoot up the fuckin' corner? What they was shootin' at us for?" Tank asked from the backseat.

"They wasn't after y'all cuz—they was after me!" the young woman answered.

When the cars arrived at the emergency entrance to Jackson Memorial Hospital, Tank and Mike quickly unloaded Brianna and the older woman and they were rushed into separate operating rooms. Tank wanted to thank the females for getting Brianna to the hospital, and he also wanted to ask their names, but he never found out because just as quickly as they had dropped Tank, Brianna, and Mike off, they were gone.

Tank could only imagine that he and Brianna had stumbled upon a 'gangster scene'. The female who'd driven him to the hospital had a mouth full of gold teeth and was wearing a blue bandanna. He then remembered the red Caddy that pulled up and saw people inside the car wearing red bandannas. The female had also told Tank that the shooters inside the Cadillac were after her and not him. Tank realized that he, Brianna and Mike were simply in the wrong place at the wrong time, and it seemed as if things were only getting worse because while Tank was awaiting Brianna's outcome, more ambulances began pulling up every now and then. The activity at the hospital was hectic this night. Tank knew New Orleans was wild, but he never knew Jackson, Mississippi was such a violent place. *"I guess it's the same no matter you at."* Tank said to himself before he drifted off to sleep.

Mike went back to the hotel after Tank told him he wanted to be alone with Brianna to await the outcome. He told Mike, who was reluctant to leave at first, to go to the hotel and get some rest. The truth of the matter was that Tank simply didn't want Mike to see him break down. If Brianna didn't survive, Tank knew he would break down and he didn't want Mike to see him like that. All would be well though; Tank wouldn't have that break down. Five hours later, doctors gave word that Brianna would survive her wounds. She was in a medically induced coma because of her surgery, but she would pull through in a couple of days. Tank was relieved, but the doctors also gave him some devastating news, news he knew he could not break to Brianna alone. Ms. Stanford would be informed of her daughter's plight the next day and she made the trip to Jackson, Mississippi after informing Brianna's friends of her daughter's plight.

Two days later, Brianna lay in her bed with bandages wrapped around her neck. Ms. Stanford entered the room and Briana immediately began to cry as she eyed her mother.

"I'm a bad person." Brianna mimicked.

"Say again, baby." Ms. Stanford said lovingly as she walked

up and sat beside her daughter.

"I'm a bad person." Brianna stated as she moved her lips, unable to speak. "When my voice comes back, I'm gone be the best singer the world has ever seen." Brianna merely figured that once her wound healed, she would regain her voice, the way Dominique had done so when she contracted 'the clap', but she was in for a shock.

"Baby," Ms. Stanford mumbled as Tank stood at her side, "the doctors, the doctors had to perform a tracheotomy to remove the bullet. Your, your voice is no more."

Brianna looked at her mother and then looked at Tank and shook her head in shock. "I can't talk no more? I can't sing? I'm twenty-three! I'm only twenty-three!"

"Baby, the most important thing is that you are alive."

"Momma, I can't talk no more? I can't sing?"

"It's, it's in God's hands, baby. Maybe one day, but the doctors, the doctors are saying—"

Brianna waved her hands and fell back in her bed and wept silently as her mother sat beside her and held her hand and wept with her. Brianna at that moment realized that she had lost the one thing she believed would propel her and Tank to a better life: her voice. She knew she was destined to be a star, but the tragic event in Jackson, Mississippi had forever changed her not only her life, but her destiny. Shaken by those thoughts, Brianna tried to leap from the bed and tried to run from the room, but she was in too much pain. She lay back in defeat and reached out for Tank and hugged him tightly. The twenty-three year-old's mouth was agape and tears flowed heavily down her face. Ms. Stanford knew her daughter was crying to the top of her lungs, but Brianna could produce no sound what so ever.

"Why?" Brianna mimicked to Tank.

"We gone get through this baby," Ms. Stanford replied as she, too, hugged her daughter. "You, you gonna be all right, you hear me? You gonna be all right! It's almost time for us to leave. To go home so you can get well. Your friends are home waiting on you and we gonna get you the best care. It's not over. Brianna." Ms. Stanford said as she pressed her tear-stained face to her daughter's face. "It's not over!"

CHAPTER 33

TALK TO ME

Tank and Mike had returned to the crime scene the day after the incident and they learned that the car was impounded and would be released in three days. Once Tank got the car back in his possession, he and Mike searched the glove compartment and saw that Brianna's money was still inside. Tank was relived; he could use the money to put towards Brianna's medical costs.

Brianna ultimately lost her voice and with that went her singing ability and her career. All dreams of becoming a musical star was destroyed by a simple wrong turn here and there in Jackson, Mississippi. She returned home to New Orleans a week later and was greeted by her friends where a party was held at her home which was also her 24th birthday. A bitter sweet moment it was; sweet for Brianna still being alive, bitter because what was once a promising music career was snatched away in an instant. Tank knew that Brianna was still popular and they could still garner sales from her first ever album, so he was now focusing on investing all of his savings into Brianna's album in hopes of reaping enough sales to earn enough money to allow he and Brianna to invest into another venture that would sustain the two of them for the rest of their lives; but at the moment, getting Brianna proper medical care was what was most important to everyone.

Over the next few months Brianna would attend speech therapy classes, and she was also attending an alternative language class in order to learn sign language. Her wound had healed, but she had lost her voice completely. She could only produce medium-pitched yelping sounds from time to time. She would sit in her home studio playing on her keyboards and string together melodic tunes, all the while staring at her microphone wishing she had been more dedicated to her craft. She reflected on Gabriella often as well. She remembered the woman's angel-like voice. She remembered being tutored by her, and she remembered the day she found out that Gabriella died. Gabriella had not only her talent taken away, but also her life. Reflecting on Gabriella's plight had given Brianna a new outlook. She knew she was lucky to be alive. Three times— three times she had come face to face with death and she survived each scenario.

"What's my purpose God? Why am I so lucky to keep surviving? Why are you saving me? Show me what you want me to do." Brianna prayed silently. She was still strumming the keys on her keyboard and occasionally offering up prayers to God when Tank came home with a small bag in his hands. Brianna turned and smiled at Tank. *"How was your day, baby?"* she asked through sign language.

"Fine. Wonderful. I got something special for you." twenty-seven year-old Tank replied through sign language. He had learned to communicate with Brianna along with Ms. Stanford.

"What is it?" Brianna asked.

"It's a ring, a wedding ring. I bought one too and I was wondering, you know if you want to—"

Brianna let out a small yelp and leapt from her seat and ran into Tank's arms. *"Yes! Yes!"* she moved her lips in lip-sync as she nodded her head rapidly.

"We don't have much money, so I figure we go to the justice of the peace and have a small reception here at the house."

"You are the best thing that ever happened to me! I love you!" Brianna said as she ran her hand across her heart.

The two kissed passionately and showered together and made love that evening, and well into the night. The following morning, they went to the courthouse on Tulane and Broad Avenues, paid $35 dollars, and was pronounced husband and wife. Brianna had printed up invitations that same day, announcing her marriage and upcoming celebration, and mailed them to her friends.

Tracey, Rolanda, and Dominique were all quite busy. They would shout out to Brianna every night over the airwaves, but they rarely came around. Brianna missed her friends dearly and she looked forward to seeing them the following weekend, which was in the latter part of September of '95. Brianna's friends weren't ignoring her, they were just real busy.

Tracey was still feuding with Mike and her mother over being a part of Angel's life; she was also taking on Brianna's portion of the mortgage and taxes on Lubby's old pet shop. Tracey was also sleeping around with various men as she and Mike were growing ever apart. She had also racked up numerous speeding tickets after speeding home across the Causeway many a night after arguing with Mike and/or her mother. Tracey had a lot of pressure in her life and she just wanted to be left alone to do her own thing.

Dominique had given birth to Calvin's son two months after Brianna had been shot. She had gotten a blood test to prove to Calvin that the baby was his, but the blood test was obsolete, however; one could just look at the baby and see that the child was Calvin's. She was now seeing more of Calvin because of the baby, and she felt confident that someday soon her husband would take her back, even though they had been separated for over a year and she was still home with her mother. On top of trying to repair her marriage, Dominique also had to ante up more money for Lubby's pet shop mortgage and taxes because Bri was simply unable to do it because of her medical expenses.

Rolanda had been having suspicions about Bobby so she decided to move out of his apartment and got her own place for her and Kilo out in Slidell not too far from Tracey's house. Bobby would spend nights by Rolanda and vice-versa, but she had an inkling that something was not right with him. Bobby was now working as a waiter in the French Quarters and had odd hours, so he said. Not sure of his actions, Rolanda started making Bobby use condoms in the latter part of July of '95 as she just wasn't sure exactly what it was that he was up to and didn't want to suffer Dominique's plight. She also had to kick up more funds to maintain Lubby's building and had been stressed out as of late. A small get together was indeed in order for the friends by the time Brianna and Tank married in September of '95.

Brianna knew of her friends' situations, and she was glad they had picked up her slack when she and Tank fell on hard times despite their troubles. She reflected on those things as she and Tank, along with Ms. Stanford, Charlotte, Mrs. Franz and Maria set up for her celebration. Brianna was eager to see her friends that day; it had been a few months since they last hung out together. She was busy with therapy, so she could understand when her friends told her they were busy. Brianna never knew, however, until her friends arrived later that day and she got to talking to them, just how much their not being around had affected her, and what their friendship really meant to her.

The celebration was well under way and Brianna sat at a table with her girlfriends while Tank, Bobby, Gerald, Mike and Calvin stood amongst themselves on the opposite side of the yard chatting with one another. Gerald was now stationed at Belle Chase Naval Station just across the river from New Orleans and was staying at Calvin's home. Mike had brought baby Angel over to Brianna's house and Tracey downright refused to go near the child. Maria was highly disappointed in her daughter. Tracey acted as if she never knew the three year-old little girl.

This was supposed to be a happy occasion, but a lot of tension was in the air. Only the parents were getting along fine with everybody; but as far as the friends were concerned they had separated themselves into separate groups. Only out of necessity did the young males and females speak to one another. Calvin and Dominique sat and talked for a while as they both spent time with their son and Tracey and Mike conversed briefly when Maria had taken Angel inside to use the rest room.

"She gettin' potty trained now." Mike told Tracey.

"That's nice." Tracey replied nonchalantly as she looked out into Brianna's backyard.

"She, umm, she be asking me do she have a momma. You know, she believe you at work. I got her believing that. The door still open for you, Tracey. I still love you."

Tracey immediately grew angry. She didn't come to hear Mike's sentimental stories. She walked off from the young man without saying a word. She and Dominique eventually rejoined the table and sat and talked to Brianna, who'd witnessed all the events taking place, and could sense the tension as well. Brianna was concerned with the nonchalant attitude being put on display by Tracey, and she wished Calvin and Dominique would just get back together because they were made for one another. This was not the day to settle issues, however, Brianna only wanted to talk to her friends about the good things going on in their lives.

Dominique, Tracey, and Rolanda were all chatting away as Brianna sat and listened. She would chime in from time to time and she would lip-sync what she wanted to say. Her friends couldn't understand her, and at times, she grew frustrated and just waved her hands in the air and brushed them off.

"Girl, Lubby would've been so happy for you, Bri. Gettin' married and all!" Tracey stated.

Brianna merely nodded her head.

"Y'all going on a honeymoon?" Dominique asked.

Brianna shook her head to say no. She tried to add that she and Tank didn't really want a honeymoon as they were saving to market her album; but she quickly grew frustrated because she knew her friends wasn't understanding her.

"What she sayin'?" Rolanda asked Dominique.

"How I'm supposed to know?"

Brianna then tapped hard on the table, startling her friends as her eyes watered. She stared at her friends with watery eyes for a few seconds before she got up and ran over to Tank and pulled him away from his friends and drug him back to the table where her friends sat.

"Tell them, tell them what I'm saying." Brianna said through sign language. Profound tears ran down her face.

"Okay, baby." Tank stated lovingly as Brianna spoke through sign language. "She said, she saying rather, that the whole time y'all were here, never once did you even try and learn her new language. Y'all still are talking as if she has a voice. She understands and hears everything y'all saying, but y'all can't understand her. She misses—wait—she want this in quotes, '*I miss talking to y'all. This is my new language. My new way of talking, and if you don't understand me, we can't talk like we used to. I be wanting to say so much, but you can't hear me. You don't know what I'm saying. I'm not a mute, I shouldn't have to tap on tables and nod my head to communicate with you all. I feel like a child around you all, but I'm still Bri and I want to talk to you all again.*'" Tank ended as he nodded his head towards his wife.

Brianna's three friends had nothing to say except that they were sorry. The rest of the day, the girls sat and tried to learn sign language from Brianna and by the time they left, they were able to say hello, good-bye, and I love you. Still, Rolanda, Dominique and Tracey knew that was not enough. Rolanda had an idea to put to use, but it would take several months to bring it to fruition. "You girls down for this?" Rolanda asked after revealing her plan.

"For, Bri? No doubt." Tracey replied.

"It's another expense, but that's our girl. And she was right. She shouldn't have to tap tables and nod her head. We have a few months to make this happen, so let's get busy." Dominique said before the ladies hung up the phones.

****

Brianna was home with Tank on Christmas Day of '95. She had baked a ham and some baked macaroni and cheese and was looking forward to seeing her friends. When her girls arrived, Brianna opened the door wearing a green velvet elf's hat, a red knee length dress and green suede ankle boots and handed each of her friends a card as they walked through the door. The girls thanked Brianna and produced one single card of their own. Tank handed the girls a glass of wine and they sat the glasses down as Brianna opened the card and began to read in silence.

"On this day," Rolanda said aloud, causing Brianna to look up, "*we celebrate the birth of our Lord and Savior, who came forth to give his life as a sacrifice for all mankind.*"

Brianna smiled and looked back down at the card, and then looked back up and realized that as Rolanda spoke, she, along with Dominique and Tracey, were using sign language to communicate and were reciting the card with their hands. "*Ask not why the Father came, only be thankful that He cared enough to give his life for us sinners so that we, through Him, can celebrate life on Earth with the ones we love with the hope and promise that we all shall have everlasting life. Merry Christmas, Brianna.*" Rolanda, Tracey, and Dominique ended in unison.

Brianna smiled a wide smile as her eyes watered, "*This is the best gift ever!*"

"*Sorry we were so inconsiderate, can you forgive us?*" Dominique asked.

"*You know, I expected you girls to learn from me, how to speak that is, little by little. But you took it upon yourselves to do all of this for me?*"

"*Yes,*" Tracey replied. "*We took classes at Delgado. Now we can talk like old times.*"

"*I'm very blessed to have friends like you. Thank you for being my friends. Thank you for doing this—this means so much to me!*"

"*Bri,*" Rolanda said, "*we lucky to have a friend like you. Remember when Lubby didn't have clothes, who was there? You.*"

"*Remember when Daphne almost killed me? You were there.*" Tracey added.

"*Who bought Dominique and Tracey their first turntable and microphone? You."* Rolanda stated.

"When Jazzy was looking for us, who was there? You." Dominique stated.

"The idea to hold on to Lubby's pet shop, that was your idea." Rolanda added.

Brianna remembered those things; she smiled as she handed her girlfriends their glasses of wine and she poured herself a drink; before she picked it up she spoke, *"To friendship!"* she lip-synced.

"To friendship!" the three friends said in unison before they all sipped their wine and sat down and talked to Bri in their new language. Once again, the friends had come together to show just how much they cared for one another. Brianna's anxiety was healed and the friends' bond was further tightened on Christmas Day in 1995.

CHAPTER 34

HOW LONG?

Dominique was on her way to drop off her one year-old son to his father's house on a sunny evening in May '96, having just taken the child to have his pictures taken in celebration of his first birthday. Dominique and Calvin were now on speaking terms and things seemed to be getting better between the two; but Calvin still harbored some ill-will towards his wife. Dominique wanted her husband back in her life more than anything above all else; but Calvin could never look at her for more than a few seconds before turning away. She knew he was still hurt over what she had done nearly two years ago and she understood fully.

Dominique, at twenty-four years of age, had toned up her 5' 125 pound figure. After having the baby, she began to hit the gym often with the goal of becoming more appealing to Calvin. Many a man hit on Dominique, she could have easily pursued another relationship, but she only wanted Calvin. She rode to Calvin's house with baby in tow, listening to Natalie Cole's song *I Live For Your Love* playing in the CD player as the song reflected exactly how she felt in May of 1996. Dominique sang the lyrics as she drove, reflecting on her past mistakes and contemplating on what it would take for Calvin to forgive her. She would repeatedly apologize to Calvin for what she had done to their relationship, and Calvin would only nod his head and turn and walk away; but Dominique would not give up. For whatever reason, on this day, she felt that she would indeed take a huge stride towards regaining Calvin's love. She pulled into the driveway and shut off the ignition and pulled her baby boy from the backseat. As she approached the front door to the home she and Calvin once shared, she could hear an argument between Gerald and Calvin taking place just inside the foyer. Calvin and his brother were arguing so loudly that they didn't hear her arrive to the house. She quickly walked back to her brand new, white on white 1996 Toyota Lexus and placed her baby in his car seat and let down all four windows and walked back to the front door and looked to the ground as she listened to the two brothers.

"Dominique the one stepped out me! I did everything! Everything!" Calvin yelled aloud to his brother inside the foyer.
"Everything except take care of your woman in the bedroom!"

"What business is it of yours what Dominique and I had going on in our marriage, Gerald?"

"Look, man! You came to *me* with this shit! I only told you what *I* thought you should do! Now you upset because of what I said?"

"How you gone side with her over your own brother?"

"You told me yourself how much you still care about her! But you too scared to tell her you want her back! Why? Because you scared of gettin' hurt again? Life is about risk Calvin! Man, I'd give anything, *anything* to have Lubby standing before me, brother! Just, just to say one last time 'I love you'. You got a beautiful wife who fucked up one time and she literally begging you to take her back. If you love her, put the past just where it belongs, in the past!"

"That shit still in my head, brer! I just can't get the image of Dominique lying in that hospital bed with that shit running all through her body! Every time I see her—*every time*—all I see is the fact that she cheated with another man!"

"Yea, well at least the woman you love still around Calvin! All I have left of my woman is memories! Let me say this, Lubby knew what I was doing out there, the first night we made love, she asked me not to hurt her again. She tolerated what I did but I knew if I had fucked up again after that night, I woulda lost her for good. And for all the right I did from that point on, I still lost her."

"What that gotta do with me?"

"Dominique tolerated you neglecting her needs for five years before she stepped out Cal. *Five years*! Don't get me wrong, I'm not condoning what she did—but *man*! Most women woulda been long gone, Calvin! Five years? What ever happened to Dominique, she did it to herself. *She* got sick, and *she* lost the home! *She* taking care of the baby most times and she wants you *back*! How long you gone make that woman suffer? If you still love her, you better make a move before she stops caring young brother."

"I can't get past that shit!"

"Look at you, dude! You lying to yourself, Calvin! You really don't care if Dominique find another man?"

"Shit been over for us two years ago, Gerald."

"If was so over for y'all almost two years ago—how come you never divorced the woman, Calvin?"

Everything went silent between the two brothers after that question was asked.

Dominique could hear footsteps so she quickly ran back to her car. When Gerald opened the door to the house, Dominique was opening the rear door to her car. Gerald spoke and called for Calvin before walking to his car, getting in and driving away.

Dominique grabbed the diaper bag and swept the baby into her arms and carried him to the front door where Calvin greeted her. The two spoke as Dominique held her baby and waved his hand towards his father. Calvin smiled and grabbed his son and he and Dominique stared at one another for a few seconds before Calvin turned away. Dominique heard a good portion of the brothers' discussion and she was glad someone besides her mother, father, and girlfriends sympathized with her plight.

"Well, I guess I'll see you tomorrow, Cal. I'll pick up CJ up around six tomorrow evening, is that okay?" Dominique asked as she stared up at her husband.

"That's fine."

"Okay. Well, see you tomorrow." Dominique replied as she turned and walked away. She wanted to ask Calvin the same thing her brother had asked him at that moment. Why hadn't he divorced her yet? Not that she wanted him to, but Dominique never really looked at her situation from that angle. Her hope was ever rising that someday Calvin would be able to look her directly in the eyes and say he loves her again, the way he used to do before she ruined everything. Dominique's heart was aching as she walked back to her car. Deep down inside she was hoping that Calvin would realize that the two of them belonged together, she hoped Gerald's words had sunk into his heart.

"Dominique," Calvin called out as he stood in the doorway holding his son.

Dominique's heart pounded rapidly. She was prepared to turn and run into Calvin's arms and apologize once again. She believed they were about to be reunited.

"Yes, Calvin?" Dominique stated as she turned and faced her husband with a pleading look in her eyes.

"You still got the baby diaper bag on your shoulders. I think I'm gone need that later on."

Dominique's heart dropped. She bowed her head and walked back to Calvin and handed him the diaper bag, never even look his way as she was too embarrassed to do so. She quickly walked to her car, got in and started the car and rolled all the windows up and turned the radio up loud as she rode away dejected.

"How long he gone put me through this shit?" she asked herself as she drove down the street.

After that incident, Dominique became more nonchalant whenever she saw Calvin. She would drop the baby off and 'keep it moving' so-to-speak.

****

"What's up CJ? What you starvin'? Daddy ain't feed your light-weight ass last night?" Gerald said to his nephew through laughter one early Saturday morning in June of '96, a month after the argument he'd had with Calvin was overheard by Dominique.

As Gerald was feeding his nephew in the dining room, he saw a slender black-skinned female walk out of Calvin's master bedroom and head towards the front door. She waved politely at Gerald as she passed him and walked towards the front of the home. Calvin followed the woman through the house in his silk robe, thanking her as the two headed to the front door.

Gerald stared at the sexy woman as she walked through the kitchen and out of sight and then smiled at Calvin who had reentered the kitchen. "Who the hell was that fine mutherfucka?" Gerald asked.

"That's a li'l chick work in the mail room."

"I know you knocked the *bottom* out that thang right there!"

"Yea." Calvin said softly as he looked to the floor somberly.

Gerald stared at Calvin before he smiled and said, "Nooo! You ain't even touch the li'l chick, huh? Scary ass!"

"No, man. She wanted me to go down on her first. You know, for the first time I felt uninhibited with the opposite sex? I wanted to do everything to that female, but I didn't."

"Why?"

"I was like, 'baby I can't do this. I never did nothing like this with my *wife* and here I am about to get my freak on with *you*'."

"What she said?"

"She laughed at me. Then we just started talking you know? After a while she up and said 'no wonder Dominique stepped out'. She then said she was surprised to hear that it took Dominique five years to do so. She came at it from a non-objective point of view."

"Shit I coulda done that! Matter of fact I *did* that!"

"How? When?"

"When you asked me a while back, Calvin! Man you don't listen to shit! Or you hear what you wanna hear! I told you what the deal is! I guess you need to hear it again!"

"Yeah, take me to school big brother." Calvin stated as he grabbed the spoon from Gerald and began feeding his son.

"Dominique showed tremendous restraint given the circumstances. It was only a matter of time before the right situation presented itself. You don't think men at the grocery store where she used to work, college professors and students, and all those business men in the Amoco building and everywhere else downtown weren't trying to get next to Dominique?"

"Ole girl said the same thing. It was only a matter of time. We talked for good while, Gerald. She helped me to understand some things. And just like you, she didn't condone what Dominique had done, and then ultimately, she felt bad about being in our home, in our bed. She slept in a chair, rather, she watched me sleep while she sat in a chair. She told me when I woke up this morning, my heart would tell me what I should do." Calvin said as Gerald got up from the table and tugged his nephew's cheek. Gerald went into a spare bedroom and grabbed a duffel bag and walked towards the front door. "Where you going?" Calvin asked his brother.

"Going stay with mom and dad till I find my own place."

"You can, you can just stay here, I got plenty of room."

"Nahh, li'l brother. I don't like being a third wheel." Gerald ended as he turned and headed to the door.

Calvin then knew why Gerald was leaving that morning. "Hey Gerald," he called out aloud. Gerald turned and Calvin told him, "Thanks, brer. Umm, you was right about everything."

Gerald nodded and walked out of the house leaving Calvin and his son alone.

****

"How long I'm gone have ta' wait for the damn cookies?" Rolanda asked aloud over the airwaves inside WYLD studios. It was a week after Gerald had left Calvin's home. It was a hot summer Friday night and the show was in its eight 'o' clock hour.

"Now wait a minute, I won the tickets fair and square and you holding my Mary J. Blige tickets hostage over some homemade cookies?"

"What? What we agreed on? When I met you in the lobby you was eating some cookies right?"

"Right!"

"I said, 'bring the cookies, and I'll give you the tickets'. You said 'deal'. So whether you won or no—I got the tickets and I *wants* my cookies!"

"Man she *trippin'* on some cookies man!" the caller spoke over the air as she laughed. "Alright Mrs. Jones, I'm a bring the damn cookies Monday! Now please can I have the tickets?"

"On Monday! On Monday, when you bring the damn cookies! And don't have me waiting too long! Or I'm going back on air to regive your tickets away!"

"Regive ain't even a wo—"

Rolanda abruptly hung the phone up on the caller and spoke to her over the airwaves, "Hey, don't insult my intellectionalism! Regive *is* a word, it means to give again! Reissue! Rehandeded out! I'm tired of settin' you people straight about what is and ain't ain't a word! Just bring the dam cookies and you will get your damn tickets!" Rolanda said as Jazzy and the girls laughed aloud. The show continued on at its lively pace before coming to another successful end at eleven that night.

"Hey Dee, you wanna hit Razoo's tonight?" Tracey asked as the girls walked through the underground garage.

"Nahh, I got CJ tomorrow. How's Angel?"

"I don't know! Last I heard she was reciting her ABC's. She fine right there with her daddy!"

"Girls? I'm going home to my buddy, Kilo. I know he got my slippers ready and I got a new video we gone watch tonight." Rolanda sighed.

"Well ladies," said Tracey as she hopped onto her motorcycle, "I'm going to the clizzub, and find me a young stizzud, and take 'em to the hizzome, and get my freak izzon!" Dominique and Rolanda shook their heads and laughed at Tracey as she placed her helmet on her head and sped off through the parking lot. The girls went their separate ways that night, each looking forward to the weekend.

Early that Saturday morning, Dominique was up waiting on her son's arrival casually dressed in a t-shirt and sweat pants. She was planning on taking her son over to Brianna's home and together, they were scheduled to head to the zoo with Rolanda. The doorbell rung and Dominique answered and quickly grabbed her son from Calvin. She went to close the door, but Calvin asked her how she was doing.

"I'm fine, Calvin. We, umm, me and Rolanda, and Bri taking the baby to the zoo today."

"Ohh, okay, well, I'm just gone hang out at the house with Gerald and Tank."

"That's nice." Dominique stated as she tickled her baby, completely unaware of Calvin's intent. She had all but given up on her marriage and was slowly beginning to get over not being with Calvin.

Calvin now knew that; he could see the change in his wife and he knew he was on the verge of losing this woman, in spite of what she had done. Dominique's mother came into the foyer and grabbed her grandson and walked back into her living room bouncing the baby on her hips.

"Looks like she been missing li'l CJ." Calvin stated.

"Yes she has. She's spoiling him rotten, too. He wants everything to go his way all the time." Dominique said as she smiled back at her son from the front door.

Dominique's statement was meant just the way she said it, but Calvin saw another meaning to his wife's remark. "Kinda like his father right?" he asked as Dominique turned to face him.

Dominique was surprised to see that for the first time in two years, Calvin could look at her without turning away after a few seconds. She closed her mother's front door and the two stood face to face on the side walk.

"Can I tell you something?"

"Anything, Calvin." Dominique replied lovingly as she gazed into her husband's eyes.

"I umm, I. I just wanted to tell you that I put him some new tennis shoes in with his clothes, and his vitamins in there as well."

"Ohh, okay. Well, we gotta get ready for the zoo. Tell Gerald I said hi." Dominique stated as she smiled up at Calvin, trying as best she could to hide her disappointment.

Dominique was expecting Calvin to say something much bigger than announcing he had bought new tennis for his son. When he nodded and turned away, she grew sad again. She said she wasn't going to pity herself over Calvin anymore, that she was not going to cry behind him anymore, but she couldn't help herself anymore. She not only let the tears flow, she grew angry. *"For two years, two years, I've been celibate! Apologizing repeatedly to this man, and he just won't, he won't! How long must I pay for my infidelity?"* Dominique cried to herself as she went to turn the door knob to her mother's home.

"Dominique!" Calvin called aloud.

Dominique was now crying heavily. Just hearing Calvin's voice caused her to desire the man and her soul was tired of being tormented by being separated from her true love; but her true love would just remain distant and she couldn't tolerate it any longer. "What," Dominique screamed through her tears as she turned towards Calvin. "What do you want from me now? I'm sorry alright? I'm sorry! How long before you give me? Will you ever forgive me? Because I gave forgave myself a long time ago!" Dominique yelled as neighbors tuned in to what was going down.

Calvin balled up his fist and bowed his head, "Don't you do that shit again!" he yelled. "Look at me," he said as he spread his arms and looked around at the neighbors who were watching. "Look at me! I'm a grown man—and you got me out here in front all these people crying over you? Dammit! I love your ass! I fuckin' love you! But you hurt me bad!"

"Calvin! Baby," Dominique said as she began crying heavily. "I need you!" she screamed as she dropped to her knees on the sidewalk. "I'm so sorry! On our son! I'm sorry, Calvin! I'm sorry for what I did to us!" she yelled aloud as her body heaved.

The sight of his woman on her knees in broad daylight begging for forgiveness was more than Calvin could take. Sincerity comes on all forms and bares no shame. Dominique was unashamed to admit her wrong, unashamed to beg for forgiveness for all to see, and she was no longer embarrassed. "Let them stare I don't care! I want you back! Take me back!"

Calvin looked down into his wife's eyes and gazed upon the want, the need, and the love that this woman possessed for him. She'd fucked up. She'd paid the price. And she was contrite over the matter. Calvin walked over to Dominique and picked her up and she grabbed hold of his silk shirt and cried loudly, repeatedly thanking him and promising never to hurt him again. When Calvin tilted her jaw upwards and pressed his lips to hers, Dominique's whole body shook in ecstasy. She pulled away and stared into his eyes.

"I'm sorry. I'm so sorry. Say you," Dominique began to cry as it was a hard question to ask after what she had done, but still, she had to ask, "say you forgive me!" she said through tears as she continued to hold onto Calvin not wanting to let him go. She pressed her face into Calvin's chest and pounded her fists lightly against his shoulders, pleading with the man, "Say, say, you, forgive, me! Please!" she heaved as she clutched her husband tightly.

"Let's go home. You and me. Just you and me." Calvin requested of his wife as Dominique nodded her head to say yes.

"Thank you! I'll never hurt you again! I promise!" Dominique said with her face pressed to Calvin's chest. Calvin held her tightly, keeping her on her feet as he knew if he let her go, Dominique, in her weakened state, would just fall to the ground.

Mrs. Franz was watching everything through the living room window. When she saw Dominique and Calvin approaching her front door, she quickly walked back into the living room, with baby in tow and sat on the couch, happy for Dominique and Calvin.

"Momma," Dominique said softly as she held Calvin's hand and walked into the living room. "Momma, me, and Cal, we umm, we—"

"Shh, shh," Mrs. Franz whispered. "Go! You two go! I got my grandson to deal with and you two have each other back in each other's lives! Go be together!" the woman said as she smiled upon her daughter and son-in-law.

Dominique rode with Calvin back to the home they once shared. They were barely inside the home before the two of them began stripping off their clothes in the kitchen. Calvin picked up his wife and carried her to their marital bed and lay Dominique down gently and stared at her body. Her firm 32-c cup breasts heaved up and down in anticipation. She spread herself for Calvin as he got on the bed and sat at her feet. Dominique stretched her arms and reached for her husband, ready to be taken at that moment. What happened next, however, surprised Dominique. Calvin leaned forward and dove right into her glistening vagina. She let out a guttural groan of shock and delight as Calvin began to suck on her outer lips and lick her clitoris. Dominique's mouth was agape and she stared at the ceiling; her arms were flung back to either side of her head and all she could do was produce sweet groans of shocking delight. She surrendered her soul to Calvin, crying out from the pleasure; this was all she ever wanted. Calvin delivered to Dominique one of the most powerful orgasms she had ever received.

Dominique hadn't been with no one since she and Calvin separated two years ago, but the orgasm she had on this day was special because it came from her husband; the one man she wanted to take control of her body and use it for his pleasure. She wanted to be Calvin's everything. Calvin sat back and Dominique sat up on her elbows staring at him. She then looked down upon his throbbing penis and her mouth watered. Calvin knew what she wanted so he stood beside the bed and Dominique crawled across the bed and came face to face with his hardened member. "Can I?" she asked.

"Do whatever, baby. It's all yours." Calvin whispered.

"No, I belong to you." Dominique stated as she stared up at her husband.

Dominique leaned forward and took Calvin's dick into her mouth. He was shocked at the pleasure, never had something felt so good. He called Dominique's name repeatedly as she moved her head back and forth across the length of his rod. She licked the underside and the side of his shaft, taking Calvin to newfound boundaries of pleasure. He was savoring his wife's loving tongue, and Dominique was in exquisite delight, she loved being able to please her husband, she adored the sounds emanating from the depths of his soul and she smiled from within as she listened to Calvin's loud moans. She knew, Dominique knew all along, ever since they met, that she could take him there, now Calvin came to know of the sexual prowess his wife possessed. His breath became more rapid and his hips began bucking and Dominique knew he was close. She was moaning as she fellated her husband, Calvin steadily calling her name, his hips rocking to and fro in rapid motion. Dominique engulfed Calvin's dick fully, her nostrils were pressed against his pubic hairs as he ejaculated down her throat. She orgasmed herself as Calvin's seed blasted the back of her skull and slid down her esophagus. She released her husband's member from her mouth and breathed heavily as she licked her lips free of semen. To her surprise and delight, Calvin was still rock hard. The two of them fell into each other's arms and kissed passionately. Dominique lay on her back, but Calvin flipped her over and lowered her down onto his dick. She placed her hands on Calvin's chest and held on for the ride. Calvin thrust up into her snug vagina as she stared him in the eyes. "Yes," she said as she leaned down and pressed her breasts to Calvin's chest. "Yes! Take me! Fuck me! It's yours! I'm yourrrss!" she cried aloud as she thanked Calvin repeatedly through tears.

The two of them climaxed together and wrestled for one another's affection, each wanting to show how much they cared. They kissed, they stated their love, they laughed, and they talked. The waiting, the longing, the wondering, and the crying was over. After years of separation, Dominique and Calvin rekindled their marriage and renewed their vows the following weekend. All was well in the Huntley household, by the end of June 1996.

CHAPTER 35

KITTY, KITTY, KITTY

It was now September of '96 and 25 year-olds Dominique, Tracey and Rolanda were on air with Jazzy on a cool rainy night in the latter part of the month. The show was going along quite well and many callers were calling to speak to Rolanda, who was the most popular of the four female Dee-jays. Rolanda, however, was only fielding a minimum amount of calls that night as she had announced to the listeners that she was a little under the weather. A lot of fans called and wished her well during the show's first two hours. Rolanda thanked them all and sat her headphones down when the show entered its third hour. She said nothing on air the rest of the night as she was just feeling too ill to do so. Jazzy had told her to leave early, but Rolanda stayed the duration of the show.

When the show ended, Rolanda was the first one to leave. She didn't even finish her paperwork, and Tracey had to run and catch her before she left. Since it was raining, Rolanda had to drop her off at home. Rolanda was so ill Tracey had to drive her car to Slidell. She drove herself to her apartment and Rolanda slowly got behind the wheel of her car and drove the mile or so to her own place. When she arrived, she saw Kilo waiting for her with her slippers. Rolanda smiled and walked over and rubbed the dog before flopping down on her couch. Before long, she was sound asleep.

The next morning Rolanda awoke, still dressed in her work clothes and shoes from the night before. She went upstairs to prepare for a bath and as she ascended the staircase she suddenly felt nauseated. She had to rush to the bathroom and barely made it to the toilet before she vomited. She surmised she was coming down with the flu; on top of that, she had her menstrual cycle to deal with. She thought about calling in to work, but she decided against it as she knew Tracey needed a ride to retrieve her motorcycle. That day was another grueling day for Rolanda, and she had two more days to work as well. When the weekend arrived she spent the entire time locked in her home in her bed deep under the covers and taking cold medications. Rolanda believed that a weekend of rest would be all she needed to regain her strength, but when Monday came around she seemed to be doing worse than before. Her cycle was still on, three days longer than normal and she was feeling very tired most times. She decided to call in to work that day and go to the hospital to have some tests run.

The doctor gave Rolanda a prescription for some antibiotics and told her he would call her with the results later on in the week. The next day Rolanda returned to work, she was feeling better and her cycle had withdrawn, she now believed all was returning to normal. Thursday morning, three days after she had the tests run, the doctor called Rolanda at her home and told her to come in for the results. She walked into her doctor's office and saw two additional doctors sitting with the older Black man. All three doctors had a look of concern on their faces as they pulled a chair out for Rolanda and they, too, sat at the circular table.

"Miss Jones, these two women are specialist from Tulane Medical Center. They are head of a new research program sponsored by The Mayo Clinic in Cleveland, Ohio in conjunction with the CDC out of Atlanta, Georgia."

"What kind of specialist? Why do I need specialists?" Rolanda asked as she stared at the three African-American doctors with a worried look on her face.

"Your test results have come back, Miss Jones. We've discovered that you have the Human Immunodeficiency Virus, or HIV. Now these doctors here want—"

Rolanda gasped and her heart sunk to the pit of her stomach

as she closed her eyes and began to cry. "No," she said under her breath. "This has to be a mistake! Not me! Run the test again! Do it again!" she yelled as she stood up from her seated position and stared back at the doctors.

"We've run them repeatedly, Miss Jones," one of the female doctors said softly. "We are so sorry. We ran them over and over. But we can help." the doctor ended in a compassionate tone.

Rolanda stared at the floor with wide eyes in total disbelief. "Not, not me!" she said as she looked at the doctors and held her hand across her heart, "Please," she panted. "Please, miss. Tell me this is a dream or a joke. Because if it's not, then this is a nightmare that I'm having! Because *this*? *This*? Is not happening—*to me!*" Rolanda screamed as she placed her head into her hands and hid her face.

The doctors comforted Rolanda and told her they wanted to enroll her into an experimental program. She agreed, but she told the doctors she needed a few days to notify her family and friends. She left the hospital in shock, not knowing how to tell her mother and her friends that she had contracted HIV. She didn't know if she even wanted to tell them. She began contemplating what she would do with the rest of her life as she drove towards City Park. Rolanda was scheduled to go into work early, but she called and informed Jazzy that she was running behind.

Rolanda was on her way to see the one person she knew had given her HIV: 28 year-old Bobby. She still had a key to his place, and when she arrived to his house, she let herself in. Music was heard coming from upstairs so she headed that way with the intent on confronting Bobby. Midway up the stairs, Rolanda heard moans and she began to cry. She now knew for certain that Bobby was indeed sleeping with another woman and he had contracted HIV and had given it to her early on in their relationship because she had been making Bobby use condoms for over a year.

Bobby was Rolanda's first and only lover, so she knew he was responsible for her having contracting the disease. The doctors had told her that the virus could lay dormant for months, even years before a person could feel the effects. Rolanda was heart-broken and devastated by what Bobby had done to her. As she walked up the stairs towards his bedroom, the moans grew louder and louder. Rolanda could hear Kitty's name being called and she grew enraged as she ascended to the top of the stairs and approached the threshold leading to the bedroom.

Rolanda received the shock of her life when she peered into Bobby's bedroom, however; what she had witnessed repulsed her beyond words. She covered her mouth to suppress her shock and she backed away from the door. The shocked twenty-five year-old was unable to confront Bobby at that point as she just couldn't get over what she had seen. Rolanda never saw it coming. The sounds of flesh slapping flesh echoed throughout the house, the repeated cries of pleasure emanating from Bobby and his lover's mouth were still in the air as Rolanda descended the stairs and left the house. The distraught woman got into her car and drove to Slidell, crying aloud the whole way home and barely able to maintain control of the car. When she got to her apartment, Rolanda went to her computer and began to type a letter and then printed it out for later use.

The following day, just before the show was scheduled to go on air, Rolanda was in her office on her computer retyping and reediting the letter she had brought with her to the show. She was planning on reading that letter over the air during the ten 'o' clock hour before she announced that she was leaving the Fantastic Four Show for good. Dominique and Tracey were sitting inside the studio when Rolanda entered. They greeted her in a friendly manner and asked was she feeling better.

"I'm all right." Rolanda said nonchalantly just as Jazzy entered the studio and the show's theme song began playing. The introductions were done and the show quickly got underway.

In its final hour, Rolanda began reading the letter she had typed and edited: *"Dear Fantastic Four Show,"* She read aloud over the air waves, *"My name is anonymous, and I want to make all females aware on this night. I want them to take a serious look at the person, the man, whom they profess to love, because sometimes, things just aren't what they to appear to be. My lover was a man I trusted and loved with all my heart. He was my one and only. I did everything for him, physically, mentally, and sexually, I did it all. I recently took ill, and after visiting the doctor, I went to confront my 'man', to make him aware of my situation still believing, like a damned fool, that we could get through this God-awful test that lay before us. Understand that I loved him, even with all that was transpiring, I still loved him, but he took the last bit of strength I had left in me to fight this battle. Going on is hard to do, I don't think I can, and I'm not sure if I want to. Let me tell you why I'm giving up: when I entered my man's home, I found my man, the man I loved and cared about once upon a time, making love to another man. You see, Mr. X was, back in the day, a straight up gangster, so I thought, but I now know he's on the down low. I can't go on living with this embarrassment, this terrible secret, and this ultimate act of betrayal. My friends and family shall never know of my plight. What is my plight? Well, I've contracted HIV from this man. My life,"* Rolanda said as she began to cry over the airwaves, "I, I can't do this shit no more! This is a sad and pitiful letter!" Rolanda then stated as she threw her headphones against the wall and shoved her computer screen from her desk.

Jazzy, Dominique, Tracey and the entire production staff looked up in shock as Rolanda stormed out the studio. The whole scene had unfolded live on air. Jazzy had Tracey go to commercial and the three women followed Rolanda out into the hall. Rolanda was in her office gathering her things as tears streamed down her face.

"Rolanda, you okay? I mean, that was a heavy letter, but we gotta finish so we can help this woman out. They have clinics and stuff where people can get help." Jazzy stated.

"She don't want help! She said she don't wanna go on living! How much help can she get for that shit? HIV is a death sentence for people!" Rolanda stated quickly through tears as she stuffed items into her purse.

"No it's not! AIDS is far more deadlier. People live with HIV! Look at Magic Johnson." Dominique stated.

447

"How many people you know got Magic Johnson money, Dominique?" Rolanda asked angrily. "I quit! I'm through with this *show*! I'm through with *Bobby* ass! I'm through with *everything*!" Rolanda screamed as she cried and ran out her office with letter in hand and headed towards the elevator.

Dominique followed her as Tracey stayed behind and keyed up the computer in Rolanda's office. "What are you doing Tracey?" Jazzy asked.

"I'm just checking something on Rolanda's computer."

"About that letter?"

"Yea, she mighty worked up about something." Tracey replied. "*Why she leaving Bobby all of a sudden?*" Tracey then asked herself. "Shit! She got her computer locked. You know her password, Jasmine?"

"Darius knows it. He's out of town, but I'll call him and tell him it's an emergency. Come on, let's get back on air, I'll contact Darius. Then we'll go and talk to Rolanda."

Tracey and Jazzy returned to the show and Dominique rejoined them a few minutes later. The ladies were all planning on going over to Rolanda's house after the show, which only had forty minutes left, to check on their friend. Jazzy had contacted Darius and he called her back thirty minutes later and gave them Rolanda's password. Tracey took the password from Jazzy and returned to Rolanda's office as Dominique and Jazzy did the last portion of the show. The show was uneventful over the airwaves, but behind the scenes, the drama was rapidly escalating. As Dominique and Jazzy slid off their headphones, Tracey rushed into the studio and grabbed her motorcycle keys. She was crying and yelling hysterically as she ran back out of the room.

Dominique quickly followed her out of the studio. "Tracey what's wrong?" she yelled aloud as she ran behind her down the corridor leading to the elevators.

"That letter was about Rolanda! I read the whole thing! She got HIV from Bobby!"

"Bobby?"

"Yea! He was on the down low sleeping with another man!" Tracey yelled as she trotted towards the elevator.

"Wait let me get my keys! We can take my car!"

"No!" Tracey said as she headed towards the elevator. "Rolanda ended the letter by saying she was going home to kill herself! She been home for at least ten minutes now! She probably already laying there dying!" Tracey said as she repeatedly pressed the elevator buttons.

Dominique stood in shock at Tracey's statement. She quickly regained her composure and ran back to her office to grab her car keys. She then ran towards Tracey holding her cell phone just as the elevator bell rung, signifying that the door was about to open.

"Come on fuck!" Tracey yelled at the elevator doors as they slowly opened. "Call Bri, and Charlotte! They close out that way! Tell them, tell them Rolanda got HIV and she planning on killing herself!" Tracey said before the elevator doors closed.

Dominique and Jazzy scrambled about the fourteenth floor gathering their belongings before they, too, headed down an elevator. Dominique had Tracey's helmet in her hands and she was glad she met Tracey before she left the garage. Tracey snatched the helmet, threw it on her head and sped off. Tracey rode along Tulane Avenue, pausing briefly at red-lights before she ran through them. She got onto an on ramp on Interstate-10 and headed east towards Slidell, worried sick about Rolanda, and hoping she could make it to her friend's home in time to save her life.

As Tracey sped towards Slidell, Dominique, who was in the passenger seat of her car riding with Jazzy, phoned Charlotte. Charlotte's answering machine answered so Dominique left her a message stating to call her back immediately. She then called Brianna. Brianna picked the phone up.

"Bri that you?" Dominique asked.

Brianna pressed the key pad on her phone and smiled, glad to hear from one of her friends.

"Bri, Bri listen! Rolanda contracted HIV from Bobby! We just found out tonight! If you was listening to the show, the letter Rolanda read was about her and Bobby! She—ohhh my God!" Dominique suddenly said as she panicked and cried aloud, unable to speak, "Nooo, God!" she yelled as she dropped the phone in her lap. The realization that Rolanda was planning on committing suicide had just sunk in with Dominique. She could not utter another word as memories of the friendship she had with Rolanda ran through her mind. Images of her drumming on her desk top as Rolanda danced in class back in sixth grade. The day they found Kilo nearby the beach. The blue blockers. Graduation. Their college days. She began palpating over the thought of Rolanda killing herself this night.

Jazzy snatched the phone from Dominique's lap and spoke as she drove. "Brianna, this is Jazzy! Baby, please, Rolanda, Rolanda went to her home and we think she gone kill herself tonight! You and Tank, we need y'all to drive out there and try to get in, okay? We called the paramedics and me, Dominique and Tracey headed that way!"

By then Brianna had shaken Tank awake from his slumber and handed him the phone and he'd heard everything that Jazzy had said. "This Tank right here Jazzy! We on our way!" he said as he and Brianna grabbed little of nothing but their set of car keys and dashed out the door and began driving towards Slidell.

Everyone was converging on Rolanda's house, but nobody was making the run quicker than Tracey. She rounded a curve on her motorcycle about four miles from East Shore and was quickly up to 100 miles an hour. She had made this drive many times before, but on this night, she had at least a half dozen police cars behind her; they'd spotted her running red-lights downtown and gave chase as she merged onto the interstate. Tracey had almost crashed her motorcycle when she looked back at the cops and for whatever reason, she thought of Mike and her baby girl. As she sped towards Slidell, she began to cry. Twenty-five year-old Tracey Sanchez cried for Rolanda, she cried for Mike and she cried for her daughter, Angel. She realized at that moment that if she were to have died, she would always be remembered as the woman who hated her daughter. Tracey shoved those thoughts aside for the moment, however, as she had only one goal before her: to get to Rolanda's house.

Tracey stayed well in front of the police cars. Their sirens were flashing and they were darting in and out of traffic trying to keep up with the speeding motorcycle. When Tracey approached the junction leading to East Shore, she sped through the huge spaghetti-like interchange with the police cars in hot pursuit. Brianna and Tank was coming from Chalmette and she and Tank were on the on ramp leading to Interstate-10 when they spotted Tracey's black and yellow Kawasaki Ninja speed by with at least six police cars following. Brianna grew worried as she watched Tracey disappear from sight with numerous flashing lights behind her.

Rolanda, meanwhile, was in her home crying uncontrollably. She looked over her test results one last time before she went into her kitchen and grabbed a bottle of Champagne from her refrigerator. She had placed a gun on the table, but when she went to retrieve it, the weapon was gone. She believed Kilo had taken the gun so she began searching for the muscular pit-bull and found him in the downstairs bedroom underneath the bed with the gun in between his front paws. She reached for the gun and the dog growled angrily and snapped his jaws. Kilo had saliva dripping from his powerful jowls and he looked as if he would rip her hand off if she placed it near his mouth. Rolanda backed away. "Stupid beast!" she yelled aloud as she cried and walked up the stairs towards the bathroom, locked the door behind her and stared at herself in the mirror as she cried. "You can't stop me now, mutherfucka!" she said aloud, talking directly to Kilo.

Rolanda Jones, the twenty-five year old 5' 10" 150 dark-skinned pound stallion now felt as if she had nothing to live for because Bobby had destroyed her life. She had only slept with one man, one man, and that very man had given what was to her a death sentence. Rolanda wondered if she was woman enough? Was she unattractive? Not enough woman in bed? Why would Bobby sleep with a man? She was prepared to deal with Kitty, but when she saw Bobby with another man, her heart was torn and her ability to fight was taken away. She had to face that the hard truth that Bobby was Kitty all along.

Rolanda was ready to deal with the issues pressing her and Bobby, but after witnessing what she had seen the day before, she had given up. The sight of Bobby on his hands and knees with another man standing behind him pistoning back and forth and calling Bobby by the name Kitty, repeatedly telling Rolanda's 'man' how good his 'pussy', felt, had sickened Rolanda more than the virus she had contracted. She had been a fighter all her life and she was strong and capable. She was the scrappiest of her friends when they were little and could readily handle her own, but this fight, the battle Bobby had thrust her into was a fight Rolanda Jones felt she could not win. She had no more strength to continue on. She picked up a single-edge razor blade and stared at herself one last time before she slashed her left wrist. Her eyes widened and she dropped the blade and fell to the floor and just lay there silently with her eyes open as tears ran down her face.

Kilo was outside the bathroom door barking ferociously. The dog knew something was wrong and he tried desperately to get into the bathroom. When he realized he had no way of entering the room, the dog sat down in front the door, bowed his head, and whined lowly.

Tracey meanwhile, had sped across the twin span on her motorcycle with the police still in pursuit. Rolanda stayed only a short distance from the lakefront just off the interstate. Tracey exited the highway and sped towards Rolanda's apartment complex. She was barely inside the complex when she hopped from her motorcycle and made her way to Rolanda's unit where paramedics, who could not enter her home without permission or an authorized person to accompany them, were waiting. Tracey ran up the sidewalk telling the paramedics to kick down the door. As she did so, she was knocked to the ground by New Orleans Police and St. Tammany Parish Deputies.

Tracey wrestled with the men, but she was outnumbered and being assaulted. She was trying to get up, she was screaming at the officers that her friend needed help, but all was in vain, however, as the police used a stun gun on Tracey. She stretched out on the ground unable to speak as her body convulsed. She was rolled onto her stomach and handcuffed and carried hog-tied style to the back seat of a St. Tammany Parish squad car in a semi-conscious state.

Tracey was passed out on the backseat of the squad car when Brianna and Tank arrived on the scene. Bri jumped out and ran towards the front of Rolanda's apartment and began banging on the door. Brianna grabbed one of the paramedics and placed him in front the door and made a kicking motion towards the thick wooden structure.

"Kick it? You telling me to kick the door down right?" the man asked.

Brianna nodded her head rapidly and the paramedic tried as best he could to knock the door down, but it wouldn't budge. Brianna made a futile attempt, but she clearly wasn't strong enough. She then banged on the door repeatedly, hearing Kilo barking fiercely from behind the closed door. Tank soon ran up and shoved everyone aside and jumped into the air and kicked the door. It loosened the first time, he kicked the door again and it flung open.

The paramedics rushed in and Brianna followed them closely. "Rolanda! Rolanda Jones are you okay?" the paramedics called out.

The paramedics were about to search the first floor until Kilo ran halfway up the stairs, turned and barked at them. Brianna shoved the medics towards the stairs.

"Follow the dog, Harry!" the lead paramedic announced as he followed his partner and Brianna up the stairs. They all followed Kilo to the bathroom door and this time, one of the paramedics was able to kick the door open. Rolanda's limp body blocked the entrance a little so they gently nudged her body forward with the door and entered the room and began administering aide to the young woman, who was sprawled out on the bathroom floor in a pool of her own blood. The paramedics had ordered Brianna out so she wouldn't come into contact with Rolanda's blood whilst they administered aide.

She went and stood outside the bathroom watching desperately, hoping and praying that she was still alive.

Tank, meanwhile was downstairs talking to the officers regarding Tracey's situation. As he and the cops talked, Jazzy and Dominique arrived on the scene. They saw the ambulance and they both ran into Rolanda's home where Brianna met them at the top of the stairs and beckoned for them.

"I don't want to see her like that." Jazzy stated softly as she stayed downstairs with Tank to assist in trying to get Tracey out of police custody.

Brianna and Dominique held one another as they watched the medics work on their friend. It hurt them to see their friend in the condition she now found herself. Rolanda was naked on the floor, unresponsive and soaking in her own blood. She had always been the most animated of the five and to see her in this condition was heart-wrenching and unbelievable in Brianna and Dominique's eyes. The paramedics ordered Brianna and Dominique out of the house and a gurney was brought upstairs to take Rolanda to Slidell Medical Center. She was carted from the house and rushed to the ambulance. She would survive, but the road to recovery would be a long, painstaking process that would test not only Rolanda's fortitude, but that of her mother and her friends as well.

Tracey would not be charged with resisting arrest and flight from an officer, the charges she was facing before Jazzy and Tank explained the full situation to the cops. Given the circumstances, Tracey got a reprieve, but she would still be taken to jail because she had an extraordinary amount of unpaid speeding tickets and her license was also suspended. Tracey didn't care at that moment, though, she was just glad Rolanda would survive. Had Tracey not paid attention to her friend back at WYLD studios earlier, Rolanda would have bled to death inside her own home.

As Dominique, Jazzy, Brianna, and Tank followed the paramedics to the hospital, Tracey, headed to the parish prison, exhaled, relieved that Rolanda was still alive, she had done a good thing that night; but she now had her own problems to contend with, that's what Tracey thought about as she rode in the back of the patrol car to St. Tammany Parish Prison. Once there, she was processed and transferred to Orleans Parish Prison the next day.

CHAPTER 36

SISTERS GONE WORK IT OUT

Rolanda was now in a rehab facility in Covington, Louisiana. It was two weeks after her attempted suicide. She was recovering, but she was still grief-stricken over her current situation. She had an excellent health insurance package and she did partake of her doctor's offer to enter into Tulane's research program for HIV patients. The doctors assured her that her life was not over, but Rolanda didn't believe them; the enrolling into the research program was for her friends' sake because she didn't want them to think she was a quitter. Rolanda was expecting to die in a short period of time, but before she did, she was planning on paying Bobby a visit.

She called Bobby's home from the rehab center during the latter part of September '96 just to see if he was home. When bobby answered, Rolanda quickly hung up the phone and gathered her purse. Bobby was now aware that he had HIV, but he was still going on with his life as if he were a healthy citizen. The young man wasn't living life afoul on purpose, he was simply uninformed about the ways a person can contract the disease and was ignorant of the facts. To Bobby, hearsay was medical fact. Instead of doing the proper research and seeking help, he relied on 'street doctors' to gain his knowledge about the HIV virus. He was unknowingly spreading his disease around to both males and females.

Rolanda knew the facts about the disease, and whether Bobby knew what harm he could possibly cause people or not, she was aiming to put a stop to it. She told the staff at the rehab facility that she was going out for lunch and caught a cab to her home. She entered her apartment and went straight into the bedroom where Kilo was with the gun the night she tried to kill herself. No one, not even Charlotte, knew Rolanda had a gun. She looked under the bed and saw the pistol lying exactly where Kilo had left it. She grabbed the gun and ran upstairs to shower and put on a new outfit. Kilo was in the back yard unable to intercede.

Rolanda was exquisitely dressed in a cream-colored Gucci silk dress with a thick, black leather Gucci belt around her waist, and a black pair of leather three inch-heeled Gucci shoes. Her hair was neatly done, flowing to right side of her head. She had on clear lip gloss and wore a pair of 1 karat diamond-studded ear rings. She looked stunning—dressed to kill so-to-speak. She calmly grabbed the keys to her car and began heading for the door just as Brianna entered her home. Brianna was only there to check on Kilo, she never expected to see Rolanda, but in an instant, Bri knew she had stumbled onto something.

"I didn't expect to see you here! Where are you going?" Brianna asked as she quickly eyed Rolanda hide the gun behind her back.

"I'm going take a ride right quick and then I'm going by Charlotte and—I mean I'm going back to the rehab center after I take a ride. After I take the ride, I'm going, going back to the rehab center." Rolanda replied as she looked down at the floor.

"You know we don't talk like that girl! Talk to me with your hands!"

Brianna could careless whether Rolanda spoke through sign language or not. She had seen the gun, and she knew Rolanda was not being honest with her on this day. Bri had a feeling that Rolanda was planning on killing Bobby and herself. She understood, because if it was her, she would do half of what Rolanda was planning on doing. She would kill Bobby no doubt. Brianna then realized that if it were she that was in

Rolanda's position, she would hope that one of her friends would be on hand to stop her from making a terrible mistake. She now had a responsibility, an obligation to her friend. Fuck Bobby, Brianna's sole ambition was to save her friend. *"Come on sister. Talk to me now. Can I take the ride with you?"* Brianna asked as she smiled at Rolanda, trying to ease the tension that was mounting.

Rolanda wasn't going to play Brianna's game, however, "You know I got this fuckin' gun behind my back! You know what the fuck I'm 'bouta do!"

"Why?"

"He still out there spreading that shit around! How many lives he gone ruin? I'm a stop his ass! Today everything ends! *Everything* ends!"

"Rolanda, sister, it's not meant for us to determine what happens to Bobby."

"Bullshit! It wasn't meant for this *shit*—to happen to *me*! Bobby fucked me over, Bri! You can't see that? Move out the way!" Rolanda screamed as she started to cry.

"No! I'm not going to step aside and watch you destroy your life!"

"What life? I'm dead! You can't see that shit? I'm fuckin' dead!"

"No! You a fighter!" Brianna said as her eyes welled up. *"I watched you!"* she then said as she turned and pounded the back of Rolanda's door. It was the only way for Brianna to reinforce what she was saying. Tears ran down her face as she turned to Rolanda. *"I watched you whip four, four bitches' asses at one time! Another time, three, in front of Footlocker on Canal Street back in the day. The lady at the store in East Shore when you were only eleven, and the two females at the club that night with Jazzy! You a fighter! Always was a fighter!"* Brianna said before turning back to the door and pounding her fist hard against the back of the wooden structure. She then turned around and faced Rolanda again as Rolanda stared back at her with tears running down her face.

"Now, if you wanna go and kill Bobby, fine! But you gone have to kill me too! I been shot before! I've stared death in the eyes before! More than once! And I ain't afraid of dying no more! After you kill Bobby you gone kill yourself inside your momma house. I don't wanna be around for that! Kill me!"

Rolanda cried as she slowly raised the gun to her own head. Brianna's eyes widened and she dropped to her knees and stared up at her friend. Her mouth was wide open and her face was covered with tears. She moved her head from to side as she clasped her hands together and shook them rapidly, literally begging Rolanda not to kill herself, only she couldn't say it out loud.

Rolanda looked down at Brianna as she held the gun to her own head and stared at her friend, who was on her knees pleading with her. Bri crawled over to Rolanda and wrapped her arms around her legs and with her mouth wide open, she let out a high-pitched, short yelp. Just then, six gunshots rang out loud. Brianna grabbed hold of Rolanda and she dropped the gun and fell to the floor and grabbed hold of Brianna. Rolanda, out of anger, self-pity, fear, doubt, a feeling of betrayal, and love for Brianna, emptied her gun into her couch. The six bullets, to Rolanda, released all of her emotions. She had five bullets for Bobby, which was her original plan. The last bullet was to be farewell, the one she would take her own life with; only Brianna had changed Rolanda's plans. She'd saved her friend's life.

As Rolanda held onto Brianna, both females sprawled out in the center of the living room, Brianna grabbed Rolanda's face on either side, checking to see if she was all right. Rolanda cried aloud and Brianna grabbed the gun and began slapping her lightly on the shoulder with her free hand. She placed the gun behind her body and said, *"Don't ever do that! Don't ever do that again! God, what if I woulda came later or missed a green-light? We woulda lost you too! Don't ever do that again! You hear?"*

"I'm sorry! This shit fuckin' with my head, Bri! I'm not that strong, sister. I'm not that strong!" Rolanda cried as Brianna held her head against her chest. She then moved in front of

Rolanda and pulled her to her feet.

Rolanda stared down at her friend as she cried. Brianna cried also. *"Maybe not on your own,"* she told Rolanda. *"But together the five can conquer anything. Only if you let us know what the problem is. Lubby snuck away that day, that wasn't none of our fault. But for me to just step aside and allow you to kill yourself in your mother's home would be wrong on my part. We fight! The five always fight! Mentally and physically, we fight! This here is not just your fight! This is our fight! The five's fight! You hear? We love you Rolanda, don't go out without a fight. Forget Bobby, save yourself."*

"I need help, Bri. Them people at the rehab not helping me. They don't touch me, they don't talk to me? I'm not a bad person, but they treat me like a junky, or some kind of prostitute. Bobby was my first and my only lover. Why they treat people like me like that when they supposed to help me?"

"Let's go by Charlotte. She can call your doctor and we can get you the right kind of care, okay? Come on. Our real fight starts here and now. I'm not gone let nothing bad happen to you, sister."

Brianna took Rolanda to her mother's home and from there, her doctor was notified of her patient's current status. The next day Rolanda was moved to Tulane Medical Center in downtown New Orleans not too far from the Amoco building. She received many well wishes from fans of the Fantastic Four Show, and Dominique and Brianna were there every day. Dominique spent her days with Rolanda before work, sitting in on her therapy sessions and helping Rolanda to mix her cocktail medications. Brianna came later in the day and she almost always brought fresh flowers with her and sat with Rolanda and listened to the show while the two ate dinner.

After Rolanda was situated in her new locale, the first thing Charlotte did was pay Bobby a visit. She rode over to his home in City Park and tapped loudly on his door. Bobby answered and saw Charlotte and Tank standing outside his home and had nothing to say. Charlotte stared him in the eyes coldly for a few seconds before she smacked him with an open handed back hand. Bobby fell against the threshold and immediately stood up and charged Charlotte.

"Hit her bitch!" twenty-nine year-old Tank yelled as he got between Charlotte and Bobby. "My dog? My, my partner in crime? We drew *down* on niggas together! And you go out like this, B?" Tank asked as he shook his head in disbelief.

"What the fuck you want from me, brer? I'm sorry 'bout Rolanda alright? I ain't even know I had this shit!"

"Don't matter, B! You shoulda told her you like men! That shit right there wasn't fair to Rolanda, brer! She never had a chance because you never gave her the option! Know that shit right there nigga! Rolanda almost killed herself! Twice mutherfucka! And all you say is you *sorry*?"

Tank and Charlotte both were about to go up under their shirts and pull out revolvers to deliver retribution to Bobby, but an older black male came to the door wearing a police uniform. They covered their weapons and watched as the man came up and stood close behind Bobby, pressing his crotch against his ass. "Problem here, baby," he asked as he rubbed Bobby's shoulders and kissed his neck softly.

Tank was devastated. Bobby was his boy from back in the day. They drew down on drug dealers together, and had even murdered a time or two; he Gerald, and Bobby. When they were younger, they chased females together. Tank never knew that Bobby was gay. He hid that part of his life very well.

"This me Tank," Bobby said as his eyes welled up. "I'm Kitty. I been Kitty ever since high school. Why you think Kitty never came around," he asked somberly as he kissed the older man's hand and looked Tank in the eyes.

Tank clasped his hands to his head and walked away in shock and disgust. At the same time, Charlotte became nauseated and vomited onto the sidewalk as she walked away from the door in total disgust.

"Tell him!" Tank then turned to Bobby and stated angrily. "Tell him!"

"Tell me what," the older male asked.

"The nigga got HIV! Maybe AIDS! A woman, a *real* woman

—loved him once upon a time! The nigga got HIV and he gave it to her!"

"Kitty? You been seeing another man?"

"Is, is you fuckin' stupid? Didn't you hear me, mutherfucka?" Tank yelled aloud. "He gave it to a *real* woman! A real woman who thought he was a straight man! He didn't tell her he was on the down low, and now she have to live the rest of her life with HIV!"

"Bobby, you infected," the man asked as Charlotte and Tank walked off. Brianna was sitting behind the steering wheel of Tank's Oldsmobile; she cried, but only for a short time because she knew Bobby was out of Rolanda's life forever. Bobby would later move to Atlanta and take up a new life.

****

Charlotte had been going to the rehab center every day when Rolanda was in the St. Tammany parish facility, and she began spending much more time at the Tulane facility when the doctors moved her daughter to the medical center in downtown New Orleans. The day after the incident in front of Bobby's home, Charlotte told Rolanda she had 'slapped the shit outta Bobby' and she only smiled politely. To Rolanda, Bobby was getting off easy. Numerous hot bullets to various parts of his torso would have felt much better to the twenty-five year-old. Charlotte explained to Rolanda, however, that Bobby's lover was a police officer and his presence had prevented her and Tank from inflicting the bodily harm upon Bobby that they had planned on doing that day, and after thinking it over, both she and Tank agreed that Bobby was not worth going to jail over.

Rolanda understood, besides, it was time to put Bobby out of her life and move forward. Charlotte was hoping and praying that her daughter would conquer this monumental, highly stressful, and seemingly-bleak crisis that was unfairly thrust upon her. The supportive mother believed—getting her daughter to believe was the only obstacle; but Charlotte knew Rolanda had it in her to win this battle, only she couldn't see it at the time.

Dominique and Brianna were big helps, but Charlotte knew

Rolanda needed her more than anything else. The two would talk a lot, and Charlotte had noticed a serious change in her daughter during that period of time. Rolanda was no longer the animated and outgoing female she once was; but who would be after living through such troubling times? Still, Charlotte was not going to let her daughter give upon life. She walked into her daughter's suite at the rehab center a month after the incident with Bobby and smiled at Rolanda lovingly as she placed a bouquet of carnations onto the dresser and asked, "How are you doing, baby?"

Rolanda didn't answer, but her eyes spoke volumes. She had a look in her eyes that said she wished she were dead. She turned her head straight and stared at the ceiling and remained silent.

"I know you devastated. I'm devastated. I'm still shocked just like you. But I don't feel sorry. And I don't want you to feel sorry for yourself either, Rolanda." Charlotte said as she grabbed her daughter's hand. "We still have a lot to look forward to you know?"

Rolanda cut her eyes at her mother as she frowned. "What the hell do I have to look forward to, momma," she asked lowly. "Wasting away in my own excrement as I slowly rot away from the inside out? Becoming a vegetable unable to speak? Unable to express my thoughts as I slowly slip into a coma and die a solitary death?"

"Don't say that," Charlotte said under her breath as she stood up. "That's not gone happen to you! Not my daughter! Not Rolanda Jones!"

"Momma, these people look at me as if I'm some kind of sex-fiend or a drug addict. They have stereotypes here about how people catch this disease, but I'm not a stereotype. This disease is not a stereotype. This is real life. They have no right to treat me like they do."

"That's in your mind, Rolanda. I've seen this entire staff in action here at Tulane and they are only here to help. If they were treating you the way those people in Covington were, believe me, they would be hearing about it. You're fine here."

Charlotte said as she turned her daughter's head towards her. "Now you listen to me," Charlotte had to pause briefly because she could no longer see a twenty-five year-old Rolanda. She was staring at a scared little girl who was in desperate need of assurance and affection. Charlotte smiled upon her daughter as Rolanda stared her in the eyes. "Rolanda, you, you have *always* been strong. *Always* been beautiful. And you still are. And you *always* will be beautiful. You are a *Jones*, and we never let *anything* conquer us. We go down swangin' and bangin'."

"Momma, this is too much for me. I don't think I can win this fight." Rolanda said lowly as her eyed welled up.

Rolanda rarely called Charlotte 'momma', ever since she was able to speak clearly she had been calling her mother by her first name. It was a term of endearment that mother had come to adore. It brought sorrow to Charlotte to hear her daughter calling her 'momma'; which was a term Rolanda often used when she was in a weakened and/or frightened state. The saddened mother wanted to be called Charlotte again by her daughter; which signified to her that Rolanda was at her strongest, vibrant, and full of life.

"I don't think you have it in you to quit, Rolanda. I'm not just gonna let you wither away. If you believe, you can conquer. Believing is the first step, and I will walk side by side with you. I'll run with you. I'll run ahead of you and knock down barriers if I must! I am your rock! Jesus will be the light that leads the way! And *He* and *I say*—'you can't give up on us'! My name is *Charlotte*! You call me Charlotte like you always have. I know you want momma, and I *am* momma! Momma is here! Momma is right *here*! You hear me, Rolanda?" Charlotte asked as she cried aloud and hugged her daughter. "Don't give up on me! Fight for me! I love you more than life itself and I need you! I need my baby in my life! Say you gone fight with me! Say it, please!" Charlotte pleaded loudly.

Rolanda stared at her mother, bit her bottom lip and closed her eyes and let the tears flow as she slowly shook her head up and down to say yes. When she felt her mother embrace her, she exhaled and opened her eyes wide and closed them back as she cried aloud. "I didn't deserve this, Charlotte! But if you willing to fight for me, I'm damn sure gone fight for you! I'm gone *fight*, for *you*!" Rolanda said loudly as she and her mother held one another tightly and rocked in unison.

Rolanda needed the reassurance she'd just received from her mother. It was the nudge that would propel her head first into the fight of and for her life. Had Charlotte been a parent who acted as if the world had come to an end, it would have only perpetuated her resolve to give up. Charlotte was a strong woman, however, just like her daughter. And on this day, mother had transposed a great deal of her inner strength onto her daughter, who took the baton of strength and ran with it. The finish line lay far off in the distance, but whenever Rolanda looked back, whenever she grew tired, she knew she would be able to count on her mother running behind her, telling her to 'keep going, don't give up, I'm running with you'. If the obstacle was too big, Rolanda knew Charlotte was willing and able to run ahead of her, telling her to 'hold on' as she ran pass her yelling aloud, 'I'll pick up the slack for you'. Rolanda would keep this metaphoric synopsis in her mind and heart and face whatever lay ahead with full confidence, knowing full-well that Charlotte would have her back always.

"You know," Charlotte said as she sat back down and wiped her tears, "for whatever reason, I think of Lubby right now."

"Why?" Rolanda asked lowly.

"Because, secretly, we always thought Lubby was foolish for trying to make Cynthia love her. Lubby was stronger than we ever thought. She fought to the end to gain her mother's love. She never gave up, as futile as it was, Lubby never gave up. It cost her her life, something she never expected to happen, but until the very end, Lubby never gave up. Use your friend's fortitude, baby. I know she's looking down on you hoping you don't give up."

"I won't, Charlotte. I'm, I'm gone deal with this head on. And if I lose this battle, at least I can say I tried. The same way Lubby tried. My friend was an angel. God took her, not Cynthia. If I get called home, it wasn't because of what Bobby did to me, it's because God called me home." Rolanda said sheepishly, bringing a smile to her mother's face.

"Yes. And, Rolanda? God may be calling my, child, but right now," Charlotte said as she placed her hands to her daughter's cheeks and cupped them softly, "right now the line's busy."

****

That same day, inside Orleans Parish Prison, Tracey, who had been down for over six weeks, had just been transferred to the medium security ward where she argued with the guards as she was taken to her new cell, telling them repeatedly that she was only supposed to be serving forty days for traffic violations. She asked them why her release was being delayed and why she was being held in medium security when she was only in for traffic violations.

"Tracey, we don't have any room in minimal security, we don't want to place you in max facilities so we got you a solo cell until we can work things out. Your paperwork was screwed up. It's a mix-up with St. Tammany Parish. We're trying to get you released A.S.A.P. We know you shouldn't even be in here for tickets, but until St. Tammany gets their paperwork in order, we can't release you. Two more days at the most," the guard said as she escorted Tracey into her cell and locked it.

Tracey lay down on the bed and began to think about Mike and her daughter. Ever since the night she raced out to save Rolanda, she had been thinking about Angel and her former lover and she was now experiencing a real change of heart. The time spent behind bars had caused her to realize exactly what mattered in her life: her friends and her family. Tracey now understood what the love of another means. All the men she'd slept with were long gone. That wasn't love and she knew it. She couldn't go to neither one to ask for bail, if she had one, because they didn't give a fuck about her if she wasn't putting out, and all she had ever received out of each sexual encounter with those men was a quick nut, a wet ass and a fucked up hairdo each and every time.

It felt good back then, but those good feelings were only

fleeting moments of pleasure that compensated the guilt she carried around within her for all the ill-will she was dishing out without rightful justification. And while she was out living up, real life was happening. Her daughter was missing her, and a man who loved her more than anything only continued to hold out hope that someday they would all be a family. Her mother had just about given up on her being a mother ever, and her brother, who once looked up to her, had been avoiding her. All Tracey had were her friends, but even they were moving on into new phases of their lives. Only she seemed to be getting left behind. If she were to get out and do the same things, become the same selfish person she'd been ever sense the age of fifteen, Tracey knew that she would lose everything. Everything that now mattered would be lost forever. This was her final chance to show the people who loved and cared about her, what a good person she really was deep down inside. Her lonely and reckless lifestyle had run its course. It was time to be a grown woman.

During dinner, Tracey decided to take a chance and called Mike. It had been months since they last spoke and she sincerely was hoping Mike would accept her call. The phone rung and before long, Mike answered.

"Hello?"

"You have a collect call from Orleans Parish Prison from—"

"It's Tracey."

"To accept press one, to decline press three." The computerized voice stated. Tracey waited anxiously, hoping Mike would accept her call. She was elated when the call went through. "Mike?"

"How you doing, Tracey?" Mike asked in a concerned tone.

"I'm good, I'm good. I umm, I got like two days left. I was wondering if you could come and pick me up when I get out because my bike still in the pound."

"Mike baby, we have to hurry! Me and Angel is starving and we're going to be late for our reservations!" a female voice yelled aloud in the background.

"Who's that?" Tracey asked in a surprised manner.

"That's my friend, Yvette. We dating. We going out to eat, me her, and Angel."

Tracey's heart dropped. She never believed that Mike would start seeing another woman, and to be honest, she'd always believed that she wouldn't care whether he did or not. She'd always told herself that it wouldn't bother her, but to learn firsthand that Mike was dating someone else, and to know that another woman was becoming involved in Angel's life had caused her to want Mike and her daughter in her life more than anything else. "Mike, I know, I know I been fucking up for a long time. I just called to say I'm sorry, and when I get out I hope we can start over. That's all. If you say no, then don't come and pick me up, and I promise I won't bother you again, but if you do, I promise to be a permanent part of you and Angel's life. Tell my baby, tell her, tell her that momma says she love her. We have a lot of loss time to—"

Mike was feeling Tracey all the way, but when the time had expired on the call and it ended abruptly, he grew angry and slammed the phone down. "She gone call back. I'm just gone talk to her for a minute and then we can go out and eat." Mike said to his girlfriend Yvette, a 5' 6" 135 pound dark-skinned black female with short brown hair.

"You gone wait around for that jail bird to call back, Mike? For what?"

"Don't talk about Angel's mother like that, Yvette. You don't even know Tracey."

"I know enough to know that she don't care about you or Angel! We been getting along just fine! Angel even called *me* momma once before! Why you wanna mess up what we have over some jailhouse bitch?"

"Angel go to your room!" Mike yelled to his four year-old daughter before turning his attention back to Yvette. "As long as you live don't ever talk about her like that! Especially in front of Angel! She's tryin! At least she's tryin now!"

"Hey," Yvette said as she smiled at Mike, realizing he was

still in love with Tracey, "I shoulda seen this coming. You could never stop talking about Tracey. You always brought her name up in our conversations. Even when you and I were in the bed together—remember that night? I looked beyond that —but I should have known right then and there that you would take her back if she ever asked. I can't be mad at you. I was willing to take a chance on you knowing you still loved another woman, and for whatever reason, you willing to give that woman another chance. Goodbye Mike, and good luck. You're a phenomenal man. For Angel's sake, I hope that woman doesn't hurt that child, or I'll kick her ass myself." Yvette concluded as she walked out of the door, and out of Mike's life forever.

Back inside the prison, Tracey was trying to call Mike back, but the other inmates had the phones on lock. She returned to her cell and turned in for the night. She was planning on calling Mike back in the morning to find out where she stood, but she would never be able to make the call.

The sounds of clinging gates stirred Tracey from her slumber. The night before she dreamed of her daughter and Mike. She saw the three of them inside the justice of the peace with her mother and brother at their sides as they signed their marriage certificate. Tracey only had one day left, and she was looking forward to calling Mike to talk to him and possibly her daughter. She was feeling real good on this cold morning during the first week of October '96. As she waited on the tier for the guards to unlock the doors to allow the prisoners to enter the galley to receive breakfast, Tracey was cornered by three females.

"What's up, Tracey Sanchez?" one of the three females yelled aloud as she stood in the walkway on the second floor of the tier.

Tracey recognized the female that called her name. She was on Canal Street back in 1986 when she beat Daphne down in front of Footlocker. She was also one of the females that had jumped on her the day she was stabbed and nearly killed by Daphne. Those incidents took place over ten years ago, but these females were still instigating the same propaganda they were pushing when they were teenagers growing up in New Orleans East.

"I know you, bitch! What the fuck you want now?" Tracey asked as she stood facing the three females in her orange jumpsuit.

"This here is a wake-up call, Tracey! We listen to your show! You and Dominique think y'all the shit? Y'all gone bail out just like that bitch Rolanda with her AIDS out the pussy having ass! Yea, people talk! And the word out on ya' home girl. I *would* make ya' eat out my fuckin' pussy, but ya' probably got AIDS when ya' ate Rolanda stankin' ass cat!"

Tracey was not going to stand by idly and let another female disrespect her and Rolanda in that manner. She began swinging on the female before the other two females jumped in. Prisoners began yelling aloud as they watched the fight unfold. The guards caught wind of and they rushed the tier. As they did so, Tracey fought for her life. She got the better of one female, but she was hit from behind in the back of her head by another female and fell to the floor. The three females then swarmed her when they heard the guards rushing the stairs. Tracey was on the ground kicking up at the three females when one of them jumped into the air and came down on her lower left leg and snapped her bone. Tracey screamed aloud in pain clutching her leg as the three females kicked her repeatedly. A swift kick to the forehead sent her unconscious. The females then stomped her body continuously before the guards rushed the scene. The three female prisoners were escorted to solitary confinement and Tracey was rushed to Charity Hospital and placed under guarded care.

Phone calls went out to Maria and Tracey's friends as well, but since she was technically still a parish prisoner, only Maria could see her. She walked into Tracey's room and gazed down upon her twenty-five year-old daughter's battered and bruised body. Tracey's right eye was swollen shut and her left leg was in a cast. She was now conscious and she watched in a weakened state as her mother came and sat beside her.

"The doctors say you gone be just fine. You gone be just fine, Tracey."

"I know, momma. But I deserve this. This is God paying me back for me for fuckin' over Mike and Angel. And everything else I did wrong in life. I tried, before I got my ass whipped, I tried to tell Mike I was sorry. Being in jail was the best thing that ever happened to me. I'm not mad at nobody, not even the girls that jumped me. I deserved that ass kicking—it was a wake-up call for me. Hopefully I can wipe the slate clean, and, and be a mother to Angel." Tracey said seriously.

"For four years I prayed to hear you say those words. 'Be a mother to Angel'. I'm ashamed to say, but I believe you already know that I nearly gave upon you. You umm, you have a lot of work to do, but it's not hard work, and that little girl, that *precious* little girl is just aching for her mother to be a part of her life. She stares at pictures of you when she's at my house and she repeatedly asks your brother does he know when you get off work. God, she is just as her name says, she's an angel. You don't know how blessed you are to have a daughter like her."

"I do, momma. I didn't know at first, or maybe I didn't care. But now I know. I only hope it's not too late."

"They both still love you, Tracey. They both still care. You'll see in time." Maria ended as she sat beside her daughter and the two talked about the future.

****

The Fantastic Four Show was running on half-mast now and had been doing so since Rolanda's attempted suicide took place almost six weeks ago. Jazzy and Dominique were the only ones on air. They were still fielding calls, but many of the show's segments were old segments from the show's glory days. It pained Dominique to hear the old excerpts from the show, the excerpts that took place before the wheels fell off in her and her friends' lives. The listeners all came to know what had transpired behind the scenes of the Fantastic Four Show and most tuned in in hopes that the show would return to its dominant ways of old. They missed Mrs. Jones, they missed Sister Spanks' tirades, and they longed for the unity that once existed when Jazzy and her girls were at the top of their game. They would have to wait, however, because the Fantastic Four

472

was on a semi-hiatus during that period of time.

Through it all, Jazzy and Dominique had grown ever closer. Jazzy told Dominique that no matter what happened to the show, she her to be a permanent part of whatever she had going on in the future. Jazzy was a very popular Dee-jay throughout the radio industry and she knew she would have other options in the future and she wanted Dominique to be there by her side. The two had a heart to heart talk about the show's prospect two days after Tracey entered the hospital.

"What do you think about relocating, Dominique?" Jazzy asked as the two sat inside Dominique's home on a Saturday afternoon in early October of 1996.

Dominique watched her son run around her huge living room before calling for Calvin to come and grab the 1 ½ year-old toddler. After Calvin spoke to Jazzy, he removed his son and the conversation continued. "Relocating wouldn't be bad if the pay is right. I have to talk it over with Calvin, but if he agrees, I don't see a problem with relocating. I mean, it seems as if things down here could never return to what they were. In a short period of time, we have been through some unimaginable drama you know? I know listeners respect us, but a change of venue may be the right move. I think that's what Tracey and Rolanda need right about now."

"I'm not talking about Tracey and Rolanda—just you. We can hire new staff if we make a move out to Las Vegas next year."

"Without my girls? Why would you knock Tracey and Rolanda from the show, Jazzy?"

"They have some serious issues right now. I tolerated your situation, but even you came this close to losing your job Dominique, but you held on."

"Rolanda holding on. And Tracey will be all right, Jazzy. Look, I appreciate all that you have done, but I'd rather quit before I go on without my girls. I'm sorry, no Rolanda, no Tracey, no Dominique. I'm sorry. And I might not be able to even make that request, but at least give them a chance."

Jazzy sat back and thought for a minute. She knew Dominique knew her friends better than she did, and if Dominique felt her friends weren't capable, she would have said so. Dominique took a stand that day, and by doing so, she saved Tracey and Rolanda's careers.

CHAPTER 37

THE RESOLUTION

Tracey was gathering her belongings from her hospital room in preparation to leave after spending a week in the hospital. The parish prison had released her the day she was beaten to shore up space inside the facility and Brianna and Maria were scheduled to pick her up this morning. She grabbed her crutches and began to walk out of the room and head towards the hospital lobby. When she entered the hall, she saw Mike and Angel sitting in a row of chairs. Mike stood up and stared at Tracey, who stood before him dressed in a pair of burgundy sweat pants and a burgundy hooded sweat shirt, her hair in a ponytail wearing no make-up. The 5' 8" 140 pound dark-eyed, caramel skinned Black/Latina looked more beautiful than the painting of the Mona Lisa to Mike. The twenty-five year old eyed his woman with a look of want, a look of desire and love in his eyes.

Tracey stared back at Mike, and when she smiled and shook her head up and down, he read her mind. He knew at that moment, Tracey was ready to reconcile, to make amends for all the wrong she had done. She was ready to take her rightful place in his life; which was at his side, hand in hand, so that the two of them could raise their daughter in a loving atmosphere. Mike believed it, he hoped for it. Tracey knew it, and she wanted it.

As Tracey and Mike stared at one another from at least thirty feet apart, Angel, the four year-old, amber-haired green eyed 3'

2" little girl, who looked like a living baby doll, stepped from behind her father and looked up at him. Tracey's eyes watered at the sight of her daughter. *"How could I do what I did to my own flesh and blood? God, please, let me know she wants me."* Tracey prayed silently as she watched the little girl, who was dressed in a pink and white flowered dress with white Stride-Rite shoes, with thick buckles and pink bobby socks approach her.

Angel handed Tracey a folded sheet of paper and ran back to her father and wrapped her arms around his legs and hid her face. The little girl had not the courage to look at her mother because she felt she would get mad at her for what she had written inside the folded paper.

Tracey opened the sheet of paper and read her daughter's words which were written neatly in ink: *"Do you have to go back to work? Please say no momma so you can home. I love you."*

Tracey broke down and maneuvered herself to the rows of chairs and sat down and cried as she stared at the note, her tears staining the white piece of paper she held in her hands. Mike's eyes welled up and Angel began to cry.

"Yes, Angel!" Tracey yelled aloud.

Angel turned around slowly and rubbed her hands together. "Yes?" she asked lowly. "Yes you going back to work?"

"No, Angel. Yes I'm coming home. Momma's coming home!" Tracey said as she stretched out her arms.

Angel didn't know what to do at that moment. She looked up at her father for reassurance, not sure if it was okay for her to approach her mother.

"Go ahead." Mike said proudly. "Go hug your momma."

Angel walked slowly towards her mother, but before long, she was running. She ran into Tracey's arms, gripped her mother's back tightly and sighed a sigh of relief as tears streamed down her face. "I love you, momma," she cried as she held onto Tracey for dear life.

For so long this little girl had hoped that someday her mother would get off work and be able to spend the night with her. Angel was somewhat troubled by what Tracey had done to her, but she was also young enough to quickly forget. All she knew was that she had a mother that worked all the time, but on this day, her mother was coming home for the first time ever. The two held onto one another as Mike joined them. He knelt down behind his daughter and placed his arm around Tracey's back, placing Angel in between her two parents.

Tracey looked up at Mike with a face full of tears and said, "Please, tell me you forgive me. I'm sorry, Mike. I'm, I'm really sorry, baby."

"We know. We know. Come on, let's go home." Mike said as he and Tracey kissed passionately.

Rolanda's statement to Tracey, "Girl, that white boy gone make you fall in love with 'em watch," quoted in October of 1986, had come to pass ten years later, mere days away from the actual date it had been quoted by Rolanda, who was only fifteen at the time.

Tracey thought about her friend's statement and smiled to herself and kissed Mike harder. *"Rolanda was right after all."* she said to herself.

When Tracey and her family got into the hospital lobby, her mother and brother greeted her and welcomed her back. She was then greeted by Dominique, Brianna, and Jazzy and she hugged them all. She then felt a tap on her back and turned around and came face to face with Rolanda.

"Miss Thang? I do believe I owe you my life!" Rolanda said as she smiled at her friend.

Tracey smiled and grabbed hold of Rolanda and the two screamed aloud inside the quiet complex, causing the other visitors to look on in wonderment.

"Rolanda you all right? You, you okay and all?"

"Thanks to you and everybody else here today, I'm in this new program. Looking back on everything, I'm *glad* you looked into to that letter that night. That's where it all started for me. I owe you my life, Tracey."

"I wouldn't be going home with my daughter and future husband if it wasn't for everybody that's here today! We have a lot to be thankful for Rolanda, namely life, family and friends."

"Amen to that." Rolanda said. "Amen to that."

****

Thanksgiving of 1996 was one of the best holidays the four surviving friends had ever enjoyed. They had so much to be thankful for, namely life. Rolanda was flourishing in the HIV experimental program and she had a renewed vigor for life thanks to her mother and Tracey's keen insight that fateful night. Brianna and Tank had finally raised enough money to begin marketing her album. Her video for her song *You Don't Have to Cry* debuted on Thanksgiving weekend on BET. Her friends watched with adoration as Brianna recreated the five friends' life from childhood up until the day Lubby died. The video ended with a shot of five pre-teen females, all resembling the five, straddling bicycles while staring out into the camera with wide smiles planted on their faces and waving goodbye to the camera. It was the same image in which many people in East Shore often saw twelve year-olds Rolanda Jones, Brianna Stanford, Dominique Franz, Tracey Sanchez, and Lubby Williams when they were all alive, innocent, happy and healthy. Times had indeed changed for the girls, who were now full grown women minus one, but finally, as 1996 came to a close, all had become well.

Brianna's debut album, her first and only release, sold only 31,000 copies, but she and Tank were able to keep 85% of their profits. They had grossed over $310,000, and with the profit from her first and only album, Brianna and Tank opened a talent agency. Things were slow in the beginning, but through Angel Michelle Fuller, their business would flourish. Tank and Brianna moved to New York in 1998, and later moved to Los Angeles in 1999 to be closer to their friends.

After a two year hiatus, and much rearranging, promoting, and marketing, Dominique and her family, Rolanda and Charlotte, along with Kilo, and Tracey Fuller and her family, including Maria and her son Marcus, all moved to Las Vegas in February of 1999. Dominique, Rolanda, and Tracey started their new syndicated radio show right beside Jazzy in March of '99 and they all now earned low six-figure incomes.

Mike became a foreman for Coca-Cola Bottling Co. in Las Vegas and Calvin had become a real estate agent. His first deal was an investment for Rolanda. She and Calvin had gotten together and had sold Lubby's pet shop back in New Orleans, and in the year 2000, Rolanda bought a medium-sized retail lot in the suburbs of North Vegas and opened a successful pet shop called *L&R's Animal Kingdom*, in the year 2001. The drama was now over; and over the next eight years, the four friends would only continue to prosper while living peaceful, harmonious lives.

CHAPTER 38

ANOTHER DOOR OPENS

Tracey sat forward in her chair and looked over to Dominique, who was sound asleep in her lounge chair under the warm sun beating down on Vegas that warm autumn evening in October of 2008 and shook her awake from her slumber.

"Girl, how long I been sleep?" Dominique asked as she stretched.

"About two hours almost. I was replaying all that shit from the time Bri got shot up until we came out here to Vegas."

"Yeah?"

"Umm hmm. Those were some trying times, Dominique. Rolanda came *that* close to killin' herself. A few more inches to the left or right, up or down, Bri coulda been dead. Bri almost lost her life three times. I almost lost my life twice. I can't believe Daphne's friends was still with that shit ten years later. I thought about how you used be all sad when you and Cal split up, too. Now everything all right. We blessed, Dominique," thirty-seven year-old Tracey stated as she looked over to Dominique.

"Eh, when we were younger, did you ever think we would've made it this far in life?"

"Hell no! I thought I was gone die in a crash on my

motorcycle one day. Drivin' like a bat outta hell whenever I got mad. And all those different men? I'm lucky I didn't get —" Tracey paused before she went further.

"Lucky you didn't get the disease I had or the one Rolanda has to live with?" Dominique asked, picking up the slack.

"Yea," Tracey said as she looked to the ground sadly, "Rolanda—that shouldna never happen to our friend, Dominique. Rolanda didn't deserve what she got early on. Lubby neither. Bri neither."

"None of us did Tracey. Well, except my dumb ass! Sometimes I think back to how stupid I was when I had that affair with Brian and I just—"

"Brad," Tracey said correcting Dominique, "his name was Brad."

"Right, whatever that nasty man name was. Sometimes I wish I could turn back time and just go a different way you know?"

"I don't regret anything. Lucky for me Angel didn't remember much of what I did. But when I finally told her, she forgave me outright. She said all she remember was me being at work. If I could go back, the only thing I woulda done different was to get dress by Rolanda house the day Lubby died. I wouldna let Lubby leave my eyesight that day." Tracey stated just as her cell phone rung.

"Hello?"

"Hey momma! Me, uncle Tank Head and Auntie Bri back in town! Where you at?"

It was 16 year-old Angel calling her mother.

"Hey, who you calling Tank Head?" forty year-old Tank yelled aloud as he drove down the streets of Vegas in a black on black '07 H1 Hummer. "They didn't call me Tank because of my big head—they called me Tank 'cause I was hard back in the day!"

"Yea, you might have been hard back in the seventies!"

"The nineties! The nineties!"

"Man, that was twenty somethin' years ago when y'all was out there! What 84, 85, somethin' like that? This the next generation pops!"

"I got your pops right here ya' little whipper snapper!" Tank stated as he mocked an old man's voice and shook his fist causing Angel and Brianna to laugh.

"Momma," Angel said as she laughed aloud, "momma where you at? This funny big head man making fun of old people!"

"I'm by Dominique. How'd your audition go?"

Angel was being managed by Brianna. At age sixteen, she was a beautiful 5' 7" 135 flat-stomached well-toned female with long amber hair and green eyes that were all so captivating. She was easy to look at, a real pleasure to the human eye. Brianna saw Angel's beauty early on and ever since Angel was seven, Brianna had been getting her gigs in commercials, small roles in feature films, and straight to DVD, and TV movies. Brianna had a roster of at least two dozen models, actors, and dancers, but sixteen year-old Angel was her most talented client. Angel had netted over $370,000 in personal income the nine years she and Brianna were working together, somewhere around $41,000 a year. For a child Angel's age, that was good money. By age eleven, Angel had a healthy five figure bank account; at sixteen, she had more money saved than most adults. Tracey was banking all of Angel's money for her college tuition and future investments. Despite the money she was making, Tracey still took care of her daughter the way a mother should. She and Angel were more like sisters than mother and daughter. "My audition went well, real good. We shot a commercial for Old Navy out in Santa Barbara too! I did a li'l dance routine on the beach for that one. We stopping at Starbucks, you want something?"

"No, thanks. Tell Bri to bring you out this way, sugar. We going to Phoenix next week, so we going to the mall to pick up some clothes so you can have something nice to wear."

"Momma, can I spend some of my money? They gone deposit my check for the commercial. I'll have it by next week."

"I told you, you going to a good college. That's to help you out later on in life, Angel."

"Alright, alright," Angel said dejectedly as she said good-bye to her mother.

"Hey, why you didn't tell her the whole story?" Brianna asked Angel.

"Because I knew she was gone say no. Auntie Rolanda told me not to tell her until the check come in."

"You and Rolanda is gone stop messing with my friend like that." Brianna ended as Tank pulled into Starbucks. Rolanda and Angel were real close. When Tracey and Mike married, they Christened Angel and asked Rolanda to be her Godmother. Rolanda was over-joyed at being a Godmother, and she had somewhat spoiled Angel. Rolanda, to Angel, was 'the cool auntie'. The two of them loved to pull pranks and crack jokes.

"I just love to see her get excited, my momma funny to me when she get like that." Angel ended as the three exited the 2007 H1 Hummer on thirty-two inch chrome wheels.

The following Friday morning, Rolanda, Dominique and Tracey ran a best of show and were all preparing to head down to Phoenix to meet Ben and his family. Rolanda had a '06 silver Porsche Roadster with a T-top and chrome mag wheels. She loved her car, so did Angel. Rolanda would often let Angel drive when the two were together, and today would be no different. Angel sat behind the steering wheel of Rolanda's car eager to get on the road. Tracey, Dominique, and Brianna were riding to Arizona in Tracey's Land Rover. Tank, Mike, Calvin and Calvin's son CJ were going to ride down the following day as both Calvin and Mike had to work, CJ had school, and Tank wanted to ride down with his boys.

The women headed out, but Rolanda had to stop and put gas in her car. They pulled into the service station and Rolanda leaned over to Angel and told her to ask Tracey for fifty dollars. "Watch she flip out!" she said to Angel giggled and exited the car and walked towards her mother's jeep.

"Momma, I need fifty dollars to fill up the Porsche."

"I'm, I'm not driving that thing! That ain't my car!"

"I know. But Rolanda ain't got no money and I can't cash my check."

"Hold up! This ole nigga-rich, skinny black heifer ridin' in a damn Roadster with a t-top on chrome wheels and can't put gas in the son-of-a—"

"Momma, momma," Angel said as she started to sniggle whilst watching her mother climb from her jeep and walk to Rolanda's car.

Rolanda was sitting in the passenger seat laughing aloud when Tracey walked up and said, "You gone stop tryin' me, chick! How you going outta town with no money? How you gone have a $90,000 car with no gas money?"

Dominique and Brianna started to laugh as well; they knew Rolanda and Angel were fooling with Tracey. "Momma," Angel said, "I got the money and can give it back. Look at my deposit slip."

"How much was your check?"

"Just look at the deposit slip," Angel replied as she handed the paper to her mother.

Tracey was dressed in pair of light blue jeans and a black tight-fitting tank top with a white sweater tied around her neck and a pair of platinum Ted Baker glasses on a rope hanging down on her breasts. The women all laughed when she took the deposit slip and held it far away from her eyes. They couldn't wait until she put the glasses on. When she did, they burst into laughter.

"Maria!" Rolanda and Angel yelled aloud at the same time as Dominique and Brianna burst into laughter. Tracey peered over the top of her glasses at Brianna and Dominique and they cried aloud in laughter.

"Girl you look just your *momma* with them grandma glasses on!" Dominique yelled from the back of Tracey's jeep.

Rolanda was bent over the side of her door laughing

uncontrollably. Tracey's friends, and her daughter loved to mock her when she wore those glasses.

"Laugh it up ya' li'l midget!" Tracey said to Dominique. "You too Bri, ya' ole Charlie Chaplin actin' behind! What you laughing at Rolanda? Sitting there looking like a black licorice stick!" Tracey snapped as she stretched the deposit slip out again.

"Hey, Tracey! Girl how you doing?" a voice called out.

Tracey leaned back and peered over her glasses and said, "Ohh, hey, baby! How's everything? Y'all all right?"

"Yea we fine, nice seeing you again."

"Same here sugar, tell, tell everybody I said hello!" Tracey ended politely as she eyed the people as they left the gas station.

"Who that momma?"

"Angel I don't know them damn people! Now back to this slip y'all been all giddy about. Okay that's, seven hundred eighty, wait, seven thousand, shucks I can't see these numbers! Wait that's seventy eight, seventy eight thousand seven hundred, seventy eight thousand seven hundred fortyyyy-two! Seventy-eight thousand?" Tracey whispered and looked over to Bri. "What y'all doing in L.A.? Moving bricks?"

"Come on, mini-Maria! Cough up fifty flat so we can ride out!" Rolanda stated through laughter.

After filling Rolanda's tank, Brianna told Tracey that Angel was to be one of the leading models in L.A. for Old Navy's young women's department. She had a four year contract that paid $78,742 every three months. Angel was now set for life thanks to Bri. She was being brought up under good care and supervision and would not experience the trials that her mother and her mother's friends had experienced when they were coming up if they had anything to say about it.

Three and a half hours later, the friends rode into Ben Holland's neighborhood in Mesa, Arizona and Rolanda called Ben to let him know they were approaching his home. Tracey, Dominique, and Brianna, as well as Angel and Rolanda eyed the huge homes lining the street leading to Ben's home. "Man these people, what the hell Ben been doing?" Tracey asked as she eyed mansion after mansion. "This some 90210 shit right here, Ben 'nem rich!" She added.

"He got what Gabriella would've gotten had she not been killed. God is good." Brianna said.

"You ain't lying Bri. Ben came a long way." Dominique stated from the backseat as she eyed the lavish mansions.

"Auntie, who this man is we going see? He famous or something?" Angel asked as she drove slowly through the neighborhood, being guided by Rolanda's GPS.

"No, baby. He blessed. Just like you. You can have all this someday you know?"

"I like my life the way it is, auntie. I don't need a mansion to be happy, although it wouldn't hurt none." Angel said as she and Rolanda laughed.

"Right, that's the attitude. Material things mean nothing if the ones you love not around to share them with you. I'd give up all I have to have Lubby around. You know, this man here lost his momma and daddy? They got killed right in front of his eyes when he was just nine years old. Imagine that." Rolanda said as she stared at Angel.

"Aww, that's so sad auntie."

"It is. That happened in 1984, over twenty-four years ago. Me and your momma 'nem was good friends with him way back in the day. Learn from us older folk Angel; take nothing for granted, and live each day to the fullest, because no one inside this big blue bubble we call Earth is promised tomorrow, no one. So every chance you get to spend it with friends and family, do so, because you never know when you or the ones you love might get called home." Rolanda ended as she rubbed Angel's arm and squeezed it tightly just as Angel stopped in front of the Holland Estate.

The five females exited their two vehicles just as Ben and Katrina exited the house hand in hand to greet them in the cobble-stone driveway. Ben remembered only four of them; he was searching for Lubby, but when he didn't see her, he stopped, closed his eyes and smiled.

"What's wrong, Ben?" Katrina asked.

Ben opened his eyes and looked own at his wife and said lowly, "Lubby? The girl I was telling you I saw in my dream or whatever when I died after Manhattan shot me?"

"Yea, what about her?" Katrina asked as she scanned the five females. "That's not her with the brown-like hair?" she asked, referring to Angel.

"Nahh, that's not her. Lubby dead, Katrina. I'm willing to bet that she dead and that was who I saw dancing when I saw my mother that day." Ben remarked as Katrina looked out at the females, hoping Ben was wrong.

"Maybe she had to stay at her pet shop." Katrina then stated as she rubbed Ben's back.

"I doubt it. I just had a feeling she had passed away. Not seeing her here only confirms what I already knew." Ben replied as he went and hugged his childhood friends one by one. Tracey then introduced her daughter and Ben introduced his wife.

Just then, Henrietta walked out of the house. "Is that Rolanda Jones over there?" she yelled aloud.

"Hey lady how you know my name?" Rolanda asked as she and Henrietta recreated the first day the two of them had ever met over twenty-five years ago.

The two women laughed aloud and walked towards one another and gave a tight hug. "Good to see you Rolanda. Wow! Almost twenty-five years have gone by since we last spoke and that was a sad, terrible day, but not anymore!"

"You right, Miss Henrietta."

"Child, please! Call me Henrietta. Nobody calls me miss."

After a long greeting, Ben and Katrina along with Henrietta invited their guests inside and explained their financial successes to the five as they toured their home, leaving the females' jaws agape as they toured the pristine mansion.

Before long they were all outside by the pool house sipping cocktails and lattes and chatting away. Ben found out that Lubby had indeed died in 1994. He was saddened, but he told them he had died and he saw her in his dream. They talked about Lubby for a good while and Ben and Henrietta both got to hear Lubby Williams' whole story.

"I remember that little girl. I can't believe her mother did that to her." Henrietta stated.

"We were all shocked by that, Henrietta." Rolanda stated.

"Bri, what happened to your voice?" Ben then asked.

Brianna then told her story with the aid of her friends, and it touched everyone. She spoke again in sign language when her story was completed and had Angel translate.

"She said she always thought of your mother every time she sung back in the day." Angel said as Brianna handed him a copy of her CD. "She said your mother was a big influence on her early on and she only wished she could've gone further and become a superstar. Just as she believed Gabriella would have been a superstar. Your mother was her idol when she was a little girl and she was heartbroken by your mother's death. My auntie said she felt your pain for a long time, Ben."

"Thanks, Bri." Ben replied. He and Brianna then stared at one another briefly and smiled slyly. They both were thinking of the day Ben had saved Brianna's life, but that was something to be spoken on only amongst the two of them, not now.

"I'm sorry about your voice, Brianna," Katrina chimed in. "This is supposed to be a happy occasion though, right? Let's listen to your music, Bri!" she added as she got up and ran to her pool house and began setting up her stereo equipment.

As they sat and listened to Brianna's CD, Rolanda shared her story. She thought she would be treated oddly once she revealed she had HIV, but to her surprise and delight, Ben and his family acted as if Rolanda hadn't even revealed to them her health status, and after hearing Tracey's story, the friends' conversations turned to the present.

Music was flowing, and so were the drinks, laughter abounded. It was as if Katrina had known Ben's friends all her life, and Ben and Henrietta acted as if the four females were around all their days. It was a family atmosphere out by the pool just as Samantha, Tre`, JoAnne, Dana, and Alicia walked into the huge pool area with Ben and Katrina's two sons, Ben Holland Junior, and two month old Kenyan. Samantha had her twins Gabby and Tabby in a double stroller and she smiled at her brother as she wheeled her daughters out to the pool area.

"Ohhh, twins!" Angel said as she hopped up and ran towards Gabby and Tabby. "They look like little baby dolls! Can I hold one, Samantha?"

Samantha looked at Angel and smiled as Rolanda, Dominique, Tracey and Brianna all got up and walked briskly over to her and stood before her with wide smiles. Samantha widened her eyes and smiled as the women took turns hugging her. She looked at her brother with a confused look on her face as if to say, *"Who are these people?"*

Ben only laughed. He knew the girls had never gotten to see Samantha, and for years they'd all believed that she was dead.

"You look *just like* Gabriella!" Dominique said as she backed up and stared at Samantha with the rest of her friends, who nodded in agreement.

Samantha, on the other hand, was overwhelmed. She had a strange teenager holding one of her twins and four grown women staring in awe at her, but she was open-minded and very much down-to-earth and slid into her role easily.

"I'm sorry I don't know all of your names. I'm guessing you Rolanda. My brother said you were tall. Girl, you gotta twin! JoAnne come see your twin!" Samantha yelled towards JoAnne, who was unloading a pan of potato salad from the back of Samantha and Tre's Suburban.

JoAnne rounded the corner toting the dish and she stopped suddenly. "I know this woman ain't tryin' ta' look like me!" she said playfully as she eyed Rolanda.

"Uh, uh! You look like me sister child!" Rolanda said as she smiled at JoAnne.

"How old are you?" JoAnne asked.

"Thirty seven!"

"Ha! I'm thirty eight! You look like me!" JoAnne stated as she and Rolanda laughed and walked off together, engaging in laughter and chatter.

Ben introduced all of his friends and before long everyone had sunk back into the family atmosphere. Samantha really liked Ben's friends. They were funny and down-to-earth. In turn, Rolanda and company got along well with JoAnne and company. The night went by all too fast and the entire group couldn't wait until the next day in which Ben had planned a huge cookout.

Early Saturday, the girls returned from their hotel suites and helped set up for the cook out. Conversations abounded along with the joking and laughter. Later that afternoon, Calvin, Tank, Mike, and CJ arrived at the Holland home. Ben greeted the men and the young boy and when he got to Cal, he laughed.

"This man saved my life! I almost got hit by a train going to the beach back in the day!" Ben said as he laughed, still remembering the day Calvin had saved his life when he was rushing to get to Lubby.

"You mean to tell me I owe you a spanking, young man?" Henrietta said as she approached Ben whilst laughing. "You know Gabriella hated you going around them train tracks! Your mother would have scolded you for going to that beach! Now I gotta do it for her! Samantha, go and get my belt so I can spank this young man for Gabriella!" Henrietta snapped as the group laughed and talked about what Calvin had done back in the day.

The group made Calvin blush, calling him a hero. "Man, I was scared myself! Those tracks were dangerous back in the day. A dude got hit that same day not too long before we got there. But umm, ole Ben was a cool li'l fella back then and he loved him some Lubby," thirty-seven year-old Calvin said as the group laughed. "Sad what happened to her brother." he ended as he and his son walked over to his wife.

JoAnne was working the grill when Ben Holland Junior rolled a basketball towards her area. Rolanda picked the ball up and began bouncing it and JoAnne quickly took note.

"Oh, oh." Alicia said lowly to Dana.

"Rolanda! Put that rock down before you hurt yourself, girl!" JoAnne yelled over the music. Rolanda and JoAnne hit it off well, they were close in age and resembled one another a great deal, and they also had the same tastes in clothes and music.

"You lucky, you lucky. That's all I'm gone say." Rolanda stated as she sat the ball on the ground. "You lucky."

"Scared?"

"Nah, just that you know, with my illness and all, I just don't wanna—"

"Aww girl please! HIV ain't nothing! You been alive all this time and you gone keep on being here! What other excuse you got?"

"None really." Rolanda stated as she picked the ball back up and bounced it clumsily.

"Hey, Katrina! Go get my Manute Bol shorts so I can dunk on this rookie right quick!" JoAnne stated as she flipped chicken wings on the grill. "Dana y'all get this grill so I can school this young buck right quick!" JoAnne said as she broke and ran into the pool house.

When JoAnne changed, she came out in a high pair of daisy duke shorts wearing a white headband with an old pair of converse—a ridiculous looking outfit that she wore on purpose just to make people laugh.

"She do look like Manute Bol!" Tracey stated as she laughed aloud.

"Man, these people off the chain right here! Come on Rolanda! Go Manute Bol!" Angel then yelled as everybody laughed and watched the contest.

JoAnne gave Rolanda the ball first. Ever since she dunked on Timothy in 2005, JoAnne felt as if she owned the Holland basketball court. Rolanda would change JoAnne's thinking this day, however; she clumsily began dribbling the ball and when JoAnne went to reach in and steal it, Rolanda, who was baiting her in all along, swatted her hand and broke left. JoAnne watched surprised as Rolanda ran up to the basket and slammed the ball in and clapped loudly.

"What the hell just happened? How you do that?"

"Well, JoAnne, down at the health center, we work out all the time on a full—length— regulation—sized—basketball—*court*!" Rolanda ended as she tossed the ball to JoAnne.

"Not your court no more JoAnne! A new sheriff in town!" Katrina stated over the laughter.

"She hustled me," JoAnne said as she shook Rolanda's hand. "Eh, next time you come back ta' Phoenix, let me know. I'll challenge you to a full game. But give me like a month notice so I can work out the kinks."

"Sure thing girlfriend, sure thing, my friend."

"That was funny right there." Calvin said as he stood beside Ben. "Ben, they tell me you restore old cars," he then said.

"Yeah, brer. Me and my homeboy Tre' over there. We the best on the west coast, ya' dig? When ya' ready to fix up somethin' hollar at me."

"No doubt, no doubt. I need me a fun mobile. Dominique gotta Lexus jeep now and I gotta Chrysler 300. Maybe I can fix that 300 up. Put some rims or something. I like them old cars though. I remember back in the day, when umm, when me and Dominique was separating, man I saw this convertible—"

Calvin paused and immediately recalled that strange day. "Hey y'all didn't tell Ben about that day huh baby?" Calvin asked Dominique as she passed by with a bowl of potato salad.

"What day, baby?"

"The day when you came by my momma house after you left the—"

"The day we were splitting up?" Dominique asked as she cut Calvin off. "Why would I mention that? I mean, Ben know we split up and got back together and all, but, what about it? You wanna tell him what happened in every explicit detail? What was said, what was—"

"No!" Calvin said angrily as he cut Dominique off.

Ben looked on at the married couple believing an argument was about to get underway. "Cal," he said, "Cal, it's not that serious, man."

"It is, Ben! Dominique! I thought that woulda been the *first* thing said! Wait man, I forgot about it myself!"

"What? What did you forget about Calvin? I don't know what you are talking about! Come on now baby, we here ta' have a good time, don't—"

"You right, you right baby." Calvin said as he hugged his wife. "I forgot you didn't hear what happened. And I never told you. I'm not mad at you, just, just mad at the situation and all the lost time!"

"Well, everybody turned out okay. We all good right now, right?" Dominique asked as she looked up at her husband and shared her potato salad.

"We all good, but it can be a lot better for Ben and his family!" Calvin said as he savored the potato salad. "Damn that's good!"

"What are you talking about, man?" Dominique asked inquisitively.

"Hey! We ain't smoke nothing on the way down here, so unless Cal popping pills—"

"I ain't popping no damn pills, Tank!" Calvin stated as he cut Tank off abruptly and loudly.

"What's wrong Calvin?" Rolanda asked as she and the rest of the group walked towards him, all under the impression that Calvin, Dominique, Tank, and Ben were arguing over something.

"Everyone was getting along just fine and now someone

about to have it out? This is what happens when a bunch of black folk get together. We was having fun too." Angel said to herself.

Angel had it wrong, however; she watched as Calvin smiled and shook his head and said, "Ben, Henrietta, Samantha, I know y'all told Dominique and my friends what happened back in the day and who killed Gabriella and I'm glad y'all found justice—but y'all never said nothing about y'all daddy people."

"Sam didn't have any family. He was the only child. His parents were junkies and they gave him up." Henrietta stated.

"No, no! It's more to it, something else." Calvin said as he gathered his thoughts about what he knew to be true.

"What else, Calvin?" Dominique asked.

"The day me and you were arguing Dominique, a lady came. Ben I swear to God, if I knew where you were, I woulda told you, but after all these years, and all that happened I never brought it up because I forgot about it. And I had no reason to remember until now because we had all went our separate ways, you know?"

"Bring what up, Cal?" Ben asked as the entire group grew silent and waited for Calvin to speak.

"The day me and Dominique argued, a lady came looking for Sam. I told her Sam and Gabriella died. I asked her if she knew Sam, and she said, she said she was his sister!"

"Calvin!" Dominique said aloud as she dropped her bowl of potato salad and everybody gasped.

Everyone was shocked. Henrietta and Samantha's eyes and mouth were wide. "How you know she was kin to my daddy?" Samantha asked.

"Because she told me her name was Mary Holland and that she was Sam's sister! She told me to my face that Sam was her brother! That's what she said, Sam was her brother!" Calvin said excitedly as Henrietta placed her hands to her face. Samantha smiled and hugged Henrietta as she squeezed her brother's shoulder.

"That's not all Ben. I believe her man."

"Why, and how?" Ben asked seriously.

"She had a dimple in her chin, and a beauty mark under her left eye, just like you Samantha. And she resembled Sam a whole lot. On top of that," Calvin stated as he turned and looked at Samantha, "she had a set of female twins riding with her in the backseat. She had female twins just like your daughters Samantha. You got more family out there Ben...Sam had a sister. And she may have even had children!"

...TO BE CONTINUED

Made in United States
Orlando, FL
05 April 2024